Mama always told me bad things happen on Wednesdays, 'cause it's the middle of the week and the Lord just ain't looking then. I never really understood what she meant by that, because I thought the Lord was always supposed to be looking.

I'm grown now, and Mama's long since gone. But, oh, how I pray she was wrong about Wednesdays and that the Good Lord is looking down on York County, Pennsylvania this day.

Smart, hard-working, educated. A proud wife and mother. As a free woman of color in the 1830s, Margaret Morgan lived a comfortable life and envisioned a good future for her family, until the day her former owner sent a vicious bounty hunter to return her and her children to Maryland. Thrown back into a brutally cruel system, Margaret did the unthinkable in that era: she took her case to court. Her fate would be determined by the laws of a time when one state considered her a citizen and another saw her as property. The landmark case of *Prigg v. Pennsylvania* sewed the bitter seeds of the states' rights battle that would lead eventually to the Civil War.

Yet, the heart of this story is not a historic Supreme Court ruling. It is the remarkable, unforgettable Margaret Morgan. Her life would never be the same. Her family had been torn apart. Uncaring forces abused her body and her heart. But she refused to give up; refused to stop fighting; refused to allow her soul to be enslaved.

This vivid story, inspired by actual events, will draw readers deep into the heartbreak, terror, courage and indomitable pride of one heroic woman.

All Different

Kinds of Free

JESSICA MCCANN

Bell Bridge Books

Bell Bridge Books
PO BOX 300921
Memphis, TN 38130
ISBN: 978-1-61194-005-3

Bell Bridge Books is an Imprint of BelleBooks, Inc.

Printed and bound in the United States of America.

We at BelleBooks enjoy hearing from readers.
Visit our websites – www.BelleBooks.com and www.BellBridgeBooks.com.

10 9 8 7 6 5 4 3 2

Cover design: Debra Dixon
Interior design: Hank Smith
Photo credits:
Woman (manipulated) © Ron Chapple Studios | Dreamstime.com
Landscape (manipulated) © Rox_amar | Dreamstime.com

:Ldak:01:

Dedication

For Mike, Caitlin and Jake

Acknowledgements

There are so many people involved in the success of a book (not the least of which includes you, my cherished reader) that it's difficult to acknowledge them all. Still, there are several people without whom this book would never have seen the light of day, and they deserve special thanks. I want to thank my parents, and all the family, friends and colleagues who have supported and encouraged me as a writer. Immeasurable thanks go to my generous, loving husband Mike, and my two remarkable children, Caitlin and Jake; you guys are the reason I was able to write this book and have the fortitude to see it through to publication. Among the many other people and organizations who contributed their expertise and support in the development of this work are: Melissa Crytzer Fry, Wayne Ude, The Historical Society of Harford County, Paul Finkelman, the Dana Awards and the Faulkner-Wisdom Creative Writing Competition (both of which gave semi-finalists nods to my novel-in-progress), and the Mackinac Center for Public Policy (which honored this work with their inaugural Freedom in Fiction Prize). Finally, gratitude to my agent Natalie Fisher, the team at Sandra Dijkstra Literary Agency and everyone at Bell Bridge Books for believing in my book.

Part One

It is 1837, and America is divided.
For how can one man boast of freedom,
while his neighbor lives in chains?

Chapter 1

Margaret

Mama always told me bad things happen on Wednesdays, 'cause it's the middle of the week and the Lord just ain't looking then. I never really understood what she meant by that, because I thought the Lord was always supposed to be looking. But her explanation still consoled me when the goats got into the saltbox and Mr. Ashmore took the switch to me for it, or when my stomach was growling at night because rabbits had gobbled up our small garden and all we had to eat that summer was Johnnycakes.

I'm grown now, and Mama's long since gone. But, oh, how I pray she was wrong about Wednesdays and that the Good Lord is looking down on York County, Pennsylvania every day.

"Margaret, hello," Nellie shouts to me as I cross Lombard Street. She works as a housekeeper for the Forten family on the north end of town. The Fortens are the wealthiest colored family in Philadelphia, maybe even the whole country, so Nellie is paid well and always dresses sharp. The bell of her bright red dress dusts the ground as she glides along the planked sidewalk. "I didn't expect to see you in town in the middle of the week," she says.

"I heard a new shipment of fabric arrived at McFarland's yesterday, and I wanted to take a look before it gets picked clean," I say.

"Of course, they did get in some fine bolts, but it sure is strange to see you here because I was just talking about you yesterday. There was a man up here from Maryland asking around about you."

"What man?" I ask.

"Said his name was Mr. Prigg, and he needed to find you right away. I hear he's a bounty hunter."

"No, Ed Prigg was our neighbor when we lived in Mill Green down in Maryland. He worked for Mr. Ashmore at the mill. I can't imagine why he'd be looking for me, though."

"Well, he sure is looking for you," Nellie says, lowering her voice and looking around. "I didn't say a thing about where you lived, Margaret, but I know he was heading to the Constable's. So you best be watching your back."

Nellie doesn't trust white folks. She was bought as a housekeeper in Connecticut when she was just ten years old. Her mistress had her working from five o'clock in the morning until ten at night, washing, cooking, sewing, cleaning, tending the children. She got Sundays off, and she was promised that after ten years of labor she'd earn her freedom. But when ten years came up, her mistress said Nellie had done such a good job, she couldn't possibly let her go. One spring evening, when Nellie was about twenty-three, she'd had enough. She went out for a walk, with nothing more than the clothes she was wearing, and she just kept walking. Didn't stop till she reached the North three weeks later.

I never had it that hard. My mama and daddy got their freedom after years of slaving for the Ashmore family, and I was born a free Negro in a town where there weren't but a handful of us to be found.

"You're a good friend, Nell, but don't you worry about Mr. Prigg. I'm sure his business with me is legitimate, whatever it is. He probably just has news from Mill Green. Perhaps the Widow Ashmore has taken ill, God forbid."

Now, it's true old Prigg has a mean streak in him. I learned early on to stay out of his way. But he was a good friend to the Ashmores, and they were decent enough for slaveholding folks.

It's been almost five years since I've thought about the Ashmores or any of the other folks we left behind in Mill Green when my husband Jerry and I packed up our children and moved here. We had planned to go far, to the northern part of Pennsylvania. But York County was the first place we came to after we crossed the Maryland border, and I just fell in love with it. We built us a little one-room cabin about two miles outside of Philadelphia, just a stone's throw from a clear lake jumpin' with fat fish. The thick, sweet-smelling woods were so different from the open, rolling hills of Harford County. I quickly forgot about my old home.

York County is a wonderful place to live, especially in spring, when the sun rises early and warm, and you wake up to the music of snow drip, drip, drippin' from the roof. Little shoots of green start peeking up from patches of black mud on the ground all around our cabin, between melting drifts of dirty snow. In the morning, deer come out from the woods to nibble at it.

But, mostly, I think York is wonderful because they don't have slaves here. A colored woman can be free here. Free to earn a living. Free to raise a family. Free to kiss her husband on the street without getting the back of a white man's hand. Of course, we were free in Maryland, too, but there's all different kinds of free.

Nellie's voice calls me back from my daydreaming to the streets of Philly.

"Land sakes, Margaret, you're a trusting soul. All the same, you best watch yourself."

"I will, Nell, to be sure. Now I better be on my way if I'm gonna get back home before sundown."

We part company, and I head east on St. Mary's Street, past the African Presbyterian Church. They say Philly is the capitol for America's black leaders and the abolition movement, and I believe it's so. The Free African Society is down a block or two, and over on 15th Street is the country's only black publisher. It's the biggest city I've ever seen. The fourth biggest city in the whole country! And I just love rambling through downtown, soaking up the place.

A dozen scents and sounds waft on the air, a mingling of all elements that make the city grand. My nose delights at the hot corn, fresh muffins and steamed oysters being peddled by street vendors shouting on every corner. The smell of hard work radiates from a gathering of men in overalls haggling outside the feed store. The sharp smell of charcoal stings my nostrils, and the charcoal man's horn bellows in my ears.

There's no law against me walking on the sidewalk in Philly, but I stay to the street out of habit, sidestepping fresh piles of manure as I go along.

Any time of day the cobbled streets are teaming with traffic— buggies, carts and wagons of all sizes, carrying everything from society folks in silk suits to bushels of fresh fruit and coal. Every now and again all the drivers get jammed up in total confusion. Traffic stops and everyone starts shouting and cursing one another. Then a policeman dashes into the center of it all to take charge. Shouting out commands, pointing and waving with complete authority, he aims each wagon in a clear path. One by one they move along, and the steady clip-clop of hooves on stone resumes.

"Apples, fresh apples! Care for some fresh apples today, ma'am?" A boy calls out to me from beside his pony cart piled high with golden fruit. His head is a tangle of flaxen curls, his light eyes barely peeking out between the thick locks.

"What's your price today?" I ask.

"Just a copper apiece, ma'am."

"They're fine looking apples. Are they good for baking?"

"Oh, yes ma'am. They're best for baking. I'll give you a dozen of these beauties for a dime, special just for you."

I reach in my purse, digging around for the shiniest coin I have. I'm rewarded with a wide grin from the young man as he carefully loads the apples into my shoulder bag.

I'll curse myself during the walk home, as I juggle the fruit and the bolts of fabric I'll purchase next. And Jerry will laugh when he sees me hobbling down the muddy rutted road leading to our cabin. But I can never resist the street vendors when I come into town, especially the children. They call me ma'am and treat me with perfect manners, even the white ones. It's so different than the vendors and businessmen back in Mill Green, where a colored woman is lucky to complete her necessary purchases during her trip. Surely, a young white boy would never have offered me a "special" price there, unless it was double what he charged his other customers.

"Thank you, ma'am. Thank you much."

"Thank you, young man. I hope you sell the whole lot today."

With this final word of encouragement, the boy laughs and bows to me, then turns his cart up the street. "Apples, fresh apples here! Get yer apples!"

McFarland's General Store is up ahead a half-block, just past the dress shop, where I stop to look in the windows displaying the latest fashions from Europe. Velvet ball gowns with yards and yards of lace flounce imported from Paris go for $300 or more, a year's wages for both Jerry and me if we got lucky. I love the traveling dresses best, made of rich black silk or velour, with their high lace collars and long straight skirts. Those go for about $100, depending upon the fabric. They're a far cry from my plain cotton dresses, to be sure, although I doubt the quality is any better. I wouldn't be braggin' to say I've got the straightest hem stitch in York County.

I make my way into McFarland's, eyeing the big clock above the counter. One o'clock. I've got to be out the door by two if I'm going to make it home in time to get dinner going. It's harder than it sounds.

I once spent four hours in McFarland's without batting an eye. Seems to me there's no end to its treasures.

I'm greeted by the smell of coffee, sugar and beans in oak barrels along the east wall. The ingredients give off a delicious crunch and fresh burst of perfume each time the patrons dig in with their scoops to fill up their sacks. A group of children buzz about the candy counter, eyeing the brightly colored taffy, peanut brittle, fudge and popcorn balls behind the glass. I scan a table of books, dozens of them, mostly dime novels with paper covers, but also a few thick leather-bound volumes. My fingers brush the spines and fall upon a fine copy of *Nature* by Ralph Waldo Emerson. Just published last year, the library's copy of the book is already well worn because of me.

Mrs. Ashmore took it upon herself to teach me to read when I was a child back in Mill Green, and I'll be forever grateful that she did. Very few Negroes where I'm from know how to read, and those who do learned it in secret. In Maryland, the law doesn't allow blacks to go to school or learn to read. Mama worried her missus would get in some kind a trouble for teaching me. But Mrs. Ashmore would just cluck through her teeth and say, "I had no vote in the making of such a law, and I have no intention of abiding by it, either." Mama always thought that was real brave of her.

I took to reading like you wouldn't believe, and Mrs. Ashmore was so pleased. I remember she used to say to me, "Margaret, a book is like the best friend you can imagine. Once you read a book, it stays with you forever." And she was right. Next to my children, reading is the greatest blessing I ever got, and Emerson is a treasure. "A nobler want of man is served by nature, namely, the love of Beauty."

But the book is a dollar today. It'll have to wait. I head toward the fabric bolts, lined up in the middle of the store, the prize of the week.

"I thought I might see you this week, Mrs. Morgan."

Mr. McFarland smiles at me from behind his round spectacles. The small circles of his glasses sit high atop his apple cheeks, making his head look even larger than it is, if that's possible. McFarland is plump all around, right down to the short chubby finger he uses to poke jovially at my thin arm.

"Yes, sir. News of your fine goods travels fast. I'm hoping to find some nice linen today."

His laugh rattles through the store, and he pulls a bolt from the rack.

"Pink, the finest linen you can buy, straight from England. You'll look lovely in a dress made of this."

I take the bolt from him and hold it up to my chest, turning to face a tall mirror trimmed in wood. The pink does look lovely against my dark skin. I can easily picture it—a striking gown with a v-neck and pointed waist, perhaps a bodice laced up with silver hooks at the back.

"I'll take five yards," I say, although the dress will not be for me. Nellie mentioned just last week that Mrs. Forten would be needing a new dress for the July 4th celebration, and this fabric will turn her eye, I'm sure. I'm her favorite seamstress, and she will easily pay me $30 for such a dress.

Three yards each of a flowered gingham and crisp white linen round out my purchase. It'll be enough to make two sets of skirts and blouses, which I can sell at the May Day picnic. McFarland hums as he carefully folds and packs the fabric into my bag. I heave the package over my shoulder and turn for the door, checking the time on my way out. Two-thirty. Not bad for a shipment week.

It's a delicate dance, working one's way along the back roads of York County in spring, all mucky and thick from the rains and heaps of horse manure. The walk's taking longer than usual because of my heavy load, but I know these roads well and there'll still be plenty of sunlight left when I get home. I hope Jerry and the boys had a good day down at that lake. Boiled fish and baked apples would make a fine dinner tonight. If not, we've got plenty of supplies for salt pork and biscuits.

Our cabin is coming into view as I make my way along the muddy road. *What a pretty sight!*

Oh, I know the place probably don't seem like much of anything to the average passerby, not that we get many of those way out here. But our tiny home is so much more than its four ramshackle walls and lopsided roof would have you believe. Inside, it's big, full of love. It's a hospital where my babies can be born. It's a schoolhouse where my children can learn. It's a mansion where my husband and I can enjoy the riches of our life together.

My eyes search the yard for the children. They usually keep watch when I go into town, but they're not running up the path to greet me. Maybe Jerry sent them down to the well to get some water for the evening. *Won't they be excited when they see these beautiful apples!*

A black wagon hitched to two massive horses is parked beside the cabin. A brass horn is mounted at the dashboard. It's the constable's wagon.

"Jerry, I need a hand with these packages," I shout, struggling through the front door.

Inside, the children are sitting straight-backed along the bed. John, my oldest, looks smart in the blue sweater I knitted for his tenth birthday just last month. He's got his arm around Emma, in that protective big-brother way he has. She's half his age, and just half his size to boot. Sammy Jr. sits on her other side, looking far less bold than his brother. His left foot is twitching where it dangles off the edge of the bed and has set the ruffle on the quilt into motion.

Jerry moves to help me with my bags, but he doesn't speak. Constable William McCleary and Mr. Prigg are seated at the dining table, drinking coffee, no doubt brewed fresh just for them.

"Jerry?" I ask, handing over the apples first, missing the hearty laugh I had been expecting from him. His face looks ashen beneath his cocoa complexion, telling me without words that these guests were not invited. Jerry worked a plantation in Georgia growing up, before he bought his freedom, so he knows how to behave around a man like Prigg. But I know his silence doesn't come easy to him.

"Mrs. Morgan," Constable McCleary speaks up, as he and Prigg stand up from the table. "This here is Mr. Prigg from Harford County, Maryland. You know him?"

"Yes sir, I know him well. We were neighbors for years and years down in Mill Green."

Prigg looks just as I remember him. His dirty grey hair combed back over his head, too thin to hide the pink scalp showing through. His eyes have that glassy look of a man who partakes in a bit too much ale and is always aching for yet another pint.

"Neighbors?" the Constable asks me.

"Yes, sir."

Prigg snorts and shifts his weight, pounding his tin coffee cup down hard on the table.

"Mr. Prigg has a different way of saying it," says Constable McCleary, looking sideways at Prigg. "He says you're a runaway. Says you and the children are the property of the Ashmore family in Mill Green."

Prigg nods along, looking all smug and self-righteous. My whole face goes hot. *Runaways!* He's got some nerve accusing me of such a crime.

"That ain't really so, Constable," I blurt out, and then I stop myself. *Easy now, Margaret, watch your mouth.* I must choose my words carefully. I may be free, but even a free Negro can easily get herself locked up for talking back to a white man, no matter what state she lives in.

"Begging your pardon, sir," I begin again, slower, more restrained. "I did live at the Ashmore estate my whole life, but I never was a slave and neither were my children."

The Constable steadies his gaze on me, looking long and hard into my eyes. Normally, I wouldn't dare look a white man square in the face, but there's something in his soft brown eyes that comforts me a little, with their golden flecks and pale lashes.

Jerry can't stay quiet any longer. "Damn, Bill, you know us. You know Margaret ain't no slave."

"Well now, I know you've been living here quite some time, Jerry. And I always believed you all were free. But I can't rightly take the word of a bunch of Negroes over that of a white businessman, now can I?"

A businessman? That's a fine fairytale. Prigg's nothing more than an underhanded drunkard. I cross my arms across my chest and cluck my tongue against my teeth in disgust.

"Does Mr. Prigg have any papers?" I ask curtly.

With that, Prigg's face turns red with rage. "Papers?" he bellows, stepping toward me, his arm raised. The Constable steps between us, thank the Lord.

"All right now, Mr. Prigg, just hold on. Near as I can tell, this is a matter for the Justice of the Peace. Let's all get in the wagon and head on down to County Hall before dark and get this settled."

Constable McCleary has always struck me as an honest man, strong but kind. Jerry knows him better than me, since they like to fish the same spots and sometimes they get to talking about the kinds of things that men like to talk about. But once, I saw the constable get after a couple a white boys for tormenting a neighbor's dog. He grabbed 'em both up by the ears and marched them right on down to the dog's owner to confess their deeds. Those boys painted fences for two weeks after that, and the constable came checking on them every day of their penance to make sure they were working good and hard. I've liked him ever since then. I figure anybody who looks to make sure a dog gets treated right is gonna be just as fair to any Negro.

"Must we all go?" I ask him. "Can't the children stay home?"

"No, I'm sorry, Mrs. Morgan. The children will have to come along. If Justice Henderson agrees with Mr. Prigg, you'll all need to go along with him back to Maryland."

Back to Maryland. I feel my back stiffen. This can't be. I'm *free*. My *children* are free.

"Damn straight," Prigg thunders, stomping a heavy boot down upon the plank floor, making a deep hollow thud. The constable shoots him a look that says he'd better tread lightly, but it does little to comfort me now.

What in God's name will we do if the justice of the peace believes his lies? I look at Jerry, and our eyes speak the same panic we work hard not to show.

"Can we ride in our own wagon, Bill?" Jerry asks, just as calm and strong as an oak tree in a storm.

"No harm in that," the constable says, and Prigg tips over his coffee cup in disgust. Emma jumps up to put a towel to the spill, but I raise my hand.

"Don't you worry about that mess, baby," I say, just as steady as you please. Then I glance at Prigg for a second. "I'll just clean that up when we get back home."

Prigg eyes me for a moment, then stomps out the door. Could he see past my calm mask and see my guts tied in knots? *I should know better than to play with him that way.*

My motherly instincts draw me to the children. I place my hand firmly, but tenderly, on John's back, then Sammy's to lead them out of the cabin. When I reach for Emma and feel her warm innocence, something buckles inside of me. I squeeze my eyes tightly. This *can't* be happening.

Into the wagon we go. We'll be to County Hall in an hour's time. I can only pray we'll be turning back for home after that.

Chapter 2

Margaret

Justice of the Peace Thomas Henderson sits on-high, behind his massive desk in the court room at York County Hall. The place looks just like the churches I've heard about where rich folks go on Sundays to praise the Lord for their blessings—mile-high ceilings, polished mahogany wall-to-wall, rows and rows of tall-backed benches. Most of the workers have already gone home for the night, and so the place is empty and quiet. Our party sounds like a herd of cattle thundering down the hall and into the court room.

"What business do we have today, Constable McCleary?" the justice asks after we file in.

"Your Honor, I have with me Mr. Edward Prigg of Harford County, Maryland. He has come to Pennsylvania as a bounty hunter under contract for Mrs. Margaret Ashmore, also of Harford County, to claim Margaret Morgan and her children as runaways and return them to Maryland."

"Margaret Morgan?" The justice seems startled. He knows me by name, if not by sight. The very shirt he's wearing under that robe could be my handiwork. Mrs. Henderson appreciates my proficiency as a seamstress and gladly pays me to do the task she has neither the skill nor want to do herself.

"Yes sir, and the children."

"Very well," Justice Henderson says furrowing his grey brow, deepening the creases on his high forehead "Mr. Prigg, please step forward with your papers of ownership, sir."

Prigg shifts from one foot to the other, scrunching his hat between his hands at his belt. He does not step forward, and he does not speak.

"Mr. Prigg?" Henderson asks again, and now the Constable speaks up.

"Mr. Prigg has no papers, sir. Seems there was some confusion when Mrs. Ashmore's husband passed on years ago, and the widow has no official documents of ownership."

Justice Henderson takes off his spectacles and sets them down on the desk. He places his other hand over his face and rubs his eyes with a thumb and forefinger, leans back in his chair.

"Mr. Prigg, I say step up, sir."

With this, Prigg shuffles up to the bench, meeker and smaller than I've ever seen him. Most times, he swaggers about like he's the biggest toad in the puddle. But now Prigg looks more like a child to me, a miniature in comparison to the bench and the honorable man seated behind it. He still does not speak.

"You've come before my court to request extradition of this woman and her children, yet you have no papers of ownership. What proof have you that she is indeed property of Mrs. Ashmore of Harford County?"

"Your Honor, I have a certified letter from Mrs. Ashmore's son-in-law, Nathan Bemis, requesting my service to locate and return the runaways," says Prigg stretching up to place the letter on Henderson's desk. "I have that, sir, and my word as a gentleman."

We wait as Justice Henderson places his glasses back upon his nose, long and straight, like it's never been broke in a fight. He reads the letter slowly. My heart beats faster, the longer we wait. What could the letter possibly say? Nathan Bemis is married to the Ashmores' only daughter, Susanna, and she's the only one who calls him Nathan. The rest of us call him Nat. He grew up just a mile down the road from us and started working for Mr. Ashmore down at the mill when he was fourteen. It just doesn't make sense to me that he's the one behind this mess. I'm mighty relieved to know it wasn't Mrs. Ashmore who sent Prigg after us, but Nat never had an original idea come to his mind. His father always bossed him something terrible, and Susanna took over the job when they were married. My daddy used to laugh and say it was a wonder Nat wasn't always tripping over the strings that Susanna pulled him around by.

"Mrs. Morgan, step up."

"Yes sir, yes, Your Honor," I step up quickly and stand beside Prigg.

"I assume you disagree with Mr. Prigg's claim. Do you have your papers of manumission?"

I shoot a glance at Jerry over my shoulder. He gives me a reassuring nod and a little wink. It gives me strength like hot stew on a cold day.

"I do disagree, sir, thank you. But I have no papers of manumission, because I never was a slave. I was born free and so were my children. We all moved from Maryland five years ago, sir, with no trouble at all. All except little Emma, who was born here in York. It's a wonderful community, sir, and Mr. Morgan and me both feel so blessed to live and work in such a fine, fine community."

Sure hope the justice is wearing his boots, as thick as I'm laying it on. But I've never been asked to step up and speak in a place so official. I'm not going to squander this precious opportunity, especially with so much at stake.

"What a load of crap, you smart-mouthed coon," Prigg turns upon me with contempt in his eyes.

A bang of a gavel jolts us both.

"You'd be wise to hold your tongue, Mr. Prigg. You're in a court of law, not some back-alley tavern. I don't allow such vulgarities ."

I can't believe the smile that breaks loose upon my face, and I quickly look down at the floor to hide it. I can hear feet shifting around behind me, a few nervous coughs, no doubt my family taking the same measures as me to hide their disbelief, their pure delight, with the reprimand.

Prigg must be just as shocked. I look sideways, only with my eyes, and can see the veins bulging in his forearms as he squeezes that poor hat of his tighter and tighter. Could be I'm dreaming, but I swear I can hear his heart pounding away in his chest.

The gavel is still in Henderson's fist, and he taps it repeatedly against the palm of his other hand as he thinks things over. With each tap, my insides jump. *Can my entire fate truly be determined by another pound of his gavel? What will become of my family if he sends us back to Maryland?*

"According to the laws of Pennsylvania, I find no legal ground for your claims, Mr. Prigg. You may not be aware, but we have a Personal Liberty Law here, created in 1826, that requires bounty hunters to provide proof of ownership before hauling off one of our Negro citizens. Not only have you no papers of ownership for this woman, but one of these children was born in Pennsylvania and is therefore free without dispute."

Judge Henderson pauses for a moment to let out a sigh of exasperation. I let out a sigh of relief.

"Your request for a certificate of removal is hereby denied, Mr. Prigg. Constable McCleary, thank you for your service today. You may release this family from your custody. And, Mrs. Morgan, you have the apologies of the court for this disruption to your life. Court is adjourned."

The gavel thunders a final time, and his words echo in my head—unbelievable words which send goose pimples up my arms and confirm my belief that Pennsylvania is a wonderful, wonderful place to live. *Mrs. Morgan, you have the apologies of the court.*

The morning after our victory at the courthouse, Jerry gathers up his fishing gear and walks down to the lake with the boys. Standing out back at the well, I can see him, sitting cross-legged on the moist bank, flanked by little John and Sammy, patiently waiting for some sign of life at the end of his line. Just the sight of him makes me smile. I breathe in a deep breath and let it go in a heavy sigh of contentment. *That's my man.*

In many ways, Jerry's method of fishing is just like his method of living. He works real hard to equip himself with the gear he thinks he'll need to get by, and then he waits with an empty stomach for some sign of real life, for something to fill him up inside.

My Jerry is mulatto, first generation. Mulatto babies are born pale, their color deepening to their final shade a few days after birth. Jerry's complexion ripened to a rich cocoa brown, his hair grew thick and coarse, and he has always been grateful for it. Despite the hardships of being colored, to be mistaken for a white man would be far worse in his mind.

His mother, Marie, was a slave on the Goodlow plantation in Georgia, where she washed and cooked seven days a week in the big house. His father, Mr. Goodlow, was the type of master who took liberties with those in his stock who caught his fancy with a submissive smile or rounded figure.

Marie had smooth, dark-coffee skin and, by the age of fourteen, the pleasing shape of a fertile woman. Her small bosoms were round and firm, and her limbs were thin yet toned and shapely from her endless days of lifting heavy baskets of wet laundry and steel pots for cooking. Mrs. Goodlow was a pious woman who ran an orderly household with a heavy hand, and Marie was her charge. The girl was educated in proper Southern etiquette and restricted to the house so she would not be "ruined by the Niggers in the field."

The summer of her fifteenth year, Marie's stomach began to protrude, and there were many whisperings among the wives of the neighboring households about who might be the father. Of course, most residences in the South have at least a few mulattoes, but no Southern lady is prepared to speculate on the pedigree of the mulattoes in her own household. And so, the larger Marie grew, the more venomous her mistress became.

Just hours after Jerry was born—pale and pink—Mrs. Goodlow took a skillet to poor Marie, beating her about the back and shoulders until the girl was a huddled mess on the kitchen floor. Already weak from childbirth, and a mere child herself, Marie could not withstand the abuse and died two days later.

Because his mama was a slave, Jerry was a slave. But being the offspring of the master brought him some benefits. By the age of eight, he was frequently sent off to run errands. Some days he would walk five hours out and five hours back, just to deliver a dinner invitation or fresh-baked pie to a neighbor. These tasks were assigned by Mr. Goodlow himself, mostly to keep Jerry out of the mistress's sight. Jerry was glad for that, for when she did catch sight of him, he would feel her loathing delivered in a broom handle across the back or steel pot flung at his head.

As he grew older, Jerry got permission to work extra odd jobs at neighboring plantations, once his assigned tasks were complete. He was also allowed to keep a portion of the pittance for himself. By the time Jerry was twenty-five, he had earned and saved $350, enough to buy his freedom and help secure passage north. With papers of manumission in hand, he traveled to Pennsylvania, where he had heard a free man of color could work as a teamster transporting goods by wagon for three dollars per week.

Jerry had generally been spared the backbreaking field work and cruel treatment of the overseer that his kin experienced daily on the plantation. But he saw plenty, which I think hurt him a lot more than if he had endured the hardships himself. Those miseries gnawed away at his guts, bit by bit, day by day, eating him alive from the inside out. By the time I met him, Jerry Morgan was a shell of a man.

It wasn't until after we were married that Jerry seemed to find the kind of nourishment that could really fill him up, that could give him life—a life of sitting on a moist bank, flanked by little John and Sam Jr., waiting for some sign of activity at the end of his fishing line.

"Mama, we got fish for dinner, four big fat fish!" Sammy rushes through the door of the cabin, jubilant, proud, bringing the cool perfume of the lake and the pines right along in with him. John follows, more solemn, with the honor of being the one chosen to carry the bucket with today's prize. The ice in the lake only just melted a few weeks ago, and this is the first catch of the spring season.

"Here you go, Mama," John says to me. "Should be 'nough there for seconds tonight. I'll clean 'em up for you."

Trailing in behind is Jerry, beaming like a fat jack-o-lantern. But this is not his silly grin, the one he gives me at the end of a long week, after we get the kids to bed and he's had a cup or two of rum with dinner. No, this is his fishin' smile, a peaceful one that says "the Lord takes care of those who take of themselves," and that the world can't be too awful bad when a man and his boys can bring home a good meal for his family.

"Looks like you boys did some fine work down at the lake today," I say to him. I'm at the table, up to my elbows in dough, as little Emma and I work on a batch of apple dumplings to go with dinner. Jerry steps up close behind me and slides his arms under mine, around my waist, squeezing me tight. He places his cold, windblown face against mine, eyeing our project at the table. I turn to give him a little kiss, leaving a flour nose print on his brown cheek.

"Looks like my girls are doin' some fine work here, too."

Pride fills me up like warm bread from the oven. *What have I done to deserve such blessings in my life?*

The boys get busy to cleaning and cooking the fish, and Emma and I work at our dumplings. And in no time, we all sit down to a dinner fit for royalty. The table is heaped with fish, boiled tender and white, golden dumplings, pickled greens and steaming corn biscuits— more than we lay on for Thanksgiving Day itself. Jerry asks me to say grace, and I'm glad to. I have so much to be thankful for on this evening.

"Dear Lord, thank you for this bountiful dinner tonight, and for all the blessings you've bestowed upon us. We know you been watching over us careful, especially at the court house yesterday, and we're just so thankful for that. We ask that you continue to keep us in your loving light, and give us the strength to continue working hard and living right by your Word. Amen."

After dinner, Jerry and I wash up the dishes and get the children tucked into their bed. Then we settle ourselves outside in the crisp night air to bask in the starlight and in one another's happiness.

After some minutes of quiet, Jerry says, "I'm gonna tell Mr. Mitchell I can't make tomorrow's delivery up to Trenton."

Mr. Mitchell runs a shipping yard in Philly. He hires Jerry to transport all sorts of goods around Pennsylvania and down across the border to Maryland—baskets of corn and apples, barrels of whiskey and kerosene—nearly every week. The white teamsters don't like to be driving loads on the weekend, so Jerry usually fills that need and Mr. Mitchell pays him nice for it.

"What do you mean, Jerry? Why would you go and do that for?"

"Trenton takes three full days. I don't wanna leave you and the chillun all alone for that long, not after the trouble we had with Prigg yesterday."

Jerry has good reason to worry, of course. He's never had a run in with Prigg himself, but he has heard plenty of my stories about the old man's temper.

One time, when I was about fourteen or so, Mr. Ashmore sent me up to Prigg's place to tend his pigs and goats just like I did on the Ashmore estate. I arrived early in the morning and worked through near until dark. My heart went out to those poor creatures. The goats' hooves were overgrown, their fur all matted in some places and gone altogether in others. The pigs were slow-moving. I could count the bumps on their back bones and the ribs along their sides. After shoveling out the pens, I brought the animals out, one by one, down to the creek and cleaned them up good with buckets full of water and a wire brush. Then I hauled fresh hay up to the pens, and filled all the water and food troughs. Prigg watched me the whole day through, from a chair on his side porch, his boots propped up on the railing. From time to time he'd disappear into the house and emerge with a pint of ale from the keg he kept tapped in the cellar.

When I had finished the job, I walked up to the house to collect my pay. The Ashmores always paid me for my work, so it never occurred to me that Prigg wouldn't do the same.

"Job's done, sir, if you'd like to take a look and see if it's to your satisfaction," I said, looking down at the mud and manure caked to my shoes.

"Can see from here," he said.

"Ok, thank you, sir," I said timidly. "I'll accept whatever wage you see as fair."

"Wage!"

I was still looking down, so I had no time to dodge the heavy mug full of ale that Prigg flung at me from the porch. It struck my shoulder with such a force that I stumbled and fell onto my backside. Then Prigg jumped to his feet and leapt over the porch railing, charging at me like an angry hog. I scurried back on all fours, still dazed from the impact of the mug. By the grace of God, he lost his footing somehow, stumbled a bit and paused to catch himself from falling. The sun had dropped below the hills and the dark had come upon us fast. Without a moment to lose, I scrambled to my feet and ran like a deer down across the creek and disappeared into the Bemis's apple orchards. I never looked back, although, for a short time, I could hear him wheezing after me as I darted through the shadows.

Mr. Ashmore paid me the next day and said I needn't worry about the misunderstanding with Prigg. I never worked for nobody in Mill Green except for the Ashmores after that, and I did my best to keep a distance from Prigg.

"That trouble's done with," I say to Jerry, pulling myself away from the past. "Justice Henderson saw to that once and for all. If that old buzzard comes wheezing around here again, I'll just send Johnny to fetch the constable. We'll be fine."

We sit in the quiet again. Jerry takes a deep breath and lets it out real slow, looking up into the velvet black Pennsylvania heavens. "Still . . ."

"We'll be *fine*," I say again, trying to convince myself as much as him.

I nestle up closer to my man, my protector. The feel of his hard muscles against my body gives me strength. We *will* be fine. I tilt my head up and give him a long, tender kiss on his firm lips.

"A'right, Maggie, a'right," he says and gives me another good kiss back. "I'll leave at daybreak, and you make sure to set me a plate for Sunday dinner."

Chapter 3

Margaret

My eyes shoot open. I lie still for a minute, groggy, my heart thumping evenly in my chest. I swear I heard something—but I don't hear the sound again.

It must be nearly midnight. There's a new moon tonight, and the cabin is black around me. Suddenly, I hear it again: the sound of dry twigs crunching beneath heavy boots.

My heart starts to thunder in my chest as I sit up, blind in the blackness. I hold perfectly still, breathless, trying to fight off the dizziness from my deep sleep. I struggle to listen for it again.

Must be an animal. There's no good reason why someone would be walking around out there in the dead of night. *No good reason at all.*

The crunching draws closer, louder. This is no animal.

Fighting to stay calm, I roll out of bed and crawl through the dark to wake the children.

"Mama, what? It ain't morning yet?" John moans.

"Shhhh," I fight to control the shaking of my voice as I whisper and nudge him. "Wake up. Something's wrong. Get your daddy's rifle and don't be scared. But be quiet, Johnny. Be very quiet."

I can hear hushed voices just outside now, two or three men at least. Maybe more.

I swallow hard, looking at the door. It's made of pine branches, stripped clean and woven together in a tight lattice. One of my best quilts is sewn to the inside, thick with wool and embroidery of the lush green hills and bubbling creeks of Harford where I was born. It's strong against the cold—but not much else.

If they want in, they won't have much resistance.

I look back at my babies.

Sam Jr. lies frozen in the bed he shares with John. He is awake, and he hears them, too.

"Be brave, Sammy," I say, my own voice cracking, my palms sweating, as I crawl over to Emma's bed. She quickly climbs to me, wrapping her trembling arms tight around my neck and her bare legs around my waist. Our hearts pound wildly, in unison.

God help us. There's nowhere to hide.

The door rattles, cracks, flies open, and the cabin fills with light. Prigg charges in, looking like the devil himself, his lantern casting deep shadows onto his seething face.

His arm flies toward me, and Emma and I crash to the ground. Her panicked screams and hot tears fall upon my ear.

The hulking shadows of three other men fill in the cabin. Sammy makes a dash for the door, and he's snatched up.

"Don't let any of them pickaninnies get by you," Prigg bellows, and serves a swift kick to my shoulder as I roll and try to push Emma safely behind me.

A rifle cocks and Johnny's voice rings out, strong and strangely deep. "You get outta my house, Mister, or I'll let her rip!"

My brave boy!

"Oh, you gonna shoot me, huh?" Prigg charges at Johnny possessed, grabbing the barrel with his meaty hands and sending a shot up through the roof. Splinters fall down on us, as Prigg wrestles the rifle from my dear boy and strikes him in the temple with the butt.

"Johnny!" I scramble over to my crumpled child and plant a dozen kisses on his head, watering them with my salty tears. *Oh, Jerry. You were right. I should have never let you go.*

"Now, that's enough," Prigg announces, looking down on us. "On your feet, and I won't have to crack any more of ya."

My mind is swimming. I'll awake at any moment. This will all be a bad dream. Just a bad dream.

My lips tremble as I try and keep my body from shaking. I gather the children close around me; I can't let them be hurt. Prigg is obviously not above harming us, and I can't let that happen.

Their tiny bodies tremble against mine.

"Jake, you grab up whatever you see that's worth anything," commands Prigg, his tone more controlled now.

I watch in horror as Prigg pulls a coil of rope from his belt and tosses it to another man. *You animal!* I snarl in my mind, forcing myself to keep the insult in. It won't help to be angry.

"Here Nat, you tie up them boys and get 'em loaded into the wagon."

"No, please, Mr. Prigg," I plead, stepping in front of the children. *I've got to protect my babies. But what can I do?*

The instinct to obey is overpowering and, Lord help me, I can't seem to stop myself from begging. I raise my arms up to him, careful not to grab hold of his sweat-soaked shirt. "Please. Don't take the children. I'll go along willingly, just leave my children alone."

Our eyes meet in the dim light. He reaches out and strokes my cheek, a touch that makes the hairs on my arms raise and my stomach tighten. I try to jerk my head away, but he grabs hold of my chin.

"You always were a pretty little cherry," he says, licking his chapped lips. His eyes drift down over me. I'm wearing only my nightgown. I suddenly feel embarrassed and exposed. And frightened. Prigg is a big man. He probably has sixty pounds over me and would crack my ribs, if he wanted his way. Dear God, what *does* he want of me? The possibilities fill my mouth with acid. I try again to pull away, but his grip on my jaw tightens. He jostles my head from side to side.

"But I reckon you don't have half a brain in that Nigger head of yours."

Then he laughs, while deep inside me, something hot and threatening starts to brew. It boils up my fear, turns it to anger. I'm torn between begging for the lives of my babies and tearing into this letch with my last wild breath.

"You are the property of the Widow Ashmore, you dumb coon, and I'm just returning her rightful property. I don't care what that Nigger-lovin' boot-licker Justice of the Peace has to say."

My anger finally bubbles to the surface. Dumb coon? Nigger-lovers . . . *That's enough.* I can no longer stand the sound of his revolting voice, his hateful, ignorant words. It's just too much.

"I'm nobody's property!" I shout, and I spit in his face.

He grabs me up by my neck and lifts me off the ground with one arm, wiping the spittle from his cheek with the other hand. I struggle, pulling at his arm, his fingers clamped tight around my neck, up under my jaw. My toes stretch for solid ground, but they don't reach. *He's going to kill me! Right in front of my babies!*

My lungs burn and struggle for breath, but they get no air. I can hear the children screaming at him to leave their mama alone, yet their screams sound distant. Prigg's booming laugh is all I can seem to hear. The room is going darker. I claw at Prigg's arms, digging my nails into his clammy skin.

"Ow! Damn you!" He throws me back, and I fall, hitting my head hard on the ground, coughing, gasping.

The cabin is spinning in a flurry of activity. I lie on the floor, unable to move, and watch the men sweep my cherished belongings into canvas bags—the small mantle clock Jerry gave me for a wedding gift, the heavy Bible I got when Mama and Daddy died, the little cedar box with my sewing money, our linens, even our cooking utensils.

The children are tied together and herded out the door. Emma sobs.

"Leave the children." I try to shout, but my voice comes out barely a whisper.

Prigg walks around the cabin, circling me like a wolf circles its prey. Suddenly, he grabs my arm and lifts me from the floor. I want to struggle, to fight him off, but my muscles are limp. I want to curse him, but I'm mute. *What's wrong with me?* It's like a nightmare I've had so many times; I run as hard and fast as I can, but I go nowhere, I can't break loose. Only this is worse. It's really happening, and I can't escape, and I can't wake up.

He pushes me out the door and up into the wagon next to my heap of children. I look at their scared faces, and wings of panic beat in my chest. The other men climb aboard, and Prigg takes the reins. He shouts to the horses, and the beasts snap to, pulling the wagon into motion. I pull my babies as close as I can, amid the ropes that bind them awkwardly together.

The only sounds in the dense night are the muffled, hiccuppy cries of my daughter as she lies quivering beside a mountain of our personal belongings. *This can't be happening.*

"Come here now," I whisper to the children, and they wriggle closer to me. The warmth of their small bodies makes me shudder. I close my eyes hard and tight, and hold my breath, fighting back the sobs gurgling up from deep in my gut. After a second or two, I open my eyes again and let out a short, quick breath. Then I take in a few more deep breaths and let them go slowly. *Just keep breathing, Margaret,* I say to myself. *Keep breathing. We're gonna get through this. Somehow.*

The silhouette of our cabin quickly vanishes in the moonless night, as we jostle down the road, heading south. The McBrides' house is less than a mile away. Did the shotgun blast wake them? If I scream, would they hear my cries for help? Even if they did, could they find us in the darkness? And what would Prigg do if I cried out now? I gently run my fingers over Johnny's head, feel the smooth, tight lump rising up from where Prigg bashed him with the shotgun. *Hold your tongue, Margaret. There's too much at stake.*

I wonder how long it will be before we return home. Surely the judge will make this right. Surely the Lord will take notice of this crime. Won't he? As though she has read my mind, Emma nestles up under my arm and whispers the Lord's Prayer, and the wagon wheels rattle along the muddy road.

The cover of trees is behind us now. The clear, open sky is rich with stars that cast a divine light upon our entourage. I can see now who else has been party to this crime.

"What do you think we'll get for the whole lot of them at auction?" Nat questions Prigg eagerly, looking at him with admiring eyes, like a puppy fawning over his master.

Auction? I stiffen, my arms and legs becoming so rigid I can hardly feel my babies beneath them. *Oh Jerry . . . I should have listened to you.* Prigg never said anything about selling us when we were in court the other day. I thought he was just bringing us to Mrs. Ashmore. I try to calm myself, reasoning that there's no way she'd allow us to be sold at auction.

Nat leans back, fidgeting in anticipation of Prigg's answer, running his stubby calloused fingers through his unkempt hair. I've always found his gray eyes to be dull and empty, and the pale starlight does nothing to improve my opinion of his looks.

I'm sure his opinion of me is no better. My coffee skin is the darkest seen in Harford County. My black eyes and wide nose are my Daddy's. My small figure and my coarse hair are my Mama's. My parents came to America on boats straight from Africa when they were just babes, long before President Jefferson decided it wasn't right to kidnap people that way. Most coloreds in Harford have lighter skin, of brown or copper - lots of mulattoes. When I see their light freckled complexions and wonder about who their daddies might be, I thank God for my black skin and for sparing my mama such an assault.

"Darkies like them will fetch a good sum, I'd say," Prigg finally answers up. "The boys are young and healthy, so they could pull in a couple hundred a piece. Maybe more. The girl probably ain't worth too much. What you think she is, five, six years old? That's old enough to do house work, though, so maybe you'll fetch about fifty for her."

"What about Margaret?" Nat asks.

"Oh, she'll bring a tidy sum. She's strong, has good teeth, wide hips. With the right auctioneer, I'd wager you'll get three maybe four hundred dollars for her."

I feel sick, listening to them talk about me this way. As if I'm no more than a horse or a hog

Nat whistles, nods his head.

"Holy shit, Ed, that's great," he says, smiling. "That's just great."

Prigg's other two cronies just listen. Jake Forwood and Steve Lewis, also neighbors from my old home, were just skinny boys when we moved to York five years ago. They're men now, make no mistake.

The ride to Harford is about five hours. I'm still in a haze, still in disbelief this is actually happening. I study the faces of our kidnappers, trying to see the boys they used to be, trying to make sense of how people change as the years go by. Perhaps they really didn't change at all. Perhaps they always had evil in their hearts.

We're going to Maryland. My old home. To Mill Green, Harford County. The reality of it brings a flood of memories to my mind.

The county lies like a well-fed hog at the northern border of Maryland, its body pulsing with a thousand streams that pump life into its fat mounds like so many arteries. The people here tapped into those vibrant streams decades ago, and the waters were used to power grist mills and saw mills, iron forges and furnaces. A dozen little villages sprung up throughout the area, but the richest one is Mill Green, which John Ashmore established after the Revolution and which he named for its lush landscape.

Mr. Ashmore was a smart businessman, the kind who preferred to exercise his mind and rest his back. The idea of a grist mill fit neatly with that ambition, he believed, because it efficiently put to work the power of God Almighty Himself. I only really knew him as a broken down old man, but my daddy slaved for him back when Mr. Ashmore was young and strong and arrogant. Back in 1793, he and his fair-haired young bride used her marriage dowry to buy forty acres of land and a dozen brawny black boys and set about the task of building their enterprise. John Ashmore never really considered himself a slaveholder, though. He was just a businessman, he would say, and he treated his boys as such. He governed them like a strict father might, providing them with their daily needs, rewarding them with more when their efforts warranted, delivering the rod when necessary. And within a year the Ashmore mill stood tall at the base of the falls along Broad Creek, built off the sweaty backs of my daddy and his black brothers.

Clear water flowed down the rocky falls and over the eighteen-foot mill wheel, powering the belts, pulleys and gears that made up the machinery inside. In winter, ice sometimes formed on the wheel and had to be broken away. It's a sight I'll not soon forget, watching one of the mill workers climb up that giant frozen wheel, like a mad black spider, hacking away at the ice with an axe. But most times the mill was a peaceful operation, the rhythm of cold water dancing merrily over the wheel to the hum of the millstones as they ground buckwheat or corn into flour and animal feed.

Not long after Mr. Ashmore's mill wheel began to churn with full force, other men and women moved to the area and built residences that doubled as their places of work. Located far from any big towns, Mill Green became a real community with a general store, post office, saw mill, cider mill and undertaking establishment. Others came to farm, and they brought their grain to Miller Ashmore for grinding. Despite the hardships of the War of 1812, the grist mill and the small community that sprang up around it had flourished.

Prigg's wagon rattles across the St. Charles Bridge and into Mill Green, reminding me that everything in my life—my children's lives—might be changing. And maybe for the worst. I try to shake the cloud of doubt that has been hovering over me throughout the five-hour trip. Daybreak should be coming soon, but for now the dark remains thick around us. Still, I can just make out the silhouette of the Ashmore estate, the main house, the mill wheel far away.

My parents' old cabin, the tiny shack where I was born and raised, is coming into view and just the sight of it is making me strong again. All their sacrifice, all their sweat and toil, all their love, comes bubbling toward me just like Broad Creek, bringing new power to the mill wheel turning inside of me.

"You just wait until Mrs. Ashmore hears what you did, Mr. Prigg," I say, breaking the long silence. My mill wheel picks up speed. "She'll have your hide."

Prigg laughs. "You dumb Nigger. Mrs. Ashmore is the one who sent me to fetch you. Hunting damned runaway slaves ain't no job for a lady."

It feels as if my lungs have been squeezed tight, stopping the air from entering and exiting my body. No. Prigg is a liar. The widow has never laid claim to owning me. John Ashmore freed my parents decades ago, and Mrs. Ashmore respected that decision, even after he passed on.

"Is it true, Mama? Are we runaways like that Mr. Prigg says?" John whispers, after we're dumped into my parents' old cabin and the wooden door is slammed and bolted behind us.

"No, sir," I say loud and firm, though inside I'm in tatters. "Prigg's a dirty liar."

It's easier to speak up now, to speak the truth, when I feel safe inside my old home and Prigg stands, presumably, on the other side of the heavy door. As I speak, I gently lay Emma down. Precious thing, fear has been kind enough to let her sleep during the wagon ride. But John and Sam Jr. are wide-eyed. It will take more to get them settled down.

"But you told that judge man you don't have no papers. How do you know you're free then?"

"I know, Johnny, because my mama told me so. And now you know, because *your* mama told you so."

That gets a smile out of them, small, but heartfelt. I place my hands upon their beautiful heads, pulling both of them in for a hug at my bosom. Then we sit down upon the dirt floor, leaning our backs against the bumpy log wall of the shanty, and I rub and pat their backs just like I did when they were babies. While I find comfort in my mother's memory and my old home, I can't stop the fear that gnaws at me.

I know I'm free, because my mama told me so. Not a day goes by when I don't think about Mama. Lord, I wish she was here now, so she could tell that jackass Prigg about the day I was born. She told me that story a hundred times over, and not a single word of it ever changed, not even when she was getting on in years. Story telling was her gift from God, but if you ever asked her, she'd tell you that I was.

If Mama was here, telling my story, there's no way anybody would question my freedom. But I guess it's up to me now, to tell it, and to look Mrs. Ashmore right in the eye and ask her if she don't remember it just that way.

My mama's name was Sarah and she brought me into this world on a warm October day in 1808. Her body told her to push, and all at once she knew a baby was on the way. Hours earlier, she didn't even know she was with child.

She had collapsed in the garden, overcome by a deep, powerful ache in her back. That's where my daddy, Old Sam, found her, slumped over her basket of sweet potatoes, weeping. He lifted her up close to his chest and carried her in to the cabin. And he thanked the Lord out loud that he had refilled their mattress with fresh straw and cornhusks just that morning. Then Sam laid his wife down on the bed and took off across the yard for Master Ashmore's house.

"Oh Lord, Missus, my Sarah gonna die. I just know it."

Master's wife, Margaret Ashmore, did not hesitate. She grabbed her sewing bag and some clean towels from the linen drawer and rushed with my daddy back to the small cabin at the south end of the estate. She ducked her head into the doorway and directed Sam to fetch a kettle of water and wood for the fire. Then she knelt down beside Mama.

"What ails you, Sarah?"

"I done broke my back, I think. I finally done broke my back."

Mrs. Ashmore quietly considered the possibility of that diagnosis. She inhaled deeply through her nose and ran her hand across the top of her head, smoothing her soft blonde hair back toward the neat round bun at the nape of her neck. It was what she did when she was thinking.

Hot tears welled up in Mama's dark eyes and then escaped, leaving thin tracks on her dusty garden cheeks before falling to freedom on the mattress. Then a wave came over her, a surge that began at the knees, washed up through her body flush to her cheeks, and then flowed back down again. And then she knew.

"Oh my Lord, Missus, I'm gonna have a baby!"

"What? That's nonsense, at your age. Sarah, I believe you've lost your mind."

"No, no, Missus. There's a baby comin'. There's a baby comin' now."

Mama was no stranger to having babies. But she was past the age, or so she'd thought. At forty-something, this would be her twelfth pregnancy, though not one of her children had called this cabin home for long. Most had been sold to slave traders at about the age of eight and shipped out from port at Havre de Grace to plantations in the Deep South. Two were still born. One had been crushed to death working at the Ashmore mill when he was nine. He was the last of Mama's children to be snatched away by slavery. Mama said Master

Ashmore actually wept with her at the news, and two days later he gathered all his slaves at the mill and told them they were free.

Mrs. Ashmore had delivered many of Mama's babies, and Mama had cared for the Missus through four miscarriages and one delivery of her own. She placed a hand on Mama's belly, gently pressing and feeling all around.

"Well, I'll be . . ." she nodded. "I'll go tell Old Sam."

Less than two hours later, in a rush of blood and tears, and cries and laughter, I slipped into the world. Mrs. Ashmore wrapped me up and laid me on Mama's bosom.

"It's a wee little girl, Sarah. She can't be but five pounds."

Mama smiled down at me and wondered out loud, "Oh, sweet Jesus. What's gonna become of this tiny child?"

"I suppose you'll have to raise this one for yourself, Sarah, if you're able."

Of course Mama was able, more than able, though she had given up long before on any thoughts of watching a child of hers grow up in plain sight, much less under her own care.

"What shall you name her?"

Mrs. Ashmore had never asked Mama that before. I was the first child she ever named.

"I'll call her Margaret, after you, if that's a'right ma'am."

"Yes, Sarah, that's all right with me."

"Oh, Lord have mercy. Lord have mercy."

The splintered door pushes open, and sunlight floods into the windowless cabin. My eyes blink in the brightness as I rise from the ground, shaking off the sleep from my bones and the dust from my skirt, surprised that I slept at all. It's Mrs. Ashmore. Did she knock? I didn't hear it.

Her broad, familiar smile warms me, and her outstretched arms take me in for a welcoming embrace.

"Margaret, my goodness, it's been far too long. You're so thin, dear. How have you been managing on your own?"

"We're doing a'right, ma'am. The children keep me running, I suppose."

Why do I feel the need to somehow excuse my small frame, to comfort her? Truth is, since we moved to Pennsylvania, I never missed one meal. That's more than I can say for the years I grew up on Ashmore land.

"Well, you do seem thin," she repeats, stroking my cheek with the back of her soft, spotted hand. Her frown has more crinkles than I remember.

"It sure is kind of you to take notice, ma'am."

Her gaze turns to the children sprawled about the cabin, and new crinkles spring up around her smiling eyes.

"I remember when you were just a wee thing, sleeping in that same corner. What a scamp you were! Your mama and daddy didn't know what to do with you half the time. Good thing we kept you busy tending the animals, or who knows what would have become of you."

"Yes, ma'am."

John and Sam Jr. are sleeping back-to-back on a tattered rug in the corner, and Emma's curled up on my parents' old mattress, which is now flat and rank, littered with mildewed straw that hasn't been replaced in years. Vile as it is, it provided her protection from the cold and the hard of the ground. I can see Emma is awake, though she pretends not to be. Her eyelids flutter as she fights to keep them closed, her breathing is fast.

"Shhhhh."

A sharp twinge shoots through my shoulder as I bend down to stroke her hair, and the events of the past evening shoot through my mind just as sharply.

"Damn that fool, Prigg. Can you understand it, Missus, the way he's harassed my family?"

Mrs. Ashmore stiffens. She stares at her skirt, smoothing down imaginary wrinkles with her palms. Her posture says our lovely reunion is nearing an end.

"I suppose that's his job, dear. Perhaps if you had seen fit to come along readily, the rough treatment could have been avoided."

Come along readily? I can't believe what I'm hearing. I look down at Emma, noticing her quickness of breath is more audible, her eyes squeeze tighter shut.

"In fact, Margaret, I must say I was quite hurt when I learned that you refused to return peacefully with Mr. Prigg."

"I don't understand it, Missus. Why would you be hurt? What reason would I possibly have to leave my home and go willingly under Prigg's thumb?"

"I would have thought you'd be more loyal to the family that kept you," she says.

"Kept me, ma'am?" My mind is swirling in confusion. Surely I've misheard Mrs. Ashmore.

"Yes. And your folks."

That's not how I remember it.

I'm disbelieving at what my ears are taking in. Could it really be true? Nat and that old buzzard were acting with the blessing of the Missus? My heart beats faster and faster. I press my hands against my chest, as though I can somehow keep my heart from breaking in two.

"We sacrificed quite a lot when Mr. Ashmore freed all his slaves those many years ago. He did that for your mama, you know. I do believe it was the death of him. He did the work of five men after that."

And my daddy always did the work of ten men! I want to shout it into her self-righteous face. I try to speak up, but no words form on my tongue. And Mrs. Ashmore gives me no chance.

"Mr. Ashmore left me with precious little when he passed, as you well know. My debts are heavy. Honestly, Margaret, I should think you'd be honored to help see they get repaid, after all we've done for you."

Honored?

"Where's there honor in passing your debts on to *my* back?" I say, the disbelief, the absurdity of it all, crackling in my voice. "How can honor be any piece of you tearing my family apart?"

The missus doesn't answer. She smoothes her hand up over her head. Her hair looks coarse and dull. It doesn't have the glossy shine it once had. It's not the only thing about her that has changed for the worse in the years since we've been gone. I suddenly want to shake her. Bring her back to the truth. She *knows* the truth. Has old age made her mad?

Then the reality of my circumstance sinks in. *She* has done this to us. How could she? I put my arms straight down at my sides now, my fists clenched tight.

"So Prigg was telling the truth." I look her straight in the eye, long and hard. "Poor Mr. Ashmore must be turnin' in his grave."

The contempt in my voice is clear. She turns and walks silently to the cabin door, stopping for just a moment with one final address, her back still turned toward me.

"Auction is in two days, Margaret. Make sure the children mind."

Chapter 4

York, Pennsylvania

Jerry Morgan ran into Constable McCleary's office, tripping over the doorstep on his way, and flew sprawling across the floor into a group of wooden chairs. He was muddy and breathless, sweat seeping from his body and creating dark damp patches on his filthy shirt at the armpits, chest and back. His hair was matted and his eyes were wild with fear or anger or confusion, like a bear cornered by hounds.

"Holy Mary, Mother of God," McCleary blurted, jumping back from his desk and drawing his weapon. He gathered himself quickly and, realizing this wild beast was in fact Jerry Morgan, McCleary holstered his gun and reached a hand out to hoist the man to his feet. "Shit, Jerry. You all right? What's gotten into you?"

"They gone, Bill! They gone!"

"What? Slow down, Jerry. What is gone?"

"Margaret and the chillun. They gone, and the place is all torn up. They all gone."

Deputy Bailey charged in from the adjoining room. Only nineteen years old and inexperienced in dealing with Negroes, he too was already sweating from the excitement. Red haired and fair skinned, still wet behind the ears, the boy's face was flushed and his voice high. "You need the cuffs, Constable?"

"No, I don't need the cuffs. Man alive! Jerry ain't here to be arrested."

The constable corrected a chair and guided Jerry into the seat. Jerry clung to McCleary's arms, looking up wildly, an expression of shock and horror and disbelief still chiseled on his face. "All right now, Jerry, you take a deep breath here and tell me nice and slow just exactly what you're hollering about."

Jerry did as instructed, sucking in a lungful of musty air from the Constable's small office and letting it go in a gush of frustration.

"I left Friday mornin' on a delivery up to Trenton," he began, then labored to take in another breath and let it out.

"I come back 'bout an hour ago, and our place is all torn up, Bill, all torn up. There's a shotgun hole up through the roof, and there's furniture all turned, mud all over my Maggie's clean floor. And they gone, Bill. Margaret and the chillun, they nowhere to be found. Nowhere to be found."

Jerry stood back up to emphasize his final point, and McCleary, nodding, placed his hand upon Jerry's shoulder in silent comfort. Bailey's wide eyes blinked repeatedly as he looked back and forth from Jerry to McCleary, and he cautiously placed his hand on the black man's other shoulder. The three men stood silently in a triangular pattern at the center of the office, while wheels of thought churned in McCleary's head.

"It had to be Prigg," McCleary finally said. Of course, Jerry knew this to be true but, even in his wild panic, he knew better than to have been the first to say it out loud.

"Yes, sir, gotta be."

"Prigg?" Bailey joined in. "He that feller up from Harford who came stomping around here last week, sir?"

McCleary nodded.

"It's the only thing I can figure. But we can't go around making accusations without any proof. Deputy, you go saddle up your horse and pack some bacon and biscuits. You're riding down to Mill Green to talk to the sheriff tonight and see what you can find out. Then you haul yourself on back to York just as fast as your girl will take you in the morning."

"I'm going with him."

"No, Jerry, that won't do. I need you to show me around your place and see what we can learn there. Then we need to get you washed up and put some food in your belly. If we need to make a trip to Harford tomorrow, I want you clean and sharp. But first we've got to know what we're dealing with, so you just hold on. We'll get 'em back, Jerry. We'll get 'em back."

Jerry nodded, trusting the constable's authority and intelligence. It wasn't the first time McCleary had dealt with a kidnapping like this, and he knew just how to handle the matter. McCleary could knock heads if he had to and keep the peace, without a doubt. But he was also a true man of the law and could quote any statute or bill, word and verse, as well as any lawyer or judge in York County.

Back in 1787, when McCleary was still in diapers, the U.S. government had passed the Fugitive Slave Law, which gave slaveholders the right to hunt down and reclaim runaways in neighboring states, with or without proof of ownership. Nearly 40 years later, Pennsylvania passed its own law, saying bounty hunters couldn't just kidnap anybody they wanted to make an easy buck or two. They had to prove ownership. It was this law that had protected Margaret just four days before and sent Prigg away with his tail between his legs. And the constable knew it.

McCleary turned to Bailey, "All right, get a move on now, while you've still got some daylight."

Jerry extended his hand to Bailey. "God's speed, Mr. Bailey. God's speed."

The Deputy shook Jerry's hand, shook a black man's hand for the first time in his young life. Jerry's grip was firm and sure, and Bailey marveled at the realization that it felt no different in his grasp from any white man's. The three men exchanged one final round of glances and nods, and then silently departed on their separate missions.

What kind of a man *goes crashing into someone's home and snatches up a defenseless woman and her children? How could somebody do such a thing?* Deputy Bailey ran the questions over and over in his head as he rode out of town and on his way to Harford. He had grown up north of Philadelphia, in a predominately white community so, although he had very little understanding about slavery, Bailey also had very little understanding about Negroes. *But ain't they people, after all?* he asked himself. *Didn't that Jerry Morgan shake my hand just as good and proper as any white man? And ain't he grieving for his family just the same as any man would?*

The sun sank below the horizon, glowing like a hot iron in a blacksmith's oven, casting ominous drawn-out shadows in the fields and along the roadside. Bailey didn't like being alone at night on such a mission, and he decided to forego a break for supper and ride straight through. As the curtain of night closed in around him, he grew more anxious about what he would learn in Mill Green and he continued to ponder what motivated a man like Edward Prigg.

Mill Green, Maryland

"Sheriff Porter, good morning. To what do I owe this pleasant surprise?" Margaret Ashmore opened her door wide and invited the man in. She dried her hands on her apron and motioned toward the kitchen. "May I offer you some coffee? Griddlecakes?"

"No thank you, ma'am. I'm here on official business," answered John Porter, Harford County's Sheriff for more than thirty years. He had considered retiring on several past occasions, and on this particular morning he wished that he had done so. There had been days when the office required him to perform duties he was dead set against. This was one of those very days. The widow studied his somber expression and the purple shadows beneath his eyes, but she did not know they were the result of a late-night visit he had had from Deputy Bailey.

"What sort of business would that be, Sheriff?"

"I got a report last night of a kidnapping. And I have reason to believe the victims are being held on your property."

"A kidnapping? And you've tracked the marauders on to my land? Oh my, Lord. Jim. Jim!" Mrs. Ashmore shouted out to her slave. "Lock up the house!"

Jim walked into the foyer through the kitchen door, only slightly startled by the panicked squawking of his mistress. He had been the widow's houseboy for fourteen years, and he knew she was prone to nervous outbursts.

He took up the widow's hands in his and patted them tenderly. "There, there, now, Missus. What's got you so upset?"

The sheriff was shocked at the familiarity the Negro took with the widow. He was even more shocked that she had allowed it.

Mrs. Ashmore seemed oblivious to the matter the sheriff had brought before her. She looked frantically about the house, pulling her hands from Jim and rushing to a nearby window to slam and lock it shut. She eyed Deputy Bailey, who stood at attention beside the sheriff's wagon just outside. "Have you brought a deputy to watch over me until these criminals are captured?"

The sheriff tried a more direct approach. "Ma'am, if these accusations are true, your safety certainly is not in jeopardy."

She turned her gaze to him, puzzled.

"The kidnapper in question is Ed, Ed Prigg. The constable up in York County believes he may have kidnapped Margaret Morgan and her children and brought them back down here to Harford."

"Oh." The widow exhaled heavily and placed a hand upon her chest. "Is *that* what this is all about?"

The sheriff waited.

"Mr. Prigg went up to York to retrieve Margaret for me, sure enough. As I understand it, she did raise quite a fuss. You know she ran off years ago, and I decided it was high time to reclaim my rightful property. Nat is taking her and the children to auction today."

"So, you're saying you hired Ed to fetch her and that she's your rightful property?"

"Why, yes, of course. What on earth did you think, Sheriff?" Mrs. Ashmore didn't wait for an answer. "Well, now that that's all settled, how about some coffee?"

"Begging your pardon, ma'am, but this is not such a light matter. Pennsylvania has some pretty tough laws about this kind of action. This is a very serious affair. You'll need to take me to see Margaret immediately, and you'll need to produce your papers of ownership for her and the children forthwith."

The widow stood dumbfounded. Both her hands had moved instinctively up to her throat and her mouth gaped, as though she were choking on a piece of meat and gesturing for someone to step up and save her life. Jim moved dutifully to her side.

"Missus?"

"Oh, Jim!" The old woman collapsed meekly into his arms, which were ready to catch her. What an odd sight they created, these two bodies so opposite, as the slave cradled his mistress in his arms. She was thin and flimsy, with alabaster skin that made her seem almost transparent. He was brawny and hard, with a bronze complexion that gave him a look of durability. And, yet, the two seemed inexplicably connected, one unable to survive without the other.

The sheriff could only watch in amazement. He remembered what a handsome woman Margaret Ashmore had been in her prime, confident and proud, the virtual matriarch of Mill Green at the side of her husband, John. But after Mr. Ashmore passed, the widow became a pale version of what she once was, a lost lamb wandering in search of a new flock to follow. She had only her daughter to turn to, which was most unfortunate in the sheriff's view.

"Let me get you over to the couch, ma'am," Jim said. "You rest yourself, and I'll take the sheriff over to see Mr. Bemis."

"I'm afraid that won't do," the sheriff interrupted. "By law, Mrs. Ashmore will need to come along, so we can get this matter resolved."

This order from the sheriff seemed to infuse an unseen strength into the widow, and she rose steadily to her feet, an expression of resolve on her face.

"Very well, Sheriff. Let us get this matter resolved."

She removed her apron, folding it neatly and placing it on the foyer table, while Jim ran to retrieve her cloak and bonnet.

Chapter 5

Margaret

"Are you sure you don't want your beans, Mama?" Emma looks at me, her long lashes curling up like ribbons around her smiling eyes, eyes so black and clear they look to me like tiny pieces of blown glass.

"Yes, I'm sure, dumpling. You eat 'em up, so you'll grow big and strong."

Truth is, I'm afraid to eat. My stomach is all knots and if I put anything inside of me, it'll sure come right back up again. We've been sitting cooped up for two days now, the shadow of the slave auction hanging over my head like a blade at the gallows. When I think of my babies toiling in a field, being treated worse than barnyard animals, I have to close my eyes. Steady myself. I try to push the thoughts out of my mind. This is a life they've never known. Sadness they've never suffered. I can't bear the thought of it. I clutch the hem of my dress and squeeze. I try to squeeze the fear from my fingertips.

Wagon wheels rumble up the road and stop just outside the shack, sending whispers of dust through the cracks of the dilapidated walls. The children are sitting cross-legged on the floor, slurping up spoonfuls of beans, unaware of the horror about to befall us. I've tried a dozen times to prepare them. But how do you explain to a child something you can't possibly understand yourself?

I rise slowly and casually from the ground, smiling at the children, and move closer to the wall to get a good listen to the voices rising outside. A few more puffs of dust come through the wall, putting a taste of dirt in my mouth. I can hear feet stirring outside. But no one's coming in.

"What the hell is this about, Sheriff?" Prigg's voice is unmistakable.

"Mr. Prigg, please, watch your language around a lady," Mrs. Ashmore reprimands him with words of maple syrup, telling me she really doesn't mean it.

"Listen, Ed, this ain't up to me. You know that," the Sheriff says. "If Mrs. Ashmore had papers, that would have been different. But she doesn't, and Mr. Bailey here has orders to locate Margaret and the children and report back to York County immediately."

"He can report whatever the hell he wants. But his orders ain't a fart in a whirlwind to me. We're taking these Niggers to auction today, and that's all there is to it."

Prigg's turn of phrase draws a giggle from the widow. I still can't believe Mrs. Ashmore has turned on me. My family. I don't know how she can laugh so easily, knowing what she's done.

The Sheriff doesn't sound so pleased. "I can't oblige your wisecracks today, Ed." His voice is louder now, and another ribbon of dust wafts past my nose. I pinch my nostrils to fight off a sneeze. "Margaret and the children are coming with me, right now. They're gonna stay in the jail house until I hear word from the York County constable on what course of action he wants to take. I'm sorry Ed, but you really stepped in it this time. You really stepped in it."

Feet move toward the door, and I scurry back quickly before it opens. The children are startled, too, and jump to their feet, overturning their beans into the dirt.

"Oh, Mama, the beans," Emma whines and I shush her, pulling her in close beside me.

The sheriff steps in and removes his hat.

"Hello, Margaret."

I nod. There's a silence in the room, as if it's a cloaked stranger standing right between me and the sheriff. He doesn't seem to know what to say. I lean my head a bit, to see past him through the doorway, half expecting Prigg to come charging through to knock us over again. The sheriff must have read my mind.

"I'm taking you and the children down to the jail house, for safe keeping, until we get this runaway question settled. How are you all doing, Margaret? You got anything you want to say?"

I've got a lot I want to say, but none of it is befitting of a lady. Besides, I remember Sheriff Porter well, and I know he's not really too interested in what I've got to say. He's nothing like Constable McCleary. They are both men of the law; but they've got different laws to enforce.

"We're okay, Sheriff. Is Jerry outside?"

"No, he ain't here. Just a deputy down from York, says Mr. Prigg violated a court order bringing you here. So we need to get that settled. Why don't you all come along with me now."

Part of me doesn't believe him, but my choices are few. We either go with him to be locked up somewhere else, or we go with Nat to auction.

"Yes, sir. Come along, children."

I walk through the doorway, my little ones following behind like a handful of baby ducks, and we all step out blinking into the morning light. We march past Prigg and Nat and Mrs. Ashmore standing shoulder to shoulder, scowling at us. Jim is with them, and he looks me right in the eye, showing only the slightest smile of recognition. My, he's grown into a fine-looking young man in the years since we've been away. Must be twice my size now, all muscle. I want to throw my arms around him, kiss his cheeks and ask how he's been. But this ain't no time for reunions.

"Mr. Bailey, you want to inspect the family, so you can report back properly on their condition?"

A young man with red hair looks at me, bewildered. Must say, I'm a bit unsure myself of what the sheriff is meaning by "inspect."

"We're all fine, sir," I say to him, and he looks back at me with tremendous gratitude and relief.

"Yes, ma'am," he says, nodding and taking the reins of a horse hitched beside the wagon. He hoists himself up into the saddle and turns to address the sheriff.

"I'll let Constable McCleary know you'll be keeping them, sir." Then he turns to me and tips his hat. "And I'll let Mr. Morgan know you're safe and waiting for him to come take you home."

All I can do is smile at him, the first genuine smile to lift my tired brow in two days. The thought of being in Jerry's arms again—in my home—brings me a peace I haven't felt in days. Prigg snorts and spits, sending a giant gob of snot onto the ground between me and Mr. Bailey's horse. The deputy just lifts his head high and turns his horse toward the road.

"He-yaa!" he hollers, pulling up on the reins a bit, holding back the horse just enough to make it kick a cloud of dust and dirt in Prigg's direction. Then he gallops up the road and disappears down around the hill on his way north.

The wagon ride into town is nice, all things considered. The fresh air in my lungs and warm sun on my face lifts my spirits, after being cooped up in the dusty dark cabin. I watch the children take in the sights of Mill Green, so different from their home in York, with its rolling hills and endless bubbling streams. They seem to be excited by this new adventure, despite the horrible ordeal that brought us here.

We rattle through the center of town, quite the spectacle, I'm sure—a wagon full of Negros. It feels strange being back in a town where nearly all the passersby are white. You won't see many colored folk in Mill Green unless you go to the farms and mill operations on the outskirts. "Town" slaves are kept more discreetly, in kitchens and work rooms and back roads, out of sight whenever possible.

I recognize many of the folks who watch our wagon go by. Men and women I grew up with in this small village. They avoid making eye contact with me, then turn to one another and exchange comments out of my earshot. I can only imagine what they must be saying. My cheeks burn, being paraded through town like a common criminal. *Hold your head high, Margaret,* I tell myself. *You've done nothing wrong.* The sheriff parks the wagon alongside his office and marches us in through the back door. There are two small cells in the place, each with two cots and one piss pot. One cell has a small window on the north wall.

"I'll have to put you all together, Margaret," he says. "Got to keep one cell available, just in case."

He directs us to the cell with the window, and for that I'm grateful.

"Thank you, Sheriff," I say as the children file through the open bars. I can only imagine the permanent scars these bars will leave on my babies, even though this situation is temporary.

The metal door swings closed with a clang behind us. I jump at the finality of the sound. But I assure myself that soon we will be out. Constable McCleary and Jerry will get this all straightened out. They'll come get us. Come take us back home to Pennsylvania.

"I've got to run now and see the judge," Sheriff Porter says. "I'll lock the outside door when I go, and you'll be safe enough."

I thank the sheriff again as he leaves. John climbs up on one of the cots to look out the window. Sammy follows suit, though he has to stretch on tip-toes to see out.

Emma plops down on the other cot.

"This place is cleaner than the other one," she says.

"Yes, it is," I say.

"But there's still nothing to do."

"Here, play with this," John says. He pulls a tiny doll from his pants pocket. It is crafted of twigs and twine and fabric scraps. "I made it when we were in the shack."

Emma's eyes twinkle.

"Oh!" she says, snatching it up. "Thank you, Johnny!"

What a good boy he is, taking care of his sister that way.

The boys go back to their window gazing, and Emma settles down on the floor, talking to her new dolly in a sing-songy voice. Oh, to have that innocence of childhood—that trust that everything is going to be okay.

"I remember this place," John says after a little while. He was only about five when we packed up and left Mill Green. "I remember catching tadpoles in the stream with Nana."

"Do you?" I ask. It brings tears to my eyes, knowing he remembers happy times with my mama. "Tell me more. What else do you remember?"

He hops down from the cot and sits beside me.

"I remember helping you tend the goats and coming into town to buy feed," he says after thinking for a bit. "And I thought I recognized Mrs. Ashmore, but she's different than I remember her."

"Yes," I say. "She's different than I remember, too." A pang of anger fills my chest. I'm not sure I can ever forgive her betrayal.

My memories of her are tarnished now. The woman who entered my parents' old shack just a few days ago to announce the slave auction is not the same woman who delivered me, who taught me to read, who wept at my parents' funerals. Where did that lovely woman go?

Seems to me like Mrs. Ashmore was never quite herself again after her husband passed on. I blame that wretched daughter of hers. A young woman is supposed to mourn the loss of her daddy and comfort her mama through it all. Lord knows that's what I did when my daddy died. Susanna has a different way about her.

I remember her criticizing the widow one morning after they returned from church.

"Honestly, Mother, why you still hold an ounce of allegiance to Father's ridiculous notions is beyond me," she had said while they sat at the dining room table. I was putting out the Sunday brunch.

It was 1825, less than a year after Mr. Ashmore had died, and the poor widow was still suffering from his loss. Susanna, apparently, was only suffering from the loss of her family's money. She had always blamed their hardships on what she called her father's "unexplainable" distaste for slavery.

But even I knew that bigger things than Mr. Ashmore's ideas on slavery had contributed to the family's financial troubles. Back in 1819, a panic had swept the entire country. I remember it well, even though I was just a small thing. Children often see and hear more than they're capable of understanding at the time, I think.

In hindsight, it all seems so clear. Many things caused that panic— dropping cotton prices in the South, tightening of credit by the government to curb inflation, and closing of factories up North because of foreign competition.

But few people understood any of that during the thick of it. All they knew was that the good times that had followed the war of 1812 had come to an abrupt end—jobs disappeared, banks failed, homes were lost. The depression officially ended by about 1823, but it left lasting scars behind in Mill Green.

The Ashmores probably suffered more than most folks, because they paid their workers, instead of using slaves.

"You know darn well that's how Father nearly bankrupted the mill," Susanna scolded her mother that day after church. "If he had just listened to Mr. Prigg and put his slaves back to work at the mill, we would have saved thousands of dollars."

It probably would have been easy enough for him to do that. Mama and daddy never had official free papers. None of the Ashmores' slaves did. But Mr. Ashmore was stubborn about it. Daddy told me Mr. Ashmore sold off his other property instead, item by item, piece by piece, to make ends meet.

If Mrs. Ashmore had known about their financial hardships at the time, she never let on. Instead, she organized clothing drives and traveled to Baltimore twice a month with the Mill Green Lady's Auxiliary to volunteer at the soup kitchens that had been established to feed the poor.

"Dat woman has a heart of gold," Mama said to me more times than I can count.

Part of me is glad that Mama has already passed. It would break her heart to see how Mrs. Ashmore has changed. It breaks mine.

Chapter 6

Philadelphia

Pennsylvania District Attorney Thomas Hambly removed his riding gloves and pulled the brass bell knob at the Johnsons' massive front door. The young attorney had been invited to dine at the Attorney General's home once before, when he first was offered the district attorney job less than a year ago. Tonight, Pennsylvania Governor Ritner and his wife would also be in attendance. Tom had worn his best suit in the hope that another promotion was close at hand.

The door opened wide. Anna, the housemaid, smiled and motioned for him to enter.

"Good evening, Mr. Hambly," she said. "May I take your coat, sir?"

Tom Hambly admired the delicate sprinkle of freckles across her cheeks and nose, just as he had during his previous visit. One bouncy curl of chestnut hair had escaped from beneath her bonnet and danced seductively near her left ear.

"Good evening, Anna. Thank you," Tom said.

"Everyone is in the parlor," she said, reaching out to take his coat.

"Not everyone," Tom said, holding on to his coat for a moment, waiting for their eyes to meet.

Anna met his gaze with a demure smile, then cast her eyes down again and hurried off with his coat.

"Tom! My good man, I didn't hear you come in." Ovid Johnson burst through the parlor doors. "How long have you been loitering out here in the foyer?"

"Just long enough to enjoy a brief visit with Anna," Tom replied.

"Tom, you hound. Come into the parlor. I want you to meet the governor."

Abigail Johnson quickly took Tom's hand as he entered the room.

"Tom, it's so lovely to have you for dinner again," she said, leading him toward the other dinner guests while her husband poured him a glass of sherry.

"You're so kind to have me," Tom said. "It smells like heaven in here."

"Spoken like a true bachelor," she replied. "You must half starve to death with the hours you work and no wife to put a hot meal on the table every night."

Tom only smiled. Most evenings he dined at the tavern across from city hall. A pint of cold ale and a bowl of hot chowder in the smoky tavern were all he desired after reviewing piles of legal briefs late into the night.

Mrs. Johnson had other plans for him. She led him toward her other dinner guests.

"Have you met Miss Rose McFarland? Her father owns the general store on St. Mary's Street," she said.

"I don't believe I've had the pleasure," Tom said, bowing slightly to the young woman. "Tom Hambly."

"Delighted to make your acquaintance, Mr. Hambly," she said.

"Please, call me Tom."

Rose smiled. "I've been told your talents are highly regarded in Mr. Johnson's office. Civil rights litigation, is it?"

"Of sorts, yes," Tom replied. "Constitutional law, to be more precise."

Mrs. Johnson continued. "And, of course, you know Governor Ritner."

"Only by reputation," Tom said, extending his hand. "It's an honor to meet you, sir."

"Indeed," the governor replied as they shook hands. "This is my wife, Gertrude."

"It's a pleasure, madam," Tom said, bowing slightly.

With introductions out of the way and the first round of drinks poured all around, the group settled in to polite conservation about the weather, the vintage of the sherry and the marble chess set Mr. Johnson recently had shipped from the Orient. In due time, Anna entered the parlor to announce dinner and led the party to the dining room.

Tom dutifully took his place at the table as Mrs. Johnson directed him to sit beside Rose McFarland. He smiled and chatted with the debutante, while catching sidelong glimpses at Anna as she drifted in and out of the room serving up steaming platters of meat and vegetables and bread.

"Your centerpiece is just lovely, Mrs. Johnson," said Rose. "Where ever did you find mountain laurels this time of year?"

"Thank you, dear," Mrs. Johnson said, smiling. "The flowers came from your father's general store, if you must know."

"Oh!" Rose exclaimed. "Did they really?"

The women laughed.

Mrs. Ritner commented on how nicely the silver candelabrum complemented the blue flowers. "I just read in Lady's Magazine last month that a good table presentation is vital to the success of any dinner party," she said.

"Indeed," Mrs. Johnson agreed.

The governor leaned in toward the attorney general. "Hold on to that candelabrum, Ovid. Currency being what it is today, you may need the silver to fund your next dinner party," he said. Then he laughed and stuffed a large wad of meat in his mouth.

Rose set her fork down and cleared her throat softly.

"All due respect, sir, but I don't believe the dismal state of our economy is a matter for jokes," she said.

The governor seemed to notice the young woman for the first time all evening. He smiled broadly and leaned back in his chair.

"Is that so, my dear?" he said, his mouth still bulging with meat. "And what can you tell me about our economy?"

Rose had gained Tom's full attention now, too. Her face was flushed. Her nostrils flared just a bit. She drew a deep breath and folded her hands neatly in her lap.

"I can tell you that President Jackson's rash monetary policies thrust our great nation into a financial crisis destined to be the worst we've seen yet," she began.

The governor's expression turned serious. He began to interject, but his mouth was still full. So Rose carried on with the economic lecture he had invited.

"Inflation is out of control," she said. "I see the pain it brings every day, in my father's store. His customers struggle to pay their debts, and he struggles to decide whether their paper currency will do his own debts any good."

Mrs. Johnson commented again on Mr. McFarland's lovely flowers, hoping to guide Rose back to a topic more befitting a lady. Her efforts were in vain. The floodgates had been opened.

"Have you forgotten, young lady, that Jackson is no longer in office," Governor Ritner said. "If there is a mess at hand, perhaps President Van Buren is not doing all he should to rectify the matter."

"Ah, but Van Buren has only been in office a few months," Ovid Johnson sounded off. "It was Jackson who vetoed the national bank bill in '32. Without a federal bank, the states banks have run amok, printing money in their basements, making loans they couldn't possibly cover."

Rose nodded. "Yes, yes, that's exactly right, Mr. Johnson. And President Jackson also issued the Specie Circular, so that the federal government could only accept gold or silver in payment for taxes and for land. Why, in doing so, he practically declared paper currency to be worthless. Now, many establishments are refusing it, just as you joked only a moment ago, Governor. People are rushing the banks in a panic, and the banks are closing their doors."

The young woman's face had become completely flushed. Mrs. Johnson placed a hand on her shoulder.

"My dear, why don't we take our tea in the parlor," she said. "I'd like to show you the lovely mantle clock I purchased from your father last week. We'll leave it to the men to debate politics and banking."

"Oh," Rose said. The two elder women rose from the table, and the men immediately took to their feet.

"Oh, yes, of course, of course," the young woman said, standing slowly. Tom pulled out her chair and watched with some disappointment as she was shuttled from the room.

"She's a spirited little filly, isn't she?" Tom whispered to Mr. Johnson as the men adjourned to the study.

"Indeed she is," Mr. Johnson agreed with a wink

Tom surveyed his mentor's study. A large mahogany desk faced out the bay windows affording a panoramic view of the estate. Four supple leather wing chairs were perfectly arranged for conversation near the brick fireplace. The credenza was fully stocked with brandy and cigars. Tom felt a rush of exhilaration at being admitted to the room. It was a near replica of his father's study, in which he had been strictly forbidden to step foot as a child.

"Make yourselves comfortable, gentlemen," Mr. Johnson said. He motioned for them to sit.

"Thank you, Ovid," the governor said, helping himself to a cigar from a silk-lined cedar box.

The attorney general carefully poured three snifters of brandy and replaced the decanter stopper with a gentle clink. "You may have already guessed, Tom, that the purpose of tonight's dinner party was not purely a social one," he said. He handed the men their snifters, then took up his own.

"I always appreciate a good home-cooked meal, Ovid," Tom said. "But if you've got something else on your mind, I'm glad to hear it."

Ovid exchanged looks with the governor. Tom took a sip of brandy to settle his nerves. His suspicions had been confirmed. Something big was coming.

"The governor and I want you to take the lead on the Morgan case," Ovid said.

Tom nodded, took another sip of brandy.

"Are you familiar with it?" the governor asked.

"The colored woman who got snatched up by the Maryland bounty hunters about a month ago," Tom nodded again. "Right?"

"Yes, that's the one," Ovid said. "We need to secure an error-free kidnapping conviction for Edward Prigg and his accomplices."

"Kidnapping," Tom responded flatly. He had hoped for something bigger—a promotion or, at least, a case that might make the front page of the papers. "Criminal cases aren't really my area of expertise, Ovid. Don't you think Mr. Hines or Mr. Petrigu would be a better match?"

The governor stood abruptly. He paced back and forth in front of the fireplace, gnawing at his cigar. Ovid was silent. Tom waited.

"It's not really about the Morgan woman getting kidnapped," Gov. Ritner finally said. "She doesn't even have free papers. So it may end up she's a runaway after all."

"Then what is it about?" Tom asked.

The governor resumed pacing and gnawing.

"Ovid?" Tom wanted an answer.

"We think this case is going to end up being about something bigger than kidnapping or runaways or even the morality of slavery..."

"Bigger than the morality of slavery?" Tom interrupted.

Ovid sat down in the wing chair across from him.

"It's about states' rights, Tom," he said. "The governor of Maryland is already insinuating that Pennsylvania can't have a law that keeps the citizens of Maryland from claiming their rightful property from within our borders. He said we can't rightly prosecute Mr. Prigg for kidnapping because Pennsylvania's Personal Liberty Law is unconstitutional."

"Unconstitutional," Tom echoed. "That's a decision for the Supreme Court. Do you think the case will get that far?"

"It better not," Gov. Ritner said and took a long slow draw on his cigar.

"It wouldn't be in our best interest," Johnson concurred.

Chapter 7

Margaret

I use my hair pin to scratch a little notch in the wall behind my cot. Thirty-two. That's how many notches are there. One for every day we've been cooped up.

"I spy, with my little eye," Sammy says, "something *green*."

"Is it the ceramic spittoon by the sheriff's desk?" John asks.

"Yes!" Sammy says in disbelief. "How'd you guess so fast?"

"Because that's the same *green* thing you spied yesterday," my oldest replies in disgust.

"And the day before that!" Emma laughs.

Sammy jumps to his feet and stomps away, but there's really nowhere to stomp in this small cell. So he just goes to the other side, weaves his arms through the bars and presses his forehead against the cold iron.

"Ugly old spittoon," he mumbles.

After a moment or two, Johnny speaks up again. "Okay. I spy, with my little eye, something.... *brown*."

"Is it the floor?" Emma asks.

"Nope."

"The walls?"

"Nope."

"The sheriff's desk?"

"Mm-mm," John shakes his head from side to side slowly.

"His chair?"

"Nope."

"The door?"

"No."

Emma's quiet for a bit, thinking, looking around. I lay back in my cot, let out a heavy sigh.

"Is it the ceiling?" I ask.

"Yep," John says flatly.

"Oh, Mama," Emma says. "How'd you know?"

"Just a lucky guess."

She tells me it's my turn to spy something. But I'm really in no mood to play. "You take my turn, baby."

Emma smiles, studying the cell and the office for something tricky to spy. Sammy looks at me sideways from his post at the bars.

"Come on," I say, patting beside me. He walks over slowly, then squeezes in beside me on the narrow cot. I wrap my arm around him tight.

Thirty-two notches.

More than four weeks.

That's how long it has taken to get things only half settled in this crazy mess. Jerry and Constable McCleary came down from York right away, and they laid out the whole story to Sheriff Porter. How Prigg tried to take us away and Justice Henderson told him he didn't have the right to do it. And then how Prigg kidnapped us anyway, in the middle of the night when Jerry was gone.

The sheriff agreed that old buzzard Prigg didn't go about things in the best way, but he stopped short of saying we were right and Prigg was wrong. Fact is, he said, the Ashmores don't have papers saying they own me, and I don't have papers saying I'm free.

We were deadlocked. So it was decided by the lawmen that the children and I had better stay in Sheriff Porter's jail until some official something could be agreed upon.

Jerry is permitted to visit us for a few hours each Sunday. He brings a basket full of biscuits and bacon and apple cider, and we sit out behind the jail office and have a family picnic under the watchful eye of the sheriff. While the children stretch their legs and play hopscotch in the sun, Jerry and I share information in hushed voices.

"I overheard the sheriff talking to the mayor the other day," I tell him. "He said the Pennsylvania district attorney sent word that Sheriff Porter is to arrest Mr. Prigg and the others and send them north for a trial."

"No kidding," Jerry says. "How'd that go over?"

"Not too well. They were both cursing up a storm. The mayor told the sheriff not to do anything of the sort. He was planning a trip to Baltimore to meet with the governor and discuss their options. It sounds like they're digging in for a fight."

"Things are getting hot up in Philly, too," Jerry whispers. "Nellie said Mr. Forten raised the issue at a meeting of the Free Africans Society, and they're planning rallies to protest."

"I sure hope it does some good," I say, lowering my voice even more, to be sure the children don't overhear. "Nat and Susanna were in the other day demanding that we be released, so they can get us all off to auction."

With that, Jerry grabs hold of my hand and shakes his head.

"That ain't gonna happen, Maggie. I will never let that happen." His voice is strong and his hands steady, but I know my man. His eyes give away the fear we both share.

"Well, what are we gonna do?" I ask.

It is a question neither one of us can answer, are afraid to answer, so we finish our meal in silence.

Every Sunday, it has been just a different version of the same old story.

And every week, the children and I sit in the jail cell and watch a parade of folks come in and out of the sheriff's office to stomp and fuss and make their demands—as though it's their lives or their freedom that's on the line and not ours. First it was Mr. Prigg, then Nat and Susanna again, then Mr. Forwood, and a whole lot of other people I don't even know.

My patience is wearing thin, as we wait and wait. I find myself pacing through the cell while the children sleep at night. Praying silently for the strength to keep my mouth shut, to trust that everything will turn out right.

I scratch another notch in the wall. Thirty-six.

I'm getting that desperate, anxious feeling I used to get when I was a little girl, in trouble for one thing or another with Mr. Ashmore. "If I could just go talk to him and explain," I would say to Daddy. And Mama would just shake her head and say, "That's my Margaret. Always tryin' to jump outta the frying pan and into the fire." Things are definitely heating up all around here, and we're safe for now under the sheriff's lock and key. But I'm still aching to speak my mind. Still wanting, I suppose, to jump into the fire.

The office is quiet. The sheriff has been reading the newspaper, his dusty ankle boots propped up on the desk and his reading spectacles riding low at his flared nostrils.

"It sure would be nice to go for a walk today," I say.

"What? What's that, Margaret?"

I've been watching him some time, but he didn't even notice me staring him down.

"I said, it sure would be nice to go for a walk. Would feel good to get some fresh air, work our legs a bit."

The sheriff studies me, nods.

"You'll get you some air on Sunday," he says finally and turns back to his newspaper.

Sunday.

I watch him read a little while longer, think about jumping out of a frying pan.

"I'd rather not wait until Sunday, Sheriff. I'd like to go for a walk, with my children, today."

He looks up at me again, raises his eyebrows. He clears his throat, but he doesn't say a word. I wait for a response. All I get is a cold stare. Then, he turns back to his paper once again.

The silence roars in my ears.

"Sheriff, am I under arrest?" I finally ask, frustration weighing down my voice.

The sheriff places his feet on the floor, folds up the paper and lays it down on the leather blotter covering the desk. He removes his glasses, folds them up neatly, and places them atop the paper. Then he slowly stands, walks in a small circle and leans back on the desk, almost squashing his specs in the process. Finally, he folds his arms, square across his wide belly.

"No, not exactly, Margaret. You ain't under arrest."

"Then why am I being held captive, like some kind of criminal? And the children, too? Were we not the victims of this crime?" I tug at the bars that separate us, motion to my children as they lay sleeping.

"First off, Margaret, you're here for your own safety, until we get this matter settled. There's quite a stir happening over this affair, I'm sure you know. Not just here in Mill Green, but up in Philly, too."

He reaches behind him and picks up the newspaper again, waving it at me before he opens it wide and shakes out the crease.

"Listen here." He slips his glasses back on his nose and reads from the *Baltimore Times*. "Pennsylvania District Attorney Thomas Hambly has issued an indictment on the charge of kidnapping for four slave hunters from Harford County. Maryland officials have refused extradition. Questions have arisen as to the status of the runaway slave and the rights of property owners in slaveholding states to cross state lines and retrieve their goods. Heated communications among Pennsylvania Governor Joseph Ritner, Maryland Governor Thomas

Veazey and other high officials of both states have delayed negotiations . . . "

He stops reading and then repeats his odd ritual of folding and placing and folding.

"So, you see Margaret, this thing is bigger than all of us."

I can't accept that. No matter how big it may seem, nothing could be bigger to me than my children and my freedom. Nothing. I look at my Johnny, my Sammy and my Emma. That familiar tremble of sadness washes over my body again. And again I long for Jerry.

"What if I can prove I'm free?" I blurt out. "Wouldn't that settle things?"

"How you gonna prove that, Margaret? You haven't got any papers."

"Well . . . there has to be people in the village who remember when Mr. Ashmore set my parents free. Everybody knows for a fact that he did, right after the mill accident. They could testify." The more I talk, the more energized I get. I am right. Everyone in town *knows* the truth. "And what about the census records? You did the census survey yourself, Sheriff, just before we left Maryland, remember? I saw you write it all down the day you came out—Morgan household, one free black male, one free black female, two free black children. Couldn't I take all that to a judge as proof? Couldn't I sue Mrs. Ashmore for my freedom?"

The sheriff whistles a mouthful of air through his sparse, clenched teeth. I can't tell if he is angry at my impertinence, or surprised by my inspiration.

"It'd be a first for me, that's for sure. I never heard of a colored taking a white to court. Never heard of it."

Maybe he has never heard of it. Maybe nobody has ever heard of it. But after saying the idea out loud, it seems to me like my only hope. I want this. More than anything. I will *be* the first black woman to take a white to court. I can do it. I'm not going down without a fight and, after seeing fairness prevail in Justice Henderson's court, perhaps it can prevail again.

"Will you look into it, Sheriff?" I ask. "Please?"

"I never heard of such a thing, Margaret. Never," he repeats. "But, yeah, I'll look into it. Just don't go getting your hopes up."

Chapter 8

Mill Green, Maryland

"I'm going out to tend the goats, ma'am!" Jim called out to Mrs. Ashmore from the back door of the kitchen. Susanna had come over early, and the women had taken tea and biscuits in the parlor.

"All right," she answered.

Jim walked out to the small animal shelter about 100 yards from the house. It had a coup with four chickens and a night shelter for three goats. During the day, the goats roamed freely about the property, keeping the weeds down and the shrubbery nicely groomed. There was a hog's pen, as well, but it had been without an occupant for nearly a decade.

"Maaa!" Jim called out to the goats. "Maa-aa, maa!"

In no time, the curly-headed threesome trotted in from the pasture to see what their friend had for them on this day.

"Time to trim your toes," Jim told the animals as they entered the pen.

He set out a bucket of rolled oats and the animals circled around it. Jim looped a rope around the neck of one goat and led it to the fence. The animal went along willingly, knowing it could return to the crunchy treat as soon as Jim was through. He tied its head securely to the post and, standing alongside the animal, gently pushed it against the fence to maintain complete control.

Margaret had taught Jim how to take care of the animals when he was boy. He'd taken over her job when she'd moved to Pennsylvania in 1832. He'd just barely been 18 years old at the time.

"How am I ever gonna do all this on my own?" he had asked her. "What if the animals don't mind?"

Margaret had put her arm around the young man's scrawny shoulders and given him a squeeze.

"Just show them respect as God's creatures and give them the best care that you can. And they'll come to respect you just the same.

You'll do a fine job with this, Jim, just like you do with all your other chores."

Jim had been delighted to learn she was right. The animals always came to him when he called. The goats produced ample milk and the hens provided eggs nearly every day. Sometimes, though he thought he must be crazy, Jim was sure the animals even smiled at him.

"Relax now, girl." Jim picked up a hind foot firmly in one hand and pulled rose pruners from his pocket with the other hand. He had sharpened and washed the tool the day before to ensure the hoof trimming would go swift and clean.

"Too bad you didn't get to say hello to Miss Margaret when she was here," Jim spoke to the goat.

"Maa-aa," the animal seemed to answer.

"I know you'd remember her, what with the way she took such good care of you all those years."

Jim worked quickly, cutting the dew claw first, then trimming the outer hoof wall of the goat's toes. He moved from one hind foot to the other and then shifted up to work on the front feet.

"She looked real good," Jim continued. "And that little girl of hers looks just exactly like her. Such a pretty little thing."

"Maa."

"Wish I could'a got the chance to talk to her. I bet Miss Margaret's got some interesting stories about livin' up North."

Jim untied the goat. It smiled up at him and then pranced over to the oat bucket. Then Jim got to work on the second goat and then the third.

"Yep, I sure wish I could'a talked to Miss Margaret, just for a bit. Didn't realize how much I missed her all this time, until I saw her again. Gets lonely around here sometimes, being just me and Mrs. Ashmore."

"Maa-aa."

"Oh, you're right! Sorry. I got you girls to keep me company, don't I?"

Jim laughed, as he untied the last goat. He watched the three crunch away at their oats for a minute or two. Then he picked up an empty bucket and headed down to the well to fetch some fresh water for the trough.

Mrs. Ashmore sipped her tea. Her eyes shifted from her cup to her daughter to the parlor window. She took another sip.

"I heard Betsy Forwood is expecting again," she said.

"Yes," Susanna replied. "I heard that, too."

"Oh, you had?"

"Yes."

"Oh." The widow took another sip of tea and stared into the cup.

Susanna split open a biscuit and dabbed each half with a spoonful of peach preserves. Then she took a bite and chewed slowly.

The women had little to say to one another. They attempted to gossip or discuss fashion and recipes. It didn't suit them. Still, sometimes the silence was more than the old woman could bear. When she felt completely desperate to generate conversation, Mrs. Ashmore would bring up the one topic she knew her daughter loved above all else.

"Is business keeping up at the mill?" she asked.

Susanna's eyes came to life.

"Oh yes, Mother, we're keeping quite busy really," the young woman said. Then she giggled and shrugged her shoulders. "I suppose no matter how difficult the times get, people still need to eat!"

"Yes, I suppose," the widow said. "Although during the Depression, our mill business suffered terribly."

Susanna scoffed. "That's because Father had no sense at all for business."

"I wouldn't say that," Mrs. Ashmore said.

"You've just forgotten." Susanna stirred her tea briskly, then tapped the spoon on the side of the cup. "I remember all too well watching him run that business into the ground. If Nathan and I hadn't stepped in, we would have lost everything."

The Depression that began in 1819 took a toll on countless businesses and families. But Susanna had only been concerned with her own family's fortune. She'd seen her inheritance dwindling and knew that she, being a woman, was powerless to stop it alone. So she had made arrangements to marry a neighbor's son, Nathan Bemis, on the contingency that her father would sell his remaining real estate holdings, including the mill, to the newlyweds for a nominal sum.

Mr. Ashmore had done as his daughter asked. He died intestate in 1824, one year after the Depression had officially ended, leaving an estate valued at only $509 to his widow.

Nat had taken over operations at the mill when Mr. Ashmore died, immediately revoking the promise of freedom and fair wages that had been made to the former slaves. The mill flourished under the changes and the economic recovery that was underway.

"You know very well how much business improved at the mill under Nathan's leadership. Certainly, his decision to use slave labor helped tremendously," Susanna said.

The young woman looked at her mother, waiting for some response. Mrs. Ashmore only shrugged her shoulders a little and added a spoonful of sugar to her cup.

"Father had no business sense. He had only his twisted sense of morality, which destroyed this family, if you ask me," Susanna continued. "After all, what would they do, the Negroes, if we didn't provide them with shelter and work? It's just like the preacher said last Sunday, Mother, idle hands are the devil's workshop."

When her husband was alive, it was easy for Mrs. Ashmore to defend his positions, to support his actions. That was her duty. *But now that he is gone*, she wondered, *shouldn't my duty lie with my only daughter? And what of my duty to myself to live out my remaining years in comfort and security? Susanna raises a valid point about idle hands. Is slavery really so terrible a thing, after all?*

The widow glanced out the window at Jim. It had been a blessing to have such a loyal servant, and Jim was certainly the most valuable piece of property she possessed. When her husband first took ill, Ed Prigg had brought Jim over to the house as a gift. Jim was about 11 years old and had been purchased at auction by Prigg the year before, along with some miller's tools, a small wagon and an old mule.

The boy took over the major work of the estate—the wood pile, the cooking, the wash. He required little, if any, direction and he learned quickly. When Mr. Ashmore finally passed, Jim became the widow's primary focus. She set to the task of teaching him on the finer points of etiquette and spoken language.

Mrs. Ashmore had often considered emancipating Jim, as her husband surely would have done had he recovered from his illness. *But how would the boy possibly get along without me to provide for him and keep him from the devil's work?* she wondered.

"Well?" Susanna asked. "Mother, are you even listening to me?"

"Huh?" Mrs. Ashmore said. "Yes, yes, idle hands. Of course I'm listening to you, dear. I always do, don't I?"

"Well, yes. Good," Susanna said, her voice softening a bit. "I only wish Father would have listened. You know I only want what's best for our family. I'm just thankful that you've been more open to considering my advice."

A few years before, Susanna had proposed that the widow hire Jim out from time to time. Mrs. Ashmore had taken the advice, and the income she received for his work helped keep her debts at bay.

Not long after, Susanna began suggesting that her mother contract a bounty hunter to track down Margaret and the children. The money earned from their sale could wipe out the widow's debts entirely, she had reasoned. That took quite a bit more prodding, but the widow had finally complied.

"Yes, dear," the widow said. "I'm thankful, too."

She took a sip of her tea, but it had gone cold.

Chapter 9

Margaret

Praise the Lord. Today is the day I will finally get to speak for my freedom. Sheriff Porter proposed my wild idea to the powers-that-be in Harford County, and they agreed to let me take Mrs. Ashmore to court.

The courthouse is in Bel Air, the county seat of Harford, about an hour's ride from Mill Green. The sheriff and I leave early in the morning. Bumping along in the back of his wagon, the summer sun rising bright on the horizon, I rehearse all the things I want to say today. I'll tell them about how Mr. Ashmore freed his slaves, and Mama's story about the day I was born, and about the sheriff taking the Census all those years ago. The words run through my mind. My nerves are so rattled, I can hear my voice shaking even in my imagination. *Lord, give me the strength to speak loud and strong when the time comes.*

Bel Air is a quiet little town, which seems to exist only for the sake of having the courthouse here. You'd think the building would be grand, for that very reason, but it ain't. It's nothing like the one up in York. Small and dark, with a low ceiling and scuffed up wood floors. I sit at a small table, empty except for a few ink stains and a dozen thin grooves left in the soft wood by a lawyer's quill. But there is no lawyer sitting at this table today. The state may have allowed me to file a petition, but I have not been given the right to an attorney. Blacks aren't normally even allowed in the courthouse in Bel Air. So I'm here alone. Jerry is waiting outside, and my children wait in the jail cell back in Mill Green.

"All rise. Harford County trial docket number fifty-three, the case of Negro Margaret vs. Margaret Ashmore, petition for freedom. The Honorable William T. Archer presiding on this day, Wednesday, August 28, 1837."

Mrs. Ashmore has a lawyer, of course, a squirrelly sort of man, with sharp cheekbones and tiny ears. She's standing beside him, looking something like royalty in her finest Sunday fashion. Her hair is smooth across her forehead, parted in the middle and pulled back in a simple knot. It remains just as she has worn it for years, rather than loaded with sausage curls at the neck like Susanna's hair, which is more fashionable today. Her dress is also classic, of navy blue velvet and just a touch of vanilla lace at the cuffs and collar.

Susanna and Nat stand directly behind her, and I see them each lean forward slightly and whisper words of encouragement to the widow as the judge walks in.

The courtroom is filled to capacity and a whole row of folks are standing at the back of the room for lack of enough seats. Judge Archer motions, and the bailiff quickly moves to open a few windows, which brings a welcome breeze to the warm stale proceedings. We're told we may be seated. I sit down and smooth out my skirt to dry the sweat from my palms. I suddenly realize my fate rests with this decision. It could all be over in a short while. I could be going home. I pray another silent prayer as my foot taps nervously on the floor.

"Counsel, do you have an opening statement?" the judge asks, and Mrs. Ashmore's lawyer stands to address the judge.

"Yes, Your Honor, we do. As you know, we're here because this Negro has petitioned for her freedom from Mrs. Margaret Ashmore. Shortly, we will present testimony from numerous witnesses which will show that this Negro is the fair and rightful property of Mrs. Ashmore. The testimony will show that this Negro took her children, also the property of Mrs. Ashmore, and ran away to Pennsylvania five years ago. Finally, the testimony today will show that Mrs. Ashmore is a woman of benevolence and dignity, and that her word in this matter should be honored above all else."

The judge listens intently to the man's words. He nods stoically and smiles at the widow ever so slightly.

"Very well, sir. Call your first witness," the judge directs.

"Your Honor, the defense calls Mr. Josiah Johnson."

I've known Mr. Johnson my whole life. He managed the mill for Mr. Ashmore, kept the books and delivered the payroll. My wage for tending the family's animals on the estate was one dollar per week, and Mr. Johnson always paid me with four new quarters, which he would carefully lay out in a straight row on the table with the eagle sides up. Sometimes, just to get a rise out of him, I'd flip the coins over one by one into a little stack before sliding them off the table and into my purse. Then he'd clear his throat and say, "All right then, Margaret, you go on your way." And I'd giggle about it all the way home.

Mr. Johnson walks to the front of the court room and places his hand on a Bible. The bailiff asks if he swears to tell the truth, and he does.

"Sir, how long have you known the defendant?" the widow's lawyer asks him.

"I've known Mrs. Ashmore for more than thirty years."

"And do you know the plaintiff, Sir?"

"Yes."

"And would you describe for the court, as you understand it, the nature of this Negro's relationship to the Ashmore family?"

"She's one of their slaves."

I gasp out loud, and the judge slams his gavel down hard.

"You will control yourself, Margaret, or you will be removed from this court room."

The gallery rumbles behind me as people shift in their seats, muttering and sharing their approval of his honor's declaration. I can feel their eyes burning little holes in my back, my arms, my cheeks.

The lawyer goes back about his work. He asks Mr. Johnson some more questions and Mr. Johnson tells more lies.

"The Ashmore's were so kind to her," Mr. Johnson says. "Then as soon as Margaret's mama died, she ran off. Stole all their silver when she went, too."

With each filthy lie, my mind goes darker and darker, swimming in a blackness I've never experienced in my life. The next witness brings more of the same, and the next, and the next. They all place their hands upon the Bible and swear before God to tell the truth. Twelve people in all.

"Margaret ran away, but Mrs. Ashmore was too benevolent to have her hunted down."

"She was a slave, and her parents before her, living under the kind Christian care of the Ashmores."

"She's about as free as she is white, and she ain't that at all."

"Oh yes, sir, Margaret is a slave."

"That ungrateful Nigger ran off soon as she got the chance."

The deceit just curls outta their mouths like ribbons of smoke, filling the room with a poison that makes my eyes burn and my throat swell. I turn around in my seat to find the sheriff. He's sitting right behind me and I reach out and grab hold of his coat sleeve.

"Sheriff?" I whisper desperately. "When do *I* get to speak?"

The sheriff jerks his sleeve from my grasp and shrugs his shoulders.

Another pound of the gavel snaps me back to facing the judge.

"This is your last warning, Margaret," the judge bellows. "You show some respect in this court, or you'll end up with a lashing."

The squirrel smirks at me, straightens his coat, and continues his questions. No one mentions the mill accident and the day Mr. Ashmore freed all his slaves. Mrs. Ashmore doesn't tell them about the day I asked for her blessing to move my family to Pennsylvania and she gave it to me. The sheriff is never called to testify about the Census. And the judge never allows me to speak. Not *once.*

After what seems like hours have passed, the judge announces a brief recess so that he can review the evidence. It doesn't take him more than ten minutes. A wave of dread crashes down on me as he takes a seat.

"I've listened to the testimony given today by the fine citizens of Mill Green, and I've reviewed other evidence presented in the matter of Negro Margaret vs. Margaret Ashmore," the judge says, shuffling papers on the desk, looking up at me, then down at his desk again, then over at Mrs. Ashmore. He clears his throat and pauses a moment.

"It is clear to me that the Negro Margaret and her children are the rightful property of Margaret Ashmore, and I therefore rule in favor of the defendant. It is so ordered that the Negro will remain in the custody of Sheriff Porter until such time that the Ashmore family is ready to remove their property for auction."

The gavel echoes in my ears.

I jump to my feet in a panic, my head spinning with the sudden rush of voices in the courtroom.

"No! Mrs. Ashmore, please. Please!" I sound so small.

I reach out to her. The judge bangs his gavel hard, again and again.

"Sheriff, remove that Nigger at once!"

The sheriff grabs hold of my arm and pulls me from the room, shoving his way through a swarm of people to get us outside. The people smile and buzz all around me. They nod and hug and shake hands. Jerry is lost in the crowd, pushing and struggling to make his way through. I catch sight of him and our eyes meet for a heartbeat.

"Jerry!" I try to break free from the sheriff's grasp, to run. But he's too strong. He jerks me hard and shoves me toward the wagon.

"There'll be none of that, Margaret," he yells at me. "You're not going nowhere except back to your cell."

I climb in the wagon slowly, looking back, trying to catch another glimpse of my husband. *I've got to see him. I've got to touch him.* If I could just get back to him, somehow, back into his strong arms, everything would be okay.

"Maggie?" Jerry's voice is but a murmur in the crowd, distant, small. "What happened? What's going on? Maggie!"

The sheriff pushes me up into the back by my rump and quickly locks iron shackles around my ankles.

"No, stop," I say, but it falls on deaf ears. I reach down and try to pry the shackles open, try again to somehow break free. The sheriff just laughs at me, finally showing the true colors his position has forced him to hide these many weeks. He climbs into the driver's seat and clicks to the horses.

My eyes scour the crowd again, trying to find my Jerry. But he's gone.

"He's gone," I whisper, still searching the crowd. I suddenly feel hollow inside, like everything that kept me alive inside was just torn out of me. The iron shackles feel cold and hard against my skin, uncompromising. *My God, will I ever see my husband again? And my children...*

Mama must have been right about Wednesdays after all. The reality hits me hard, like a kick in the ribs. Could the good Lord possibly be watching this? Ain't even lunch yet, and all is lost.

Chapter 10

Mill Green, Maryland

Widow Ashmore took a sip of tea from a tiny china cup and looked out the kitchen window into the dusky night. Jim stood at the work table a few feet away, shelling peas in preparation for the evening meal. Every couple of minutes he sidestepped to the iron stove to stir a bubbling pot of creamy fish chowder.

"Why do you suppose Margaret put herself through such an ordeal at that trial, Jim? Surely, she must have known she would not prevail. Why couldn't she just accept her position," the widow said.

"Maybe freedom is just too sweet to give up without a fight, ma'am."

"What?" The widow was incredulous. She had just been uttering her thoughts out loud, mindlessly, rhetorically, certainly not expecting a response from her long-devoted servant. She set her tea cup down hard on the window ledge and stood. "Jim, of all the impertinence . . . "

Jim had turned to face her, but a jingle at the brass doorbell interrupted her sentence. They stood eye-to-eye for a moment, until a second jingle broke the silence. Jim bowed his head.

"I'll get the door, ma'am."

He let Nat and Susanna into the foyer and took their wraps, and the widow followed him out from the kitchen.

"Mother Ashmore, you look as if you've seen a ghost," Nat said, startled by his mother-in-law's ashen complexion. He kissed her cheek. "Are you feeling ill?"

"Oh Nathan, for God's sake, don't be so dramatic," Susanna derided. "Mother has been through quite an ordeal with this ridiculous property hearing. I'm sure she's just tired, isn't that so, Mother?"

The young woman did not wait for an answer. Instead, she took the widow by the elbow and proceeded into the dining room. "Jim, bring us some tea," she ordered.

The family sat about the table and Susanna rattled on with excitement about their success at trial, about the upcoming slave auction, and about what the widow should do with the financial windfall she was about to receive.

"You'll need to clear your debts at the general store and the feed market, to be sure. But the remainder should be put into real estate, I think. I've heard that plots out west are selling again. Elizabeth McCarty told me the other day that her husband bought some land that had been foreclosed by the bank. They purchased it for half of what it's worth. Real estate would be a wise investment, don't you agree, Mother?"

Mrs. Ashmore had been tracing the embroidery of the tablecloth with her index finger. "I suppose it was rather courageous," she whispered, tilting her head slightly to one side.

"What? Mother, have you even heard one word of what I've been saying?" asked Susanna.

There was a pause in conversation as Susanna stubbornly waited for a response. Finally, Nat spoke up. "What was courageous, Mother Ashmore?"

Jim walked in with a tea tray and set it down upon the beige linen cloth which covered the expansive mahogany table. He set out a cup for each and poured out the steaming beverage. Nat was the first to drink.

"Dickens! What have you done to this tea, boy?" he exclaimed, as the tea dribbled out over his lower lip and down his chin.

"It's just honey, sir. I'm sorry. Is it too sweet for ya?"

The widow couldn't help but chuckle at Jim's little prank, at his clever attempt to make amends. He smiled at her ever so slightly before bowing his head in contrition.

Nat caught the glance exchanged between mistress and slave. "Mother Ashmore, is this some sort of joke?" he asked.

"Heavens no, it's not a joke, Nat. Jim just knows I like my tea sweet. He meant you no harm."

Susanna chimed in, "Honestly, Mother, drinking your tea so sweet is positively sinful. You really should give it up." She moved all the cups back to the tray and motioned Jim to remove it.

The widow quickly reached out to retrieve her tea. "No, dear, I don't think I will," she said, pausing to take a sip. "Maybe some things in life are just too sweet to give up without a fight."

"Now what on earth does *that* mean?" Susanna balked.

Jim carried the tray back to the kitchen and the widow sat quietly sipping her tea. Susanna sighed in exasperation, and Nat reared his head back and laughed at the women in his life.

Jerry Morgan sat hunched upon an old Hickory stump outside Jake's Tavern. A half-empty bottle of gin lay on the ground between his feet. He had purchased the liquor at the back door for twice the price he would have paid in Philly. The Mill Green establishment had been closed to blacks for several years, along with most other public places, in the aftermath of the Nat Turner slave rebellion in Virginia several years before.

On an August night in 1831, Turner had led six of his fellow slaves in a bloody rebellion, which began with the slaughter of his master's entire family as they lay sleeping. The marauding band grew to more than forty slaves as they proceeded on horseback from house to house. They spared no one in their path—stabbing, shooting and clubbing to death more than fifty white people—men, women and children, alike.

Citizens throughout the South had been so shocked and horrified by the massacre that many states, including Maryland, had debated ending slavery. Instead, they'd passed more stringent laws to govern slaves and free blacks. It was one of the many reasons Jerry and Margaret had decided to move their family North.

"Well, lookee what we got here, boys." Ed Prigg and his drinking buddies emerged from the tavern to find Jerry seated outside. The group circled around the stump.

"Couldn't be a Nigger, could it?" one man slurred.

"Nah, couldn't be," said Prigg, kicking the gin bottle away from Jerry's feet. "See, 'cause Niggers in these parts know they ain't allowed to loiter around such a fine establishment."

Jerry sat in a haze, too drunk and too defeated to get up and run, as he should have.

"Wait a minute, now," Prigg said, leaning in close to Jerry's face. "This ain't no ordinary Nigger. This here Nigger seems to be having a real hard time learning his place. What you think, boys, should we give this Coon a little educating?"

The first blow came as a fist to his temple. Jerry's teeth clacked together with a second blow to his jaw. It was not the first beating he had endured in his life, and he defiantly stood to face his attacker. A cut to his abdomen took his wind away and quickly dropped him to his knees. Boots hammered his back and his front, and blood stung his eyes, as Prigg's gang joined in the fun. Jerry's limbs and ribs and face didn't know which way to jerk or curl for protection as the onslaught continued. "Maybe a rope would teach him better," was the last thing he heard before blacking out.

Jerry awoke the next morning in a jail cell. His left eye was swollen shut. A metallic taste lingered in his mouth.

Sheriff Porter had caught word of a lynching the night before and gone down to Deer Creek to disrupt the activity. Under normal circumstances, he might have looked the other way and let Prigg and the boys blow off some steam. But people were looking just a little too closely at Mill Green these days. With the cloud of a kidnapping indictment still hovering over them, the Sheriff couldn't allow his friends to make any more missteps.

Jerry moaned as he struggled to sit up from the floor. A sharp pain throbbed in his temples, and his swollen body ached. The sheriff laughed.

"Don't know what did you in worse, Jerry, the gin or the boys."

"Where's Margaret?"

"Nat Bemis took her and the children down to auction 'bout two hours ago. Too bad you got yourself so knocked out, or you could have said good-bye to them."

Chapter 11

Margaret

I exhale heavily, exhausted even though I've been asleep. The children snore softly. I put my hands on them, running my fingers across their soft faces, down their thin arms. I know this may be the last time I will ever do so. My soul aches beneath the soft touch of my fingertips.

The sheriff wakes us before the sun, gives us a basin of fresh water, clean towels and new clothes. Then he watches as we wash ourselves and change. It is his job, he says, to make sure we're clean and in fine condition today.

As we rattle along the road to auction, I still can't believe this day has actually come. I find myself wondering if it has been my entire life that was a dream. And this, now, is the real life that God intended for me all along.

Emma's eyes are dull and swollen as she blindly watches the landscape go by us. She won't allow me to hold or comfort her. My boys, though, they are clinging to me tight. They understand I'm not to blame.

Last night, the Sheriff ran out in a hurry to settle some business, and the children and I were finally left alone. We sat quietly in the dark office, as the moon shone through the bars of our cell, casting a soft blue light onto our sullen faces. I took the opportunity to talk to the children, to prepare them for what was to come.

"Something bad is going to happen to us tomorrow, children. There's just no easy way for me to tell you about it."

After weeks of rolling it over in my mind, I had decided there was no way to sugar-coat the truth. John already understood and giant tears welled up in his eyes and ran silently down his cheeks as I began my lecture. Fact is, the children all had heard people talking in the Sheriff's office in the past weeks. They all understood, at some level, in their own way, what we had already lost.

"I've been to an auction before, Mama. It ain't so bad," Sammy said, rubbing my arm. When he turned seven, just this past January, Sammy went with Jerry on a delivery up to Lancaster. They took a wagon-load of chickens to auction, and he came home with a pocket full of pralines and a mouthful of stories about the wonderful haggling and deals he had witnessed.

"This will be different, Sammy," I said, taking his hand in mine. "There will be no hogs or chickens or wagons being sold. Only people will be sold. We will be sold."

"So we *are* slaves. We're not free at all, like you always said!" Emma wailed, stomping to the edge of the cell and throwing herself against the bars.

"They're gonna sell people?" Sammy whispered, wide-eyed, turning his glance from me to Emma and back again to me. He looked deep into my eyes, searching for an answer other than the silence I gave.

"No!" Emma shouted. Her arms were straight at her sides, her fists clenched tightly. "I won't go. You can't make me!"

My throat tightened and a burning ran up through my nose and into my eyes. I could not speak, and I could no longer be strong. My body collapsed in loud, violent sobs, and my boys rushed to me, heaped upon me, until we were one massive heaving being. The fear in their eyes was unmistakable, a reflection of the fear they saw in my own eyes.

We lay there weeping for some time, until we grew too tired to cry any more. I pressed my burning cheeks down upon the cold wood floor of the cell, and it gave me some relief. It reminded me of a time up in York, after the first snow fall one winter, when the children and I had stretched out in the cold drifts and made snow angels.

After a time, I pulled myself up to sit on the cot.

"There are things you must know, must always remember," I said, wiping my eyes and nose with the edge of my skirt. "No matter what happens tomorrow, no matter what anyone says or does, we are a family, and we will always be a family. Your daddy and I love you more than life itself, and that will always, always be true. Do you believe me?"

They nodded and sniffled. I cleared my throat.

"Now, there are other things," I said, pausing a moment to make sure I had their full attention. "Your life as a slave will be hard. But you must always be smart, much smarter than your master, and you must never let him know that. Keep reading, whenever you have the chance, and learning. But never let anyone know you can read. Let other people, white or black, believe you are ignorant. It will give you an advantage over them."

John watched me intently. Sammy watched, too, but the crinkles in his forehead caused me to wonder just how much of what I was saying was sinking in. Emma played quietly with her doll. She has always had a way of paying attention without actually paying attention. I can only hope that they'll remember all I said, that some day when they're a bit older it will make sense to them.

"And, most important of all, don't lose hope. You *were* free once. Emma, you were. We all were. We lost our freedom, and it's not fair. But when something gets lost, it can be found again. Just because we don't see something anymore, doesn't mean it's gone forever. Remember that. Promise me you'll remember that."

Suddenly, the front door of the office banged open and the Sheriff and his deputy came through pulling a black man along the ground between them. They each had hold of one arm, just under his armpits, and his knees dragged across the floor. The man was bloodied and unconscious, and his head dangled from his limp neck as he jerked along. They thrust him into the adjoining cell and left him in a tangled, disfigured heap on the floor in the far corner. The sheriff muttered something under his breath, and the other fella laughed and kicked the man. Then they left just as quickly as they came in.

"Is he dead, Mama?" John whispered.

"No, I can hear him breathing. I'm sure he'll be all right."

"He stinks," Emma pinched her nose.

The poor soul. His clothes were soaked with blood and smeared with what looked like mud, but smelled of cow manure. The strong stench of gin and vomit was also noticeable. But I had no time to worry over his fate. I had to stay focused on the children.

"He'll be all right. Come now, let's try to get some sleep."

The children crawled into the cots, and I sat on the floor beside them and sang softly, every song I know. One by one, they fell into a soft, rhythmic breathing. Just before I drifted off myself, I heard John whisper, "I'll remember, Mama."

The auction will be in Havre de Grace, a port on the western shore of the lower Susquehanna River, which empties fresh and clear into the

Chesapeake Bay. Years ago, Mrs. Ashmore told me it was French, meaning "harbor of grace." Before the War of 1812, the little port was well-known for its beautiful taverns and inns, where travelers stopped in for a cup of ale and a night's rest on their way north to Harrisburg or south to Baltimore. My daddy used to tell stories about going there with Mr. Ashmore to buy up barrels of blue crabs for Mill Green's annual spring picnic.

"Oh, Maggie," he would say to me. "You wouldn't believe what a pretty little place dat harbor is."

When Mr. Ashmore thought I was old enough, I got to go along to Havre de Grace to gather the prized blue crabs. I was so excited, didn't sleep a wink the night before we left. But the place wasn't nothing like daddy always said.

We went about 1816, when I was eight years or so. The city had been burned clear to the ground, or nearly so, a couple years just before, when the British attacked the coast. The townspeople had gotten word the enemy was coming, so they ran for their lives, and the little community was pretty much abandoned when the Red Coats finally came.

In 1816, a few of the buildings in Havre de Grace had been rebuilt, but the place was still mostly beaten down. It was late spring when we went, and the air should have been filled with the sweet smell of azalea and swamp roses. Instead, it smelled of mildew and ash. The only building of significance left standing after the siege was the Episcopal church, a huge rectangular building of neatly laid brick and perfectly arched windows. But its grounds, which must have once been green and lush with blossoms, had been trampled down and were littered with makeshift tents, fire pits and heaps of wood.

I felt bad for that poor little town, not necessarily for the people who lived there, but for the town itself. Sure, those folks had lost their homes, but they also ran, when they could have stayed to defend the place. Seemed to me the town itself had lost so much more than those people had, being abandoned like that. I remember wondering if a town could feel, could have a soul, if it could cry when it was wounded. It just looked so sad to me.

Seems fitting that we're going to Havre de Grace now—a place of such despair and ruin and ugliness—to be auctioned off to the highest bidder.

"I hope you explained to the children that they better mind themselves today, Margaret." Nat speaks to me over his shoulder as he turns the wagon down a dusty road that leads into town.

The sound of his voice makes the muscles in the back of my neck tighten. His words are meaningless, because he is meaningless, a sad excuse for a man. Yet his voice seems to somehow get up under my skin and makes me want to scratch myself bloody just to be rid of it. "Yessir, Master Bemis. They gonna mind," I somehow manage to answer.

"Damn straight they'll mind," he repeats, speaking more to himself than to me.

We haven't passed a soul on the road for quite some time. Maybe we should try to make a break for it. I untie my bonnet and test the strength of it pulled tight between my hands. My mind races with a vision of the strings wrapped around Nat's neck, of me choking the life from him, while he flails and fights in vain. Then we could run! The vision quickly becomes a blur. My grip at the strings loosens. The bonnet falls from my lap.

"Where would we go?" The words escape from my mouth without my realizing it.

"What's that, Margaret?" Nat asks with surprise. "We're going to Havre de Grace. I already told you that."

The children look at me with confusion in their eyes. But they say nothing. Sammy picks up my bonnet from the wagon floor and rubs it to his cheek.

"Here we are now," says Nat.

Up ahead, a sign at the fork says, "Welcome to Havre de Grace, population 4,065." It's bright and welcoming, with fancy letters the color of oak leaves in October. Looks so new and fresh, I wouldn't be surprised if the paint is still wet.

The town is in view now. My, what a sight! It's completely rebuilt, restored, surely, to its original glory, just as my daddy had always described it. Rows of black-eyed susans—all bright and sunny with their golden petals and black faces—line the streets and fences. Red brick houses stand in stately rows, their white porches jutting out onto emerald lawns. Colorful potted plants dangle from tall black light posts and a family of geese waddles across property lines, probably headin' for the river. The storefronts are a rainbow, with gleaming windows, and wood eaves and trim painted pink and violet, yellow and blue.

To think, I once felt sorry for this little town as a small black child, free and without worry. I hardly recognize it now. It has grown, blossomed, triumphed despite its plunder. I wonder if this harbor of grace remembers me—a grown woman, no longer free or without worry—as the small girl who once took pity on it. Perhaps now it pities me. And so it should.

"Don't cry, Mama," Emma whispers, placing her hand on my lap. I didn't realize I was cryin', the tears streaming silently from my eyes and dropping down onto my skirt. Emma smiles at me wide and sweet. "Isn't it lovely here?"

She looks around, enchanted by the sights as we bump down the cobblestone deeper into town. Her eyes are clear and bright again, the picture of this pretty little town having soothed her misery from the night before. I almost feel the need to shield my eyes from her glow. My poor girl has no real idea what lies ahead. Instead of breaking into a million pieces like I want to, I nod at her, squeeze her hand, do my best to smile. The boys seem to be energized by the sights and smells of Havre de Grace, too—freshly whitewashed fences, vines filled with white and pink maypops creeping up the sides of houses, the Susquehanna river flowing clean and free just beyond the storefronts. They're sitting up on their knees, craning their necks to see over the sides of the wagon as we bounce along. Their excitement burns in my bosom. The injustice of it all lays so heavy on my heart, I can barely breathe.

I suspect it'll be just a few more minutes before we arrive at the auction house, and I'm gonna hold my tongue until then. I don't want anything to spoil these last precious minutes of happiness for the children. But it just ain't fair, really, to lose everything you've got in a place so lovely.

Chapter 12

Margaret

"Good afternoon, Mr. Bemis," a large colored man greets the wagon as we pull into the auction lot. He hitches the horses and Nat hops down, places his hands upon his hips, and takes a long look around the scene. He breathes in a big lung full of air through his nose and lets it out in a gust through his gaping mouth. Then he turns to me with a smile.

"All right now, Margaret, you and the children come along," he says, clapping his hands together like a man fixing to scoop up his poker winnings from the table. I want to reach out and slap that fool smile right off his face. How plumb ignorant, or damn cruel, must he be to even permit himself to smile at me today.

I nod to the children, and we climb down from the wagon.

"You stay along close with me, now, and keep yourselves quiet, so I won't have to rope you all together," he says, getting a more serious look about him as we approach the crowd at the auction house. We weave through clumps of people, who fidget and laugh and chatter eagerly for the activity to begin. A large placard at the entry reads:

Sale of Negroes, Mules, Hogs, Farming Tools, Wagons and Carts in Harford County at Havre de Grace Auction House on Monday, the seventh day of September, 1837.

My heart quickens as I read the words, my breath catches in my chest. My feet turn to iron, and I just stop in my tracks, staring at the sign.

"That just says there's an auction today," Nat says impatiently, motioning for me to move along.

"I know what it says," I blurt without even thinking.

He stops now, looking me square on. His eyes narrow. Time seems to freeze, if only for a second or two.

"You just keep whatever it is you know to yourself," he growls at me. "You hear me now?"

I toss my head back, thrust my chin up at him. In my mind, I have all sorts of sass I'd like to speak. *Hold your tongue, Margaret,* I tell myself. *You better learn.* I let my eyes do the talking instead, and Nat just stares me down.

A man approaches us with his hand extended to Nat. He's squat and heavy, dressed in a dark blue suit coat and pantaloons, with a dusty three-corner hat that has been sorely out of style since the war. The two men shake hands vigorously.

"Mr. Bemis, I'm so glad you were able to make it today," the man says. "So discouraging it must have been for you to have to postpone your plans again and again."

He turns a stern eye to me briefly, then smiles again at Nat. "Well now, sir, tell me what you've got here."

"Thank you, Mr. Wille. It's kind of you to recognize the hardships we've undergone to get our property to auction," Nat nods, his arm still being jostled by the auctioneer's handshake. He turns toward me and the children. "We've got some fine property, if I do say so. Margaret here is a skilled seamstress, and still young enough to bear probably five or six more children. She's quick as a steel trap, although with proper discipline, I doubt that would be a burden to her new master."

"Hmm," says Mr. Wille, walking around me, sizing me from head to toe. He squeezes my arm. I recoil from the touch of his callused fingers. He gives me a stern look, and I brace myself for more prodding. He reaches down and squeezes my thigh. Then he runs his hand down my leg and squeezes my calf. I want to slap his fat face, but I control my outrage. He seems pleased with my submission.

"She's good and strong. And the children?" he says, turning to Emma. He places one hand on her forehead and another on her chin, trying to cock back her head and get a look at her teeth. Emma will have none of that and she snaps at him like an angry bull dog.

"Blazes!" he shouts, pulling his hands from her mouth just in time to save his stubby index finger.

"Margaret!" Nat bellows, as I draw Emma in close to me.

"I'm sorry, Master Bemis. Don't you worry, it won't happen again. She'll mind, I swear. All the children will mind."

"Sorry, sir," Emma says, her eyes cast down at her skirt.

We stand quiet for a few moments, while the auctioneer seems to be in deep thought. "We better make sure these two go together, so she can keep that little heathen in line until the sale is final," he grumbles to Nat, serving a hard kick to Emma's behind.

Emma lets out a tiny yip. Then she grits her teeth and squints her eyes at him as he stomps off to greet another patron.

I know we'll endure many more humiliations before the day is through, and I'm proud at how well the children are holding up so far. I'm even proud of Emma for trying to take a piece out of that auctioneer's finger. If it's one thing I've always preached to my babies, it's that they have to fight for what's important to them.

But you also have to choose your battles and, today, fighting will do us more harm than good. This is one battle we can't win.

I've already learned that the hardest way.

Nat says the other property will be auctioned off first—the hogs and tools and such—and the slaves will go last. Just makes things go smoother that way, he says to me with a knowing look. So all the slaves are shuttled into pens to wait our turn. Me and the children are put in a pen with three men and an old granny. She looks at me carefully, then shakes her head and clucks through her sparse teeth.

"Oh, sweet baby girl. This be your first auction, ain't it?"

I nod. She pushes a bit of hair away from her face, revealing a black smudge on her light brown cheek. Jerry had told me stories about the tricks owners tried to make their slaves look younger for auction. The men were always clean shaven, and the gray hairs were plucked from the heads of the older folks. In the case where the grays were too many, shoe polish was combed through to blacken their hair. It could make a man or woman look ten years younger, and bring in an extra two hundred dollars at auction, if applied right. But shoe polish or not, there is no hiding this woman's age. Her deeply creased face, her yellow nails, her dry cracked lips all give away her long hard life. I wince. Am I looking at the future, my future, when I look into her eyes?

"Be brave child," she says, looking so deep into my eyes that she must see my whole life's story in the time it takes me to blink back another tear. I nod again. It is all I can seem to do, just nod at her like some kind of dumb fool.

"The men'll go first," she continues. Maybe she thinks it might come easier to us if we know what to expect, or maybe she thinks talking will help pass the time better. Either way, I don't stop her. She goes on explaining, and I keep on nodding.

"The boys is next. And then the mamas and little girls. They put ya up on dat platform and make ya turn around and such. Might make you drop yer dress, too, so they can make sure you ain't damaged in some way. If you got a trade, you'd be smart to talk big when they ask ya. House keepin', sewin', cookin'. That might get you a place in da house, 'stead of in da field."

We sit quiet for a moment, listening to the auctioneer sing and to the buyers shouting out their offers. Then she continues, addressing the children directly.

"You'all do ya best not to cry, a'right? Folks looking for houseboys want a quiet little Nigger, one who's gonna mind and smile nice. The chillun who carry on up dar get sold for next to nothin' to the traders and get shipped way down South. That ain't the path you be wanting to go, you hear?"

The children nod, mesmerized by the honest wisdom of this strange woman, and I slowly pace back and forth in the pen.

"I already been at auction five times b'fore, if you can believe dat," she said, shaking her head. "Five times, mmm, mmm, mmm. Got taken from my mama at da firs' one. Said good-bye to my husband and chillun at da second. The other three times, well, they just ordinary. Didn't really have nothing else to lose by then, you know. Still breaks my heart though, like today, seein' such a sight."

They came and got the men about 15 minutes ago. I can see them coming back now, for my boys. *Dear God!*

I pull them to me, squeeze tight. I clutch at their heads, cover them with desperate kisses—kisses that must last us a lifetime. They look up at me, wide-eyed with pooling tears.

"It's okay," I whisper, closing my eyes tight against the tears. "It's okay." *I have to stay strong for them. I have to stay strong for my boys.*

"Let's go," the men command and grab hold of them.

A small whimper leaves my lips as their tiny bodies are wrenched from my arms. John and Sammy cling to me for a moment, their small fingers the last memory of their touch I will ever have. I can't stop the tears now. I see the fear in their eyes, as my tears fall down my cheeks.

"It's okay," I try and say again, trying to force a smile, trying to reassure them. *Trying to stay strong.*

Then they let go. My fingertips tingle only briefly with the memory of their skin.

They're just children. Please. Oh God, please, my babies.

The old woman whispers to them as they pass her, "Remember what I told ya boys. Remember."

"Mama!" Sammy cries out to me, looking back over his shoulder in panic, pulling to break free.

"Shut up, boy!" the man shouts and delivers a swift blow to the back of Sammy's head.

"Sammy!" I cry out, lunging forward, and the old woman grabs my shoulders to hold me back. She's strong, despite her age.

"Don't make it any harder for him than it already is," she grunts in my ear.

The pain inside is crippling. I can feel my stomach turn as I realize that I have to let go. *Jerry will come,* I think suddenly. *He'll find us.*

My lips are tight with the effort not to scream out, my muscles itching to flex and tear after them, to shriek and holler like a mad woman.

Like a woman who has lost her child.

"Be brave," I finally say, the tears flowing hot and fierce from my eyes. "I love you."

"There, there child." The old woman draws me back into the pen. The gate is slammed back into place, just inches from my face, and latched.

I watch helplessly for a moment, my fingers threaded through the bars, before turning and running to the other end of the stall to stand on my toes to see over the divider. The old woman stands on an upturned bucket beside me to get a look, too. There's a clear view of the auction platform, and I watch, my heart in my throat, as my oldest boy is led up the steps. He takes off his shirt and turns around. Mr. Wille, the auctioneer says something I can't really make out, and he points out into the crowd. I can hear shouts from the men, see hands gesturing. The bids come fast.

"Sold."

Sold! My *son* has been sold.

For a moment, everything stops. All the shouts, the laughter, the cold haggling over warm, helpless bodies becomes a roar in my ears. Tears well up in my eyes, and I blink rapidly to clear them away. I have to see him. My eyes burn with the effort not to lose sight of him as he is led away.

Johnny walks off the platform and is met by a man in a silk suit and top hat. He leads my boy to a carriage and removes a small waist coat from within, handing it to Johnny and giving him some sort of instructions. Lord, I wish I could hear what he's saying. Johnny puts the jacket on and slowly buttons the front; then he takes a seat next to the driver, a good-looking Negro in a red jacket with black velvet lapels and cap. As the carriage rattles past us, Johnny gives me a little wave, but he doesn't look back.

"A houseboy," the old woman says quietly. "That'll be good for him, real good."

"Mama! What's happening?" Emma asks, pulling at my dress, jumping in a vain attempt to see over the pen walls. "What's happening?"

Her small voice grounds me, dulls the sharp pain inside. *I have to be strong.*

"Emma, settle down," I say, crouching down so our faces will be level. "Johnny's been sold, looks like to a real nice man." I try hard to smile, but my tears have not stopped.

"What about Sammy?" she pleads.

A part of me can't stand to see my other boy sold. That part pulls at me, heavy inside my stomach. Another part, a stronger side, has to know.

I jump back to my feet and crane to see over the wall.

"Sold!"

I nearly missed it!

Sammy is hiccupping and fighting back more tears. My heart pangs painfully to know that I can't reach out to him, can't kiss his head and rock him until it's all over.

God protect him, I pray, because I know that I can't. Because I know that I'll never be able to save him from the horrors he'll endure.

The auctioneer is shakin' his head and gives Sammy a little shove down the platform steps. A man in a faded blue denim suit pays the auctioneer with a crumpled wad of cash and pulls Sammy by the wrist to where the horses are tied. He binds my son's wrists together with a rope and fastens the other end to a buckle on his saddle, leaving about six feet of slack between them. He mounts the horse, clicks his heels and trots off, forcing Sammy to either run along side or be dragged.

My precious boy turns his face to me as they scuttle past the pens, tears running down his cheeks. Our eyes lock.

Be brave! I want to shout at him. *I love you,* I mouth the words.

I stifle a gasp as he stumbles a bit and catches himself. A look of fear and seriousness takes over his face, and he turns his head forward again and steadies his jog in rhythm to the horse.

"What about Sammy?" Emma repeats.

I can't speak. The old woman looks at me in grave silence as I step down and turn to face my last tiny child.

"He'll be all right. He'll be all right," I whisper, more to myself than to Emma. A sharp pain in my gut doubles me over, and I vomit into the dirt. Emma watches me, a look of horror on her face.

"We're next, child," the old woman says, as the men approach the pen once more.

I can't breathe. The old woman pats my back and wipes my mouth with her apron. Then she helps me to my feet.

"You gonna be alright," she says.

I can only look at her. I don't think I'll ever be right again.

The men lead us to the platform. The old woman is taken up first.

"Okay, folks, we have a fine Negro woman for sale today. She's got a bit of a hunch back, as you can see, but she's well suited to kitchen work. Tell 'em what you can cook, Auntie."

"Oh, yessir," the old woman plays along. "Oh, I's a great cook. I make all kinds a biscuits and breads and sweet cookies and cakes. My gumbo is tasty, so tasty. And oh, I can clean. I scrub dem pots good and polish up dat silver. My arthritis ain't so good, you know, but if I work in da house, I do real good, real good. I polish up dat silver real nice, and . . . "

"All right, that'll do," Mr. Wille interrupts. "Who'll start the bidding at $100?"

The bids come slow, but she's finally sold for $250 and led away to join a group of several other slaves who had already been purchased and were awaiting transport in a large wagon.

Mr. Wille motions for us to step up. I'm afraid that I won't be able to move. Then I feel Emma's hand link into mine, and a calm sweeps over me. I swallow down the fear. For her. We walk up the wooden steps and stand beside him.

"I like to save the best for last, and this, gentlemen, is quite a prize. We have two fine females, healthy and strong," he says.

I feel sick, more from the pain of having the men leering at my baby girl than for my own sake.

Then he leans in to me, "Take off them clothes now."

I know there's nothing else I can do. With trembling hands, I reach around to unfasten the hooks in the back of my dress. I slip it off my shoulders one at a time and let it fall into a puddle around my feet. Looking out into the crowd, my gaze is met by dozens of white faces. Some of the men nod, others rub their chins, shrug their shoulders. A freckled man off to the side removes his hat, squints at me and scratches at his head. What am I worth to these men?

"Undergarments, too," Mr. Wille commands, and I feel my face getting hot. I unfasten my brassiere and let it drop. Then I slide my bloomers down to my ankles and step out of them. I can't look at Emma. I know the horrified humiliation I will see in her eyes is the only thing that can break me now.

Mr. Wille lifts my arms out to the sides and slowly turns me around, like some kind of giant naked bird being roasted on a spit.

Up to now, Jerry has been the only man to lay eyes on my nude form. Today, hundreds of men, women and children stand gawking at me. I cast my eyes up now, over the heads of the men who will be bidding on me. Don't want their faces to torment me after this ordeal is done.

"Look at that," marvels Mr. Wille. "No scars, no deformities of any kind. She's a fine specimen, and she's a skilled seamstress. Tell 'em what you can make."

I open my mouth, but words fail me. My tongue is a huge wad of wool, and I gag on it as I struggle to speak.

"She made this dress," Emma declares, stepping out in front of me.

My eyes shoot to her. Grateful tears swim in my eyes. *My daughter. This is my daughter.*

She twirls around and curtsies, and the crowd eats it up. Is it wrong to feel so proud at a time like this? It's bittersweet, to know how strong she is, in a moment no man, woman, or child should ever have to face.

The crowd laughs and a few of them clap. "And she makes pantaloons and jackets, and lovely, lovely quilts, too," Emma continues.

The auctioneer, chuckling along with the group, tells me to put my clothes back on and I do so quickly. "Yes, yes, very nice," he says, turning to the crowd. "Now, who will start the bidding at six hundred for this charming pair of Niggers?"

"Six hundred," says a thin man in the front row.

"Seven hundred!" comes a bid from the back.

"All right, I hear seven! Who'll bid eight? Do I hear eight for these sturdy Negroes? Eight? Ah, seven fifty from the gentleman in the red hat! I've got seven fifty now. Another bid, gentlemen? Let's go eight. Who'll offer eight?"

The man in front raises his hand, and the auctioneer points to him with a smile.

"We have eight from our opening bidder! Fine, fine. Who'll give me nine, nine? Who'll bid nine hundred?"

The speed at which our future is being decided is sickening. Emma grabs hold of my wrist, squeezing so tight my hand throbs with the blood fighting to work its way out of my fingers and back up my arm.

"Nine!"

The bids are slowing down, but still coming.

"Nine fifty!"

"Excellent! We've got nine hundred and fifty, gentlemen. Let me hear a thousand! Who'll bid? Do I hear a thousand dollars for this fine stock?"

The crowd has quieted and dust is clouding up around their shifting feet.

"I've got a bid of nine fifty. Going once. Going twice. Sold! Sold for nine hundred and fifty dollars to the gentleman in the front row! Congratulations, sir!"

Wille chuckles and smiles at me, slaps me on the back. "Good, good," he mumbles and laughs again, using a handkerchief to swipe the beads of sweat from his brow. I am still in a daze.

Emma and I are led off the platform and around back where the top bidder greets the auctioneer with a vigorous handshake.

I half expect him to have horns atop his head, to look like the devil himself. But he looks just like any other man, about forty or so, with thick sandy hair swept neatly back over his head. His brown suit coat is finely tailored, the sleeves falling just where they should at his wrists, allowing the cuffs of his shirt sleeves to peek out the bottoms.

"Hell, that was a fine exchange of business," the man says. "Just fine!"

"Thank you, sir, I quite agree," returns Mr. Wille. "And who do I have the pleasure of meeting?"

"Harold Beane, up from South Carolina."

"My pleasure, Mr. Beane. You sure have traveled a ways for our auction today, sir."

"Indeed, I have," the gentleman replies. "I usually buy at my plantation from the traders who pass through, but my last few purchases were disappointing. Very disappointing. One Nigger up and died on me not a week after the money exchanged hands. Of course, I had no way of tracking down that trader to see that he made good. So I took a sizeable loss."

"Terrible, sir, just terrible," laments the auctioneer.

"Way I figure it, I come on up here myself and buy my own stock, see the merchandise up close. And if anything goes wrong, I know where to find you," Beane says with a wink. He removes his billfold and carefully counts out nine hundred and fifty dollars.

"Oh, yes sir, that's a wise decision. We require our sellers to guarantee their merchandise for thirty days after auction," assures the auctioneer, accepting the money and quickly stuffing it in his shirt pocket. "But I can tell you with almost certainty that you'll be pleased with these Negroes, Mr. Beane. They're young and strong and healthy. You'll have no complaints, I'm sure of it. Though I think they'd serve you better in house work than in the fields. But I don't mean to tell you how to run your business, sir. I don't mean to do that."

"To be sure. They will serve the lady of the house with whatever she wants," confirms Beane. "But my primary need is for good breeding stock. I aim to raise my Niggers myself, just like I do with the pigs and the chickens, and save a pretty penny in the long run. Bought myself two other females last fall, and I've already got plenty of studs to mate them with."

"Indeed, sir! What a shrewd plan for business," Mr. Wille nods.

Their words fall on me like a pounding rain, chilling me to my bones. Seems like this day is going on for a hundred hours. I don't know that I can take another minute more.

Dear Lord, I pray, *give me strength to get through this day, and all the hard days that are coming so I can keep Emma safe. I just know you've got to be listening today, Lord.* Breeding stock! Oh, have mercy. *And keep a watchful eye on my boys, Lord, and please, please don't let any harm come to them. Dear God, lift up my Jerry. Lift him up with your strength and shine a light on his path so he can come find us and . . .*

"What the hell are you doing, Nigger?" a voice pulls me from my prayers. "Open your damn eyes and move along."

Mr. Beane tightens shackles around my wrists and Emma's, chaining us together.

"Get on up in that wagon now. We've got a boat to catch."

Part Two

"For what avail the plough or sail,
Or land or life, if freedom fail?"
—*Ralph Waldo Emerson*

Chapter 13

Mill Green, Maryland

"Now that sure is strange," Sheriff Porter said as he and Constable McCleary rode their horses back down the road leading up to Ed Prigg's property. "Can't imagine where Ed could be today. Maybe he's down at St. George's this morning. The church has been needing some repairs, and Ed's always one to help out in the community. He's always helping out."

A Pennsylvania grand jury indictment had been issued for the arrest and extradition of misters Prigg, Bemis, Forwood and Lewis on the charges of kidnapping. But the Harford County sheriff made no effort to deliver the defendants. So the constable made the trip down from York to retrieve the men. He was not surprised that they were mysteriously absent when he called upon them.

McCleary rode along silently, a purple vein throbbing at his temple, his knuckles white at the horse's reins.

"Suppose we could head over to Mr. Bemis's next," Sheriff Porter said, smiling helpfully, knowing full well it would be an uneventful afternoon.

The lawmen repeated this game several times, while the governors of Pennsylvania and Maryland remained deadlocked on how best to resolve the matter.

Philadelphia

Rose McFarland had recently begun working at her father's general store four days a week. She filled the place of a young Irishman by the name of Cobb McGinty, whom her father had regrettably released from his employment two months before.

"It breaks my heart, Rosie," her father had said at dinner the night he fired the boy. "It truly does. But I just can't afford to keep him on any longer. If things keep up the way they are, I'll have to let Frankie go next. One helluva rotten businessman I've become, haven't I?"

"Don't blame yourself," she had consoled him. "The *Post* reported just the other day that national unemployment is nearly 10 percent. It's this dreadful economy. A lot of businesses are cutting back, not just you."

The young woman volunteered to fill Cobb's place at the store, and her father reluctantly agreed. Mr. McFarland's wife had passed away when Rose was just a child. He had always dreamed of a son who might someday take over the business, but Rose was all he had.

She took to the job quickly and relished every moment of it. It was a welcome break from the endless cycle of cooking, cleaning and sewing that she tended to at home.

Another benefit of her employment was the more frequent opportunity to be in town and orchestrate "chance" encounters with a certain gentleman.

"Good morning." Rose smiled at District Attorney Tom Hambly as their morning paths crossed once again.

"Good morning, Miss McFarland," he said.

"Oh, please, do call me Rose."

"Rose," he replied, tipping his hat.

"It's so cold this morning," she said, rubbing her hands briskly. "I'm sure it's going to snow today."

"Yes," he said. "It's dreary isn't it?"

"Oh no," Rose countered. "I love it when the sky turns gray. Nothing better than scooting up beside a blazing fire with a hot cup of coffee and the daily paper."

She wore a chocolate-colored wool overcoat. A man's coat, but it was becoming on her nonetheless, Tom noticed. Her head was covered snuggly with a green knit cap, and a thick braid of red hair hung down her back. He studied her carefully.

"You're off to work at your father's store, I suppose," he said.

"Yes," she said, then paused. "But he's not expecting me for another hour yet."

She laughed, just a bit, and a delicate puff of fog escaped her lips. A frigid wind whistled through the storefronts. Rose shifted her weight from one foot to the other.

"Is that so?" Tom asked. "I don't suppose you'd care to join me for a drink over at Quinn's."

"The tavern?"

"They serve coffee in the morning," he laughed. "And I've already got the daily."

He waved the folded newspaper in the air, to prove his point, and Rose laughed.

"I'd love to," she said.

They crossed the street and walked down the next block. The bell above the door jingled as they entered the tavern. Tom pulled out a chair for Rose at a table near the fire.

"Thank you, Mr. Hambly," she said.

"Please," he said. "You should call me Tom."

The couple removed their hats and overcoats, piling them in an empty chair. Quinn hustled over to take their order.

"What can I get you and the lady this morning, Mr. Hambly?"

"Two coffees," Tom said.

"And toast, please," Rose added.

Tom plunked the daily down on the table in front of her, smiling. Rose unfolded the paper, scanned the headlines and crinkled her nose.

"Nothing new I'm afraid," she said.

"There never is," Tom replied.

Quinn delivered the toast and coffee, then disappeared into the back room. The couple had the place to themselves.

"I should congratulate you, by the way, on the getting the Morgan case," Rose said. "I've been following it in the paper. It sounds very challenging."

"Mm-hmm, thank you," Tom nodded.

He took a cautious sip of the steaming coffee. The lull in conversation prompted Rose to quickly take a large bite of toast.

"I'm afraid I'm not really at liberty to discuss the case," he finally said.

"Oh, of course," Rose said, awkwardly taking a sip of coffee to wash down her mouthful of dry toast. "I'm so sorry."

"No, no," Tom replied. "Don't apologize. I find it interesting that you're following the story in the paper. I'd like very much to hear your perspective on it."

The young woman wasted no time. It was a rare occasion when a man inquired as to her opinion; and there was no one else around to reprimand her for sharing it.

Rose admitted to knowing very little about the complexities of constitutional law, but it seemed to her that the promise of life, liberty and the pursuit of happiness was fairly clear. All men are created equal, she said. In her mind, that should apply to every man, woman and child in the nation, white or black.

"I think it's important that each state maintain the right to make its own laws," she said. "But those laws should protect people, not condemn them."

Rose's pace quickened, her cheeks become flushed.

"My heart goes out to that poor woman and her family. If she can't rely on our laws to protect her freedom, what does she have? Maryland's laws? That's a sorry joke, if you ask me. Did you hear about the so-called hearing they held to determine her status? Well, of course, you did."

Tom listened intently. Their coffee turned cold.

"Mrs. Morgan had no lawyer to represent her. She wasn't even allowed to speak on her own behalf, for heaven's sake. The whole thing was a farce. They never had any intention of giving her a fair trial. They were merely covering their backsides in the hope that the good people of the North might be fooled."

She paused to let out a heavy sigh, then shook her head.

"Of course, I suppose the citizens of Maryland could have the very same conversation about our laws and your case against the bounty hunter. It's not likely they have any faith he'll get a fair trial here. So where on earth does that leave you?"

Tom smiled smugly. "Between a rock and a hard place."

"But, of course, you're not really at liberty to say," she returned.

They laughed.

Rose suddenly noticed the late time. She jumped to her feet. Tom helped her with her coat and left a few coins on the table. She thanked him for the breakfast and apologized for talking his ear off. He thanked her for the honor of both.

They parted ways hesitantly, promising to have coffee again soon.

As Tom walked across the street to his office, he listened to Rose's words again in his mind. She was right. The powers that be in Maryland would never accept a guilty verdict against their citizens; and because they must expect nothing other than a guilty verdict, they might never surrender the defendants at all.

Why put off the inevitable?

"Ovid, I've got an idea!"

Tom rushed into the attorney general's office. He didn't bother to remove his overcoat or check in with the secretary. Mr. Johnson looked up from his desk, then eyed the clock.

"If your idea is to make a point of arriving to work on time, I'm all for it," he said stone-faced. Tom knew his mentor was only teasing.

"Seriously, Ovid, I've solved our problem with the Morgan case."

Tom laid out his idea for a compromise that just might satisfy both states. The defendants Bemis, Forwood and Lewis would each pay a small fine for obstruction of justice, and Prigg would surrender himself to the court in York County for trial on kidnapping charges. The violent and devious nature with which Prigg had abducted the family would be the persuading factor for compromise by the Maryland governor.

Upon conviction, Prigg would be released on his own recognizance and the case would be immediately appealed to the U.S. Supreme Court. This point would be the Pennsylvania governor's concession. The Pennsylvania trial would be a formality, a dress rehearsal of sorts for the Supreme Court arguments.

"What do you think, Ovid?"

"It just might work," he replied. "How did you ever come up with the idea, Tom?"

"It came to me over coffee this morning." Tom smiled slyly. "You might say it did me some good to stop and enjoy the roses."

Chapter 14

Margaret

"Mama, I'm hungry." Emma's eyes are dull and sunken, looking up at me for so much that I can't give her.

"Shhhh, baby," I say.

The trip from auction has been long and slow. We traveled by boat out of Chesapeake Bay and along the Atlantic coast for nearly a week. It was my first time on a boat. Might have been a small bright spot had we been permitted on deck to taste the salt air and look around. But we spent the whole time below, chained together in the dark cargo bay, fighting against the endless rocking that made our empty stomachs churn.

When we reached port in Charleston, Master Beane picked up another 30 slaves from the traders to work the rice fields, and he hired a man to help keep an eye on all of us for the rest of the trip. We've been inching along slowly for five days now across the South Carolina coastal plains, us house slaves in the wagon with master, and a train of slaves shuffling along behind in ankle chains.

There's been one meal a day. A biscuit and a cup full of water. My tiny girl looks to have shrunk to half her size already, and I cry at night knowing she's hungry and there's not a damn thing I can do about it other than offer up my own biscuit when nobody's looking. The hardest part is not knowing how long the trip to the plantation will take or how much worse things will be when we get there.

At least Emma and I are together. I pray endlessly for my boys. They must be terrified being alone for the first time in their precious young lives. *Please, Lord, keep watch over them. Don't let them be frightened.*

We passed through some marsh lands this morning—dark and moist and smelling of mildew, with monstrous trees rising up out of the green water, blocking out the sun—and I was quite relieved when we emerged back into the open plains before we broke camp for the night.

"Dat swamp is haunted, you should know," whispers one of the women we picked up in Charleston. She's helping Emma and me make the biscuits, while the other slaves work to set up Master's camp and water the horses. The hired man stands guard with a pistol in his holster and shotgun across his chest, leaning against a tree and smoking a big black cigar.

"It's the gators," the woman continues, and Emma is riveted. "They possessed by da ghosts. You can hear 'em moaning in da swamps at night."

"I'm Margaret, and this is my daughter, Emma," I say.

"Why do they moan?" asks Emma, moving in a little closer to the woman.

My attempt at introductions is lost. The slave's eyes dart back toward the swamps and she slowly sways her body from side to side, digs her bare feet into the black soil. She closes her eyes and hums softly.

"They callin' out for yo soul, child. They callin' out for somebody to sacrifice."

Emma gasps, and I click my tongue.

"Ya think I'm playin' with ya?" the woman's voice rises and her gaze falls steady on me, the disbeliever. She grasps at her necklaces, an odd assortment of chains and twine adorned with teeth and colored beads and tiny bird's feet.

"I mean no disrespect," I say. Jerry had told me many stories about the superstitions and witchcraft of slaves from the South. He believed in it, too, until he found Jesus. "Whereabouts are you from?"

"All over. Louisiana mostly. Georgia, too," she says. "Been sold here and there."

"Why do the gator ghosts want my soul?" Emma interrupts.

"Oh, child, they angry slave spirits," the witch says. "You see, so many slaves, they try to run. Run into the swamps to hide and hope to break free somewhere's on da other side. But the swamp gators swallows 'em up whole, and they never to be seen again. Thas who you hear at night moaning, crying for another soul to come take their place."

I shake my head and put another batch of biscuits over the fire. The old woman continues.

"Me? I rather die in the sun, out in da fields, so as my spirit can go on up and join the good Lord in heaven. That's how I wanna die. Not in the swamps, where my soul be trapped for all eternity."

Master Beane breaks in and gives the woman a shove.

"Quit your jawing and be quick with my dinner," he snaps.

"Yes, Massa," she says. "We's jus now cooking up your salt pork and your coffee's near ready, too, sir."

He grabs a biscuit from the pan and stomps away. The sun is slipping below the tree line and the night is coming alive with a low buzz from all manner and size of bugs. I don't know about gator ghosts, but I can't say that I have any fondness for the dark, murky swamps either. A low steady moan rises from the marshes, and the old woman looks off into the distance with a knowing expression. Emma shudders.

I've got to think we'll be there soon. We broke camp early and have been on the move all day. Night fell a few hours ago, but Master Beane keeps driving those poor horses through the darkness. He seems to know this road even without seeing it. We turn, heading down a narrow drive and pass under a large cast iron sign too black to read at night.

"Whoa," Master calls to his team and he stands, reaches over and clangs a big bell at the gate. Within seconds lanterns flicker in a small shack down the road and we can see a handful of Negroes come tumbling out and running to greet him.

"Evenin' massa," they say, unloading his bags. "Welcome home."

"It's good to be home," he says. "I'm dog tired. Ben, you and your boys get all this unloaded. I'm heading up to the house."

"Wha 'bout dem?" one of the men asks, nodding in our direction, as another man begins unlocking the shackles we've worn for ten days and nights. It stings as the irons come off, leaving my wrists red, swollen, raw.

"The ones in the wagon are the new house hands. The others can go on down to the field house and we'll get them started in the fields in the morning. Take the witch and the little one over to Granny Gin's place, and get Tucker up here for the other woman. He'll know what to do with her."

"Yessir," the Negro says, taking Emma by the hand and pulling her down from the wagon. She looks back at me over her shoulder, too frightened to cry out, too worn down to shed any more tears. He jogs away with her across a foot bridge. "Come on now, come on," I hear him coax as he whisks my daughter away into the eerie black.

"Where's he taking her?" I demand, jumping down from the wagon. "Who's Granny Gin?"

"None of your damned business," Master Beane snaps.

Master tosses his duffel to an old Negro man, who trots along behind him as he strides up the cobblestone path to the big house. Lights had come on in the parlor windows when we rolled up, and now a petite woman in a billowy nightgown is waiting on the porch in bare feet to greet him. Her hair is draped over her shoulder in one long thick braid. She kisses him on each cheek. He strokes her hair, saying something into her ear that I can't hear from way back. Then he pulls the woman close for a long embrace, and they walk arm-in-arm into the house. A husband and wife reunited. My heart aches at the sight of it.

"Massa'd whip you raw if he knowed you be starin' at him and his woman like that," a gritty voice whispers in my ear from close behind me. I jump and turn around, looking up into the shadowy face of a hulking black man. The darks of his eyes are like stones at the bottom of a murky lake, all glassy and half buried in the mud.

"I'll stare at whomever I please," I say, throwing my shoulders back, folding my arms across my chest.

He echoes my words in sugary high-pitched mocking, "I stare at who ever I please."

The man is smiling and looking around as the audience of slaves snicker and prance about like ladies with parasols. Then, out of nowhere, his fist flies at me, striking me down. I'm on all fours in the dirt, blinded by the blow, my head throbbing from pain and hunger and so much more.

If only my Jerry were here! Jerry would tear into this brute with a force, bring him to his knees, just like Prigg would have buckled that night if Jerry had been there. But Jerry's not here. Not then, not now. I'm alone. And now Emma is gone. What will become of her? Will I lose her, too?

I'm trying to stand, but my strength has left me, can't even seem to lift my head. The men are mostly quiet now, but a few are still laughing. "There you go, Tucker. She gonna learn her place."

My place. I dig my fingernails into the soft earth, breathe in the South Carolina air, all musty and acrid from the nasty swamps. Is this my place now? Alone, in the dirt?

I stagger slowly to my feet, still hunched over, dazed, clenching fists full of earth. My hands come together, the dirty fingers of my right closing tightly around the fist of my left. I summon all my strength, rearing up and slamming my elbow square into my attacker's stomach. He coughs, sputters, caught off guard, and I take advantage of the moment to deliver a swift kick to his groin.

He catches his breath and lunges at me. His fists beat down on me—my face, my back, my arms and breasts—drenching me in a pain so heavy it soaks through to my bones. My mouth fills with blood, and I cough and spit into the dirt. He kicks me in the stomach, in the legs, in the head.

Then he stops. The hum of the bugs, the low moan of the swamps, echo in my head.

"A'right boys," he says panting. "Y'all get these wagons unloaded like Master said."

He stands over me, while the others spin into motion and disappear one by one into the blackness that surrounds us. I turn my head up a bit, to get a better look at him. Who is this Tucker, this black man the other slaves seem to fear, who I should have been smart enough to fear from the start?

He looks down at me and smiles, reaches out a hand to help me up. No. He snatches up my hair, jerks my head back! My hands fly up to my head, clawing to get a hold of his arms.

Tucker grunt as he drags me along the ground. He doesn't even flinch as I dig my nails into his flesh.

It's as though time has somehow slowed down. The roots of my hair rip away from my scalp, one by one by one. The ground beneath me is changing, from loose dirt, to soft moist grass, to dirt again as we pass by a neat row of dilapidated shacks. One, two, three, four, five of them, masked in shadow from the starlight by giant black trees. A warm trickle of blood is running out my nose, over my lips, off my chin. My whole body is hot now, like somebody forced burning coals down my throat, packing every inch of my insides with lumpy, red heat.

Tucker approaches one of the shacks and kicks in the door, heaves me across the threshold and into a wall.

"Tucker, what da hell?" a voice shouts in the darkness. Restless bodies toss and turn in various corners of the shack, and my eyes slowly adjust to the dark. Rugs hang down from the ceiling, flimsy walls to create some small trace of privacy for the bodies scattered along the floor. Tucker paces back and forth between me and the door, shoulders hunched, a wild animal.

"You'll call me sir," he says in low deliberate voice, coming at me again. I try to scramble away, but I'm overcome with the fire in me, heat rising up through my body and seeping out the gashes in my skin, the holes in my scalp. He pulls his tattered cotton shirt up over his head, exposing a heaving chest criss-crossed with pink scars. He unties the rope holding up his cotton britches. "You my woman now."

A voice calls me from my sleep. "They want you up at da house." I open my eyes to bright sunlight streaming in slivers through shabby walls. Tiny bits of gold dust glint and float through the air. Images of Mama and Daddy's old shack surround me. I close my eyes again and can see the Ashmore's house just up the green hill.

"Get a move on!" Tucker gives me a hard kick, and last night comes back to me in an instant. I struggle to sit up, to focus my mind, to ignore the fire burning every inch of my flesh. Even the smallest breath sends a dozen knives plunging into my back. My dress is torn, muddied, bloodied.

Somehow, I get to my feet and stumble out the door, down a path, not sure where I'm headed. My left eye is swollen shut, so I cock my head and take in this new world with a warped, one-eyed perspective. Time has slowed down again, taking me hours to inch my way along the path toward the fuzzy big house in the distance. I suck air in through my blood clogged nose and huff it back out through my mouth.

"Oh!" a woman screams as I shuffle closer to the house. "Harry! Harry come quickly, dear!"

Master Beane bursts out of the house and stops dead in his tracks at the sight of me.

"Aw shit," he mumbles.

"Who is this poor child?" the woman demands with an elegant accent I've never heard before. She rushes to me, and I can see now it's the woman from the porch last night. She takes me gently by the arm and leads me up the veranda steps.

"That's Margaret," Beane says, "the housekeeper I bought up in Havre de Grace."

The woman sits me back on the veranda swing and my feet dangle like strangled fowl in a shop window as the contraption sweeps me forward and back, forward and back. Drool trickles from my swollen mouth.

"My housekeeper!"

The two talk in loud whispers.

"Now just settle down, Simone. I'm sure she ain't in as bad shape as it looks," Master says to his young wife, for I can see now that he is at least ten years her senior. "Tucker respects my property. But this Nigger has a sharp mouth, I'm sorry to say. My guess is she needed to be taught a prompt lesson about respect last night."

"Oh, I see," his wife replies, stepping back from him. "Well this morning she'll receive a lesson in charity."

With that, Master Beane can only seem to smile in bewilderment. The woman calls out to "Nanny," and a round coal black woman with thick ankles and massive breasts comes waddling out onto the porch.

"Oh, Lord have mercy," she says, her chubby hands flying up to her cheeks.

"Help me get her into the house, Nanny."

"Yes, Missus, I sho will."

The women stand me up and lead me into the kitchen and set me down again on a stool. The Missus stands beside me, propping me up, while Nanny pumps water from the sink into a large basin.

"Neberdaw suchating," the words tumble out of my swollen mouth.

"What's that?" the Missus asks, leaning in closer. Nanny moves the basin to the stove to heat the water.

I suck in a mouth full of air and drool, and swallow hard. "Never saw," I say the words slowly, motion toward the sink, "such a thing." A pump for the well right in the kitchen. No need to haul heavy buckets across the lawn. Nanny nods, seeming to understand my amazement.

The Missus still looks at me with bewilderment. She's so fair— thin blond eyebrows and a slender nose with a tiny swoop at the end, cheekbones high and sharp, the perfect shelf on which to display crystal eyes. She is the opposite of me in every way imaginable.

Nanny and the Missus gently peel away my tattered dress and wash me with a soft white towel, warm with water and lavender soap. Master stands out on the lawn with a cigar, thick smoke puffing up and around his head. He glances over his shoulder into the kitchen window, watches a bit as the women wash the dirt from my bruised breasts, the blood from my broken skin. Then he turns away again and sucks at his cigar.

Chapter 15

Margaret

Emma calls out to me from the darkness.

"Help me!"

I can just barely make out her face.

"Help me, Mama! Help!"

I reach for her hand, but she disappears into the black swamp. "Emma!"

"Wake up child, wake up now," Nanny nudges my cot with her knee. "You're just dreamin' again. It's only a dream."

The missus had insisted that I sleep in Nanny's room in the big house until my wounds healed. An extra cot was set in the small nook beside the kitchen. They gave me a couple of Simone's opium pills to ease my pain that first day, and I slept off the effects for two days after. Nanny would rouse me a few times a day to feed me onion broth with pepper, hot tea and, eventually, a slice of bread with butter. But my rest was tormented by nightmares of losing my children.

"Where's my Emma?" I would ask in a haze. Nanny would say, "Oh, she fine. Old Granny Gin be taking good care of her," and force a spoonful of broth into my mouth. Then I'd fade out again, back into a fitful sleep.

After four days, Master said it was time he started getting his money out of me, and I began some of my lighter housekeeping duties.

"What you gonna fix up this morning?" Nanny asks. If her size didn't give her away, her eyes certainly did. Any mention of food and Nanny's eyes nearly dance right out of their sockets with delight.

I've been living in the big house two weeks now, and I already have earned full responsibility of preparing the meals. Even Master had to admit my skill in the kitchen. "I'll be damned for saying it, but she's got the touch," he had declared one evening, as I had served him up a second helping of sweet potato pie.

"Oh, I was planning to make ham with griddlecakes and apple butter," I say to Nanny, worrying more about hauling myself out of bed than with making breakfast.

"I love dat apple butter, I sho do." The woman gives me a gentle heave to my feet in anticipation. "Think you can save me a little dab of that? A small griddle cake and a dab o' your apple butter?"

"You know I will, Nanny."

Our meals are rationed, just like all the other slaves on the plantation. But working in the house has privileges, and no one takes any notice when a slice of ham or wedge of pie goes missing.

"Oh, you a sweet thing, you are," Nanny says.

"Naaaany!"

Two little blond heads pop through the curtain that serves as the door to Nanny's room. Clarice and Sean-Paul are Master's children, though they have nothing but their mother's fair features, and French names to boot. They pad into the room, still in their night clothes, rubbing their slender fists into crusty eyes. The twins will be five years old in a few weeks, and the Missus has been planning a party like nothing I've heard the likes of before.

"What are you chillun' doing up so early?" Nanny asks. She and I usually rise a few hours before the sun and the rest of the house, to get started making the breakfast and coffee and bread for the evening meal.

"Mama said let her and daddy sleep," Clarice says.

"Daddy said you'd tell us a story," adds Sean-Paul.

The two always speak in tandem. One starting off. The other finishing.

"Did they now?" Nanny says. "A'right then, off we go."

Nanny and the children head off for the living room, and I go into the kitchen to draw a pot of water and light the stove. Then I gather up the chamber pot from Nanny's room and walk out into the early morning to empty it in the outhouse. I take a candle with me, to scare off the snakes that like to curl up in the warmth of the outhouse in the early morning. Today it's a bright green one, with a narrow head and glistening skin. It drops down off the step and glides into the tall grass headed for the swamp. I sweep the candle around once more, on the lookout for more snakes or the spiders that like to weave their tapestries across the opening during the night. In the glow of the flame, I can see a red tint to my piss as I pour it into the hole.

Praise God! I look at the backside of my gown and see a small dark stain. My monthly cycle came in the night. The tears come to me in an instant, and I drop to my knees. My hands come together in prayer.

"Oh Lord, thank you for this blessed gift," I whisper. "I've been so fearful, God, that Tucker left his seed with me that night. But I should have trusted in you, should have known you wouldn't let that happen. Thank you, thank you, Lord. Please keep your watch over me. I will not lose another child to slavery, Lord. I swear to you. I will not."

"You lost a child?" Sean-Paul asks.

"We'll help you look for it," Clarice adds.

I hadn't noticed the twins coming down the path to the outhouse, and Nanny toddles up just behind them now. She's shaking her head in apology, out of breath.

"No, children, no one is lost," I say jumping up, wiping the tears from my face. "You two just go about your business, now."

As I hurry past them, Nanny whispers that there's a fresh stack of rags in the trunk beside her cot.

"Praise the Lord," I say, and rush off to wash and change.

The ham sizzles in the pan, while I grind the coffee beans. Nanny waddles in the back door with a bucket of fresh milk in one hand and a basket of eggs in the other. Our roles would have been reversed, if Tucker hadn't beaten me down that first night. But Nanny doesn't seem to mind relinquishing the cooking to me, even if it means more trips to the barn than usual.

"Here you go, Margaret," she says, setting down her load and sitting with a huff onto the stool next to me. "Lemme take over dis, and you start to work on those griddle cakes now."

I transfer the ham from the skillet and onto a china platter, then place it into the oven to keep it warm. A scoop of butter goes into the skillet and quickly starts to bubble and spit. The flour, soda and sugar are already blended, and I just need to add the eggs and milk to get my batter started. I pour five even portions of batter onto the skillet and leave it to cook while I stir a bubbling pot of apple juice, pulp and spices. It's setting up just right. Smooth and sweet apple butter is one of my little Sammy's favorite treats.

"Where's your mind at, child?" Nanny asks. "Why you so quiet?"

Small talk has become my savior in the past two weeks, keeping my mind and heart from aching for the past or, even worse, wondering about what sort of life my family is living without me.

"I don't know, Nanny. Just feeling a bit tired this morning, I suppose."

"Well, jus be careful not to fall asleep at the stove and let those cakes burn," Nanny says, laughing and getting up to put the coffee on.

"Don't worry," I whisper. "I'll save the burnt ones for Master Beane."

"Oh! Baby, you terrible," she says, and we share a quiet laugh at the stove.

After a few minutes, Nanny's smile fades and a small crease forms between her brows.

"I know you'all like to kid, Margaret. But you really shouldn't joke like dat about Master so much," she says.

Here it comes. Nanny has lectured me more than once before about how lucky I am to be working in the big house and not out in the fields. While I can't really argue her point, I'm still a good ways off from thankful.

"He done you a real kindness keeping you up here at da house," Nanny says.

The house slaves consist of Nanny and me, a young couple that tends the family garden and landscaping around the big house, and two men who take care of the cows, pigs, chickens, horses and other livestock. Nanny's husband keeps the woodpile stocked and sees to all the household repairs and maintenance. Two other women, the barn hands' wives, have the sole responsibility of helping Simone organize and prepare for the almost weekly social events hosted at the plantation.

It is by Master's design that the house slaves are all couples.

"And for Master to give you a man like Tucker," Nanny continues, her hands busy with folding napkins and organizing china settings on a large silver serving tray. "You lucky to get such a strong young man for a mate."

I don't bother telling Nanny I already have a husband. Someone who is ten times the man Tucker will ever be. A man who loves and cherishes me, who protects me, who would never ever raise his hand to me.

"What you mean by rolling yo eyes around like that, girl?" Nanny asks. "You don't think you could do a lot worse than Tucker?"

"Sorry, Nanny, but my experience with Tucker so far hasn't been so good. You know?"

My hand instinctively goes to my ribcage, still tender after two weeks. Nanny lowers her eyes.

"Dat's true enough."

The last batch of griddle cakes get transferred from the skillet to the serving tray, and the bubbling apple butter gets ladled into a silver bowl to cool. The sun has broken above the rice fields and the kitchen is heating up. The eggs are the last to go in the skillet. We can hear the family gathering in the dining room, and Nanny and I quicken our pace.

We take turns filing back and forth from the dining room to the kitchen. It's a regular parade—platters heaped tall with warm griddlecakes, ham, fried eggs and crisp apple slices, china pitchers brimming with fresh milk and water, steaming coffee with cream and sugar, bowls of sweet honey and apple butter. Nanny places everyone's napkins in their laps, starting with Master, and I pour the coffee. We both work to fill the plates, making sure to compliment the Missus on her dress and extend our hopes that the family all had a pleasant night's sleep.

Once everyone is taken care of, Nanny and I retreat to the kitchen to eat a quick breakfast ourselves before we set about the task of scrubbing the pots and dishes.

"Nanny," I whisper, pulling a towel from the oven. Wrapped inside it are two griddlecakes sandwiched together with a spoonful of apple butter. I pull back the towel and Nanny's eyes dance. She shoots a quick look to the door. The clatter of silver on china and a soft murmur of voices tell us we're safe. We pull the griddlecakes apart like a wishbone and quickly devour them. Then I pull a pan from the oven with two large corn biscuits and two thin slices of salt pork, and Nanny pours us two big cups of water.

"Tucker ain't got it so easy, you know," Nanny starts in again, keeping her voice low, and I just listen.

I need to hear her out. The past two weeks, I've been doing nothing but praying that I would not get pregnant after Tucker raped me. Now that I know I'm not with child, it's time to focus on making sure it never does happen. Nanny's soft spot for Tucker could give me the insight I need to keep him at bay.

That first night keeps replaying in my mind, though.

"You'll call me sir," Tucker had said to me. "You my woman now." He needed to prove his dominance. He needed his ego stroked. His job was to bed me, and my job was to let him. He proved that I'm no match for him physically. So I will have to fight him some other way.

Another week in the big house. I'm feeling strong again, despite rising at four o'clock every morning and working without rest until I lay my head down again about ten at night. I actually made it through my laundry duties this week without any help from the other house slaves.

The washing involves hauling a dozen or more baskets of laundry down to the swamp's edge, over the course of three or four days. The articles get soaked and scrubbed in lye soap in one big tub and rinsed clean in another. The metal washboard is a luxury compared to the big flat stone I used up in York, but the amount of wash each week is hard to believe. Bed sheets, tablecloths, napkins, towels, pants, shirts, dresses, petticoats, handkerchiefs. I haul the wash water over from the creek in buckets, and all the dirty water gets dumped into the swamp when I'm through. Each item gets wrung by hand, so that by the end of the day my fingers are so stiff and sore I can barely move them. Then I carry the wet, heavy laundry in baskets up the hill and hang it on lines behind the barn.

Granny Gin's place is just down the other side of the hill. I watch it closely as I hang the laundry every day. Children scurry here and there all around the rundown shack. My eyes strain in the hope that I might catch a fleeting glimpse of Emma at play, but there has been no sign of her so far.

Doing the twins' wash makes my head throb. I hang up their tiny stockings, their night clothes, their hankies in neat rows to dry. Clarice's dresses dance in the breeze. Do my children have clean clothes to wear? Have they any clothes at all? Or a warm place to sleep at night? Or food to fill their bellies? I pull a wet little shirt from the basket and press it against my forehead. It cools the throbbing, but it doesn't stop my mind from racing.

Evenings are spent ironing and folding, bed sheets and all, to the light of an oil lamp. The only breaks I get during the day are when I return to the kitchen to prepare lunch and dinner, and work with Nanny to wash the dishes after.

"It's about time Margaret gets on with her full duties at the plantation," Master Beane announces at the dinner table this evening. He's looking at me, but I don't dare make eye contact while I clear away his pie plate and replace it with a fresh cup of coffee. I know he's not referring to my housekeeping duties.

"Oh, Harry, I don't know that she's ready," Simone says. "It's only been three weeks."

"Three weeks is plenty to heal up her bumps and bruises. I want her in the slaves' quarters with Tucker tomorrow tonight, and I'll not hear another word about it."

Simone has proven herself to be a strong woman in the short time I've known her. But she is a woman, after all, a plantation owner's wife. She knows her place, and she knows mine. I can see in her silent expression that this is one battle she will not choose to fight.

"Yessir," I say and hustle into the kitchen, the tears already filling my eyes.

Nanny is close behind me.

"There, there, child," she says. "That's just the way, ya know. It'll be a'right. You mind Tucker, and he'll be a good man to ya. Jus don't fight it, child."

I pull from her, run out of the kitchen, and throw up in the azalea bushes out back. *That's just the way? Just don't fight it?* Like hell. They're in for a fight, God as my witness, and they'll never even see it coming. The soft pink petals of the azaleas bow under the weight of the vomit, as the slime oozes and drips into the dirt. I spit at the flowers, and they recoil. Then I wipe my chin, and walk back into the house. They're in for a fight.

Chapter 16

Margaret

"You go on now, Margaret. I'll finish all this up," Nanny says, shooing me toward the back door, smiling gently. "You go on, and get yo'self settled in down at the houses."

It's dusk, and I've finished preparing dinner. It will now be up to Nanny to serve the meal and clean up after. Simone discharged me from my duties early, so that I could move my few personal belongings into my new quarters.

The plan has run through my mind a hundred times today. God only knows if I'll be able to go through with it. Certainly, what I have in mind is just as vile as anything Tucker might do to me. But I can't let that cloud my judgment. The goal is to keep from getting pregnant. To do that, I will have to seduce him.

I leave the big house and walk slowly down the path to Tucker's. It takes two minutes to put away my things. I change into my nightgown and wait.

The house slaves here were either married when they came to the plantation or had paired up by their own choice afterward. Plantation owners encourage slave weddings to ensure future generations in their stock, though the ceremonies aren't recognized legally and the owners have no qualms about breaking up the families later on. But, Nanny said, Master Beane had only recently decided to play matchmaker, because allowing his slaves to pair off naturally just takes too long. Each summer, after the rains come, scores of slaves come down with the fever and Master loses a good number of his stock.

So the house slaves receive slightly better treatment, shelter and rations, to keep them healthy, happy and productive. Nanny lives at the big house, though, since she is too old to have any more children. But she gets to see her husband around the house during the day, and on Saturday night she comes to the slave quarters and stays over until Monday morning. That seems to suit her just fine.

Voices are rising up outside, as the slaves come in for their dinner. They're exhausted from the day's work, but they're happy to return home. The place is abuzz with chatter and merriment. The men build up the fire outside and head down to the stream to collect fresh water for dinner. The women come into the house to gather up the tin cups from which they'll drink their water and the cornmeal they'll use to make the ashcakes.

Ashcakes are the slaves' daily sustenance at the plantation. They're made by mixing a hand full of cornmeal with small amounts of water and a pinch of salt or sugar. The mixture is then pressed into a flat firm patty and buried beneath the coals of a hot fire until it cooks up crisp. The hard, dry cakes, still tasting of ash, can be stowed in your pockets, to be eaten during the next day, whether or not there is time to break for a meal.

I sit quietly on the floor of Tucker's makeshift bedroom, motionless, as the women come and go from the large cabin, seemingly unaware of my presence. Then Tucker comes in, his body filling the entire door frame, and the women quickly exit. They must have known I was here, but they dared not speak to me.

"You back now, huh?" Tucker says, removing his hat and tossing it on the floor in the corner.

"Yessir," I say.

He looks down at me, and I look up to meet his gaze. The firelight flickers through the gaps in the walls. Dark comes quickly here, when the sun sinks into the swamps.

"Why you in sleepin' clothes already?" he asks. "You better get dressed and make my food."

"I've already made dinner. Here, sit, and I'll get it for you."

He sits down on the straw mattress and leans his back against the wall. Earlier that night, while making the Beane's dinner, I had made up an extra plate heaped with biscuits, buttered greens and bacon. I had placed it in a basket on top of rocks I had heated in the stove and covered it with a towel to keep it warm. I pull it from the basket, now, and set it in Tucker's lap. His eyes grow large and he begins to say something, but I cut him off by touching my fingers to his lips.

"Shhh," I say, smiling. "It's leftover from the big house. No one will even notice it's gone. Would just be pig's feed tomorrow anyway."

"Why you bein' nice to me?" Tucker asks, as I remove his tattered boots and set them aside. I crawl up beside him on the mattress and feed him a piece of soft crumbly biscuit. He sucks on my fingers as I place the food in his mouth. *Disgusting.* I quickly pull my hand away, wipe off his spit on my gown. Then I catch myself and pretend to straighten my bosom instead.

Tucker watches me with those murky eyes that have haunted my dreams every night since I arrived at the plantation. I glance toward the door, only for a moment, and consider making a run for it. I take a deep breath instead. Steady myself.

"I've been watching you from the big house, working outside, the sun shining off your back," I say, placing another bite in his mouth. "Maybe I just realized being your woman might not be so bad."

Truth be told, I always looked away whenever I saw Tucker around the house. The shame of my first night at the plantation still burns, the anger still cuts. This is the first time I really got a good, close look at him for any length of time. He's young, maybe twenty. The sun and fields have already taken a toll on his skin, but beneath the sunburn and chafing, it still has the undeniable, tight look of youth. A bright pink scar runs from his left eyebrow down to his ear.

Kneeling beside him on the mat, I take the plate from his lap and set it on the floor beside us.

"You've got more than one job to do around here, Tucker. I know that much."

My stomach is in knots. I place my trembling hands on his thighs, squeezing gently, working his hard muscles.

"I know my job, woman," Tucker barks, pushing my hands away. "Not tonight. I'm tired."

I moved too fast. He needs to be calling the shots. I should have known that. But if my plan is ever going to work, it has to be tonight. The stage has already been set.

"Of course you're tired," I say, looking down demurely. My voice is giving out, and I'm suddenly feeling light headed. I clear my throat a bit and take a deep breath.

"You shouldn't have to do any more work today. I'm your woman. Let me take care of you."

I pick the plate up again and feed him another little piece of biscuit. He jerks the plate from me and starts devouring the meal with his hands, stuffing in thick pieces of bacon and slurping up the greens. I watch him. After a few minutes pass and his plate is empty, I run my hand down his arm gently.

"It was good?" I ask, smiling just a little.

Tucker gives me only a conceding grunt. I nod.

Once again, I move the plate aside. Then I lean in a bit closer, take in a deep breath and let it out slow. "Yessir," I whisper, "I'm a pretty good cook. I'm pretty good at lots of things."

I reach over and untie his belt, slowly, slowly. He watches me. I ease down his britches to expose his manhood. Oh, how will my Jerry ever forgive me? *How will God forgive me?*

"I told you, I ain't up for no more work tonight," he says, but his voice has softened and he does not push me away. His youth gives me an advantage. There's no turning back now, for either of us.

It's just like scrubbing and wringing the laundry, I tell myself, trying hard not to think about what I'm doing as I stroke him. My mouth is dry. I lean across his hips, reaching for a cup of whiskey I stole from Master's house. I take a gulp and offer Tucker the cup. He throws back his head and finishes off the drink, then clucks through is teeth.

"What you doin' anyway?"

"There's more than one way to be with a woman, Tucker. I'm sure you know that," I say, licking the whiskey from my lips. "And there's lots of ways to make a baby. You just relax now."

I close my eyes, and I put my mouth to him. He tastes of dirt. I hesitate. Tears escape my tightly sealed lids, but Tucker doesn't seem to notice. He's fully aroused now. *Dear God. I can't go through with this.*

Tucker groans and thrusts his hands to the back of my head. His hips rise and fall, rise and fall. It takes little time to satisfy him.

He leans his head back against the wall, sighs. He closes his eyes and quickly drifts off to sleep. When I'm sure he's completely out, I slip out of the cabin, unnoticed by the merry couples enjoying their evening meal by the fire.

Alone and safe around back, I scoop up a handful of dirt and stuff it in my mouth. Anything to get rid of his taste. The dirt makes me choke, and I spit it back out.

I drop to my knees spitting, spitting violently and, finally, crying uncontrollably. Yet even now, even after the sin I've just committed, I'm somehow mindful not to be heard. Silent sobs seem to take over my entire body with a vengeance. I rock back and forth on my knees, my head in my hands, eyes shut tight, mouth open wide, mud and snot and drool dribbling over my lips and down my chin. My head throbs. I squeeze my hands together tight at my chest, and I pray—for forgiveness, for strength, for answers. *Why, dear God, why?*

I'm not sure how long my hysterics have lasted. But exhaustion seems to have taken over instead, and I'm feeling mostly numb now. I wipe my face clean with the hem of my nightgown.

The crackle of the flames calls to me. The evenings have gotten noticeably cooler in the three weeks I've been here. It reminds me of home, just a little bit, and it's enough to coax me out from behind the shack. Tucker is snoring inside. I start walking, to get away from the sound, and work my way toward the couples gathered at the fire, stopping short of sitting with them.

"You Tucker's new woman, huh?" says one of the barn hands, eyeing me from head to toe, smirking. A petite woman next to him slaps his face, and everyone laughs.

"Sit down, Margaret." Nanny's husband, Elbert, pats the ground beside him. We've become acquainted in the past few weeks, and it feels good to be welcomed by a familiar face.

"Thank you," I manage to say, sitting down.

"Nanny sure has been goin' on about you and yo cooking," Elbert says.

"That's awfully nice of her," I say, looking down at the fire.

"Got any good recipes for ashcakes?" someone asks, and another round of laughter erupts.

It feels good to sit around the fire and joke with people. Almost makes me feel like a human being again, instead of someone's property.

"So that pig there, thas Joseph," says Elbert, pointing at the man who just got slapped. Everyone laughs again. "And that's his wife, Jennie. This here is Robert and his wife, Betsy. Them two work the barn and the women plan the Missus's parties for her. Now *that* be some back breakin' work, plannin' parties and all."

"Elbert, you hush yo mouth," Jennie laughs, taking the ribbing in stride. "It ain't so easy as that. You think Joseph be a pig, you should just see some of dem society ladies eat!"

More whoops and hollers rise up, and the group can hardly contain itself any longer. Everyone starts talking at once, making jokes, laughing, and getting slapped or kissed or both. I just watch and listen. Elbert finishes the introductions, pointing to the gardeners, Eli and Peter, and their wives, Hope and Lucy.

The conversation turns to debate over the weather, if this winter will be colder than last, and to gossip about the new batch of field slaves Master bought over in Charleston. The banter among the couples is strangely comforting. It makes me miss Jerry something fierce, and yet, it makes me feel somehow closer to him at the same time.

"Nanny said you don't smile so much," Elbert says, nudging at me. "So what's got you smilin' now?"

I pull my knees up to my chest and give them a hug.

"I'm thinking about a time last year when my husband and I had some friends from Philly up to our cabin for a summer bonfire," I say.

"Philly-delphia?" Peter asks.

"Mmm-hmm," I say. "We were free."

All eyes are on me now. And those eyes tell me not one of them has ever known what it's like to be free. Not even for one day. It almost makes me feel ashamed for having been free for so long.

The fire crackles and the bugs hum, but the group is stone silent. Their eyes narrow with curiosity, disbelief, waiting for me to continue. I meet their gazes, one by one by one. It's filling me with a sense of strength that I haven't felt in a long time. My plan to manipulate Tucker seems to have worked, and I'm suddenly feeling confident, fearless even, like I might be able to control my own fate after all.

"Tell us about it," someone finally says.

I nod and close my eyes so I can see it better.

"I boiled up a big pot of fish stew, with onions and turnips, and baked a dozen loaves of bread. Jerry, my husband, he put up a fire like you wouldn't believe. Had to have been ten feet wide and near as tall. My friend, Nellie, fixed a whole mess of honey-popcorn balls, all crunchy and sweet. Jerry's boys from down at the shipping yard— William and Lewis and Solomon—they came up with a couple big jugs of rum."

I pause again, for dramatic effect, and to make the memory last just a bit longer.

"Then we all sat around the fire until the small hours of the night, eating and talking and drinking. I handed out a bunch of my quilts, and we all just enjoyed the night, together under a blanket of stars."

Eli shrugs and looks up at the sky. "Jus like we is now."

"Yessir," agrees Hope, staring into the dwindling fire. "Only they was free."

Chapter 17

Margaret

The day starts at four o'clock in the morning. I cook and serve breakfast, then begin the task of hauling laundry to the edge of the swamp. Scrubbing, rinsing, wringing. When the sun is almost straight overhead, I return to the house to prepare lunch. Then the laundry gets hauled up the hill and hung all along the lines. I watch it waving in the breeze from the kitchen window, as the sun sets and I sweat over the stove. After dinner is served, I haul in the laundry to be ironed and folded. Then I walk down the path to the slaves' quarters, wishing I could wash a hundred more baskets of laundry before performing my day's final chore.

And that's how it goes here—every day except Sunday. On Sundays, I get to tend to Tucker's and my laundry. There isn't much to wash, but I spend a fair amount of time mending and trying to hold our ragged clothes together. I also tend a small garden behind our quarters that produces some fine winter squash and earns me instant popularity among the house slaves.

Tucker still struts around like an ignorant brute most times, but he hasn't raised his hand to me since that first night. I'm thankful for that.

Most evenings, I sneak him a bit of food left over from the family's meal—biscuits and greens, ham and potatoes, a sliver of gooseberry pie, maybe a swallow or two of whiskey. He's usually exhausted from supervising the field slaves all day. If I ply him with enough food and liquor, he often falls asleep before I have to prostitute myself.

Truth be told, I think Tucker enjoys the food and whiskey just as much as the other stuff I do. Maybe even more. After surviving on nothing but ashcakes and water all his life, it's no wonder.

Master Beane bought Tucker about ten years ago at the age of eleven or twelve along with his older brother. Both boys were immediately sent to the rice fields to work from daybreak to dark, six days a week.

Nanny and I were making bread one morning, when I asked her what had become of Tucker's brother. She shook her head and clucked through her teeth.

"Oh, child, that's a sad story, that is. But there be some good in it, too."

Tucker's brother, according to Nanny, didn't take well to being a field slave. He was always slow about his tasks. Whether it was from sun stroke or stubbornness, she didn't know. Every day, the overseer would ride his horse up behind the boy and shout and curse. "Get a move on, you damned lazy Nigger. Get a move on!" Tucker tried to help his brother with the work, but the overseer wouldn't allow it.

Every few months, the overseer would order the boy to report to the stables for twenty lashes to encourage him to work harder. After nearly three planting seasons had passed, the boy had had enough. One morning the overseer rode up and ordered him to report for the lash. He refused.

"You report to the stables now, or I'll shoot you where you stand!"

"Shoot away," the boy said calmly, his arms outstretched. "I won't take another lash."

With that, the overseer drew his pistol and shot the boy right in the face. Tucker watched as his brother's lifeless body crumbled into the muck of the rice fields. The other slaves didn't even look up. They just continued their work.

The overseer turned his horse and began to ride down the next row. Tucker charged after, leaping up onto the horse's hind quarter and grabbing the man by the neck. The two fell from the horse into the water. Tucker wrestled the pistol away and threw it aside. Then he punched the overseer in the head, again and again and again, until the grown man begged for his life.

"Then Tucker jus' stood up and walked away," Nanny said. "Just like that. He couldn't a been more'n fifteen years old."

"What did Master Beane do to him?" I asked.

Nanny pulled a mound of dough from the warm oven.

"Well, thas the good part of story," she said. "Tucker walked right up to the big house, all drippin' wet, bloody knuckles, and he told Master everything that done just happened. Oh! Master was mad!"

She stopped her story a moment to pound down the dough with her chubby fists.

"Anyways, Master was so mad. And Tucker says he *should* be mad. What good is a overseer who can't get a slave to put in a solid day's work, he says. Who goes destroying Master's property by shooting dead a slave that he can't get to mind him, he says."

Tucker's logic apparently got through to Master Beane. It spoke right to his pocketbook. So Master asked Tucker what *he* would do, and Tucker said he thought the slaves would work harder if they had a black overseer—one of their own.

"So Master fired that horrible overseer and put young Tucker in charge of the field hands." Nanny smiled as she finished her story. "Them other slaves, they saw how Tucker took down that man in the field and nearly beat him to death. So they got the respect for him. They work hard for him."

She cut the dough in half and patted each portion into a loaf pan.

"Every now and again, when a new batch a slaves come in, Tucker gotta show them who be the boss," she added. "But they learn quick. He gets the respect."

I could only nod, remembering all too well how Tucker earns his respect, and put the bread pans in the oven.

The Beanes have a beautiful kitchen. It's as big as my whole cabin back in York. The table and chairs are made of cherry wood, with smooth legs and pretty little leaves carved into the edges. Two large cabinets of matching style hold the china, silver and linens. All the drawer and cupboard handles are shiny brass lion heads with a ring dangling down. The kitchen has a large cast-iron cook stove, with the stovetop waist high, so there's no need to stoop over kettles in the fireplace. I've never seen anything like it. All things considered, I don't mind spending half my days here.

But I still feel trapped. I haven't had the time or freedom to venture beyond the big house or house slave quarters. All I can think of day in and day out is a way to somehow steal a glimpse of Emma. "How far down the hill is Granny Gin's place?" I ask Nanny as we finish up our evening chores.

She's washing the dinner dishes, up to her elbows in suds. I'm standing a few feet away ironing my third set of sheets for the night. Nanny looks at me sideways.

"Why you wanna know?"

"You know why, Nanny."

She just keeps washing dishes, soaping them up in one basin, rinsing them off in another, laying them out on a towel to dry. She doesn't answer.

"Won't you at least tell me what it's like down there? Are the children well cared for?"

"Oh, you needn't worry about that," Nanny answers me now. "Granny Gin take real good care of the chillun. She raised two of my own, she did."

I suddenly feel selfish, ashamed. In all my misery over losing my babies, I had forgotten that I have plenty of company in that regard. The plump woman gets a faraway look in her eyes, wrinkles up her forehead.

"I'm sorry, Nanny. We don't have to talk about it, if you don't want to."

"Naa, that's all right," Nanny finally says. "But I'll have to go a ways back, to tell it proper."

I point to the mound of laundry waiting to be ironed. "I'm not going anywhere."

"Ain't that the truth." Nanny shakes her head. "That used to be Virginia's job, you know, years ago when Master Beane's daddy run the plantation. That's Granny Gin's real name. Virginia. Wasn't until she started looking after the little ones that they all started calling her Granny Gin."

"I didn't know that," I say. "Virginia's a beautiful name."

"Yes," Nanny nods. "And she's a beautiful person."

Master Beane's daddy had no use for slave children at the plantation, Nanny tells me. Back in the day, he could get all the adult Negroes he needed straight off the boats from Africa at low cost. He maintained order of his stock with a heavy hand, and he had strict rules about keeping the men and women separate. When a baby did happen to come along, which was bound to happen from time to time, he would sell it off for whatever price he could get—usually a dollar a pound.

Then the government banned slave trade with Africa in 1808, and maintaining a full stock while keeping the books balanced got tougher.

"So Master decided he better start keeping the babies in his stock," Nanny says. "But he didn't worry none about whether they was taken care of. Most of the time, they just run around the property buck naked, scrounging for food, like wild animals. When they was big enough, he'd send 'em into the fields to work."

Sadly, the children rarely lasted more than a couple of years working the fields, Nanny explains. Skinny, weak, half starved to death their whole short lives, they just couldn't stand up under the hot sun for twelve and fourteen hours a day.

Nanny and Elbert were lucky because they worked in the big house. They were able to keep an eye out for their own children, teach them some manners. As soon as the children were able, the couple put them to work at the house, hoping the job would hold on and Master wouldn't send them to the fields.

"I raised eight babies that way," Nanny explains. "By the time they're four or five years old, they can work the butter churn, feed the chickens, bring in the eggs, polish the silver. Virginia was getting on in age, moving slower at her chores. The little ones around the house was a big help to both of us. So Master let me keep 'em close at hand that way for a while."

But as the children grew older, Nanny's plan backfired. There was no need for so many of them to work the big house. And since they had all been trained for such work, they were more valuable as house slaves than field hands. So Master sold them off, one by one, to neighboring plantations.

"Broke my heart every time," Nanny says, tears rolling down her cheeks and into the dish water. "You know how it is, Margaret."

I try to say yes, but a lump in my throat won't let me speak. So I just nod.

"Then Virginia started taking ill from time to time." Nanny clears her throat and continues. "Master had enough of that, so he sent her down to the old creek shack to live out what days she might have left. Pretty soon, all the little ones started keeping her company down there. And before you know it, she was Granny Gin and all the babies got sent down there to live with her until they was old enough to work."

The timing of Nanny's story doesn't add up right in my head. I sit down at the table to fold the napkins I had been ironing.

"How long ago was that, Nanny?"

"Oh," she says, drying her hands on her apron. "Let's see. My youngest has gotta be twelve by now. So it's been a good while."

"But you said Granny Gin had taken ill?"

"Yes," Nanny confirms.

"And then she got better?"

"That she did."

I stand and walk across the kitchen to put the napkins in the linen cabinet.

"Maybe taking care of the little ones gave her new life somehow," I say, turning to face Nanny. "A reason to keep pushing on."

"Maybe it did." Nanny smiles at me broadly. "All I know is I sent her my last two babies, and she loved them like they was her very own. They're working in the fields now, but I get to see them every Sunday."

"You-you do?" I say, nearly speechless. "Master lets you visit them?"

"Oh, sure child," Nanny says. "Master ain't so bad as his daddy was."

My mind is racing. Nanny eyes me carefully, as if she knows my thoughts. A mother's thoughts.

"But you'll have to get permission from Tucker, too," she says, and my heart sinks.

At 22, Tucker is only eight years younger than me. Yet, most times, he seems more like a child than a man. He never had a mother or father to teach him the ways of the world. This wretched plantation *is* his world. As the Nigger overseer, Tucker is both respected and feared. He has no friends.

I think that's why Master decided to buy Tucker a woman. The poor boy would never have figured out how to get one himself.

Tucker knows very little about the relations between a man and woman. His only education has come from watching the mating rituals of the plantation livestock. I told him the pleasures we enjoy are how the higher class of God's creatures makes babies. He believes me, and I pray every day for God's forgiveness.

Since I've come along, Tucker is no longer alone. I have provided the human touch he has never had. It has only been a short time, but I believe he has actually become sweet on me.

In the mornings, we rise early. He smiles sheepishly at me as he heads over to the fields and I head up to the big house. Sometimes, Tucker brings me back a flower from one of the gardens—an act that would earn him a lash or two if Master Beane found out. I will never love Tucker, but I do despise him less than I once did. Now that I know the tragedy and torment he has endured in this place, it's hard not to feel some measure of compassion for him.

He's been acting so good to me the past few weeks, I've worked up the courage to ask him for permission to visit Emma at Granny Gin's. First, I have to get him in the right mood.

I unveil tonight's meal—buttered carrots and potatoes, a few scraps of ham—and his eyes light up. He gulps down the food almost without chewing, washes it down with a cup of water. He pats his stomach. We exchange smiles.

"Glad you liked it," I say, moving the plate and cup aside. "I like to see you smile."

Tucker laughs. He knows what's coming next.

"Is it okay if I make you smile a little bit more, hmm?" I ask coyly.

"If you want," he says, quickly removing his pants.

I lie down beside him and do what I must.

"Oooh," he moans. "That feels so good, woman. I just know we gonna make a baby tonight."

We lounge together for a bit, after it's done. I twirl my fingers in the hair on his chest. He's getting sleepy.

"Tucker," I whisper.

"Mmm?"

"I was thinking, this Sunday, I might just run down to Granny Gin's for a little while. Would that be all right?"

His muscles stiffen a little. "Granny Gin's? What for?"

"Well," I hesitate. "You know my daughter lives down there, Tucker. I'd just like to visit with her a bit. That's all."

Tucker sits up, pushes away my hands.

"What you need to visit her for? Granny Gin's taking care of her now."

He's never had a child. He just doesn't understand.

"I miss her, Tucker. I think about her all the time."

Tucker stands up, still naked, and paces the floor. He doesn't even have the decency to cover himself. He's an animal.

"That just means you ain't keeping busy enough with your work." His voice is tinged with anger now. "You don't have enough work to do if you got time to worry about how she's getting on down there."

How can he be so cruel? I was a fool to think he cared for me even the littlest bit. My eyes fill with tears. Tucker towers over me. I go to my knees, cling to his bare thighs.

"Tucker, please."

"Quit your begging," he hisses and slaps my face hard. I fall back to the ground. "Keep it up and I'll make sure you never see that girl again. You hear?"

All I can do is nod. The bastard. One day my Jerry is going to show up and take us away from here. And when I tell him what Tucker has done, he'll show him a thing or two about respect.

Chapter 18

Mill Green, Maryland

The Widow Ashmore had made a habit of reading the daily paper to Jim as he prepared her evening meal. "There's an advertisement in today's paper for scented candles," she said idly.

It was easy conversation, and Jim was her only company. Nat and Susanna had stopped coming around with any frequency. They had visited on her birthday with a basket of flowers and pair of lace gloves, and, of course, Christmas dinner had been hosted at the widow's home. But for what other occasions must they be forced to visit the old woman?

"It appears they make them with mint leaves and vanilla beans right inside the wax. Doesn't that sound lovely, Jim?"

She set her newspaper down on the kitchen table and tilted her head up, as though she could see those lovely candles lining her pantry shelves.

"Yes ma'am. Sounds lovely."

Mrs. Ashmore glanced back down at the advertisement. "Oh, for heaven's sake. They're selling for twenty-five cents apiece at Bailey's down in Baltimore. Can you imagine paying twenty-five cents for a candle?"

"Some folks do, I suppose."

"Well, I suppose I would too, if I were more comfortable," the widow admitted.

The money she had made from the sale of Margaret and the children had helped the widow pay off her debts and make several long-overdue repairs to her home. She was comfortable now, despite the depression, but certainly not to the point of extravagance. Certainly not to the point of buying twenty-five-cent candles.

"You could make them candles for yourself," Jim said, stirring a large pot of bubbling broth at the stove.

Mrs. Ashmore chuckled and scanned the society page.

"It looks like Mary Jane Coleman is to be married next month. Isn't that splendid? She's such a darling child," the widow said. "And the McCafferty String Quintet will be playing at the Fifth Street Theater in Bel Air next month in honor of William Stone. It says here, 'Mr. Stone will be retiring from the position of commissioner after twenty years' service to the county government.' What do you think of that, Jim?"

"Twenty years sure is a long time."

"It certainly is," the widow replied, turning the page. "Oh, here's an advertisement for curtains, at a reasonable price, I'd say."

"I like the curtains you got now, ma'am, with them little pink flowers all along the trim."

"Yes, they are lovely. Margaret made those for me years ago," the widow said, her voice trailing off to a whisper.

"Miss Margaret, did you say? Well, I'll be darned," Jim exclaimed. "Those curtains are so fancy, I always thought they come from an expensive store in the city."

"She always was a talented seamstress," Mrs. Ashmore said.

"I'm sure she still is," said Jim, never taking his eyes from the boiling broth.

The subject of Margaret and the children rarely came up after the auction, but when it did Mrs. Ashmore always referred to the Morgans in past tense. It was easier to say they were "gone," on holiday perhaps or simply vanished into thin air, than to acknowledge they had been sold into bondage. But at night, the reality was unavoidable. After the weather had turned cold, Mrs. Ashmore had pulled one of Margaret's thick, warm quilts from the hall cedar chest. Sleeping under the weight of it was suffocating. The house was full of such reminders, ones that would not go away as neatly and easily as the Morgans had. But what choice did she have? Did she not have debts which had to be settled?

The widow continued reading to herself. After a minute or two had passed, she glanced up again at her imaginary candles. "Do you really think I could make a candle like that?" she asked.

"Like in the paper? Yes ma'am, sure do. You could make hundreds and sell 'em for *thirty* cents apiece."

With that, Mrs. Ashmore laughed out loud, throwing her head back and bringing her hands together under her chin.

"I ain't kidding you ma'am," Jim said grinning. "I can show you how to make them candles yourself, if you want me to."

Mrs. Ashmore quieted down and watched Jim as he stirred the pot in a steady motion to prevent the broth from scalding.

"Where did you learn to make candles?" she asked.

"Oh, I don't know. Just something I picked up somewhere," he said, shrugging and stirring.

Jim was being vague to avoid offending his mistress. She provided him with two candles on the first of every month, along with a pound each of flour and coffee, a cup of sugar, a cup of salt and four thick slices of pork. It was the standard slave ration, but it took creativity to make such supplies last for four weeks.

Mrs. Ashmore watched Jim stir the broth. She looked down at her newspaper again, and an idea came to her, a crazy idea, which seemed quite sensible nonetheless.

"Jim," she said, "Would you like me to teach you to read?"

"R-read ma'am?" Jim dropped the spoon into the broth and then frantically searched for another utensil with which to retrieve it.

"Yes, read," she said.

A few minutes of quiet passed, as Jim, bewildered and a bit frightened, worked to fish the spoon from the bubbling brew. Mrs. Ashmore finally broke the silence.

"I will teach you to read, Jim, if you will teach me to make scented candles."

Finally, Jim retrieved the hot, dripping utensil and carefully wiped it clean with his apron. He leaned against the worktable beside the stove, still clutching the spoon tightly in his fist, and looked out the window for several more minutes. Mrs. Ashmore quietly folded the newspaper and set it in her lap, resting her hands neatly on top. She waited as Jim contemplated the offer. The hall clock chimed six.

"I'd like to read," he said.

Mrs. Ashmore smiled at him.

"Good. We'll begin tomorrow," she said. "Now then, let's see how your broth has turned out. Do we have bread tonight?"

Philadelphia

Golden firelight flickered through the decorative windows of the Forten house, beaming a galaxy of tiny rainbows out into the black, across a thick carpet of snow. Pennsylvania winters are always dark, but the winter after the Morgan kidnapping was the beginning of an especially dark season for the city of Philadelphia.

"James, be a dear and put another log on the fire, won't you?" Mrs. Forten always addressed her husband by his Christian name. He was not a Jim, certainly not Jimmy. He was the wealthiest black man in Philadelphia, perhaps in the country, a philanthropist, an abolitionist. His ship-making business employed both blacks and whites.

"Yes, my dear," James Forten nodded, setting his reading glasses and Bible on the table beside his chair. He was not so important as to put off stoking the fire on a chilly night for his bride of forty-plus years.

Nellie entered the dining room with a fresh stack of linens just as her mistress made the request.

"Oh, Mr. Forten, please just stay right where you are," she said, moving quickly toward the fireplace. "There's no need for you to get up when I'm at hand, sir."

Mrs. Forten set her quilting ring in her lap with a huff of exasperation.

"Nellie, it's nearly nine o'clock. I didn't even know you were still about. You should have retired from your chores hours ago, child."

"Don't you worry, Mrs. Forten, I don't mind. I really don't," Nellie insisted.

Truth be told, Nellie liked to work long days. It was all she had ever done. She had no family to tend, so her work did not take her away from more important things. There was little to do in her room beside the kitchen. Nellie could not read, she did not enjoy sewing and, lately, she did not sleep well. Her dreams were corrupted by the loss of her dear friend Margaret and the upcoming trial of the man responsible, and keeping busy helped her avoid thinking of things she could not change.

One task that Nellie relished was stoking the Forten's fireplace. The stones of the hearth were smooth and warm, neatly stacked and sealed with grout to a height high above her head. She required a stool to dust the crystal figurines that lined its marble mantel. Of all the artwork that graced the walls, of all the silver that adorned the tables, of all the silk that upholstered the furniture, Nellie believed that fireplace was the biggest show of power and money in the Forten residence. That fireplace was larger than the room in which Nellie had lived most of her life, before she'd escaped slavery.

"Thank you, Nellie," Mr. Forten said, settling back into his chair. He watched as she gingerly placed a fresh piece of wood onto the fire, causing a smoldering log to crumble and send a flash of sparks up into the dark expanse of the chimney.

"I suppose we're all a bit anxious about tomorrow," he said, to no one in particular, his white billowy hair glowing orange in the firelight. Mrs. Forten nodded silently. Nellie poked at the fire.

It had taken nearly a year, but Edward Prigg finally would face a Pennsylvania jury for his deeds. Margaret had been the seamstress for many of Philadelphia's elite, and her kidnapping quickly drew public ire. Both Pennsylvania law and territory had been violated by this rogue from Maryland. What's more, many debutantes had had to attend numerous social gatherings in dresses from the previous season.

"Do you think we'll be able to find her, James, and the children, too, after they convict Mr. Prigg?" Mrs. Forten asked. "Oh, how could they not convict?"

Mr. Forten did not answer. The fire crackled, as Nellie gave the blazing wood a little poke.

The old man had no idea how the jury might rule. But he worried that even a conviction would do Margaret and the children little good. To a life of bondage, they were surely lost; and, he felt lost, as well. It had been a bad year for the black community in Philly, after nearly a decade of prosperity and hope. It seemed that the city had tumbled like a house of cards the very day she was snatched up.

Just eight short years before, the Fortens had attended the first National Negro Convention in Philadelphia.

"Do you remember the convention, dear?" Mr. Forten asked his wife.

"Mmm-hmm, of course," she said. "It was the first political rally our girls attended, and it was there that talks first started on creating the Institute for Colored Youth."

Mrs. Forten addressed Nellie when she spoke of the convention. She was proud of her city and its black leadership, and she seized upon even the smallest opportunity to boast. But Mrs. Forten was preaching to the choir.

"Oh, yes ma'am," Nellie lit up. "Didn't your Miss Charlotte go to school there?"

"She certainly did. Charlotte was among the first class to graduate after the institute opened in '32." Mrs. Forten beamed.

The early 1830s had been a time of optimism, expansion and economic boom, not only in Philly, but throughout America. But when the Great Panic took hold in 1837, the social order in Philadelphia had deteriorated quickly. Family fortunes crumbled and white aristocracy fell below the financial status of many blacks.

The upper-class white community in Philly had consisted of old money, assets that had been inherited over many generations and increased through stock investments and land deals. The wealth in Philly's black community, however, had largely been accumulated through business operations built up in recent decades.

Men like James Forten, Benjamin Stiles and other members of Philadelphia's black elite owned manufacturing companies, coal dealerships and other durable businesses. These black business owners had not been left unscathed by the economic depression. Yet, the wheels of commerce continued to turn, if more slowly, and their products and services were still in demand.

"Thank goodness Mr. Stiles stepped in to help save the institute last year, when the bank called in its loan," Mrs. Forten said.

Stiles had contributed $5,000 to the Institute for Colored Youth to keep it afloat during the depression. Few other institutions had such generous benefactors. Hundreds of banks and white-owned businesses collapsed throughout the North, and thousands of people lost their land or their jobs or both.

Resentment and anti-black sentiment in the Free state exploded almost overnight. Early in 1838, the Pennsylvania legislature amended the state constitution, denying blacks the right to vote. Rioting had become commonplace in the city, as angry white mobs lashed out at abolition rallies and torched homes, churches and businesses in the black community.

Now, in the midst of all this, in the bitter cold winter of 1838, Edward Prigg would face a Pennsylvania jury for kidnapping Margaret Morgan and her children.

A frigid wind rattled the decorative windows of the Forten house, the fire spat, and Nellie gave the smoldering logs another good, hard jab.

Chapter 19

Philadelphia

Jerry Morgan tried to stamp the cold from his feet as he paced the planked sidewalk. Nellie and the Fortens huddled around an open fire nearby. Free or not, colored folk were not permitted inside the Philadelphia courthouse. Nearly a hundred people had gathered outside in the early morning, many whites among them, to show their support.

The clock at Town Hall had just struck three, and rumors were humming among the crowd that the jury had already reached a verdict.

The trial itself lasted less than three hours. The lawyers on each side presented their cases as to whether Prigg had broken Pennsylvania law in seizing Margaret without permission from the state.

Prigg had testified that the Morgans were the rightful property of the Widow Ashmore. Then Justice Henderson testified that Prigg did not have the proper papers and that he had denied the bounty hunter extradition of the Morgan family. That was pretty much all it took. The jury deliberated for about thirty minutes and found Prigg guilty of kidnapping.

Authorities quietly shuttled Prigg out the back door of the courthouse, and by the time news of the guilty verdict had reached the crowd waiting out front, he was five miles into his journey home to Mill Green.

"Oh, thank the Lord!" a woman in the crowd exclaimed, and Nellie threw her arms around Jerry's neck.

"You go on and get them now, Jerry. You go find Margaret and your babies and bring them home," she said, smiling and blinking back tears.

Jerry extended his hand to Mr. Forten and a dozen other men, exchanging hearty handshakes and pats on the back. "A hell of a year," one of the men said to him.

It had taken nearly two months for Jerry to recover from the beating delivered by Prigg and his thugs down in Mill Green. But that was just the physical injury.

"You've just got to be patient," the constable would say when Jerry staggered into his office demanding to know why Prigg had not been locked up. "These things take time." And then Deputy Bailey would haul Jerry home and stuff him into bed to sleep it off. But how long can a man sleep? Truth be told, the constable was equally frustrated with the days and weeks and months that had passed. He was tired of being made the fool by the Harford County sheriff every time he traveled to arrest Prigg and returned home empty handed.

Friends from church had come over to help clean up and repair Jerry's cabin after the crime. Nellie had brought biscuits and salt pork to him every Sunday to help raise his spirits. But it wasn't until Prigg had surrendered himself to the authorities, and a date had been set for trial, that hope began to grow within Jerry once more.

Now that Prigg had been found guilty, Jerry believed he would get his family back. His employer, Mr. Mitchell, had helped Jerry arrange for travel to Harrisburg, Pennsylvania, to meet with Governor Ritner. There he would ask for assistance in locating and retrieving Margaret and the children.

"Congratulations, Mr. Morgan. What a joyous day for you," said a gentleman from church. "When will you be leaving for Harrisburg?"

"Thank you. Tomorrow morning. I'll be leaving tomorrow." Jerry smiled broadly. "First thing."

By the time the sun broke on the horizon, Jerry was packed and nearly ready to begin his journey to Harrisburg. He had been awake all night, making preparations and planning for his family's homecoming.

The house was clean and tidy, and the kitchen fully stocked with fresh sugar, flour, coffee and salt. Jerry had carefully washed and dried the pantry cans before filling them. Then he lined them up along the shelf above the fireplace just the way Margaret liked it, from smallest to largest. He had washed the quilts and made up the beds.

Jerry saved ironing his shirt for last, and it had taken nearly an hour with little success. He did the collar and cuffs first, the way Margaret always had. The sleeves were next, then the back, and then the front. But when Jerry had finished the front panels, the sleeves had somehow gotten wrinkled again; and after the sleeves were once again smooth and neat, he noticed long creases down the back that just shouldn't have been there.

"Gimme a wagon full of fifty-pound barrels to unload instead of ironing just one damned shirt," he grumbled.

A knock at the door nearly sent him flying out of his shoes.

"Jerry? You still here?"

Nellie pushed open the door slowly, peeking in to see the shirtless man hunched over the ironing board. Should couldn't help but laugh at the sight of him.

Jerry laughed, too, realizing how silly he must have looked. Margaret could iron half a dozen shirts in an hour's time. She would stand at the board, her back straight, her hands working with ease over the fabric, while she sang one hymn after another. He had watched her do so hundreds of times in the ten years they had been married.

"Margaret always made it look so easy," Jerry said.

"Yes," said Nellie, setting down her packages and taking over the iron. "Margaret made everything seem easier than it really was."

Jerry nodded in silent agreement.

"I made up some biscuits and preserves for you to take with you," Nellie continued, quickly finishing up the shirt and holding it up for Jerry to put on. He slipped in one arm, then the other. Nellie eyed the long thick scars covering his back, before she pulled the shirt up over his shoulders. They both knew, too well, what it meant to live a life of slavery.

"You hurry now and bring your family home just as fast as you can, Jerry Morgan," she said.

Harrisburg, Pennsylvania

The trip up to Harrisburg took about three hours by canal boat up the Susquehanna River. Jerry stood on deck, his coat drawn tightly around him to block out the cold.

As the boat crept along, his mind mulled over the challenge that lay before him. He didn't know much about where his family had ended up, only that his girls had gone one direction and his boys another. What he did know, without question, was that he would spend the rest of his living days trying to find them, if that's what it would take.

"I promise to spend all the rest of my days loving you." That's what Jerry had promised Margaret on their wedding day, and she had vowed to do the same.

Jerry leaned back against the boat railing. He turned his face toward the gray winter sky. He closed his eyes, remembering that brilliant day in Mill Green, the summer sun warming his cheeks.

Margaret and Jerry had exchanged wedding vows beside the pond at the Ashmore estate. The gathering had been small. Jerry had no family. Margaret's daddy had died a couple years before, not long after Mr. Ashmore had passed. The widow Ashmore and young Jim had waited with Jerry by the pond, while Margaret's mama had helped her get dressed in the cabin.

"She's ready!"

Mama had hurried down the path to the pond, and Mrs. Ashmore had played the wedding march on her flute. Margaret had walked slowly down the path, smiling broadly. Jerry had watched her, palms sweating.

The young bride had tiny pink wild flowers woven through her thick hair, which rested in long, wavy tresses down her back. Her dress was of white lace, drawn in at the waist with a silk ribbon. Short puffy sleeves had sat just off her shoulders. Her flawless brown neck, shoulders and arms had glistened in the sun.

Jerry had always respected Margaret's conservative nature; but his heart had swelled with pride and yearning to see her look so striking on their wedding day.

"You're so beautiful," he'd said.

"And you're as handsome a man as there ever was," she'd said. Then she'd pulled a flower from her hair and tucked the stem in his shirt pocket.

Margaret had sewn new clothes for her groom, as well. A crisp white linen shirt, with long sleeves and shiny little black buttons down the front. Tan cotton pants, which she had starched and ironed. It was the nicest set of clothes Jerry had ever owned.

There was no preacher to officiate the wedding. Maryland law didn't recognize marriage among blacks. It made Jerry angry, but Margaret didn't care. "Ours is a union blessed by God," she had said. And so it was, as they stood barefoot in the grass and vowed to love one another forever.

"The governor will see you now." A stout woman in a black, high-collared dress led Jerry down a hallway and into a large office at Harrisburg Capitol Hall. "I'll take your coat."

Gov. Ritner nodded at him from behind a massive mahogany desk and waved the woman away. The woman draped Jerry's coat across her forearm and used both hands to pull the large double-doors shut as she retreated.

"Good morning, Governor. I sure do appreciate you meeting me like this today." Jerry remained standing, and the governor did not offer him a seat.

"Yes, your employer, Mr. Mitchell, has been a supporter of mine for some time. I was happy to extend him this favor."

"Yessir."

Gov. Ritner had been signing papers at his desk, dipping his quill into the ink pot and scratching out his signature while he addressed his visitor. He did not look up from his work.

Jerry stood motionless, silent, unsure of what to say or how to begin. For some time, he only watched as the governor worked. Finally, the man seemed finished with his task, slid a stack of papers to the side of his desk, leaned back in his chair.

"Tell me what it is you seek today, Mister . . . uh . . . Mister . . . " he finally said.

"Morgan, sir. My name is Jerry Morgan. My wife Margaret and my children were kidnapped by that Mr. Prigg from Maryland."

"Ah, yes. What a terrible crime. I'm only glad we were able to bring justice in the matter. All's well that ends well, as they say. You must be pleased with the conviction?"

"Yessir," Jerry answered. "I'm quite happy the jury convicted him. Thank you, sir."

"Very good, very good. I do appreciate your visit, son, but there was no need for you to travel all this way just to thank me."

Gov. Ritner turned his attention back to his papers, and Jerry stood fixed where he had been since first entering the room. He cleared his throat and shifted his weight from one foot to the other.

"Sir, I-I do thank you. But I really came to ask your help in getting my family back. Since y'all convicted Mr. Prigg of kidnapping, I thought maybe you would help me find the people who bought up my wife and children. You could make 'em give my family back."

The governor raised his hand.

"Stop right there, son. You have to understand there's nothing I can do about that. Mr. Prigg broke Pennsylvania law, and he was brought to justice, but your family is the property of the Ashmores down in Maryland. That's a whole other matter."

"But, I . . ."

The governor raised his hand again. Jerry stopped speaking, but he stomped his foot in frustration and Gov. Ritner quickly jumped up from his seat.

"You hold it right there, boy. I'll have no disrespect from you!"

"Yessir. Uh, no sir. I mean no disrespect. I really don't," Jerry stammered. "I just, I just want my family back. That's all."

"Your family is gone, son. You best accept it, and you best be on your way now."

The governor brushed past his visitor, opened the office doors wide and returned to his desk.

Jerry stood there dumbfounded. *Is that it*, he asked himself, *a half-day's journey just to be belittled by this smug son-of-a-bitch for two minutes.* His face grew hot, and his teeth began to ache under the strain of his clenched jaw. For a moment, Jerry pictured himself pulling the governor from his chair and thrashing him within an inch of his life. But that wouldn't bring his family home.

"I said you best be on your way, boy," the governor growled.

Jerry backed slowly out the giant doors, then turned and barreled down the hall and out of the building. By the time he reached the street, he had broken into a full run. He sprinted for five blocks, stumbling in the rutted street, knocking into pedestrians, blinded by heartbreak, until he reached the canal boat lock house. Jerry lumbered across the ramp, sweating and flushed, and fell into a seat on deck.

"What's this?" a ship's hand said, eyeing the breathless black man. "What's the rush, boy? What are you running from?"

Breathless, Jerry could only look up at the man and shake his head from side to side.

"No? You're not running from nothing?" the man asked. "Where are you headed? Show me your ticket."

Jerry nodded yes, and reached his hand up to his chest, where he had placed his boat ticket in his left-hand inside coat pocket. A hot flash of panic washed over him. The man squinted and took a step closer.

"It's in my coat, sir," Jerry finally managed to sputter, as he rose from the bench. "I'll just go fetch my coat and be right back."

The crewman pushed a hand against Jerry's chest, sending him off balance and plopping him back down on to the bench. By this time, the scene had gained the attention of several people on board, passengers and crew alike.

"You're gonna just go get your coat, are you? Where did you leave it?"

"It's in the governor's office."

The crewman burst out in laughter.

"Oooooh. You left it in the *governor's* office. Sure. I know lots of Negroes who just go waltzing into the governor's office and forget their coats when they leave."

Jerry tried to stand again, but a man at his left took hold of him and forced him back. He was soon surrounded by half a dozen men who looked down at him with dark, suspicious eyes.

"You got your free papers, boy?" one of the men asked. Jerry fidgeted and grasped again for his invisible coat pocket.

"Oh, let me guess. Them are in your jacket, too, right? Over at the *governor's* office."

An elderly passenger snickered.

"He doesn't have any free papers!" one of the hands shouted.

"He's on the run!" another chimed in.

Jerry jumped to his feet again, but it was too late. The men converged on him quickly, binding his wrists behind his back with a rope. In the course of all the commotion, the boat had already moved away from the lock and begun its slow journey down the canal.

"You just sit yourself back down," the crewman said to Jerry. "We'll run you on over to the sheriff when we get into Columbia. I don't allow runaways on my boat."

Defeated for the second time in just a few minutes' time, Jerry sank down onto the seat and leaned back against the boat railing. He shivered as the cold air blowing up from the river chilled the sweat that covered his body. He listened as the passengers and crew speculated on his fate. He realized he would soon lose the one thing he had left in the world—his freedom.

Jerry watched the scenery pass by at what seemed to be lightning speed, despite the canal boat's slow pace. His heart raced throughout the three-hour journey. His head felt light. But he could not accept that all was lost. He would not give in, not while he still had breath within him.

As the boat finally eased into the lock at Columbia, Jerry sprang to his feet and bolted across the deck.

With great energetic strides, he leapt onto a bench, up to the railing and over the water to the wall of the canal. With his hands still tied behind his back, Jerry fought to catch his balance, teetering dangerously on a loose stone in the wall.

Shouts and curses rose up from all sides, as the ship's crew scrambled to intercept him.

The mortar beneath his feet suddenly gave way, and Jerry fell backward into the lock. He sank like a stone in the icy water, and the boat passed over him, pushing his body down into the muddy canal bed.

Jerry struggled madly against the weight of the boat, against the ropes that bound him, consumed by total darkness, total silence.

Mud oozed into his ears and nostrils, as he writhed and fought and sank deeper, deeper into the muck. His lungs burned.

Then a faint voice called out to him from far away.

"Fear not, Jerry."

He tried to relax his body, strained to hear the instructions of his rescuer.

"Fear not."

But the voice he heard was not his rescuer, as Jerry hoped in the mere seconds he had to consider his fate.

"You are coming home, my child."

It was his redeemer.

Chapter 20

Margaret

The days turned to weeks, and the weeks to months, almost without my realizing it, and summer is suddenly upon us at the plantation.

The rains come every morning, but it's not cool summer rain like up North. Not the kind of rain that refreshes you, washes you clean.

It comes in hot, heavy drops that cling to the air and to your skin long after the showers have stopped. And it brings all sorts of bugs and vermin with it—rats, snakes, mosquitoes, ticks, leeches—creatures that eat at your flesh, that buzz and hiss and torture you day and night. The rain brings poisonous leaves and vines and weeds that lurk within the swamps and fields and gardens, just waiting to infect your skin, make you burn and itch and swell for days. Worst of all, it brings the fever, which plagues the field slaves all summer long and already has killed more than a dozen at the plantation. South Carolina is a hideous place.

The Beanes left the plantation in early June to vacation on Pawley's Island, off the Atlantic coast, until the fall. It's common practice among wealthy planters in South Carolina, Nanny informed me, to escape the heat and disease of the summer. They have overseers to run the plantations and bankers to manage the business of selling the crops, so planters are free to focus their energy on enjoying life. On Pawley's Island, the men hunt and fish, race horses and play billiards. The women and children spend their days on the beach, playing in the surf and picnicking in the shade. Evenings bring formal dinner parties and cotillion balls.

Preparations for the trip went on for weeks. The family took most of their worldly belongings with them—even the piano was loaded onto a wagon. Dozens of slaves also went along, including Nanny. Mrs. Beane said she wouldn't be a good Christian if she separated a husband and wife for so many months, so Elbert went along, too. As washwoman and cook, I would have been among them, but Master insisted I stay behind. He's expecting to find me bulging with motherhood in the fall when he returns.

Tucker is still in charge of the plantation during the summer, but Master also hires a white overseer to come in one day a week and make sure order is maintained.

"Damn you, woman, where are my ashcakes?" Tucker barks.

I dig the hot cakes from the fire pit, brush away the large bits of dirt and ash as best I can. Then I wrap his meal in a piece of cloth. Last month, I stole an empty flour sack from Master's pantry and cut it up for us to use as towels and napkins at the slave's quarters. Just another of my lame attempts to feel more like a human being than chattel.

"Here you go," I say.

Tucker snatches the package from me and hustles down the path to the fields. The overseer will be coming this morning. His visits always put Tucker on edge.

"He's a mean cuss, that one," Tucker said to me about a week before the Beanes left for the island. "You make sure to keep out of his way, Margaret. Just let me deal with him. You hear?"

I've done just that. If this man makes Tucker fearful, I can only shudder to think how horrible he must be.

We've taken to eating dinner on the veranda up at the big house, so we can enjoy the slight breeze that blows at night from the Santee River. On Sundays, I take prized salt pork and beans and sweet potato pies down to the field slaves, so they won't tell the overseer about the privileges Tucker and I have been stealing.

"Margaret, tell me again about yo' cabin in up in York," Tucker asks.

"I'm not really up for a story tonight," I say, pushing the buttered greens around my plate.

Tucker knows nothing about the world outside this plantation and often begs me to tell him story after story about Philly, Mill Green and Havre de Grace, about McFarland's store, May Day picnics and freedom. I tell him stories about my sewing business, about the wealthy black families of the North.

Most times, I like storytelling. Guess that's a piece of me I got from my mama. And, now that I've lived a piece of her life, I understand why.

Losing my family caused a relentless pain inside me that I can't even begin to understand or describe. But sometimes, when I'm scrubbing bed sheets down by the swamp or pouring Master a cup of coffee in the kitchen, my mind goes blank and my body just takes over for a brief moment, and I don't feel anything at all. It's a horrible sensation, that numbness.

Indulging Tucker with stories of home helps keep the pain inside of me, sharpens it, like a stone sharpens a blade. I want that pain to stay strong, so I'll never forget, never give in.

"Come on, Margaret, please," he says. "You know how I love yo' stories."

His childish begging reminds me of Sammy, and it cuts just a little too deep today. Since that first night at the slaves' quarters, by the fire, I haven't spoken of Jerry once. And of all the stories I've told Tucker and the other slaves, I've never talked about my kids. I guess I just didn't want to share them with anyone.

"Tell me something new," Tucker pleads. "Something you never told me 'bout before. Something exciting."

"I almost died the day my daughter was born," I finally snap. "Is that exciting enough for you?"

Tucker is stunned, but pleased, and nods his approval. My distress is lost on this simple boy. I give in.

"We moved to York when I was pregnant, about half way along," I begin. "John, my oldest boy was five, and Sammy was just two. We got the cabin built in time for the first snowfall, but it wasn't much more than a wobbly roof and four walls at that point. Lord, it was cold that winter.

"My friend Nellie stayed with us for about a week, waiting on the baby. When the time finally came, she helped me deliver. After the baby was born, she cleaned us up and then went out to haul in some more firewood from the pile out back. The children and I were all cuddled on the bed. Nellie wasn't gone more than two minutes when we heard a creaking and groaning overhead. Then the roof gave way to the heavy snow and came crashing right down on top of us!"

Tucker gasps, leans in with anticipation. "How'd you escape?"

"Well, thank the good Lord Nellie wasn't in the cabin for the collapse. So she ran to the neighbors. Mr. McBride and his whole family raced back in their wagon, and they all set about the job of digging us out. We just laid there, waiting, barely able to breathe, freezing for about an hour or two. I was bleeding something terrible from the birth. I could feel the warm blood flowing out of me and soaking the bed beneath us. But our bodies kept each other warm enough, and baby Emma was tucked nice and safe right in between me and my boys. It's a miracle we all survived with only a few cuts and bruises. The midwife who came out to check on me and the baby the next day said it was probably the snow and cold that kept me from bleeding to death."

I haven't thought back on that day in a long time.

"It always amazes me," I say, feeling my eyes beginning to well up. "To think about the peculiar ways the Lord goes about taking care of us. He saved us all that day. But now I don't even know where my boys are. And Emma . . . "

The words elude me. Tucker brushes a tear from my cheek.

The tears now stream from my eyes. My throat tightens and my stomach aches for my babies. I did not speak of Jerry, but he'd been there, too. He'd always been there. I can see him just as clear as if he were sitting beside me on the veranda, rocking one of our babies to sleep. I've cursed him a thousand times for not saving us from Prigg and the auction, and I've cried for him just as often. I'd give just about anything to be in Jerry's arms right now. His strong embraces make me feel I could handle anything, as long as we're together.

Tucker slides closer to me and moves the plate from my lap.

He kisses me tenderly on the mouth, something he has never done. He pulls me to him, hugs me. I bury my face in his wide chest, imagining that he's my Jerry, the man I love and ache for. The damp of his skin, the smell of his sweat. His breathing is rhythmic; his heart beats steady at my cheek. My mind wanders to happier times, lying naked beside my man in the cabin we built, skin against skin, the cool scent of pine in the air, our life just the way we wanted it to be.

"Let's go on down to the quarters," Tucker whispers, shattering my perfect dream. He looks at me with a longing I've come to understand well in the past several months. But I can't go through with it tonight. Not feeling the way I am, all warm inside, longing for my husband.

"I'm sorry, Tucker. I just can't tonight. I miss my children."

"I can give you a new baby," he says. "I can make you happy again."

A new baby. The words hit me like Master's switch, snap me quickly back to reality. My weakness nearly drew me into a terrible, terrible mistake. I must remain strong, focused. I must never lie with this man as I once did with my husband. Never.

"That's very sweet of you," I say, kissing Tucker's cheek. "You do make me happy. Let me clean up dinner here, and I'll meet you on down at the quarters in just a bit. Okay?"

I smile sweetly. He spent a long day in the heat of the rice fields and enjoyed a few cups of Master's whiskey with his dinner. If I take enough care with the washing, he'll fall asleep before I join him.

"You can clean up when I'm through with you," Tucker says, the softness evaporating from his eyes and his voice. He grabs hold of my wrist and pulls me down the veranda steps. I stumble along, fighting to stay on my feet.

"Tucker, wait, please!"

"No," he says.

He pulls me around the side of the house, throws me down into the tall grass. I know I shouldn't fight him, but something deep inside tells me to run. I scramble to my hands and knees. In a flash, Tucker grabs around my waist and flips me onto my back like a rag doll. He's too strong.

Holding my neck with one hand, he unties his belt with the other and drops his pants. He pulls my dress up, tears my bloomers clean off.

I gasp for air, and he releases my neck. He pins my shoulders to the ground and thrusts himself into me.

"You're my woman," he grunts, leaning his full weight onto me. "My woman, my woman, my woman."

I hold my breath, waiting for it to end.

Then he's done. With a huff, he rolls off me, onto his back in the grass.

I roll away from him, onto my side, and curl into a ball. I fight back the sobs. That only makes him angry.

"That was real good, Margaret," he says, patting my back. "You're a good woman. We'll get you a baby, yet."

Chapter 21

Margaret

Despite the torment I continue to endure by the hand of Tucker, in some ways, the summer has been an unexpected blessing.

Because the Beanes are away, my daily chores have changed. No family to cook for every day, no mountain of laundry to conquer every week. Master doesn't want me down in the fields over the summer, 'cause he doesn't want to risk me getting the fever and dying before he gets his money's worth out of me. So my job until November is to sew and get pregnant.

The sewing part is a dream. Finally, I feel like Margaret again.

A few weeks before the family left, Missus Simone presented me with a seamstress kit in a wicker basket. It's the most beautiful thing I've ever possessed, even if it isn't really mine. The top opens on brass hinges, and the inside is divided into compartments, all lined with blue velvet. This treasure box is filled with all colors of thread and embroidery yarn, shiny needles of various sizes, all manner of buttons and hooks, and a little silver thimble with matching scissors. It has a numbered tape, too, which I used to take measurements of each family member before their retreat.

The Missus was taken aback, almost angry, at my ability to measure, calculate sizes and write it all down.

"Margaret, you never told me you could read," she had accused.

"Naaaa, ma'am," I had said in my best slave dialect. "My old mistress, she done taught me how to do numbas, so as I could figure out the sewin' and such."

Pretending to be a little thick in the head has gotten me out of more than one pinch here at the plantation so far. It would be funny, if it weren't so depressing. The Beanes, and probably all slave owners, seem to get pleasure from believing their slaves are dim-witted and helpless.

"Well that was very generous of your mistress," Simone had said. "She must have been quite a woman to be able to teach you such a complicated task. Although with plenty of repetition and patience, I suppose it would be possible."

Oh, the willpower I had that day to hold my tongue!

Simone told me what articles of clothing she wanted made, and I told her how much fabric would be needed. Two days later, Master Beane returned from a trip to town with a wagon full of fabric bolts. And as soon as the family's wagon train left the plantation for Pawley's Island, I set about my sewing work with a vengeance.

I've already made matching Sunday outfits for the twins, a winter suit coat for Master, a lovely dress that the Missus will wear for the Thanksgiving ball, and two dozen embroidered cotton napkins for Christmas dinner. Also on my list are several shirts and pants for Master, and nightgowns for the children.

The Missus originally didn't want any dresses for herself, because she is "partial to the latest fashion from France." She even showed me pictures of French dresses in the *Lady's Book* magazines that the postman delivers to the plantation each month. Because she had grown up in Paris, Simone believed no one could match the quality of dresses made there.

My pride got the better of me—guess it's one of the few things I haven't lost in the past year—and I cajoled her into letting me make just one. Then I set about designing and crafting a dress that will make the Missus and her society friends go weak in the knees. It has a wide, bell-shaped skirt and a corset with a low, rounded waist, boning in the front and plenty of padding at the bosom to highlight Simone's womanly curves. Both are made of cream-colored velvet, and I embroidered delicate vines and leaves in copper, gold and red along the bodice. The bustle and draping behind are of lush copper fabric, which I also used to make a small jacket with a high open collar and long, narrow sleeves.

It's far more stunning than any dress I ever made for Mrs. Forten or her daughters, who had to be careful to always present a conservative disposition. Simone's sultry French character demands something a little bolder. When she wears this dress to the ball, Master Beane will be the envy of every rice planter in South Carolina, and I will surely be promoted from washwoman to seamstress.

The other part of my job at the plantation has not been as productive. My monthly cycle came again this morning!

I remember a time when I cursed it each month—the tight pain it brought low in my gut and the extra work of soaking and washing out the bloody rags in lye every night. And when it did not come, it meant that I was pregnant with Jerry's child, an indescribable joy.

Now, I drop to my knees and praise God each month it comes to me. The pain, the mess, the assurance that I am not with child—it's a gift I never dreamed I would celebrate.

The new bit of freedom that summer brought has given me the courage to attempt another visit with Emma down at Granny Gin's place.

My approach with Tucker was different this time. I didn't ask permission. I told him I planned to visit her and that he would not stop me. Thank goodness the overseer visits the plantation for the summer. That gave me the leverage I needed.

I made sure Tucker knew that if he held me back from visiting Emma, then I would let our secret slip about the meals and whiskey at the big house. The offense would bring a dozen lashes for each of us, but I didn't care, and Tucker knew it. So he played the big man and said I could go to Granny Gin's.

The day of my visit, I awoke early and baked a small peach cobbler for my own little peach. Just before dawn broke, I trotted through the shadows toward Granny Gin's. The chatter of tiny voices in the distance made me quicken my pace until I was sprinting full speed down the path. I stopped at the edge of the trees to take in the view before me.

The sun has broken on the horizon, and the morning is already hot, the air thick with steam. I've waited so long for this day, yet I can't seem to get my feet to move. *What on God's green earth is wrong with me?*

A dozen or so children are meandering around Granny Gin's dilapidated shack. They range in height, some barely knee-high to a grasshopper, but they all have the same look about them—thin, barefoot, half naked, covered in dirt from head to toe. It knocks the wind right out of me to see them that way. *Poor babies.*

I scan the group, desperate to spot Emma, but she is nowhere to be seen.

"Mama?"

The voice is familiar, but I can't spot her face in the horde.

"Mama!"

A child emerges from the group, runs at me, arms outstretched. She's wearing nothing but an oversized cotton shirt that hangs to her knees. Bits of grass and leaves seem to sprout from her matted unruly hair. She stops abruptly in front of me. Only her eyes give her away.

I drop to my knees and pull her in.

"Oh, sweet God in Heaven! Is that really you, Emma, under all that dirt?"

Emma laughs and squeezes me tight. Then she pulls away. Her smile fades.

"I haven't had a bath in months, Mama."

I hold her out at arm's length and give her the same once-over I've done a hundred times before. *It's all coming back to me now, as though not a day has passed since I was a proper mother to this child.* Without saying a word, I lick my thumb and rub her cheek until a small patch of her chocolate skin finally peeks through the dusty coating.

"Mmm, mmm, mmm," I say. "Wouldn't your brothers be jealous of that!"

With this, Emma laughs again. Her eyes sparkle.

A lump suddenly forms in my throat and uncontrollable sobs erupt from my mouth. All that grief and anger and fear I kept buried since the auction is just bubbling up out of me like lava from a volcano on some deserted island. I can't hold it back.

"Oh, mama," Emma smiles, cradles my face in her grubby little hands. "Don't cry. Don't cry. Oh, please, don't cry."

Her sweet smile only makes me cry more. I close my eyes and pull her close to me again. Emma gives in to my embrace completely, collapsing on me and sending us both tumbling over backward onto the ground.

"Well, thas quite a sight! Oh Lordy, Lordy, what a sight!"

An ancient frail woman, no bigger than the children around her, stands above us. Emma laughs again and pulls away to stand up.

"This is my mama, Granny Gin!"

"Yessum. I done figured as much."

Emma helps pull me to my feet and brushes the dirt from my dress. "This is my Granny Gin."

I've gotten my sobbing under control, but I'm still hiccupping and sputtering like a fool. All I can do is to reach out my hand and smile hello. Granny sandwiches my hand between hers, all skin and bones, warm and dry.

"Little Emma been talking about you nonstop," she says, laughing. "I figured it was just a matter a time before you figured out a way to get on down here for a visit."

"I brought peach cobbler," I finally manage to say. The other children have gathered around, wide-eyed. "There's probably enough for everyone to have a spoonful."

In a flurry of shrieks and dust, the children rush this way and that, disappearing into the shack and behind the trees, and re-emerge with primitive spoons in hand. Granny leads us to the shade and we all settle down into a circle on the ground. Emma pulls the cobbler from my basket and hands it to a small boy sitting beside her. He digs in his spoon and plunges a scoop of the sweet orangey mass into his mouth. A broad grin spreads across his face as he chews, and the whole group bursts into laughter.

The dish makes its way around the circle. My heart aches as I watch, knowing it's the first taste of anything more than ash cakes and boiled weeds for any one of these children. Granny only dips her finger in for a small taste, smiles and passes the treat along. I do the same.

"You finish it, Emma," one of the older boys says as the dish completes the circle. A couple bites remain. "Yes, Emma, you finish it," a few others chime in.

"Oh, thank you!" She wastes no time devouring the last fruity bites and sweet crumbles.

The food gone, the children quickly disperse. Granny Gin smiles and retreats into the shack. Emma takes my hand and leads me on a tour of her new home. She introduces me to every child and recites their histories.

"Little Ben's mama died when he was born. Mary's daddy died of the fever last summer. Her mama's still working the rice, but she hasn't seen her for about three years. Tommy is almost 10 now, so he'll be going to live with his daddy and mama next summer. He'll be working the rice then, too."

Is this really my little Emma? She seems to have aged a year for every month we've been at the plantation, suddenly so wise beyond her years.

The rest of the morning passes like a dream. The sun is high overhead, and I realize I must hurry back up to the big house and my chores.

"Emma, I've got to go now. But I'll be back again very soon, I promise."

Emma nods and throws her arms around me. Neither of us wants to let go.

"Tomorrow?" Emma asks, still clinging tightly.

"Oh, baby." It's hard to find the words. "No, not tomorrow. But soon, and often, if only for a couple minutes for a hug and kiss. Okay?"

She pulls away slowly and looks up at me, searching my face for the truth. Finally, she nods, silent tears running down her dirty cheeks. One more kiss and hug. Then I hurry up the path to the big house, my heart swelling so much with joy and grief it feels as though it's gonna burst.

Another unexpected benefit of the summer, and of having the big house mostly to myself, has been the chance to devour the Beane family library. They possess all the latest volumes. Most haven't even had their spines cracked, even though the pages have been cut. The library exists in their home merely for show, and the books have never been read. Until now! To prevent any future discoveries, I am careful to open the books only a few inches as I read, keeping their smooth spines well intact.

In the mornings I sew, and in the afternoons I read to my heart's content. Their collection includes a large number of almanacs and cookbooks, which I enjoy. Sadly, Emerson is not to be found. But I've been drawn to the novels in a way I never have before, a temporary escape from reality that makes me laugh and cry and forget where I am.

James Fennimore Cooper, with his *Leatherstocking Tales*, *The Spy* and *The Last of the Mohicans*, has become a new favorite. And Mary Shelley's tale of *Frankenstein* kept me sleepless for three nights!

But now the days are shorter, and the weather has turned. The harvest is almost complete, and the slaves have begun preparations for the Beane family's return to the plantation.

There will be no more opportunities for me to sneak bacon and buttered greens and pie down to the field slaves on Sundays. No more solitude of the big house for me, to read and dream of a better time. No more pilfered whiskey and late-night dinners on the veranda. And, for Tucker, there will be no growing bump of motherhood in me when Master returns.

Chapter 22

Margaret

It's Sunday—my usual day off—and I've been called up to the big house. I can hear Master yelling in there from across the lawn. He's been spitting venom ever since the family returned from Pawley's Island in September, but the past few months have been getting worse. I know why he's so angry. It's been more than a year since I moved into Tucker's quarters, and I have yet to produce a child for Master to add to his stock.

I enter the big house from the back kitchen door—not even the house slaves are allowed to enter from the front—and see Mr. and Mrs. Beane standing beside the kitchen table.

"Sit down," Master growls at me, pointing to the stool where I usually sit when shelling peas or cutting biscuits.

"Yessir," I say and quickly take my seat.

"Margaret," the Missus says. She pauses, ringing her hands, and looks over at Master. "I hope you know I've been quite pleased with your cooking and washing this past year, and your seamstress work is superb."

"Thank you, ma'am. I so glad you's pleased."

"However," she quickly continues. "You also must know that the privilege of working at the house comes with other responsibilities on the property."

The Missus glances over at Mr. Beane, then lowers her eyes.

"Aw, for Christ's sake," he interrupts. "I bought you to breed, Margaret. We thought the ease of housework would be favorable to that, but I have Niggers in the field multiplying like rabbits, and you've produced nothing. You're infertile."

"In-feer-tul?" I play along, pretending to be ignorant of the terminology of childbearing. Truth is, I've probably read more books just about pregnancy and medicine and womanly topics than all the books Master has read in his entire life.

"It means you can't have children," the Missus says to me sympathetically.

"Oh?" I say, trying hard to look confused. "But I done had three already."

"Well, then, why the hell haven't you had any more?" Master shouts.

Oh, how I want to tell him! *Because the Lord is on my side, Master Beane, not yours. Because I've outsmarted you, you damned ignorant fool.* Instead, I just stare at him blankly.

He takes a wild swing and knocks a basket of breakfast rolls to the floor. It doesn't scare me. Compared to Tucker's brutal temper, Master's fit seems no worse than a toddler's tantrum. I have to stifle a laugh, so I play like I'm fixing to cry.

"Harry, please," Simone pleads. "I'm sure it's very distressing to her to realize she can't have any more children."

"I don't care if she's distressed," Master shouts again. "Don't you think I'm distressed that I haven't gotten a fair return on my investment? She was supposed to produce!"

The Missus takes a deep breath and lets it out slowly, crossing her arms across her chest. She waits for him to finish spouting off.

Master paces back and forth a few times and collects himself.

"The point is, Margaret, I need to make sure I get my money's worth out of you," he says finally. "So you'll no longer be working up here at the house. Move your things out of the couples' quarters today and down to the field house near Granny Gin's cabin. You'll be working the fields starting tomorrow."

"I'm sorry, Margaret," the Missus adds.

How do I possibly contain myself? This is one of the happiest moments I've had at the plantation!

"Oh, Master!" I cry out, burying my face in my hands.

"Go on now," he says coldly.

I stand and bolt out of the kitchen, down the foot path and across the lawn toward the couples' quarters. "Ey-ey-ey-eeeee," I howl, feeling like one of those Indians I read about in *The Last of the Mohicans*, shouting a victory cry after battle. The war has been long, but I can finally claim victory in one battle. I lick the salty tears from my lips, tears of pure joy. My new home will be near my dear Emma. I'll see her every day now. Every glorious day!

"What on God's green earth are you hollering 'bout?" Hope asks as I run past the row of slave houses.

I laugh and run around in a small circle, my arms outstretched like an eagle, before tracking back and stopping in front of her. She is kneeling near the door stoop, grinding her week's ration of corn on the big flat stone. My smile is uncontainable and Hope breaks out into laughter at the sight of me.

"You finally lost yo mind," Hope says.

"No," I reply. "I've finally won!"

"You won? What do you mean?"

I kneel down beside her and pick up a stone to help her grind. She looks at me sideways. My eyes survey the grounds to be sure Tucker is not nearby. The giddiness is subsiding and my common sense returning. I must still be careful not to divulge my secret.

"I've been demoted to the fields," I say to her quietly. "Master doesn't think I'm able to have babies, so he wants me out of Tucker's quarters."

Hope raises her eyebrows and nods, taking a quick look around, as well.

"Really?" she says. "Well, Massa's smarter than any of us, thas for sho. I reckon he know best."

We share a quiet, knowing smile. Hope is illiterate, as are all the slaves here at the plantation, but she is wickedly smart. I would never have told her my secret. She figured it out for herself one night, after overhearing Master and Tucker arguing by the barn. She approached me the next morning, as I sat beside the stream, letting the cool water flow over my aching feet.

"Overheard the most interestin' thing last night," she said, kicking off her shoes and plopping down on the stone beside me. "A funny little chat 'tween Tucker and the Massa."

"Oh?" I said.

Turns out, Mr. Beane had been questioning Tucker's manhood, wanting to know why he had not succeeded in getting me pregnant after so many months.

"You do know how it's done, don't you boy?" the Master had yelled. "You do know what to do with a woman, don't you?"

Tucker had insisted that he most certainly did, and that he worked at it nearly every night. After some deliberation, the men had agreed that there must be something wrong with me.

"She had babies before she came here, Tucker," Master had said to his stud. "If you damaged her by beating on her that first night, so help me, I'll take it out of your hide."

Hope giggled when relating the story to me. She dangled her toes just above the bubbling stream.

"Privacy in bed ain't something any of us got much of around here, you know, Margaret," she said, grinning slyly. "I know what y'all been doing, but I don't think that's quite how it's done."

"I haven't the slightest idea what you're talking about, Hope."

"A'right," she said, turning serious. "You just be careful Tucker don't ever get the idea neither."

Hope and I finish grinding her corn, and she offers to help me pack up my belongings. It doesn't take long.

Once a year, each slave receives a pair of cotton pants, two cotton shirts, one wool blanket and a pair of roughly-made leather shoes. I have a few additional items of clothing—a cotton dress, a head scarf and pair of Mary-Jane shoes—since my appearance at the big house needs to be more refined. I also still have the nightgown the missus gave me when I slept up at the plantation house.

I wonder if they'll let me keep these things now that I'm a field hand. No matter. I'd walk around buck naked all my days for the privilege to be near my Emma again and free of my obligations to Tucker.

"You better wipe that silly grin from yo face when you walk on down to Granny Gin's," Hope says, folding a dress and placing it on my blanket with the other items. She wraps everything up like a big present and stands back for a long look at me.

"Oh, Hope," I say.

We hug good and tight. There's a big divide between the house slaves and the field hands down by Granny Gin's place. We'll still see each other from time to time, but we won't be close like we have been.

"Don't you think about it," Hope says, reading my mind. "This is a happy time. You're gonna be close to your baby now. Thas all that matters."

I hug her again, quickly kiss her cheek, and then pick up my bundle and walk out of the cabin and into the sun. This is the closest thing I've felt to free since that old buzzard Prigg came crashing through my door in York.

I turn down the lane to Granny Gin's, and I don't look back. Oh what a treat it will be to see the look on Emma's face when she learns we'll see each other every day!

I had managed visits a couple times a week during the summer. When the Beanes had returned, Sundays had been my only chance, but

Tucker had become less tolerant of my visits without the threat of the overseer. He wanted desperately to get me pregnant and make me forget about the family I had lost. He wanted desperately for me to love him.

The ignorant bastard. I'm glad I won't be there when Master tells him I'm no longer his woman.

Chapter 23

Mill Green, Maryland

"Ed, wake up."

Joseph Forwood gave his old friend a kick in the pants to rouse him. Edward Prigg lay sleeping on the floor where he had passed out from drink the night before. It was nearly noon, but what did the time of day matter anymore?

Prigg lifted his head, revealing a puddle of drool on the floor. "I'm sleeping!" he bellowed and rolled over. Joe kicked him again, a little harder this time.

"What, you think you need your beauty sleep?" Joe chided. "Get up already. Someone's here to see you about a job."

The words burned through the fog in Prigg's brain. A job. He rubbed his crusty eyes and lumbered up into a chair. "A job?"

"Yeah," his friend replied. "Joe Jr. was in town this morning and heard this fella, Mr. Slater, talking about how his slave ran off last month and how he can't keep up with the work around the house and…"

Prigg jumped to his feet and bolted toward the door. "Hot damn," he said, smoothing back his sparse greasy hair. "I knew it would just be a matter of time."

The Great Panic had brought hard times on a lot of folks, North and South. Jobs were hard to come by, especially for a convicted felon. Prigg had been one of the first in Mill Green to lose his property when the banks started calling in loans. He would have been camped out in a ditch somewhere, if Joe hadn't offered up his old storage shack rent-free.

"Just hold on, Ed. Hold on a minute." Joe tried to catch Prigg's arm, but he was too slow.

"Mr. Slater!" Prigg called out, extending his hand as he crossed the lawn. "Ed Prigg, bounty hunter at your service."

"Bounty hunter?" The gentleman was puzzled; but he removed his hat and politely shook Prigg's grimy hand.

"Yes," Prigg nodded. "And a damn good one, too. Joe here told me you've got yourself a slave that ran off. Well, I'm your man, sir."

The slight man only stared at Prigg, eying him from head to toe. He was a sorry sight, to be sure. His clothes were soiled and crumpled, his eyes bloodshot, his breath rancid.

"I'm afraid there's b-b-been some con-confusion." Mr. Slater turned to Joe for help.

Prigg eyed the timid, stuttering little man carefully. They all stood quietly for a moment, while Joe struggled to find the right words.

"You didn't let me finish, Ed," he said finally. "You see, Mr. Slater here is having trouble keeping up with work around the house since his slave boy ran off. So he, uh, he's looking for someone . . . well, the job he's offering is for fixing the well pump and chopping wood and things like that."

Prigg's eyebrows crinkled in. He nodded slightly. He stared at Joe, his old friend, unblinking.

"Fixing the well pump?" he said with a slow deliberate tone.

Joe sighed heavily and rubbed his forehead.

"Fixing the God-damned well pump!"

Mr. Slater, startled by Prigg's outburst, took a couple steps back.

"Now, Ed, just settle down," Joe said. "It's honest work."

"It's Nigger's work!" Prigg lunged toward Mr. Slater. "Do you want me to w-w-wipe your ass for you, too, mister?"

This second outburst was about all the gentleman could take. He thrust his hat back atop his head, turned and ran to his wagon parked by the main house, looking back over his shoulder a couple times to make sure the mad man wasn't in pursuit.

"Fixing the well pump," Prigg hissed and gave his friend a shove. Then he spat into the dirt and staggered back into the tiny outbuilding.

Joe let out another heavy sigh.

"Well, that went better than I expected," he muttered. "Stubborn old mule."

York, Pennsylvania

Mr. Mitchell paced the floor of his shipping office. Jerry Morgan hadn't shown up to work for a month. The Negro had always been Mr. Mitchell's most reliable teamster. Even if Jerry had left Pennsylvania to retrieve his family, he would have sent word to his employer.

After the first couple of weeks had passed, Mr. Mitchell had penned a letter to Gov. Ritner to inquire how the meeting between he and Jerry had gone. The governor had responded promptly with a letter thanking Mr. Mitchell once again for his generous campaign contributions in the past. The letter had also stated, however, that there was nothing the governor could do to help Mr. Morgan retrieve his family and that he had "told the Nigger just that." The governor had concluded his letter with a note as to how ill-mannered Jerry had been—leaving without so much as a thank you or even retrieving his coat.

Mr. Mitchell knew Jerry never went anywhere without his free papers, which he kept safely in his jacket pocket. Something just wasn't right.

Jerry's employer had sent a driver to check on the Morgan house and another to Harrisburg to inquire if anyone had seen Jerry there since his meeting with the governor. Now all he could do was wait. A knock on the office door disrupted his pacing.

"Come in," he called out.

Nellie opened the door just a bit and poked her head in.

"So sorry to bother you, Mr. Mitchell," she said.

"No bother, my dear," Mr. Mitchell said. He motioned for her to come all the way in to the room. "Please have a seat."

"Oh, thank you, sir. I was just wondering if you had heard any news about Jerry yet."

Nellie removed her cloak and draped it across her lap as she sat. Her eyes were fixed on Mr. Mitchell. She dared to smile, just a little, praying it would encourage some good news.

"Lewis said there's been no sign of Jerry up at the house," Mr. Mitchell began. He leaned back to sit on the edge of his desk, arms folded across his chest.

Nellie nodded, casting her eyes to the floor. Her smile faded. She had been stopping in at the house every few days hoping to find Jerry and the family back home.

"Solomon went up to Harrisburg to ask around," he continued. "But there's been no word yet."

"Do you suppose he found out where Margaret is and traveled to get her?" Nellie asked.

Mr. Mitchell shook his head no. He told her about the letter he'd received from the governor. He began pacing the floor again.

"Well perhaps . . . perhaps he . . . " Nellie's voice trailed off. She couldn't think of anything else hopeful to say.

Another knock at the office door broke Mr. Mitchell's stride once again. His secretary hustled in with a stack of parcels.

"Postman came," she said, depositing the stack on his desk. As she turned to leave, she added, "There's a letter from the governor on top."

Mr. Mitchell snatched up the letter and broke the wax seal. His eyes ran over the note. His face contorted. Nellie edged forward in her seat.

"It's about Jerry," he told her, reading the letter to himself a second time before continuing. "There, there was an accident of some sort, on the canal boat. Jerry fell overboard. It doesn't say how. It just says it was an accident. He drowned."

Mr. Mitchell looked up at Nellie bewildered. She stood and took the letter from him. Nellie couldn't read, but she studied the paper nonetheless, searching for some clue.

"I don't understand," she said. "Jerry knows how to swim."

"It says his hands were tied behind his back," Mr. Mitchell said.

"Tied? But why?"

"It doesn't say. It only says it was an accident."

Nellie set the letter down on the desk. They stood there for a moment, as the news of Jerry's fate worked its way slowly through their minds. Suddenly, she picked up her cloak and bolted out of his office.

"I have to go now," she called back.

He heard her sobbing as she rushed past the secretary's desk and out into the street.

Chapter 24

Mill Green, Maryland

Mrs. Ashmore worked together with Jim, making candles. She combined carefully-measured proportions of mutton tallow, beeswax, camphor and alum into a large vat and heated it just enough to melt the ingredients without scorching them. She had gotten the recipe from Mrs. Child's 1836 edition of *The American Frugal Housewife*. When the mixture had cooled slightly, and just before pouring it into the molds, Mrs. Ashmore mixed in a combination of herbs and spices. Peppermint leaves were her favorite, but she also liked to experiment with vanilla, cinnamon and flower petals. When lit, Mrs. Ashmore's candles burned with a bright, clear light and released a warm fragrance that lasted for hours. There was nothing else like them in the county.

Every few weeks, the widow would head into town with several boxes of candles. She would leave a box on consignment at the general store, and she would pick up her money and the empty box during her next trip. She had a number of regular customers who bought the candles for their homes and businesses. These candles were left for pick up at the post office, neatly labeled with each customer's name and amount due. The widow also spent time distributing leaflets to the local businesses, advertising her "fine scented candles" at thirty cents apiece, or a discounted rate of one dollar and fifty cents for six.

"I'm thinking of adding coffee beans and rose petals to the next batch, Jim," she said, while stirring the vat with a long wooden dowel. "What do you think of that?"

"Sounds good to me, ma'am."

Jim laced string into a wire rack that, when placed over the molds, allowed the wicks to hang straight down while the wax was poured. He had taught Mrs. Ashmore how to make candles and had been helping her distribute them in town. In return, she had not only been teaching Jim to read and write, but she also had been giving him a small percentage of the sales.

When he finished stringing the wicks, Jim turned to the widow and asked, "Are you okay pouring this batch on your own, ma'am? I got something I need to go fetch from my room."

"Well, of course, I'll be okay," she said.

Jim scuttled out of the work shed, and Mrs. Ashmore repeated the statement to herself. *Of course, I'll be okay.* She looked down at the vat and the molds. Then she thought of something else that made her laugh out loud. Just a year ago, the widow would never have been able to make candles on her own. Yet, thirty years ago, she would have thrown a sharp right cross at any man who might have dared to imply such a thing.

Mrs. Ashmore put on a pair of scuffed leather gloves and grabbed hold of the vat. She eased it over, pouring the warm thickening wax into the molds. When the vat was empty, she returned it to the fire, to soften any remnants of wax and make clean up a bit easier.

"You about done there, ma'am?" Jim asked from outside the shed door, poking only his head through the opening.

"Mm-hmm," the widow tilted her head.

"Good! Close your eyes now. I got a surprise for you!"

"Oh, for heaven's sake, Jim."

"No, ma'am," he interrupted her protest. "You gotta close your eyes."

Mrs. Ashmore decided to indulge in the game.

"Very well," she said, and closed her eyes.

She soon caught whiff of fresh whitewash paint as Jim entered the room and told her to open her eyes. He stood before her, glowing brighter than one of the widow's very own candles, holding a large wooden placard. It was rectangular with rounded corners and had perfectly-formed script letters in green paint. "Margaret Ashmore's Fine Scented Candles"

"Oh, Jim," the widow gasped.

"I wrote the letters myself, ma'am."

"It's lovely," she said, taking the sign from him and holding it at arm's length for a full inspection. "Perfectly lovely."

The same day, Mrs. Ashmore and Jim made preparations for dinner in honor of Susanna's birthday. It was one of the few times during the year that the widow could cajole her daughter and son-in-law to come out to the house for a visit.

Mrs. Ashmore sat at the kitchen table thumbing through her recipes, in search of Susanna's favorite dishes. The young woman was partial to roast beef, potatoes and onions topped with butter sauce. For dessert, Mrs. Ashmore always made a German chocolate cake. The roast and the coconut for the cake always cost the widow a pretty penny each year, yet Susanna had never acknowledged either the cost or the work involved. The old woman exhaled loudly.

Jim stood near the stove shelling peas and cast a watchful eye toward his mistress.

"Gonna be a fine meal tonight," he said.

"Yes." The widow turned the pages without reading them.

"You making that special chocolate cake of yours?"

"Mm-hmm."

The faint tick-tock of the grandfather clock in the dining room echoed into the kitchen. Steam hissed from the covered pots on the stove. Mrs. Ashmore sniffed.

"I'll be sure to make up a big pot of sweet tea," Jim finally said. "I know how much Mrs. Susanna loves that sweet tea."

Mrs. Ashmore looked up from her recipes, and examined Jim. He was grinning wide, but his eyes were fixed on the bowl of peas he was working. When he finally looked her way, their eyes met and the pair erupted in laughter.

After a moment, when she was composed enough to speak, the widow said, "I just might add an extra cup of sugar to the cake, too!" Jim roared, and Mrs. Ashmore stifled her laughter by throwing both hands over her mouth.

It was just the right amount of levity. Mrs. Ashmore loved her daughter deeply, but she had equally deep regrets about how cold-hearted the young woman had grown.

"I suppose I better just leave the cake alone," Mrs. Ashmore said, still giggling a bit and joining Jim at the worktable.

"Yes, ma'am," Jim agreed. "It *is* her birthday, after all."

He smiled at the widow, and she patted his hand.

Within a few hours, the pair had fixed a meal fit for royalty. Then the widow adjourned to her room to wash and dress for dinner, and Jim set the dinner table.

The doorbell jingled promptly at five o'clock.

"Good evening, Master Bemis, Mrs. Bemis. May I take your coats?"

"Atta boy, Jim," Nat said, slapping the servant on the back.

"Where's mother?" Susanna asked.

"Happy birthday, sweetheart," the widow came down the stairs and into the foyer. Her eyes were bright and her motions quick. Any sadness or resentment she had felt earlier had melted away during the dinner preparations.

"It's so wonderful to see you both," she said, distributing hugs and kisses to her daughter and son-in-law. "Did you have a nice ride in?"

Nat returned the kiss. "It's good to see you, too, Mother Ashmore. We had a good ride. I bought a new set of horses for the wagon last month. They're strong and fast, and they mind well. They gave us a smooth ride."

"Is that so?" the widow replied. "Well, I'd love to see them."

"Mother, we just arrived," Susanna protested, but Nat and her mother were already half-way out the front door.

"Come on dear," the widow extended her hand to Susanna. "It'll just be a minute. Jim will get dinner set up while we're taking a look."

The young woman grudgingly took her wrap back from Jim and walked outside. Nat and the widow didn't bother with their coats.

They walked to the back of the house. Many years ago, John Ashmore had built a small fenced corral there with sweet grass and a water trough. Back in the day, the Ashmores had had dinner parties several nights a week. John believed any self-respecting host should provide just as well for his guests' horses as he did for the guests themselves.

Standing at opposite ends of the pen were two stallions, their heads held high.

"They're twins," Nat said, pointing out their matching copper coats and black manes.

"They're magnificent," the widow replied. She opened the gate and walked up to the closer of the two.

"Mother, leave those filthy things alone," Susanna demanded. "You can't have your dinner smelling like a horse."

Nat enjoyed a laugh at his wife's expense, while the widow cooed and stroked the horse. The animal's muscles rippled as she ran her hand along its side. It lowered its head and gave her a playful nudge. Mrs. Ashmore laughed and scratched behind its ears.

Susanna huffed and turned her back on the scene to emphasize her disapproval. Horses, and all manner of livestock for that matter, were a bore. She pulled her wrap up around her neck, pretending to be cold, and looked lazily around the property. Her eyes fell upon the bright white sign hanging above the work shed door.

"Margaret Ashmore's Fine Scented Candles?"

Nat turned to look at his wife, then followed her gaze to the work shed.

"Yes," said the widow. "That's my new business."

"Your business?" Susanna scoffed.

"Come, I'll show you," Mrs. Ashmore said, leaving the corral and practically running toward the shed.

She threw open the doors, and the setting sun cast an orange glow into her little candle factory. The far wall was lined with shelves containing all shapes and sizes of canisters, stacked, labeled and alphabetized—from alum, beeswax and camphor, to mint, vanilla and wicks. The potbelly stove stood cold in the corner, the empty vats stacked beside it. A large oak table in the center of the shed was heaped with molds. Near the door were two boxes of candles, which she and Jim planned to deliver the next day.

"I'll be damned," Nat said. He plucked a candle from the box at his feet and pressed it up against his nose. "You sell many of these?"

"We most certainly do," the widow beamed. "Four dozen a week, on average."

Nat whistled through his teeth and took another sniff of the candle.

"We?" Susanna finally spoke.

"Jim helps me," Mrs. Ashmore said.

"It's a suitable hobby, I suppose," Susanna said. "But you can't call it a business, Mother."

"I can, and I do."

The widow handed her daughter one of the leaflets she had had made up at Buck's Printing Press in town. Nat looked over his shoulder at the paper and whistled again.

"Thirty cents apiece!"

Susanna's eyes narrowed. She was not about to give up the fight.

"It doesn't matter how much you sell them for, if you spend all your profits on printing up leaflets and ordering fancy signs." The young woman waved the paper in the air with one hand and pointed sternly toward the sign with her other.

"For your information, I can have fifty of those leaflets printed for about a dollar," the widow said. The light in her eyes had extinguished, and her voice was low. "And Jim made me that sign."

"That's enough, Mother! I won't listen to your lies. If you want to say you're running a business, you go right ahead and fool yourself. But you can't fool me into believing that you're making any kind of profit or that some illiterate Negro made that sign."

"I will not be called a liar!" The widow stormed out of the shed toward the corral.

Susanna was right on her heels, shouting. "You don't think I can find out where you bought that sign, Mother?"

"Come on now," Nat tried to soothe the women. "Let's stop this fighting and go eat a nice meal. I've been looking forward to Mother Ashmore's cake all week."

Susanna folded her arms across her chest and stared down her husband.

"Fine," she said. "I'm cold, let's go inside and eat."

"No," said Mrs. Ashmore. "It's not fine."

She entered the corral, took the first horse by the reins and led it to her son-in-law.

"Get these horses hitched up, Nat. I'll get your coat and a slice of cake for you to take home."

"Aw, come on, Mother Ashmore," he pleaded. "Susanna didn't mean any harm. She's sorry."

"Don't speak for me, Nathan," Susanna said.

"If Susanna apologizes for her rude comment about Jim, I will forgive and forget, and we can go eat dinner," the widow said.

Susanna's jaw dropped, and Nat laughed.

"That's the spirit, Mother," he said. "There's nothing a good laugh can't fix."

The widow wasn't laughing. She retrieved the second horse and began hitching the beast herself.

"Mother, you can't be serious?" Susanna threw her hands up in the air.

"Jim is my friend," Mrs. Ashmore said. She kept her voice steady, to keep from frightening the horses.

"You sound just like Dad with that nonsense."

"Your father was a good man, Susanna," the old woman said, her emotions beginning to get the better of her as she struggled with the harness buckles. The horse nuzzled her cheek, and her tears dropped onto its snout.

With that, Nat was ready to choose sides. He had never understood his father-in-law's opinions about blacks and slavery; but Nat still respected the man and the business Mr. Ashmore had built from nothing. It made him angry when Susanna spoke disrespectfully about her own father. He eased the widow's hands from the harness and took over the job of hitching the horses. Susanna, unwilling to admit defeat, climbed in the wagon and demanded that he take her home.

Jim appeared on the front porch with Nat's coat. The argument had been loud, and he knew the Bemises would be heading home. Nat led Mrs. Ashmore up to the house, gave her a kiss goodbye. Then he handed the old woman over to Jim, in exchange for his coat.

"Can I get you anything for the ride home, sir?" Jim asked.

Nat just shook his head no. He studied Jim—the worried crease between the young man's eyebrows, the tightness of his jaw, the way he gently but firmly ushered the widow into the house. He couldn't understand how it was possible, but a friendship had formed between this black man and his mother-in-law.

Chapter 25

Margaret

"Margaret, fetch my beads!"

Here we go again, I think. Two slaves come through the door carrying another poor soul stricken by the fever, and the witch springs into action.

When I first moved to the field houses, I learned that the crazy old witch who told Emma and me about the gator ghosts had been hand-picked by Master to be the plantation's slave doctor. Madame Zeta is the first and only witch doctor I've ever met. Her methods are bizarre, but I've read enough about herbs and home remedies to know that her potions and concoctions do help.

"God in heaven, cast out da demons! Cast 'em out!" She dances around her patient, digging her bare, misshapen feet into the dirt floor of our makeshift slave hospital at the plantation. I run to her medicine table, retrieve the beads and deliver them to her. She holds them high over her head, chants in gibberish, kisses the tiny bird feet dangling from the chain.

"You can set him down over here on this cot," I say, and the men lay the patient down. It is only the first week of June, and this is already the fifth patient to be brought in this month. Seven died of the fever in May.

"He gonna die?" one of the men asks me.

"Madame Zeta will do everything she can," I say, but the answer is yes, he will die.

Each summer the plantation loses about a third of its field hands to the fever. Each fall, Master buys forty or so new slaves to replace them. When he bought Madame Zeta, it was with the hope that she would reduce the number of deaths and ease the strain on his bank account each year. I don't know if she has reduced the number of deaths at the plantation, but I do believe she has helped to reduce the suffering.

When I was demoted from the big house last fall, I'd first joined the other slave women in the task of milling the harvested rice. Ten to twelve hours a day, using wood mortars and pestles to pound and grind the rice, separating the tiny white grains from their rough brown husks. I found it to be no worse than scrubbing and rinsing laundry all day, and at least I had company to help pass the time with stories and songs. But when spring arrived and the men returned to the fields, Madame Zeta had asked Master if I could be assigned to help her in the hospital.

"She a smart one," she'd said, and Master had reluctantly agreed. Although I was not going to produce any babies to increase his stock, he still seemed to hope that his investment in me was not entirely lost. It was my skill as a seamstress that finally convinced him.

"Margaret can sew up dem ones that get cut in da field," Zeta had pointed out. And that's how I went from washwoman to field hand to nurse in less than two years' time.

Rice farming has got to be the hardest, most dangerous job there is. From spring to fall, each month seems to bring its own kind of misery into our hospital.

Slaves head to the fields in March to plow and level acres upon acres of land for the coming crop. Some use picks and shovels to clear weeds and muck from the intricate maze of canals, levees and floodgates used to water the crop. Others make repairs to the bridges and boardwalks that crisscross the fields. Many come into the hospital each week with deep cuts and gashes inflicted by their tools or pieces of broken, rotted wood. The wounds must be cleaned and sewn. Madame Zeta first packs the injury with a pungent compound of boiled leaves to fight off what she calls "the green." The next day, the patient is given "sleeping tea" which eases him into a calm state and enables me to sew up the wound with little protest.

It sounds easy enough, but it's not.

Skin and fabric are not the same. The first time I set my needle to a patient I nearly fainted with fear. Skin is alive. It recoils from the needle. It is tough to penetrate, and yet it tears more easily than linen or silk. And the blood. The blood is the worst of it. The bright red liquid oozes from each tiny needle prick, soaking my thread and seeping under my fingernails where it dries and turns black. The blood disgusts me, and I've developed an elaborate ritual of scrubbing and rinsing my work area with lye soap and boiling water each morning and night to remove all traces.

In late April, the seed is sown, and the fields are continually flooded and drained until tiny sprouts are visible. Once the plants reach about five inches tall, water must be kept on the fields for the rest of the growing season. As the rice grows, the water level is gradually increased with flooding from nearby tidal creeks. This process brings all sorts of lethal snakes and creatures into the fields—cottonmouths, copperheads, alligators, swimming spiders. The floodgates keep them prisoner, keep them angry.

From May through September, field slaves live in the mud and the water twelve hours a day. They weed the fields, at first ankle deep and eventually knee deep, on constant watch for the quick slither of a cottonmouth or the ridges of a gator's back as it sits and waits for its prey. There is no shade. There is no rest. They burn in the sun. They swat mosquitoes. They breathe the foul steam and vapors rising from the stagnant water that surrounds them as far as the eye can see.

At the end of the day, they come to Madame Zeta for relief. Indeed, she has a variety of nasty-smelling remedies for most afflictions—from sunburn and bug bites to heatstroke and strained muscles.

But the fever is hard to fight, and there is nothing we can do for the slave who crosses paths with a cottonmouth. Our newest patient appears to have been stricken by both.

"Look here." Zeta points at two neat punctures at the back of his calf, just below the tattered edge of his short pants. The man's body gently trembles and convulses in the bed, sweat trickles down his head, arms and chest. The corners of his mouth are dry, cracked. He won't be long in this world.

I kneel beside him and dab at his face and neck with a cool, wet towel. He smiles faintly. Madame Zeta smears a yellowish paste on his calf, covering the bite. It will help ease the pain.

"My name is Margaret." I smile at him. "What's your name?"

It takes him a minute or so to answer.

"Charles."

"Close your eyes, Charles," I say, still washing him gently with the towel. "Try to sleep."

The witch dances slowly around us, chanting quietly, shaking her beads. His convulsions slow.

"Would you like me to pray for you, Charles?"

He nods slightly. I close my eyes.

"Dear Lord in Heaven, take Charles into your arms today and cradle him with your everlasting love. He's a good man, Lord. He works hard in the field every day. Let him rest and feel your strength. Please, God, fill him up with the love and peace only You can give."

I open my eyes and dab at his forehead again with the towel, but he is already gone.

Emma watches the black smoke billow up into the sky from the north end of the rice fields. I watch her, amazed at how old she has grown in the short time we've been here at the plantation. We kneel in the garden, pulling weeds out from between the rows of vegetables.

"Why can't they bury them when they die?" she asks. "I don't understand why they have to burn them like that."

"Too many die. Their graves would fill half of Master's acreage," I say.

"That's how it should be," she says. "To remind him."

"I agree."

The garden has been a nice escape for Emma and me.

No one at the plantation takes much notice of the children under Granny Gin's care. Not even their parents. A few of the field slaves make occasional Sunday visits to their little ones, but most are too exhausted from their work to put forth the effort. Master checks in once in a while, just to make sure Granny's doing her job and the children are kept healthy enough to go to work in the fields by the time they're 10 or 11 years old.

It's hard to believe, but Emma and I are the lucky ones. We're still a family.

The garden began with the idea of us growing the herbs and plants that Madame Zeta needs for her concoctions. It quickly grew into much more. The plot spans nearly a quarter acre and produces enough vegetables to supplement the weekly rations of every field hand at the plantation—turnips, celery, collard greens, cucumbers, carrots, sweet potatoes, onions.

Emma and I started the garden together, but she does most of the work to keep it going day to day. She's only just approaching eight years old, and yet she seems intent on making sure no one here goes hungry ever again.

"The cabbage is coming in nice," she says, pulling a stray weed out from between two large heads. She looks back out toward the smoke.

"Maybe we should put together an extra box of vegetables for his quarters," I say, and it seems to brighten her mood a bit.

"Yes, we should," Emma says, "with extra garlic to fight the fever in case anyone else in his quarters has taken ill."

Each Saturday, the two of us put together large boxes of vegetables and haul them to the slaves' quarters and to Granny Gin's for the children. Madame Zeta instructed us to include at least five heads of garlic in each box, and each week we remind the field hands to eat one raw clove every day to fight off the fever.

"Extra garlic is a good idea," I say. "I could make up a couple of pies today, too. I've been saving up some flour, and we've got plenty of nice gooseberries."

"Okay," Emma says. She smiles at me, but tears are streaming down her cheeks. Her shoulders begin to shake violently as she fights to control her sobbing.

I rush to her, and she collapses into my arms.

"Oh, Mama," she bawls. "This is the most horrible place in the whole world."

There's nothing I can say to comfort her. She is right.

My heart is breaking for her, but my own eyes are dry. I seem to have run out of tears for this place. We rock gently back and forth, sitting together in the soft garden soil

In time, Emma quiets.

"Why can't we just run away?" she asks, pulling away, wiping the tears from her cheeks with the back of her muddy hand.

"Oh, Emma," I sigh, searching for the right words. "It's just not as easy as it sounds."

"You always say that!"

"That's because it's the truth," I say, trying hard not to mirror her anger. I stroke her hair, look her square in the eye.

"For one thing, when a slave runs, Master doesn't just let it go. He would hire bounty hunters, men like Mr. Prigg, who track down runaways and drag them back to the plantation. You remember what happened that night with Mr. Prigg, don't you? And we weren't even runaways."

Emma nods.

"For another thing, I don't like the idea of running away, no matter how awful it might be here. I'd rather stay and fight. God brought us here for a reason, Emma. I'm just sure of it, even though I don't understand His reasons."

Emma listens intently. She takes in a deep breath and lets it out slowly.

"I'm just so tired, Mama. All this work. I want to play with my dolls. I want to fight with my brothers and kiss my daddy on his cheek."

"I miss them, too."

It's all I can say. Words just don't do it justice—the pain, the emptiness.

Emma seems to understand. She turns back to weeding, pulling the prickly intruders out by the roots, careful not to disturb the precious vegetables beside them. Her eyes are puffy, her cheeks sunken, her skin rough. She's an old woman at work in this garden, not my bright-eyed, rosy-cheeked child.

"I'm sorry, baby. I'm so sorry."

I kneel beside her, and we weed together in silence.

"Plannin' a trip on the railroad, are ya, Miss Margaret?" Madame Zeta asks as I walk up the path to the hospital.

"I have no idea what you're talking about," I say, sitting down on the door stoop. Zeta rocks back and forth in a creaky old chair in the hardened dirt in front of the building. "Any patients yet today?"

"Nope. No patients," she says, rocking, rocking.

"Summer ain't a good time to go on a trip, you know," she says after a minute or two.

"Honestly, Zeta, I really don't know what you're getting at."

"Oh, I heard ya, Margaret. I heard ya talking in the garden with dat girl of yours. I heard you talk about runnin.'"

Madame Zeta stops rocking and shifts in the chair to face me. She plants her feet square on the ground in front of her, leans forward and parks her elbows on her knees.

"Is that so?" I say, leaning forward myself and trying to get just the right tone of indignation in my voice. "Well, if you were doing such a good job of listening to a conversation that didn't include you, then you also must have heard me say we won't be running anywhere."

"Easy now, child. Easy," Madame Zeta says, waving her hands in the air. "I'm not accusing you of nothin'. All I'm tryin' to say to ya is this place got ears. You gotta to be careful how you be talking 'bout things. You see?"

Her point is well made. I do feel safe when I'm working in the garden, almost happy sometimes. It hadn't occurred to me that I couldn't speak freely with Emma there, especially when Master and the family are away for the summer. But Zeta's right. The plantation has ears.

"Yes, I see."

The old witch smiles and goes back to rocking, rocking, looking out over the rice fields. My head is swimming with new thoughts, new frustrations, new fears about my life here.

"Now, if I was gonna plan a trip on the railroad, I'd go in da spring, right before the rains come and just after the massas go away on they own trip. Mmm-hmm. Thas what I'd do."

She pauses, thinking, then continues.

"Course, it ain't so easy. You was right about that. White folks like to travel during the day, but us Negroes do best to ride at night."

Her gaze stays steady on the rice fields. Her chair creaks back and forth, back and forth. I look out, too, at the distant tiny figures moving slowing through the rows of green.

"Maybe you know someone else who's planning a trip, hmm?" I ask.

"Oh, child, I done met my share of travelers."

Madame Zeta turns, fixes her eyes on me, clutches at her beads.

"Met dem in the hospital, you know?" She looks around, then lowers her voice. "With their heel strings cut so they can't run again. Their thighs ripped open by the bloodhounds. Their backs shredded by the lash. Lord have mercy, I done met my share of travelers a'right."

Thank God I've never been witness to such horrors, though I'm no stranger to the stories.

"Why would someone take such a risk, Zeta?" I ask.

A rare summer breeze blows up from the fields, bringing with it the stagnant stench of the flooded crops and the smoky scent of the funeral fires.

"I guess we all gotta decide for ourselves, Margaret, what's the lesser of the evils we gots to face in life. We all gotta decide," she says, her voice breaking up just a bit, her eyes growing moist. "Lord have mercy."

"Amen to that."

Chapter 26

Philadelphia

"In non-slave-holding states the presumption is that every man is a free man until the contrary be proved," Tom rehearsed softly, as Mr. Johnson nodded along. "It is like every other legal presumption, in favor of the right. Every man is presumed to be innocent until proved guilty."

The pair was sitting on the steamboat deck, bundled in wool overcoats, mulling over notes for the upcoming proceedings. They were preparing, at long last, on their way to Washington, D.C., where Pennsylvania District Attorney Tom Hambly would present his argument in Edward Prigg v. the Commonwealth of Pennsylvania before the Supreme Court.

The sun finally broke on the horizon, an immense orb that brought some warmth and an orangey glow to the few passengers milling about.

A young couple stood near the far railing, cooing quietly, the man's professions of love interrupted only by his frequent need to turn and spit a dark, rank stream of tobacco juice from the plug bulging inside his cheek. Occasionally, he hit the sloshing spittoon three feet to his left. More often, he defiled the deck and the railing, which already sported untold yellowy stains from others before him who shared his practice of chewing and his disregard for proper aim.

The light brought more passengers from the cabin onto the deck, though their manner was subdued still by the early hour and the bitter chill that lingered in the air. Tom scribbled notes on a tablet.

"In a slave-holding state, color always raises the presumption of slavery," he recited. "If, under this monstrous assumption of power, a free man may be seized, where is our boasted freedom? What says the article of the amendments to the Constitution of the United States? The right of the people to be secure in their persons . . . that no person shall be deprived of life, liberty or property, without due process of law."

With Tom was Pennsylvania Attorney General Ovid Johnson, not because he was his boss and wished to supervise, but because neither had had the occasion before to visit their nation's capital. With an air of adolescent giddiness, the men had left Philadelphia just before daybreak one cold morning in January, 1842—four years after the kidnapping of Margaret Morgan and her children.

Mr. Johnson was leaning forward, his elbows resting on his knees, tapping the tips of his outstretched fingers on one hand against the tips of the other. A deep crease extended from the top of his nose, up between his eyebrows and into his ridged forehead. "Indeed," he said, nodding again.

Tom smiled, blew on his icy fingers, and went back to jotting feverishly in his tablet.

A vibration of excited chatter rippled through the passengers now assembled on deck. For a moment, Tom immodestly thought it was in response to his speech. Then he saw the gathering had their backs to him, as they shifted and jockeyed for a view of something near the cabin doors.

The crowd parted, and a European couple strode out the door and across the deck tailed by a gathering of socialites, all smiling, laughing and jockeying, ever still, for position. The gentleman was cleanly shaven, dressed in a navy blue waistcoat and slacks, with a yellow silk ascot and vest. His lady wore a high-collared dress, also navy blue, with a large bustle that would not become a staple of American fashion for another decade or more.

"Mr. Dickens, I'm quite a fan of your work," crowed a fat woman in a tight lace collar and tiny pillbox cap.

"I do love that dear little Oliver," chimed in another.

Charles Dickens had a high forehead, with thin lips, sharp nose and a certain air of nobility. The author and his wife, Catherine, also were headed to Washington, about halfway through an extended holiday. It was their first visit to the United States, taken in celebration of Mr. Dickens's thirtieth birthday.

The couple made their way around the steamboat deck, engaging in polite conversation and shaking hands with fans who endeavored to prove their loyalty by noting favorite characters from his works.

"I just loved your *Pickwick Papers*, Mr. Dickens. That Wackford Squeers sure is a mean one, is he not?"

"Thank you, madam. Actually, Squeers is a character from *The Life and Adventures of Nicholas Nickelby*."

"Yes, yes, of course, *Nicholas Nickelby*. I loved that book, as well. I've read them both, you know. "

A waiter rang the breakfast bell, and the crowd began working their way toward the cabin for a warm meal inside, still chattering about their brush with fame.

"That's an odd tie he's wearing," a young woman remarked to her companion. "You suppose all Englishmen dress that way?"

Her companion shrugged. "Hair's a bit funny, too."

Ovid Johnson shook his head with disdain, watching the parade of passengers march below deck with Dickens as their Grand Marshal.

"How do you suppose," he asked Tom, "that people in the presence of such a talented mind can think of nothing more intelligent to remark upon than the man's head of hair?"

"Indeed," Tom said, as the two gentlemen fell in for the breakfast parade.

The spectacle surrounding Mr. Dickens continued throughout the day's long journey, but Tom was too deeply engrossed in his own mission to pay much notice. The twelve-hour trek from Philadelphia to D.C. included a transfer to railcars just after breakfast, back to steamboat, the rails once again and ended, finally, with a coach ride to the Fuller Hotel just south of the Capitol building. All the while, Tom Hambly fussed over his notes, reviewed the case files, and tested out one line or another on his travel companion and mentor. With the rigors of the trip and the enormity of the next day's task, he had momentarily forgotten the significance of their final destination.

"Put away your tablet, Tom," Mr. Johnson said, as the coach rattled through the streets of Washington. "This is it. Just look."

Tom looked up from his writing and took in the sights of the city. A gentleman in a wool waistcoat and black boots slogged his way down muddy Pennsylvania Avenue igniting the street lanterns one by one. The sun had not yet fallen below the horizon, but this was a job best begun well before dark. Across the street, lurking in the shadows of a tavern alley, were two figures that seemed to watch the lantern lighter's progress with great interest. The gentleman, taking note of his audience, stepped up his pace.

The Capitol Mall was nearly deserted by this hour, except for the pigs and cows that stood in cramped fouled pens between the stately U.S. Patent Office and pillared Congressional Library. They rustled and snorted as the coach rattled past, vapors of steam erupting from their snouts into the cold January air. The men and women who worked in the government buildings by day—Congressmen and kitchen hands alike—had since escaped downtown to their orderly mansions or shabby row houses on the outskirts of the city. This exodus had brought a hush to the scene, a bit enchanting and a bit eerie at once. Elegant maple saplings lined the road, casting skeleton-like shadows upon the ground as the sun dimmed and the lanterns glimmered.

"Go on now, you tiny beast!" The coachman berated a goat meandering across the road. The animal continued on its way unaffected, and the driver was forced to pull hard on the reins, jolting the coach to an abrupt stop. Tom laughed. He slipped his notes into his attaché and leaned into the small window for a better view.

Another set of pens stood out among the elegant capitol buildings, framed by the pink glow of dusk—slave pens. A low chatter of voices could be heard from the street. Here and there, between the splintered planks of wood that constructed the high-walled pens, Tom could pick out a stray brown elbow or bare foot. A placard on the street announced a slave auction to be held there the following day. The snowy lawn of the White House was just a stone's throw away.

Tom let out a soft short whistle and turned to his mentor.

"What are we stepping into here?" he said.

Mr. Johnson crinkled his nose, but it was not the smell of the pens that offended.

"Well, Tom," he said. "If Philly is the capitol of abolition in America, then I dare say Washington just might be the capitol of slavery."

The goat made its way safely across Pennsylvania Avenue and was free to gnaw at the juicy bark of a weeping willow. The driver clicked to the horses, and the coach rattled back into motion.

After a fitful night's sleep, Tom awoke to a jingle of the bell at his hotel room door. He had requested the wake-up call and a breakfast of coffee and toast for the morning of his arguments before the Supreme Court. His stomach wouldn't tolerate a more substantial meal with the task that lay ahead of him.

Hambly washed and then placed his chamber pot outside the door. He ate breakfast and dressed slowly. He had laid out his clothes the night before. Formal clothes consisting of a black knee-length morning coat and grey striped trousers. Had he appeared before the court in anything less, he risked being turned away even before his arguments were made.

Johnson stood waiting for him on the steps of the Capitol Building at nine o'clock sharp, just as they had agreed. The men shook hands and exchanged nods. They spoke not a word, but instead turned and walked together through the massive doors of the Capitol. After declaring their business to the doorman, they were directed down a long hallway to a door that opened on a narrow staircase leading down. The United States Supreme Court, in all its glory, met in a borrowed space in the Senate chambers basement.

A marshal greeted the men and pointed the way to their seats. Jonathan Meredith, counsel for the plaintiff, was already settled at his desk. He rose to shake hands with Tom and Mr. Johnson, a formality the men had shared numerous times before during the course of the Pennsylvania trial.

"Mr. Meredith, I trust your travels went well," Tom said with an outstretched hand.

"Indeed, Mr. Hambly, they did," Meredith replied. "And yours as well, I hope."

"Yes, thank you."

Court proceedings were open to the public, and a small collection of spectators were already seated in the gallery—mostly a handful of Senators interested in good debate, a few journalists covering the political beat, and one or two citizens wanting a respite from the bitter cold outside. The nature of the cases to be argued before the Court each session was not announced in advance. So those present had no idea what *Prigg v. Pennsylvania* was about or what implications it might have on their nation's future.

"All rise!" the marshal shouted as the justices entered the courtroom from a hidden door to the side of the bench.

Nine men of varying ages and heights streamed quietly into the room. Their flowing black robes dusted the floor, creating the illusion that they were floating rather than walking. One by one, each justice turned and shook hands with the other. The tradition was intended to show a harmony of purpose among the men, even if they may later disagree in their ruling. The men finally took their seats at the bench— Chief Justice Roger Taney in the center seat and the other eight men alternating at his sides, first right and then left, by seniority.

With a bang of the gavel from the bench, the marshal stepped forward to shout the traditional welcome.

"Oyez! Oyez! Oyez! All persons having business before the Honorable, the Supreme Court of the United States, are admonished to draw near and give their attention, for the Court is now sitting. God save the United States and this Honorable Court."

Tom felt a shiver of excitement shoot through him, awestruck by a sight he had dreamed of since his youth. He was relieved to finally take his seat and remove his tablet from his attaché. Busying his hands helped to settle his nerves as he quickly scanned his notes.

The marshal once again stepped forward. "To be argued before the Court today is the case of *Prigg v. Pennsylvania*. Counsel for the defendant, Mr. Thomas Hambly, are you prepared to present your remarks?"

"Yes, sir," Tom answered as he rose and walked to the center podium. "May it please the Court. The final decision of a great Constitutional question, it appears to me, should at all times be regarded as a subject for grave consideration and reflection, as it may affect the happiness and prosperity, the lives or liberties of a whole nation."

He paused to take a small sip of water from the glass at the podium. Then he briefly relayed the chain of events that led to his appearance before the nation's highest court. In 1793, the U.S. government had created the Fugitive Slave Law, which gave slaveholders the right to track down and reclaim runaway slaves in neighboring states. To protect its free black citizens from kidnapping and violence, Pennsylvania in turn created the Personal Liberty Law of 1826, which required bounty hunters to provide proof of ownership before seizing runaway slaves.

Justice Taney suddenly shook his head and interrupted.

"But doesn't the rule of the Constitution vest the power to legislate over this subject exclusively to Congress?" he demanded. "As such, no state can pass any law in relation to it, much less a law which contradicts it."

Tom was not rattled by Taney's sudden interruption. Pointed questions from the bench were common during oral arguments. The give-and-take repartee brought an intriguing air of informality to the otherwise decorous proceedings. Tom relished such debate. He quickly responded by drawing the Court's attention to the second section of the Constitution, article four.

He read, "No person held to service or labour in one state under the laws thereof, escaping into another, shall in consequence of any law or regulation therein, be discharged from such service or labour; but shall be delivered up, on claim of the party to whom such service or labour is due."

The panel of esteemed judges nodded their heads in unison. They knew the verbiage well and had committed their lives and careers to uphold it.

Tom continued, his voice gradually rising. "Some contend this article means that the owner of a slave has a right, without reference to the regulations of the state or territory where he happens to be, to seize and carry away any alleged slave; that the word 'claim' means demand and surrender without enquiry or investigation. On the contrary, I contend on behalf of the great state of Pennsylvania, that the language of the Constitution not only presupposes legislation, but that this legislation should be established by the states!"

Taney fired right back.

"Aye, but state authorities are prohibited from interfering with the right of the master in the recovery of his property," the justice said. "One could even argue that it is the duty of all states to protect and support the owner when he is endeavoring to claim property found within their respective territories."

"But what is the meaning of 'claim?'" Hambly asked. "The very word implies a challenge of ownership, that the right to property is in dispute or doubt. 'Claim' has a technical legal meaning, and those gentlemen who wrote the Constitution of this United States, being eminent lawyers and well-versed in the use of language, may possibly have chosen to use it for that very reason.

"If, under this term 'claim' the stretch of power is so very great that a man from a neighboring state can venture into Pennsylvania or Maryland, and upon simple allegation seize and carry off any one whom he may choose to single out as his fugitive from labor, it is a most astonishing violation of the true spirit and meaning of the whole Constitution," Hambly insisted.

All throughout this rapid exchange, the court reporter feverishly took down every word in shorthand—quickly filing his tablet pages with graceful squiggles, loops, arcs and dashes; adeptly re-inking his quill whenever the speaker of the moment paused for breath or dramatic effect.

Tom continued. "In non-slaveholding states, the presumption is that every man is a free man until the contrary can be proved. In a slaveholding state, color always raises a presumption of slavery."

"Must I point out, Mr. Hambly, that slaves are no parties to the Constitution or the rights it preserves for Americans?" injected Justice Peter Daniel from the left end of the bench—the newest member of the court and a resident of the state of Virginia.

"I admit to that most cheerfully," Tom replied. "But I am not arguing the want of power to claim and take a slave, but to claim and take a free man! If, under this monstrous assumption of power, a free man may be seized, where is our boasted freedom? What says the fourth article of the amendments to the Constitution of the United States? 'The right of the people to be secure in their persons, houses, papers and effects against unreasonable searches and seizures;' and article five, that no person shall be deprived of life, liberty or property without due process of law?"

"But the case before us is not a matter of personal liberty," noted Justice John Catron in a leisurely Tennessee drawl. "It is a matter of states' rights. As Chief Justice Taney already noted, it is the sole responsibility of Congress to legislate over matters of Constitutional regard."

"How can legislation respecting slaves be national when only a part of the states hold them?" Tom countered. "Such legislation cannot assume a national aspect or attain a national purpose."

To illustrate his point, Tom described a hypothetical case, in which a man is seized in the streets of Philadelphia simultaneously by a citizen of Georgia and a citizen of Virginia, each claiming the man as his slave. And what if that man claimed himself to be free? If only the simplest interpretation of the Fugitive Slave Law were to be applied, both the Georgian and the Virginian would be entitled to carry him off on mere allegation.

"What is to be done then?" Tom asked. "Allow these parties to wrangle it out in the streets to settle the question with dirk and bowie knife, or execute the judgment of Solomon?"

Justice James Moore Wayne, a Georgia boy born and raised, pounded his fist upon the table. "Would the law be better served by allowing the slave to escape?"

"Better a thousand slaves escape," Tom replied with calm composure, "than should one free man be thus carried into remediless slavery."

Nearly an hour of debate had passed, and the marshal indicted that the defense had two minutes remaining for summation.

"It is being asserted by the plaintiff that Pennsylvania's law is unconstitutional," Tom began. "But let us remember one critical fact in this case—Mr. Edward Prigg, a bounty hunter from Maryland, first sought the aid of Pennsylvania law to seize his slave. Then, in contempt of that law, he forcibly, indeed violently, removed the Morgan family without making claim, obtaining certificate, or doing anything to procure the warrant of the law."

Tom paused, looking up from his notes. He scanned the bench before him, from one end to the other. He endeavored to make eye contact with each man before looking to the next. He then continued his summation.

"The language of the Fugitive Slave Law punishes those who interfere with the rights of the slaveholder; but is silent as to the rights of Negroes wrongfully seized, and of the states whose territory is entered by men like Mr. Prigg to violate the laws and carry away those who are living under their protection. These cases are clearly left to the guardianship of the states themselves. The tenth article of the amendments to the Constitution secures this right; and self-respect, if not self-protection, demands its exercise. Thank you."

Tom stacked his notes in a neat pile and turned on his heels to walk back to his seat. Mr. Johnson rose to greet him with the slightest nod, hand outstretched, eyes beaming.

"Nicely done," he whispered.

The marshal once again stepped forward. "Counsel for the plaintiff, Mr. Jonathan Meredith, are you prepared to present your remarks?"

Meredith rose and indicated he was prepared. Another hour passed, as he presented his case and the justices fired off equally challenging questions and rebuttals. During this session, the judges from the northern states—New York, Massachusetts, Ohio and Pennsylvania—were more vocal in the debate.

Justice John McLean sounded off. "The act of 1793 authorizes a forcible seizure of the slave by the master, not to take him out of the state, but to take him before some judicial officer within it. The act of Pennsylvania punishes a forcible removal of a colored person out of the state. The execution of neither law can, in my opinion, interfere with the execution of the other. The laws stand in harmony with each other, do they not?"

Whether those laws stand in harmony was moot, according to Meredith, for the Pennsylvania law should not even exist.

In his summation, Meredith asserted, "The Constitution of the United States declares that slaves escaping from service shall be delivered up, on claim, to the person to whom such service shall be due. Thus the argument before you is simpler than the defense would have you believe. It comes down to one question. Where does authority over the Constitution reside? To this there is only one answer—not with the states, but with the federal government. Thank you."

Meredith turned from the podium and took his seat.

"The Honorable, the Supreme Court of the United States is now in recess," the marshal announced. "The Court will reconvene tomorrow at nine o'clock in the morning to announce its ruling in this case. All rise!"

Chapter 27

Washington, D.C.

In the afternoon following their court appearance, Tom and his mentor enjoyed a lunch of coleslaw and dodgers—corncakes filled with minced beef—at a small café on Pennsylvania Avenue. Mildly superstitious, they refrained from discussing the case or the arguments presented that morning. They ate in near silence, then took to the streets of Washington like schoolboys to visit the Congressional Library and Patent Office and to walk along the bank of the Potomac. That evening, the men attended "The Yankee in Time" at The National Theatre two blocks from the White House.

The next morning, Tom and Johnson arrived at the Capitol Building amid a horde of journalists, Congressmen, businessmen and other onlookers. News had quickly spread regarding the nature of the case and of the impact the Court's ruling could have on a nation already divided on the issue of slavery. Inside, the courtroom was standing room only. Reporters from the *New York Tribune*, *The Liberator* and *Daily National Intelligencer* positioned themselves at the rear. With them, artists sat at the ready with pencils and tablets to illustrate the scenes that would play out.

Tom and Johnson maneuvered their way through the crowd, finally taking their seats just before the marshal stepped forward.

"Oyez! Oyez! Oyez! The Honorable, the Supreme Court of the United States is now sitting. Justice Joseph Story of Massachusetts shall deliver the opinion of the Court in the case of *Edward Prigg v. the Commonwealth of Pennsylvania.*"

In the hushed room, one could hear the gentle but hasty scratching of pencil to paper as the artists sketched Justice Story. Their hands danced over the pages, capturing the details of his manner and expression—the square jaw and deep crease between unruly gray eyebrows; the thin white hair, beginning far back from the forehead, neatly combed down; the round spectacles set upon a long thin nose.

"Few questions which have ever come before this Court involve more delicate and important considerations; and few upon which the public at large may be presumed to feel a more profound and pervading interest," Story began.

A gentleman in the back of the room coughed nervously. A few others fidgeted impatiently in their seats. Tom held his breath, frozen, waiting.

"Section two, article four of the Constitution clearly indicates that those who have escaped service or labor shall be delivered up on claim. The true design and purpose of this law was to guard against the doctrines and principles prevalent in the non-slaveholding states, by preventing them from intermeddling with, or obstructing, or abolishing the rights of slave owners. As such, we hold the power of legislation on this subject to be exclusive in Congress."

Murmurs slowly moved through the crowd. Chief Justice Taney pounded his gavel, just once, and a hush again befell the room.

"Upon these grounds," Story continued, "we are of the opinion that the law of Pennsylvania upon which this indictment is founded is unconstitutional and void. It purports to punish as a public offense the very act of seizing and removing a slave by his master, which the Constitution of the United States was designed to justify and uphold. The judgment against Mr. Prigg must, therefore, be reversed."

Tom let go of his breath and turned dumbfounded to his mentor. Johnson could only look back at him with equal disbelief. Beside them, the newspaper artists captured their raised eyebrows, their mouths slightly agape.

At the plaintiff's table, Meredith was inundated with hearty congratulations, slaps on the back, handshakes.

The marshal announced the Court to be adjourned and called the room to rise. As soon as the justices made their full and ceremonious exit, the journalists quickly closed in on the Pennsylvania attorneys.

"Mr. Hambly, are you surprised by the Court's ruling?"

"Surprised would be an understatement, sir."

"What does this reversal mean for the citizens of Pennsylvania?"

"It means," Tom began, pausing to rub his upper lip. "It means they must come to terms with the fact that their nation, their federal government, has for the first time formally and publically endorsed the institution of slavery. It means they must now know that the southern states may advance that cause without any regard to the personal liberties of free men in their state."

"What will you do now that the court has ruled, Mr. Hambly?"

"I intend to retire to my hotel room with a bottle of Scotch and drown my disappointment," he said flatly.

The reporter chuckled as he jotted in his tablet.

"It's no laughing matter, sir, I assure you!" Johnson interjected.

"Indeed!" A voice rose from the back of the gallery, that of Pennsylvania Senator William Reed. Having what they needed from the attorneys, the journalists quickly turned and converged upon the Democratic Senator. Tom and Johnson, much relieved at the shift in attention, bolted for the exit.

It was three days before the men could arrange for passage home to Philadelphia. Because they had not known how long the Court's deliberations might last, they had not purchased their tickets in advance. Tom and Johnson were stunned not only by the ruling itself, but also by how quickly it had come.

True to his word, Tom had spent those days nursing a bottle of Scotch in the seclusion of his room at the Fuller Hotel. He had requested his meals and newspapers to be delivered. He did not step out in to the light; he did not wash. With the curtains drawn to block the sun, he strained his eyes to read the articles that had graced the front page of the *Daily National Intelligencer* each day since the ruling. The reporters dutifully relayed the Court's proceedings and featured wide speculation from local politicians and businessmen on what the ruling would mean for the states, both north and south.

"The high court is meddling with states' rights to pass laws which protect their citizens," one northern politician was quoted as saying. "It's an abomination, a frightening example of Federal rule."

The South saw it differently. A senator from Tennessee was quoted, "This is a shining example of democracy at work. The Supreme Court has upheld our Constitutional rights to keep and protect our property."

Tom drained his glass and leaned back in his chair, eyes closed tight. The paper lay before him on the desk, beside an empty Scotch bottle. He twirled the glass in his ink-stained fingers. His mind raced with frustration at the reality, the finality, of the court's ruling. There would be no appeals, no more reasoned debate, only a greater divide among states.

"Damn it all to hell!"

He hurled his glass at the wall, where it shattered with a piercing crash. He pushed over the desk, sending its contents flying. Then he stood and with a howl and one violent sweep of his arms, cleared the dresser top of its items. The porcelain wash basin smashed to the ground. The leather-bound Bible landed with a thud atop the white shards.

In the room next door, Mr. Johnson could only sip his tea and wince as his protégé expressed the outrage he, too, was feeling.

The journey home lasted an eternity. There was nothing to discuss, no work to be done. From daybreak well into the dark of night, from coach to train to steamboat, Tom could do nothing more than watch the scenery pass with bloodshot eyes.

There had been a certain tension in the air when they left Philly the week before. While the state of Pennsylvania denounced slavery, there still were many people who opposed the notion that free blacks should have the same rights as white Americans. Many citizens would be frustrated with the Supreme Court's ruling and the limitation it put on their state's rights. Yet, just as many would equate the ruling to confirmation of their belief that blacks, free or not, were indeed "less than."

Chapter 28

Philadelphia

The steamboat approached Federal Street ferry landing about midnight, yet an orange glow on the horizon gave the illusion of sunset. Passengers had been gathering on deck with their bags, preparing to disembark. At first, the light baffled them. But as the tinge of smoke wafted on the night breeze, the source of the glow became startling clear. A large fire was ablaze near the center of town.

Earlier that day, a free black man had been speaking at the African Presbyterian Church on St. Mary's Street. New Yorker David Ruggles was perhaps the most hated abolitionist of the times. His audience often included not only white men sympathetic to the anti-slavery cause, but blacks and women, as well. Sitting in the pews on this day, together in the front row, were the Fortens' daughters Charlotte and Margareta, Jerry Morgan's former employer Mr. Mitchell, and black philanthropist Mr. Stiles, among other Philadelphia elite.

Such mixing of races and genders angered many in the community, especially the large number of Catholic Irish immigrants, who believed social order was being turned on its ear by such gatherings.

"Oppression, in any form, but most certainly the form in which a man is made into property, is evil," declared Ruggles, founder of *Mirror of Liberty*, the first U.S. magazine published solely by blacks. "As my good friend and fellow publisher William Lloyd Garrison has so aptly said, freedom is of God, and slavery is of the devil..."

With a piercing din, a rock crashed through the stained glass window and landed at Ruggles' feet. A woman in the congregation screamed. Ruggles raised his palms to calm the group, just as another crash sent multicolored shards clattering to the pulpit floor. Shouts could be heard rising up from a mob on the street.

"This is the very evil of which I speak!" Ruggles fought to maintain the attention of the group and prevent a stampede.

Another rock sailed through the air, striking a white-haired gentleman in the temple, and the whole congregation took to their feet at once.

"We've got to get out of here!" someone cried.

Rose McFarland, who had been seated in the back row near the aisle, stood and spun around just as the front door of the church burst open. A group of working-class men rushed into the atrium with torches. Suddenly she was face to face with the young man leading the charge.

"Cobb?" she gasped, recognizing the fair-haired clerk her fathered had had to lay off from his employ a few years before. He waved the torch in her direction, forcing her to retreat into the cathedral.

"That's Mr. McGinty to you, cherry," he shouted. Then he flung the torch down the aisle and ran out. The carpet runner ignited quickly, sending a path of flames roaring down the center of the church.

"The back door!" The clergyman shouted, waving his parishioners toward the rear exit.

On the street, the mob continued throwing rocks at the church, as the abolitionists poured out the back exit. The attackers clapped and cheered as flames inside grew taller and flickered through the broken windows.

Charlotte and Margareta wasted no time. They kicked off their shoes and ran through the back roads and across the meadow toward home to warn their family.

Several fire wagons pulled by muscular Clydesdales barreled up the street, their brass bells clanging loudly. The men directed their hoses at the neighboring buildings to protect them from the dancing flames. When one wagon tried to douse the church, its men became the object of the other wagons' hoses and the crowd cheered once again. A police wagon moved slowly down the street, surveying the scene without interceding.

Seeing that their actions would go unobstructed, the mob expanded their assault down Lombard Street and into predominately black neighborhoods. They set fire to Smith's Hall, another popular abolitionist meeting site. They looted and burned homes. They beat and terrorized black citizens. By nightfall, all hell had broken loose in the city's fifth race riot in as many years.

The passengers aboard the steamboat stood silent. The captain, upon getting an update from his crew ashore, addressed the group.

"A party of abolitionists has once again incited rioting in the city," he said. "The protestors have taken to the streets and much of downtown is ablaze."

"What shall we do?" a woman exclaimed. "How will we get home?"

"The streets will be too dangerous to travel tonight," the captain warned. "I implore you all to stay onboard the ferry until daybreak. My crew will bring blankets and put coffee on the stove."

"I'm not going to wait around here and just do nothing," one man spoke up. "Thank you for your advice, sir, but who will protect my home?"

The man shook the captain's hand, picked up his suitcase and walked across the gangplank into the smoky glow. A low chatter rose up among the other passengers, as they debated their course of action. The state attorneys exchanged looks.

"Shall we stay aboard for the night?" Tom asked.

"Yes," Johnson answered. "I think that would be wise."

They walked into the cabin to accept blankets and steaming cups of black coffee. Then the men found a bench on deck near the railing facing the city and took a seat.

"I failed them." Tom shook his head and took a gulp of the hot brew, his eyes trained on the horizon.

"No, Tom. They have failed you."

Just outside of town at the Forten residence, the lights had been doused and the doors barricaded. The riot fire's glow in the distance had become an all too familiar scene, and the family had developed a plan for just such emergencies. The butler crouched on the floor at the front window. His eyes scanned the snow-crested yard. His rifle lay at the ready. Mrs. Forten packed travel bags for herself and her daughters, containing food and a change of clothes. A stack of bills lay on the table. She counted out one hundred dollars, tightly rolled the money and tucked it neatly into her brassiere.

Mr. Forten sat in his chair beside the cold, dark fireplace. Every now and then, he raised a glass of brandy to his lips.

Nellie hurried into the room and placed her hand on Mrs. Forten's shoulder.

"They're coming," she whispered, her eyes wide, her breath short.

The old woman handed Nellie a wad of bills.

"Take this, Nellie, and go get my girls. We'll go out the back."

Mrs. Forten rushed to her husband's side, dropping to her knees and taking his hand in hers.

"Please, James, please. Come with us, dear. Come with us."

"Be safe, my darling. Keep our daughters safe. We'll hold our own."

Mrs. Forten looked out the front window. The faint roar of the mob could now be heard, and the soft glow of the torches grew brighter in the distance. She turned her gaze back to her husband, pleading.

He lifted her hand to his lips. His eyes said I love you.

"Go now," he said, and she obeyed.

Nellie was waiting at the back door with Mrs. Forten's dark cloak. She, along with Charlotte and Margareta, were also clad in black. With their travel bags in hand, they slipped out into the night. When the women reached the tree line at the forest's edge, they took cover in an old root cellar and stared back in horror at the house.

The mob had reached the yard.

Mrs. Forten threw her hands over her ears, to block out the violent shouts, the shattering glass, the shotgun blasts. She watched the throng charge the front door and enter the house. By the glow of the torches, men barged in and then emerged wielding paintings, trunks, silver trays. It all happened so quickly — but it seemed to go on forever.

The flickering light inside grew. Soon, flames burst from the windows and the home was engulfed.

"James?" Mrs. Forten trembled, her eyes darting frantically to spot her beloved. But he did not emerge from the chaos.

"Oh, mother," Charlotte cried. "We must flee. Now!"

The two women tugged at their mother, pulling her from the cellar, nearly dragging her through the pine needles and snow. Nellie took up the rear with their bags. Finally, the old woman took to her feet, and they all disappeared into the night.

That same evening, in Mill Green, Ed Prigg's friends raised their glasses at Jake's Tavern to toast the Supreme Court's ruling.

"Order has finally been restored," Ed declared, smiling.

For two days more, a violent mob would rage through the streets and neighborhoods of Philadelphia.

Chapter 29

Margaret

"Push, Hope! Just once more. You can do it!"

Hope squeezes my hand and gives in to the contractions. She pushes, wails.

"I got da head," Madame Zeta says. "Just a bit more now. Keep pushin' child."

Hope takes a couple of short, quick breaths and leans in again, crying.

A tiny shoulder comes out, then the other, and then the whole baby just comes slipping out into Zeta's hands.

"Good," she says. "You done good. It's a boy!"

Hope is still crying, and laughing. Me, too. I hug her and kiss her head.

"You take care of mama now, Margaret," Zeta directs. "We'll get this babe cleaned up."

Zeta turns and nods to Emma, who had been hanging back in the shadows during the delivery. She's eleven years old now, and I wanted her to see this miracle of life. As soon as Zeta and I knew the baby was coming for sure, and that the delivery looked to go well, I ran and got Emma from down at Granny Gin's.

"I've got more cramps, Margaret," Hope says to me with a touch of alarm.

"Don't worry, that's just the afterbirth coming," I say. "Just give us another push, and you'll be all through."

Hope pushes, but nothing comes.

"Oh, it hurts," she cries.

"You're okay," I say. But I'm a bit worried, too. It shouldn't be this hard for her. "Just breathe again and try to relax. Now, give another push."

She leans in and struggles, and another hairy head begins to emerge.

"Sweet Jesus!" I laugh. "There's another baby coming!"

Hope laughs. Zeta leaves the first baby with Emma and comes running to give me a hand. It takes just a few minutes more, and Hope's second beautiful baby comes slipping into the world.

"Another boy!"

I finish caring for Hope, while Zeta and Emma clean up the babies. They bring them over, all swaddled and sweet, and lay them at their mama's breast.

Emma wraps her arms around my waist. She looks up at me, smiling wide.

"They're beautiful," she says.

I nod in agreement and give her a squeeze.

Zeta opens the hospital door and leans out.

"Y'all can come in now," she says to Hope's husband, Eli, and Master Beane, who had been waiting outside since dinner.

Master comes in first, then Eli. They look at Hope, lying with her twins, and I can't say who looks more pleased. Eli runs to her side, embraces all three and showers them with kisses and tears.

"Two!" Master Beane says. "Well, that's fine work. What have we got?"

"They both boys," Zeta answers flatly.

Master smiles and slaps Eli on the back.

"Two boys. I can't tell you how pleased I am, Eli," he says. "I want you both to take the day off work tomorrow. You've earned it."

"Thank you, Massa," the parents respond simultaneously.

"I'm going to go tell the missus," Master says. He faces me as he turns to leave. His eyes lock on mine. Out of respect, I should look down. But I don't.

"Two boys," he says, sticking two fingers up in my face.

I fold my arms across my chest, raise my eyebrows a bit, shrug my shoulders. Our eyes are deadlocked. My cheek burns, as Master gives me a good hard slap. I saw it coming, but I didn't flinch.

"Mama!"

Out of the corner of my eye, I can see Zeta pull Emma to her, signal her to hush.

Master hits me again, with the back of his hand this time, and I can't help but stagger. He smiles this time and sticks his two fingers back up in the air.

"Two boys," he hisses at me before walking out the door.

The room is silent, but for the contented gurgling of the twins in their mama's arms.

"Oh, Margaret," Hope says, her face contorted with worry.

"Never you mind about that," I say. My face burns, but I'm smiling, and it's genuine. "You and Eli just be happy. Enjoy those babies."

Zeta nods. Emma takes my hand. The three of us walk out of the hospital into the cool night and give the new parents some privacy. We start a fire and sit together. The flames dance. Emma finally breaks the silence.

"Why did he hit you?"

Zeta and I exchange looks. She picks up a stick and pokes at the fire.

"He's angry because I haven't had any babies at the plantation."

"But Daddy isn't even here," she says, her eyebrows scrunching together. "Besides, why does he care if you have a baby or not?"

I inhale deeply. Let it out slowly. It just keeps getting harder and harder, this damned life. Another day, another question I can't answer, another question I'm afraid to answer.

"That's why Master bought me, Emma," I finally say. "He wanted me to have babies with Tucker, so he wouldn't have to buy as many slaves."

The fire crackles and pops. Eli and Hope coo and laugh softly inside the hospital. The wind picks up, and the leaves rustle high in the trees. Emma's eyes narrow.

"Is that why he bought me, too?"

How can I possibly answer that? The words won't come to me this time. I look to Zeta for help, but her gaze is fixed on the fire. My mouth opens, but I just can't say it.

Emma nods her head. *God, help me.* She understands.

It's been nearly six months now, since the twins were born. Hope named them Washington and Jefferson, because she had heard those were the names of two great presidents who were kind to their slaves.

What a hard time she had those first few months. She had been coming up to the hospital about six times a day to nurse the boys. Master finally granted her permission to sleep here, so she wouldn't have to come over in the middle of the night. Hope thought that was real nice of him. But I know he only allowed it so that she would stop falling asleep while polishing the silver.

Then the Beanes left again for summer at Pawley's Island. Hope and Eli usually go along, but Master didn't want to deal with two crying, smelling babies. He decided Hope and the twins would stay behind this time. So, she finally got some much needed rest and the proper food to nurse her babies.

"They're already so big," Hope says.

The boys lay sleeping on a blanket in the shade outside the hospital. Hope kneels beside them. She reaches out her hands to measure Jefferson from head to toe. Then she holds her hands at the same length to her stomach and laughs.

"Can you believe they both came outta here just six months ago," she marvels.

"Before you know it, they'll be walking around and talking," I say. "You won't believe how fast it goes."

I nod in Emma's direction. She stands up from her work in the garden, her tall thin frame silhouetted against the bright sunlight as she stretches. I point to my stomach.

"Can you believe *she* came out of here?" I say, laughing.

"Oh, Lordy," Hope laughs, too. "I'm not gonna think about that right now. I'm just gonna think about today."

She lies down beside the twins, closes her eyes and hums softly.

Zeta's coming up the path from the big house. She waves to me, so I get up and meet her part way.

"We got seeds up at da house," she says.

The first Monday of the month, Mr. Gales brings a selection of seeds, spices and herbs for us to purchase. Master opened an account for two dollars a month, and he lets Zeta select the items she needs for the hospital.

"Why don't you run over and pick out some things today," Zeta says.

"Me?"

"You."

She walks right past me without missing a step and plops down in her rocking chair on the hospital stoop. That Zeta. She always keeps me guessing. I turn toward the big house and put a hustle in my step so as not to keep Mr. Gales waiting.

"Good morning, Margaret."

"Morning, sir. Zeta asked me to make the purchase today."

"Yes, I know," Mr. Gales says. "Take a look at the seeds."

I walk to the back of his wagon and look over the baskets containing the seed envelopes.

"Just got in a batch of strawberry seeds," Mr. Gales suggests.

"Mmm, we haven't had much luck with strawberries, I'm afraid."

Corn would be nice. Maybe some squash. I let my fingers tip-toe over the envelopes and pull out the ones I want.

"You'll like the strawberries, Margaret," Mr. Gales insists. "They're a special batch, up from Harford County."

"Maryland?"

"Yep," he says, looking over his shoulder. "Special delivery from Mill Green."

"But . . . how . . . I mean, what . . . " I stammer like a fool at the mere mention of my old home.

Mr. Gales pulls the strawberry envelope from the basket and adds it to my stack. He winks.

"That's about two dollars' worth, I'd say." He nods knowingly. "You be sure and let me know what you think of those berries."

With a tip of his hat, Mr. Gales climbs up to his wagon seat. I quickly grab up the envelopes. He clicks to his horse and rolls off. I watch until he pulls away from the front gate and is nearly out of sight down the road.

The overseer gallops up on his stallion from the other direction for his weekly inspection. He rides through the gate and heads toward the fields. He looks my way, just for a moment, and fear comes over me like burlap blanket, all prickly and hot. He knows Mr. Gales. Would he question why I made the purchase today instead of Zeta? Would he ask to see my seeds? Would he take them from me?

"Pff, don't be a fool, Margaret," I say out loud. "Why would the overseer care about these confounded strawberry seeds?"

But I can't talk away my worry. So I turn and walk quickly up the path to the hospital, seeds clutched in my sweaty fist.

"Whatcha get, Margaret?" Zeta asks from the hospital.

Hope and the twins are fast asleep in the shade. Emma continues her work in the garden. I look through the open doorway. No patients yet today. So I shrug and drop the envelopes in Zeta's lap.

She rocks back and forth in her chair, flipping through the envelopes, sorting them.

"Here, baby, you keep this one."

She hands me the strawberries.

I take the envelope, still utterly baffled, and wander into the hospital. Squatting in the corner, near the window, I hold it up to the light. The packet is too thick to see through. Suppose it makes sense to open the blasted thing. I slide my finger under the wax seal, and the flap opens up. I peek inside. No seeds at all.

A trickle of sweat runs down my temple. Part from the heat, part from the fear. With a deep breath, I remove the contents from the envelope—a pencil and several sheets of paper folded over and again. Hands shaking, I unfold the paper. It's a letter. A letter from Jim in Mill Green!

> *March 25, 1843*
> *Dear Missus Margaret,*
>
> *I'm sure my letter to you is quite a shock. I pray it finds you healthy and well, although I fear that is not the case. Very much has happened since we last saw each other. It is hard to know what to write.*
>
> *To begin, let me tell you that I am still in bondage to Mrs. Ashmore, but I am quite well. With the horror she brought on your family, believe me when I say you have all rights to damn her. But she has since befriended me and taught me to read and write. In exchange, I taught her to make candles. She sells these, and kindly shares the profits with me. Thus, I have saved nearly two hundred dollars and I hope to one day buy my freedom.*
>
> *I traveled with Mrs. Ashmore to Havre de Grace in the fall to sell candles and I happened to overhear a man by the name of Beane haggling with an auctioneer. I nearly dropped over when he made mention of an impertinent slave by the name of Margaret that he bought more than five years past!*
>
> *It was like a message to me from God himself. With further spying, I learned it was indeed you, Margaret, and learned from where this Master Beane hailed. So I took it as my mission to write to you.*
>
> *There's a secret network used to transport escaped slaves to the North. I learned this network could also be*

used to relay messages to slaves still in labor. And there you have it!

Please write me back, Margaret, and assure me that you are well. Are the children with you? Give your letter to the messenger who brought mine to you. And do it in the same manner and form.

Yours very truly,
Jim of Mill Green

I turn the letter over, then flip through the blank papers. I read the letter again. And again, once more. Jim wrote me a letter! Wonderful, dear, Jim. Am I dreaming? Can this really be so? Maybe I should read it again. Yes, again, just to be sure.

A knock at the door breaks through the delightful fog in my mind.

"Got a patient coming up da path," Zeta hollers to me through the door.

I quickly fold up the letter, stuff it back in the envelope. Where will it be safe? I tuck it in my sewing basket for now, beneath the spools. The door swings open and a field hand limps in, blood trickling down his calf.

The fat moon is high overhead now, and the plantation is asleep. With the strawberry envelope in hand, I slip out of the hospital and creep down to the creek bed. A crooked old cypress tree stands watch. I crouch down and rub my pencil back and forth over a nice flat rock to sharpen the point.

Jim sent three blank sheets, and I intend to fill every inch of that paper. The questions flow fast and clear, like the creek after a spring rain. Every now and then, I have to stop and sharpen the tiny lead along the rock again. As the last page fills, I begrudgingly sign my closing.

P.S. Please send another pencil!

I saw Tucker yesterday, down by the field houses. We haven't exchanged one word since I was demoted, but he always seems to be lurking about, watching me. I avoid his stares, afraid of what his eyes might tell me. Would they speak of anger and resentment? Of sadness and longing? I pray they would speak of acceptance, maybe forgiveness. But I'm afraid to look, no matter how many years have passed.

Master gave Tucker a new woman just a few days after I was sent to the field houses. A pretty young thing, she couldn't have been more than fifteen years old at the time. Tucker got her pregnant straight away. And her belly was already bulging with Tucker's third child when she left with the Beanes for Pawley's Island. Emma says Tucker never comes down to Granny Gin's to visit his babies. Why would he? That's not his job.

Summer continues to be a season of small blessings. My greatest joy in life is the time I get to spend with Emma.

At the end of a long day, we like to go down to the creek bed and cool our feet in the bubbling water. I tell her stories about our home back in York, about the lake and the snow and her bed by the fireplace. She's having trouble recalling some of it, and I want to make sure those memories stay with her forever.

Every few weeks, I sneak to the big house in the middle of the night to raid the library. Teaching Emma to read has been such fun! She's smart as a whip and has picked it up quickly. I tempted her first with *Grimm's Fairy Tales* and then with dime novels about cowboys and Indian maidens, shipwrecks and pirates' treasures. We've read John James Audubon's *The Birds of America*, all four volumes. We've read *The Life and Memorable Actions of George Washington* and *The Last Days of Pompeii*.

When the moon is full and bright, we steal away to the creek to read into the wee hours of the morning. Sleep is a rare gift for either of us. Emma is tormented by nightmares of being snatched up in the middle of the night, and I'm cursed to stare wide-eyed into the dark no matter how tired my body is. So we read the nights away.

Sometimes, when the hospital is quiet, we also read in the garden during the day, behind the bean poles.

I was tickled to realize that Emma's favorite books, far and away, are the farmer's almanacs. She loves to study them, reading up on weather statistics, seasonal trends and crop predictions. Then she talks like a lightning storm, telling me all her ideas for the garden.

"We should plant an extra row of cucumbers this fall," she says. "They're predicting more rain than usual in October, so they should come up nice."

"Good idea," I say.

"Collard greens will be good. They worked out so well last year. Do you remember, Mama?"

"Yes," I say. "Seems like they kept growing right through to January, didn't they?"

"February, I think," she says. "We'll do carrots again, of course. But we should plant them closer together this time, to save space. According to this, they don't need much room to produce a bunch."

Her voice is like a lullaby. It sends my mind into sweet day dreams of my garden back home, of mornings spent with little John and Sam.

The boys are forever on my mind. Lord only knows what hardships they suffer each and every day, alone. Do they get enough food to keep away the ache in their stomachs? Do they suffer the lash? Have they been sold over and again since we said our good-byes a lifetime ago?

I pluck a feverfew blossom from a nearby row and pop its bitter petals into my mouth.

"Another headache?" Emma asks.

"It'll pass," I say, forcing a smile. But it never passes. The dull ache lives in the back of my neck. It slithers up into my skull like a king snake and squeezes my brain every time I think about my boys.

"You should boil the petals first," Emma says. "A tea works better."

"Maybe later," I say, pulling at a few weeds. "I'm feeling better already. Tell me more about your plans for the garden."

Emma gives me a long steady look. Finally, she returns to the almanac, flipping the pages slowly in search of inspiration. She stops, reads, raises her eyebrows.

"I wonder if we could get rhubarb to grow down here," she says. "You made the best rhubarb pies back home. Remember how Daddy and John used to arm wrestle for an extra piece?"

"How could I forget? Our silly boys."

It brings a smile to my face knowing that she remembers it, too. Emma laughs and turns another page in the almanac. These are the precious moments that help me lift my head every morning.

It took me nearly the full month leading up to Mr. Gales' next visit to figure out how I was going to give him my envelope without being questioned. Jim's letter had said to give my note to the messenger in the "same manner and form" that I received mine. But how could I possibly return an envelope of strawberry seeds to him? It would be strange enough if Zeta sent me in her place again to make the purchase. If I pretended to be unhappy with the seeds and returned them, word might get out and I'd end up with the lash for my impertinence. If I were to be seen giving him some sort of gift, rumors would fly.

Now that I have my plan, it's hard to contain my excitement. It's sure to work. I can't wait to receive another letter from Jim. The idea of having a secret connection with home is thrilling and terrifying all at once.

"Good morning, Margaret," Mr. Gales says as I near his wagon.

"Morning, sir."

Mr. Gales pulls a handkerchief from his back pocket and wipes the sweat from his brow. He leans against the wagon and looks up toward the sky. My stomach tightens with butterflies.

"So," he says. "How did those strawberry seeds work out for you?"

"The strawberries? We couldn't grow a single one. But I was so pleased to get them. I'd love to try my hand at another batch sometime."

Mr. Gales nods. I wonder if anyone is watching us, but I resist the urge to look around. It would look too suspicious.

"We, uh, we clipped some herbs," I say, holding out my envelope. "Madame Zeta likes them for her fever rub, but she doesn't know what they're called. I was hoping that you . . . that, maybe, you could take them. That you would know what do with them."

He takes the envelope and stuffs it into his shirt pocket.

"Sure thing, Margaret," he says. "I know what to do. With a little luck, I'll have a new batch for you next month."

"I would be so grateful for that," I say. Then I just stare at him, like a fool, not knowing what to do next.

He points to the wagon. "You best pick some things out."

I scramble up and clumsily snatch up a handful of items without even looking to see what I've got. He chuckles.

"You get what you wanted?"

"Oh, yes, sir," I say, trying to stifle my own giddiness.

We say our good-byes, and I watch the wagon pull away. I glance around before heading back to the hospital. Across the lawn, Tucker leans against the porch railing of the big house, arms folded across his chest. His eyes pierce through me. He has been watching.

I look at my feet and turn quickly up the path. Just keep walking, I tell myself. Don't look back.

Chapter 30

Mill Green, Maryland

Mrs. Ashmore had a special surprise for Jim's reading lesson.

When their efforts first began, the lessons had revolved around *McGuffey Readers*—the same primers the local school teacher used to tutor the children of Mill Green. When Jim graduated from these, the widow had turned to the weekly newspaper and various magazines for their lessons. His skill had improved dramatically.

To reward the achievement, Mrs. Ashmore had purchased a new book, fresh from the presses.

"I'll get dinner started tonight," the widow announced. "You go get the basket with your lessons."

Jim had learned to read the old woman almost as well as he had his *McGuffeys*. He knew she was up to some mischief, and he humored her. He retrieved the basket containing his pencils, writing tablets, books and newspapers.

"Feels a bit heavier than usual," he said, setting it on the kitchen table, looking at her sideways.

The widow laughed. She rushed to the table, reached into the basket and pulled out a hefty book. With a gleeful smile, she opened it and fanned through the pages. The cover smelled of tanned calfskin, the pages of fresh ink.

"It just came in a shipment from England!" She snapped the book shut and handed it to Jim. The title was stamped in gold letters on the cover—*American Notes* by Charles Dickens.

Jim smiled. He and the widow had read Dickens's *Pickwick Papers* together, which was serialized each month in the *Bentley's Miscellany* magazine from London.

"It's about Mr. Dickens's visit to the States last year," Mrs. Ashmore explained. "Do you remember when we read about that in the paper?"

"I sure do, ma'am."

"Don't you think it will be fun to see what he thinks of America?" Mrs. Ashmore asked.

"Yes, ma'am. Great fun."

Jim opened the book and began reading aloud, while the widow set about the task of scrubbing and dicing vegetables for the soup.

So it went for nearly a month. Every Wednesday and Friday, Mrs. Ashmore prepared the evening meal while Jim read a chapter from *American Notes*.

"What are we up to this evening?" the widow asked.

"Chapter eight," Jim answered. "Washington: The Legislature and The President's House."

"Oh my," Mrs. Ashmore said. "That ought to be interesting."

Jim nodded in agreement and cleared his throat.

"We left Philadelphia by steamboat at six o'clock one very cold morning, and turned our faces toward Washington," he read. The widow smiled with closed lips, raising her eyebrows and her shoulders in unison to show her approval. Jim read Dickens's account of the journey, stumbling at times over the author's acerbic prose. But he licked his thumb, turned the page and continued reading. "We stopped to dine in Baltimore, and being now in Maryland, were waited on, for the first time, by slaves."

Jim's voice trailed off, but his eyes stayed on the page. He continued reading in silence, until the widow suddenly snatched the book from his hands. She held it open in one palm. With her other hand, she ran a finger down the page until she found the spot where Jim had left off.

Then she read aloud.

"The sensation of exacting any service from human creatures who are bought and sold, and being, for the time, a party as it were to their condition, is not an enviable one. The institution exists, perhaps, in its least repulsive and most mitigated form in such a town as this; but it is slavery; and though I was, with respect to it, an innocent man, its presence filled me with a sense of shame and self-reproach."

The widow stopped, staring at it a minute. Then, very slowly, she eased the book shut. Several quiet minutes passed as she stood motionless in the center of the kitchen, staring at the book in her hands. Jim stared at the floor. Finally, Mrs. Ashmore stepped toward the table and gently laid the book down.

"I'm not hungry," she whispered. Her hand lingered for a moment over the book. Then she slipped through the kitchen door and out of sight.

Jim waited. He listened to her footsteps as she walked upstairs and closed her bedroom door. Then he picked up the book and devoured the words.

The next morning their routine returned to normal. No mention was made of the night before. Jim's next reading lesson once again featured the week's edition of the *Harford Republican*. The book—dreaded by one, treasured by the other—was kept hidden away in Jim's room. And the writings of Charles Dickens were never again discussed in the Ashmore residence.

Ed Prigg threw a gold coin onto the bar at Jake's Tavern and smiled.

"That ought to cover my tab."

Jake whistled. He picked up the coin and clamped it between his teeth.

"Yes, sir, I'd say we're square," he said with a laugh and filled a pint for his old friend.

Since the Supreme Court had overturned Prigg's kidnapping conviction, the bounty hunter had become somewhat of a legend. Requests for his services came from all over the South. He had made nearly a dozen trips into Pennsylvania, New York and Massachusetts in the past year on the hunt for runaways. His success record was perfect. His commission averaged fifty dollars a head.

"It's good to be back in the game," Prigg said. He emptied his glass and motioned for a refill.

Nat Bemis walked into the tavern and took a seat. He removed his hat, placing it on his knee.

"Hello there, Ed. I didn't know you were back in town. Good to see you."

"Good to see you, too, Nat. Just got back this morning. Let me buy you a drink."

"Hiya, Nat," Jake said. "What can I get you?"

"Just coffee for me, thanks. I've got to head back to the mill in a bit," he answered. "But you can put it on Ed's tab."

The men chuckled. Jake retrieved a brown ceramic mug out from under the bar and filled it with steaming black coffee.

"You've been on the road a lot these days," Nat said, nodding at Prigg. "Business been good?"

"Sure the hell has," Prigg said, and the two men raised their mugs before taking a drink. "I feel like a kid again."

"Glad to hear it, Ed. You deserve it after all you've been put through."

"Thanks, Nat. I appreciate it. I only wish your mother-in-law saw things that way."

"How's that?" Nat crinkled his brow with feigned ignorance.

It was no secret that Ed Prigg was sweet on Margaret Ashmore. The two had been friends for decades. After Mr. Ashmore had passed, Prigg had made it a habit of checking in on the widow with some frequency. He had also started attending Sunday services at the church again, and she'd often saved him a seat in her pew. Their relationship had never turned romantic, though the town grapevine had speculated it was only a matter of time.

Then Nat and Susanna had convinced the widow to hire Prigg to track down Margaret Morgan. Prigg had always done everything Mrs. Ashmore asked of him, and this was no exception. He even did it free of charge, for an old friend. But in the aftermath of the slave auction and the criminal trials, their friendship had turned cold, and he couldn't understand why.

"I tried to catch up with her at church a few weeks ago," Prigg said. "She gave me the brush-off. Said she didn't have time to visit because she had to get back to her candle-making."

Prigg scowled into his empty glass.

"Mother Ashmore has been busy making candles like you wouldn't believe, Ed. I can attest to that."

"Well she could have her Nigger doing that for her," Prigg scoffed, motioning to Jake for another pint. "Nah! She's got a thorn in her paw about something."

Nat shifted in his seat. He decided it was best not to say that Mrs. Ashmore and Jim had been working *together* at making candles. It's not that Nat approved—far from it. But his fear of Ed Prigg was greater than his disgust for the widow's unorthodox friendship. So he just shrugged his shoulders and took another sip of his coffee. "Women."

"It's getting to be about lunch time," Jake interjected. He dawdled at filling Prigg's mug with another pint of ale. "You fellas want something to eat? I've got chipped beef simmering in the Dutch oven."

"Hey, that sounds great," Nat said. "You got any biscuits to go with it?"

"Sure do."

"I ain't hungry," Prigg hissed. He waggled a finger at the empty mug still in the barkeep's hand. "Something wrong with your tap, there, Jake?"

"Nope," Jake said, finally filling the glass. "It's just not used to working so hard this early in the day. That's all."

He put the mug on the bar and slid it toward Prigg. The old friends stared at each other, stone-faced. Nat looked sideways at the bartender, as if to ask why he had to go poking at a sleeping bear. Finally, Prigg erupted in rasping laughter.

"Ah ha, that's a good one, Jake! You got me there."

Nat exhaled with relief, shaking his head. It was all in a day's work for Jake, dealing with angry drunks. He winked at Nat and started serving up the chipped beef, while Prigg drained another pint.

A short brick wall ran along the north property line at the Ashmore estate. Once a week, the postman left letters and the newspaper for Mrs. Ashmore in an oak box at the main gate. On occasion, he also left a letter for Jim hidden beneath a loose brick in the wall, fifth from the mailbox. That spring, Jim received his first letter from Margaret.

May 1843
Dear Jim,

I can't begin to tell you how wonderful it was to receive your letter! There are a hundred questions I want to ask, but I will begin by answering yours. Mr. Beane bought Emma and me at auction. Sam and John were each sold to different gentlemen. I do not know where they are. But not a day goes by that I don't think of them and pray they are safe.

Life at the Beane plantation has brought one horror after another. I won't waste paper detailing the wrongdoing I have witnessed and endured. But I will tell you that, as each year passes, I grow more shocked and distressed to learn that the injustice seems limitless. Living my whole life in freedom in Mill Green and then in York, I often marveled at how there can be all different kinds of free. And yet, after hearing news of Mrs. Ashmore's recent kindness to you and after living here at the plantation, I suppose now I've learned there are all different kinds of bondage, too. It lifts my heart to know you are being treated well, Jim. But I also pray the day will come soon when you can buy your freedom, like my Jerry did when he was a young man.

Have you heard any news of Jerry? Do you know, has he been searching for us? It breaks my heart to realize it has been more than five years since I have laid eyes on my dear husband. I become more desperate with each passing day to get some word from him, and I cling to the hope that he will show up here one day to buy our freedom. Emma is growing into such a fine young woman. In just a few more years, Master Beane will surely think she is old enough to breed. The thought of it is unbearable, yet escape from this wretched place seems impossible.

If there is any way you can get word to Jerry concerning our whereabouts, I would be forever in your debt.

Yours truly,
Margaret

P.S. Please send another pencil!

Jim set about trying to contact Jerry in Pennsylvania straight away. He soon learned it would be no simple task. It was one thing for Jim to travel with Mrs. Ashmore to local towns, where the widow could sell her candles and he could eavesdrop on various conversations for bits of information. It was another thing entirely for him to communicate with a Negro in a free state.

There was no way Jim would be allowed travel to the North, even if he could somehow persuade the widow into making a trip that far away. His only option was to send a letter using the secret network.

When his letters to Jerry's home went unanswered, Jim wrote again to Margaret. He asked for the name of someone else, someone safe, to whom he could write in Pennsylvania and inquire as to Jerry's whereabouts.

> *August 1843*
> *Dear Jim,*
>
> *My good friend Nellie works as a housekeeper for the Forten family in Philadelphia. They are the wealthiest colored family in the city. Mrs. Forten hired me to sew for her many times. Mr. Forten is a leader in the freedom movement. I can think of no safer party to whom you could write. Mr. Mitchell, Jerry's employer at the shipping yard, is another man I trust would keep your correspondence secret. I only pray they will reply with useful news.*
>
> *Yours truly,*
> *Margaret*

Jim sent a letter off to the Fortens straight away. Again, weeks passed and he received no response. Would he never receive word from the North? Were his letters even getting delivered? Jim attempted to contact Mr. Mitchell next. Finally, he found a reply tucked beneath the secret brick by the mailbox. Enclosed with the letter was a newspaper clipping from the *Pennsylvania Inquirer*, dated 1838. The notice was one line. It simply read, "The Negro Jerry Morgan of York drowned."

Jim read the letter again and again. The detail and compassion it contained, juxtaposed with the newspaper's single-sentence obituary, were heartbreaking. What was worse was that somehow he had to find a way to relay this tragic news to Margaret. Jerry had died nearly five years ago. She'd been waiting ever since, waiting on a dead hope.

The agony of the truth tortured him for days.

"What's gotten into you, Jim? You've hardly said ten words to me in a week." Mrs. Ashmore examined her friend closely as they prepared candle molds in the workshop one windy afternoon in November. "Have you taken ill?"

Jim shrugged his shoulders. "No ma'am. I feel jus' fine."

"Hmmm," the widow replied. Her eyes narrowed, as if squinting would help her see some clue hidden in his face.

"I don't know," Jim said after a moment. "Maybe I have taken ill. Not been sleeping too good lately."

Mrs. Ashmore nodded.

"I knew it," she said triumphantly. "I just knew something was wrong. You go to your room straight away, Jim, and get some rest. I won't have you work yourself to death."

Jim obeyed. He stepped out of the work shed and into the autumn sun—bright, though providing no warmth. A chilly wind stung his cheeks. He shrugged it off and stopped to watch a pile of crisp leaves take to the air in a whirlwind of red and gold. He extended his arms out at his sides, closed his eyes, wished he also could take flight on the wind and drift away in a burst of color.

After a minute or so, Jim retreated into his small room. The cold suddenly gripped him. He stoked up the potbelly stove. As a reward for Jim's hard work, the widow had increased his monthly rations considerably, which included unlimited access to the woodpile. He added another small log to the fire.

While Jim soaked up the warmth, he couldn't help but wonder if Margaret lay shivering somewhere at that very moment. His eyes turned to the stack of blank paper on the table beside him.

"Oh, Miss Margaret," he said. "A hundred years of schooling could never teach me the words for what I must write to you."

Jim hung his head. He took in a deep breath and exhaled hard. Then he turned himself to the table. He placed his quill to the paper and carefully wrote a few lines. He scribbled out the words and began anew. Again and again, he labored. The sun disappeared behind the hills.

Each time Jim had spoiled an entire sheet of paper with his scratchings, he crumpled it up and tossed it into the stove, where it crackled and shrank into the fire. Then he confronted the next blank page, and the next.

The task before him became unbearable. He decided to be brief and be done with the torment. On a fresh piece of paper, he wrote a short note.

November 15, 1843

Dearest Margaret,
I regret this letter contains no good news. Please see the enclosed newspaper notice and letter that Mr.

Mitchell was good enough to send in reply to my inquiry.

With deepest sympathy,
Jim of Mill Green

He placed the letters and obituary clipping in the envelope, along with several blank sheets of paper and a fresh pencil. Lifting his candle, Jim carefully poured a few drops of hot wax to seal the flap. He closed the door on the stove and blew out the candle, bringing total darkness to the small room. With a heavy heart, he cautiously slipped out the door and down to the front gate, where he tucked the letter beneath the secret brick for the postman.

Chapter 31

Margaret

I hate Decembers at the Beane Plantation. This is my sixth one.

The weather is cold, but there is no lovely snow. Preparations for Christmas in the big house are underway, but for the slaves there is no merriment, no holiday. The scent of roasting goose and ginger cookies wafts on the air from Master's home, but the stench of relentless hunger and unending despair fills the fields.

Hospital patients come few and far between; that's the season's small blessing. During the lull in work, Mrs. Beane fills my time with sewing duties.

Two weeks ago, she came to me with bolts of red and black velvet in hand. The children would need outfits for the coming holiday party. I made a smart black blazer with red lapels for Sean-Paul, and a slim red dress with a black stole for Clarice. The dress is exactly Emma's size. How I wish it could be for her instead.

Mrs. Beane instructed me to bring the outfits to the house when I was finished.

"Missus?" I call into the kitchen from the back entrance. I knock on the door. "Nanny?"

"Oh, child!" Nanny greets me with a big smile and hug. "I don't see enough of you around da house these days."

I sneak into the big house at night all summer long, while the family is away at the island. But when they are home, I have few reasons to come around. Can't say there's anything I miss. Even Nanny, who'd befriended me when I had no friends, has become an annoyance. The handful of times we've spoken in the past couple of years, she falls into lectures about how lucky we all are to have such a benevolent master. It's a load of manure.

Mrs. Beane joins us in the kitchen. I hold up the garments, and she shrieks with delight.

"Margaret, they're wonderful!"

Nanny and the missus coo and fuss over the outfits—the unique design, the craftsmanship, how charming the children will look in them. I smile, but the compliments mean nothing to me.

"If it's alright, ma'am, I should get back to work at the hospital now," I say after a bit.

"Yes, of course. You may go," Mrs. Beane says, still admiring the garments. "Merry Christmas, Margaret."

Go to hell, Simone. That's what I'd like to say.

"Merry Christmas, ma'am," I say instead and leave.

On the path back to the hospital, I meet up with Madam Zeta.

"Mr. Gales sure brought a nice batch of goodies for us today, Margaret," she says, winking. She hands me an envelope from the stack. The feel of it in my hand lifts my spirits.

We part ways when we reach the hospital. Zeta heads inside, while I head for the solitude of the garden to read my letter.

I open the envelope, pull out the papers. A small newspaper clipping falls out and flutters to the ground. I pick it up quickly. *The Negro Jerry Morgan of York drowned.* The words knock the air right out of me.

Frantically, I unfold the papers. *I regret this letter contains no good news.* Dear God. *With deepest sympathy.* No! Why? How? It can't be true.

A second letter, from Mr. Mitchell, offers more detail.

1838. Returning home from Harrisburg . . . Jerry had sought the aid of the governor in locating his family . . .

He was trying to find us. Of course, he was trying to find us.

An accident at the lock . . . hands were bound behind his back...

My Jerry is dead. Dead five years.

I knew it. In my heart, I knew he must be dead. There's just no other way to explain how so many years could have passed without any word from him.

Jerry, you damn fool! How could you go and get yourself killed? How could you leave me? My throat tightens, and I gasp for air. Sobs escape from my mouth, violent, uncontrollable. I fall into a heap on ground and pound my fists into the raw soil. *Damn you, Jerry. Damn you.*

"Mama?" Emma calls out to me from the gate. "Are you all right?"

No, not now. I can't bear to see her right now. I can't bear to tell her. I grope at the papers, try to stuff them all back into the envelope.

"I'm fine," I manage to sputter, jumping to my feet. My head reels. For a moment, I feel as though I'll fall right back to the ground.

"Did we get seeds today?" Emma comes into the garden. Her eyes take me in from head to toe. "I'll help you plant them," she says doubtfully.

"No," I snap, swallowing hard to dislodge the knot in my throat. "We didn't get anything. Go on back to Granny Gin's."

I brush by without looking at her.

January brought the New Year; but there is never anything new in this place. The days just keep tumbling by. February brings more pointless days in an empty pointless life.

The hospital remains quiet, but I can't seem to bring myself to work in the garden with Emma. Mrs. Bean brought more fabric a couple weeks ago, but I haven't touched it. Her spoiled children don't need any more damn clothes.

Mr. Gales came yesterday with another letter. I didn't open it.

"Come on inside, Margaret," Zeta calls to me from the hospital door. "You'll catch yo death sitting out all night."

It's near midnight, but the time of day or night doesn't matter. I sit in Zeta's creaky old rocking chair outside the hospital, wearing the nightgown Simone gave me my first night in the big house. After six years, it's threadbare. The full moon shines brightly overhead. My naked toes and fingers sting from the cold.

"I'll be there in a bit," I say.

"Mm-hmm," she says and tosses a tattered blanket into my lap. Zeta knows me well enough by now to know I'm not coming in any time soon. She disappears back into the dark, warm hospital.

I drape the blanket over my lap. It does little to block the cold. The wind cuts through the worn threads and bites at my bare legs. When I feel good and numb, I pull the envelope from my brassiere. My icy fingers fumble to unfold the letter.

January 30, 1844

Dearest Margaret,
I know you are wanting for good news, and I regret to say I have failed you once again. My efforts to find your sons has produced nothing.
The auctioneer in Havre de Grace told me he knows nothing about the boys. I suspected that he was reluctant

*to tell a lowly slave any information of value, so I said
Mrs. Ashmore had asked me to inquire about it because
she wished to purchase the boys back again. But he still
insisted that he keeps no records of his slave auctions
other than the payment he received. Say a prayer for me,
that word of my lies doesn't make its way back to
Master Bemis or Mrs. Ashmore.*

    *I wrote again to Mr. Mitchell in Pennsylvania, but
he had no further information to share regarding your
family. I've run out of ideas. There's just no way that I
can see to learn where your boys were sold so long ago,
or if they've been sold yet again since then.*

    Please forgive me, Margaret.
    Yours truly,
    Jim of Mill Green

So that's it then. Jerry is dead. My boys are gone. After six long years, the truth has finally rolled over me like a badly stacked wood pile. There's no hope. All is truly lost.

I stand from the rocking chair and walk inside. The letter goes in the basket with the others. I slump into my cot, pull the blanket over me. The world goes dark.

"Well, what the hell is wrong with her?" The master bellows from outside the hospital door.

"Could be a touch of the chills," Zeta tells him.

He came around last week, too, when Simone complained I had not yet delivered the outfits I was supposed to make for the twins. Zeta told him I had taken ill. It's true, something ill has taken hold of me.

Emma has slipped in and out of the hospital several times. She stares down at me lying in my cot. But we never speak. I'm too tired. Six years of tired, finally taking hold. *What's the use of fighting it any longer?*

"It's been days," Master Beane complains. "Is she going to die?"

Zeta has been doing all she can to see that doesn't happen, though I wish she would just let nature run its course.

"No, no, Massa Beane," Zeta assures him. "She's been taking the broth I give her. She gonna pull through. Margaret just needs a bit more rest, thas all."

That's right. I just need to rest.

After six sleepless years at the plantation, I finally get to rest. Lying here in my cot, my back to the world, I sleep day and night. It's all I can seem to do.

Who could have guessed, in all these years, it was nothing but hope that was keeping me on my feet.

"What are you fixing to do, Mama?" Emma stands at my bedside. "You gonna just lay here forever, waiting to die?"

Her words are harsh, but her voice is gentle. I heard her slip into the hospital a moment ago and bolt the door behind her. She went straight to my sewing basket and retrieved the stack of letters I've kept hidden beneath the basket's velvet lining. I should have gotten up, should have stopped her. But I couldn't. I could barely open my eyes.

Emma kneels beside me now, the letters clutched in her hand.

"I read them, Mama."

Words won't come to me, only tears. I never told Emma about the letters or the terrible news they contain. How did she find out about them? Maybe Zeta told her. Perhaps Emma spied me reading them. It doesn't matter. I should have told her.

"Open your eyes," she demands. "Look at me."

I follow her command and meet her stare. Tears are flowing from her eyes, too; but she's calm, quiet. She pushes the wad of letters in my face.

"I read them, Mama. I read them."

She pauses. I close my eyes again, tight as I can. Seeing the loss in her face is just too much. It's too much.

"You're all I have left," she says. "Don't you disappear, too."

Emma drops the letters and grabs hold of my arms. Rising to her knees, she pulls and pulls at me until I'm sitting upright. *How can she be so strong?* Her grip stays tight on my arms, and her power seems to flow right through her fingers, into my limbs and into my heart.

"You're all I have," she says again.

"Oh, Emma!"

I throw my arms around her. We pull together in a fierce hug. And we just sit here holding on, holding on tight, as the minutes tick by.

"Let's never let go," I whisper.

"Never," she says.

After a bit more time, I loosen my hold. She sits back on her feet, and I slip down on to the floor beside her, never letting go of each other's hands.

"How do you get the letters?" Emma finally asks. She must have so many questions.

"They come through a secret delivery. Jim calls it the Underground Railroad, but I don't really know how it all works. There's just a bunch of nice people in the North, and the South, who think slavery is wrong, and they do what they can to help us. Mr. Gales brings me the letters hidden away in the seed packets."

Emma nods.

"I thought Mr. Gales was mean to you. You would cry, sometimes, after seeing him," she says. "But it was the letters that made you cry."

I pull her close to me again. "I'm so sorry, Emma. I should have told you. I should have told you everything. I just . . . I just didn't know how."

"It's okay, Mama. I understand."

Emma smiles, strokes my cheek. I'm stuck silent by her words. How could she forgive? My baby girl. So strong. I suddenly feel so ashamed. The past month is nothing but a blur in my mind. *How could I have let myself abandon her the way I did? How could I be so selfish?*

"It's going to be different now," I promise her. Promise *myself.* "I won't shut you out ever again. I'll tell you when the letters come, and we'll read them together. We're gonna get through this life together, forever."

"That's good, Mama. That's the way it should be."

I swallow back tears as I look at her, soak in her strength. We sit quietly for a moment.

"But," Emma adds, "if we're really gonna stick together now . . . " She pauses, crinkles her nose. "We need to get you a bath."

"Oh, Emma!" I laugh for the first time in months, and I pull her in for another hug. "You're terrible!"

"No, Mama, really," she continues to tease. "I ain't kidding you. You stink!"

But she doesn't pull away. She holds me tight, stink and all.

Chapter 32

Margaret

Spring is upon us, and our work at the hospital is increasing. The slaves have taken back to the fields—clearing away the winter weeds, cleaning out the levees, repairing the boardwalks. My days of sewing only velvet or silk are over once again.

Zeta and I are working this morning on grinding up dried plants and herbs for her various concoctions. We need to stock up, ready ourselves for the rains.

The sound of wood banging against wood makes me look up with a start. Then all I can do is stare, eyes wide. Tucker fills the door frame. He holds out his hand, revealing a deep gash in his palm.

"Got it caught fixing one of the floodgates," he says.

Madam Zeta jumps to her feet. She takes him by the arm and leads him back to her own stool. I stand and back away.

"You bes' take a look, Margaret," Zeta says.

Somehow, I get my feet to move. I edge toward him. He looks up at me from the stool. I decide to remain standing. Feels better to look down at him, rather than sit eye to eye. Tucker extends his arm, and I take his hand, all warm and dry but for the gash. The familiar feel of his skin against mine alarms me.

"It's a nasty cut," I manage to say. "But not too deep."

Zeta looks over my shoulder, agrees with my diagnosis. I turn to address her, rather than Tucker.

"I think it would be best to just clean and bandage it," I say. "Stitches would only tear away in the palm."

There's a gentle knock at the door, and a small boy stands were Tucker had just been a moment before.

"Madam Zeta," he says quietly. "Granny Gin needs you. Says her 'thritis be killin' her."

Granny's joints take to hurting something fierce every year before the rains come. Zeta nods to the boy. She gathers a couple of jars from the table and turns to me.

"You take care o' Tucker here. I'll run on down and see to Granny Gin."

I want to grab hold of her, beg her to stay. The thought of being alone with him is too much. But she's out the door before I can say a word. Tucker stares at me, blood puddling in his palm. Fear grips my heart, makes me still.

"Well," I say, and clear my throat. "It'll just take me a minute to pull my supplies together."

I can hear my heart in my own ears as I walk over to the work table and collect what I'll need—a water basin and towels, herbs for the poultice to fight infection, fresh bandages. I can feel Tuckers eyes burning into my back. When I turn to face him, he's watching me still.

"Does it hurt?" If I keep him talking, I think, keep his mind on the cut, maybe nothing will happen. Maybe he doesn't have anything to say.

He shrugs his shoulders.

"Because I could put something together for the pain, if you want."

"Nah," he says. "Jus' wrap it up."

I take a seat beside him. He watches me intently as I work. He doesn't even flinch as I clean out the wound.

"Got me a new woman, you know," he says. "Her name's Mary."

Afraid to look up, I only nod, continue my work.

"She a pretty little thing," he continues. "Already had three babies by me. Did you hear about that, Margaret? I got me three kids now."

I stand and hurry back to the work table. There's nothing in particular that I need, other than distance between us.

"Yes," I finally say, turning back to face him now. "I heard about that. That's real nice, Tucker. I'm happy for you."

He raises his eyebrows, cocks his head slightly to the side.

"Happy for me?"

"Mm-hmm," I say, forcing a smile. It used to be so easy to lie to him. But it's been a long time. I'm out of practice.

I sit back down beside him and spread the poultice over his wound. Then I carefully wrap the clean bandage around his hand— weaving over and around his thumb, under and back across, so it won't slip.

Tucker watches.

"All done," I say, tying off the knot.

He inspects my handiwork. He flexes his fingers open. He curls them in to make a fist. He does this again, and again.

"There's lot of different ways to make a baby," he says, his hand frozen in a fist now. "That's what you told me, Margaret. Remember?"

He doesn't really want an answer from me, I know. So I rise and carry the basin and supplies back to the table. *Distance. Distance is good.*

"There's a funny thing about that," Tucker continues, standing now. "It was real easy making a baby with Mary, and we only work at it one way."

I busy myself at the table, stacking towels, arranging jars, careful not to turn my back to him.

"I've been thinking about that," he says. "You and me, we hardly ever did it that way."

Tucker walks toward me. I step to another side of the table and start fiddling with my sewing basket. He moves in closer, runs his fingers down my arm.

"We did other things," he leers at me. "But we hardly ever did it *that* way."

I spin away from him, scuttle to the other side the table. Our eyes connect, and we stare each other down. He makes like he's going to dart to the side, making me flinch in the opposite direction. He laughs. It's a game now. Cat and mouse. I don't want to play.

"I'm glad to know you've got a woman who makes you happy now, Tucker." My voice cracks just a little. *Steady, Margaret.* "It was nice visiting with you. You take care of your hand now. Try to keep it dry, and come back in a couple days for a fresh bandage."

Tucker smiles. He begins to turn away.

Then he spins back around and shoves hard against the table. It slams into my stomach. I stumble back, winded. The bloody water basin sloshes. Tiny jars and canisters tumble and roll off the edge of the table. My sewing basket crashes to the ground, scattering its contents across the dirt.

The letters!

I drop to my knees, frantic to shove everything back into the basket before he figures out the envelopes contain more than just seeds. Tucker laughs again.

"You know what I think, Margaret? I think you don't know so much about making babies after all."

He creeps toward me. My fingers fall on my sewing scissors.

"I think I need to teach you a thing or two."

I jump to my feet, swipe my small weapon through the air between us. The light from the window glints off the silver blades.

"Get outta here, Tucker! You leave me alone!"

He hesitates. But I can see the rage boiling up inside him.

My hand is shaking. *Dear God, is this it? Is this where it's all gonna end?*

Suddenly, Zeta comes crashing through the hospital door. She's got her necklaces and beads clutched tight in her fist. She raises her other hand high in the air. She chants gibberish, spewing venom at Tucker in a foreign tongue.

Tucker seems startled by her display. I dart behind the table again.

Zeta's eyes roll back in her head. Her crippled feet dig into the dirt as she circles around Tucker.

"What? What the hell is she doing?" he stammers.

"It's a curse!" I shout.

Tucker's eyes grow wide. Zeta shakes her chains at him again. He spies the blood red beads, the teeth, the tiny bird feet.

"You better go, Tucker," I say quickly. "Before it's too late."

He contemplates the warning for a second or two. Then he bolts for the door.

"Crazy old witch," he yells back over his shoulder as he takes off down the hospital path.

When he's out of sight, I sink to the floor in a trembling fit. I gasp for air. My whole body shakes. Zeta pulls herself from her trance and rushes to my side. She wraps her thin arms around me.

"There, there, Margaret." She rocks me gently. "Easy now. Easy. It's all over."

"Oh, Zeta," I sob.

"Shhhh. It's all over now."

I hiccup and sputter, but my breath starts to come easier. Zeta brushes my hair back from my face, starts inspecting me from head to toe.

"Are you hurt, child?"

"No. I'm all right."

She cradles my face in her hands.

"I'm so sorry, Margaret."

"Zeta, you saved my life."

"No," she says. "I never should'a left you alone with him. I never should'a left ya."

Chapter 33

Mill Green, Maryland

Spring came early to Mill Green in 1844, and by May the weather was unseasonably warm. Mrs. Ashmore and Jim had taken to eating dinner on the porch, where they could escape the heat of the kitchen and enjoy what little breeze might blow.

Jim carried out the serving tray loaded with the evening's meal—steamed oysters, sliced peaches, sourdough bread and water—the newspaper folded and tucked beneath his arm. The widow brought the napkins, plates, glasses and utensils. Together they set the table. Jim pulled out the chair for his missus and slid her gently up to the table.

"Thank you, Jim."

"Yes, ma'am."

Jim cut a big hunk of sourdough and placed it on the widow's plate. Then he cut himself a piece. Mrs. Ashmore served up the oysters and peaches. Jim poured the water. Then they dined. A light breeze ruffled the tablecloth. In a nearby oak, a black and gold oriole twittered softly, as if singing along with the gentle clinking of silver to china.

"You're awful quiet tonight, ma'am," Jim finally said. "Not taking ill are ya?"

"Oh." The widow sighed. "No, I'm not ill. I've just been thinking."

"Thinking, ma'am?"

The widow set down her fork and looked out over her property.

"I was at the pond the other morning," she finally said. "A bird flew overhead and dropped a twig. I suppose she was intending to use it for her nest. It fell in the water instead, and the ripples worked their way to the very edge of the pond. But the bird just kept flying. She didn't see the ripples."

Jim nodded and stabbed an oyster with his fork.

"It just got me thinking, I suppose," she said, shrugging.

"About the pond?"

"Well, yes, in a round-about sort of way," the widow said, taking a sip of her water.

They ate in silence for a few minutes more.

"Do you suppose she understands the ripples she caused by dropping the twig?" Mrs. Ashmore asked.

"The bird?" Jim crinkled his brow.

"What I mean to say is, do any of us really understand the ripples we cause?"

"In the pond?"

The widow waved her hands in the air and let out a heavy sigh. "Oh, never mind. I don't know what I'm trying to say."

Jim swiped his bread along the plate, soaking up the last bit of juice from the oysters, and stuffed it in his mouth. When he finished chewing, he wiped his mouth with the napkin.

"Shall I read, ma'am?"

The widow nodded, and Jim unfolded the paper.

"What hath God wrought?" he said.

Mrs. Ashmore dropped her bread. The morsel fell into her glass, sending water sloshing over the edges. "What did you say?"

"That's the headline, ma'am," Jim explained. "Right here on the front page."

He turned the paper toward her, so she could read it for herself.

"What hath God wrought?" she whispered. "What does it mean, Jim?"

Jim read the article aloud. It reported that Samuel Morse had just sent the first message using his telegraph invention. The historic communication, sent from Baltimore to Washington, D.C. earlier that week, had relayed the message, "What hath God wrought?"

The words seemed to question the widow's very soul. Her hands trembled as she tried to fish the bread from her glass. Her face was ashen.

"Are you sure you're not taking ill, ma'am?"

"Maybe I'll go lie down," she said.

Jim jumped up and went to the old woman's side. He took her by the elbow and guided her to her feet.

"Shall I help you inside?"

"No, no," the widow said, regaining some of her composure. "I'll be fine on my own."

She went into the house and sat down in the parlor. Her gaze moved slowly about the room, taking inventory of her few possessions—the walnut desk her husband had purchased in Baltimore for their anniversary; the sparsely filled bookcase; the family Bible; one of Margaret's carefully-crafted quilts, draped over the back of the settee. She watched Jim as he moved in and out of the house, taking the dishes to the kitchen.

Mrs. Ashmore went to the desk and opened the drawer where she kept her important papers. She filed through a number of documents before pulling out the sheet she had been searching for. The old woman held it up to the waning light coming through the front window and read it. She pursed her lips. Then she shot a furtive glance toward the kitchen.

"Jim," she called out. "Would you come in here please?"

"Yes, ma'am." Jim hurried into the room.

The widow settled back down on the settee and patted the bench. Jim hesitantly sat beside her. After a moment, she handed the paper to Jim.

"Can you read this?" she asked. "Do you understand what it says?"

Jim read over the paper and nodded.

"It's a deed of property," he said. "That means proof of ownership."

"And do you read what that property is?"

"One able-bodied Negro boy by the name of Jim," he read.

The widow nodded. She took in a deep breath.

"I'm giving you that deed, Jim. It's yours. I can no longer lay claim to such property."

"Ma'am?"

"We'll have to visit the judge to make the transfer official, I suspect," Mrs. Ashmore said. "We'll go see Nat in the morning and have him make whatever arrangements are needed."

Jim studied the paper again.

"I'm not sure I understand," he finally managed to say.

Mrs. Ashmore put her hands on top of his and waited for him to look up at her. Then she smiled, tears rolling down her cheeks.

"You're free, Jim."

"Free?"

The widow nodded vigorously, tiny sobs escaping through her wide smile.

"I'm just so sorry, Jim, that I didn't do it years ago. I'm so terribly sorry."

"It's alright, ma'am. Don't cry now," Jim said. But tears had come to his eyes, too.

They sat for some time squeezing each others' hands, crying and laughing and nodding.

Chapter 34

Margaret

I hurry down the path to meet Mr. Gales, hoping he has another delivery for me.

Jim writes to us regularly about news in Mill Green, the widow's candle business and the progress he's making in his reading lessons. Sometimes he includes articles from the newspaper that he thinks would be of interest to us—about the United States settling their land dispute with Canada, about the giant wagon trains setting out on the Oregon Trail, about how the Kingdom of Hawaii out in the middle of Pacific Ocean just became an official nation. It doesn't seem to matter what sort of news it is. There's just something about having a connection to someplace far away from here that helps us hold on.

Emma and I read the letters over and again for a day or two, and then we burn them. It breaks our hearts every time, but after my last run in with Tucker, we know it is too dangerous to save them.

"Good morning, Mr. Gales."

"Good morning, Margaret."

I look over the baskets in the back of the wagon and pull out a few envelopes that Zeta said she wanted—chamomile, peppermint, garlic.

"The rhubarb should turn out fine this year," Mr. Gales says. "With all the rain we've already had."

"You sure know better than I do, Mr. Gales," I say and pull the rhubarb envelope from the basket. "Do you have any sage today?"

"Yes."

He pulls a couple of seedlings wrapped in newspaper from one of the baskets. "That's the last of it, but I'll have more next month."

I cradle my purchases in my apron and thank Mr. Gales. We say our good-byes, and I turn up the hospital path as his wagon rattles down the plantation drive.

Madame Zeta is stationed in her rocking chair at the hospital.

"Good delivery today?" she asks.

"Very good," I say. "Only a few seedlings of sage, but Mr. Gales said more would be coming next month. He had everything else you were wanting."

I show Zeta the envelopes. She eyes the rhubarb and smiles.

"You best get planting these right away," she says. "There ain't no new patients yet today. Things is quiet enough around here."

Off to the garden!

Emma is crouching between the rows, carefully plucking the thorny weeds that pushed their way up from the black soil overnight. I open the gate and walk over to her.

"We got a nice delivery of seeds today."

"We did?" Emma looks up excitedly, then looks left and right, scanning for anyone who might be within earshot.

All the field hands are ankle deep in the mud by now, watching over the rice seedlings. The children are all down at Granny Gin's. We're alone, except for Zeta and the patients fast asleep with the fever in the hospital. Even so, I suggest we move deeper into the garden plot, away from the hospital building. That way, if any new patients come up the path, we'll see them before they see us.

We squat down beside several poles thick with snap bean vines. Safely hidden from sight, I open the envelope and take out the letter. Several pages. It's the longest letter we've gotten so far. Emma smiles.

"Read it," she says.

July 15, 1844

Dear Margaret,
I have the most miraculous news! It would seem the Lord has finally worked his way back into Mrs. Ashmore's troubled heart and helped her to see a new path. One joyous day last spring, she sat me down and declared me to be free! We went with Master Bemis the next morning to visit the judge. The deed of property that she held over me was destroyed and the judge drew up papers of manumission that say I am a free man. Master Bemis and the judge were not too happy about the procedure and tried to talk Missus into a different course of action. But she stood firm, and that was that!

*Because you are a good friend and good Christian,
I know this news by itself will be enough to lift your
heart. But I have still more good news!*

*After gaining my freedom, I continued working at
the candle-making business with Mrs. Ashmore. She
pays me a fair wage, including room and board. Things
didn't seem too much different for a while. It took me
several weeks, but the idea of being free finally became
clear in my mind.*

*I realize it is owing to you, Margaret, that I now
have my freedom, for Mrs. Ashmore has been so
tormented by her hand in your fate. So I worked up the
courage to tell her about my letters to and from you. She
was distraught at first, to learn I had kept such a secret
from her. But then we talked and came up with a plan
that will make us all quite happy.*

*I have managed to save $428 with the hope of
freedom. That hope is still strong in my heart. So I am
leaving in October for the Beane Plantation. And I will
use the money I've saved to buy yours and Emma's
freedom! If the price is set higher, Mrs. Ashmore will
provide a letter guaranteeing that she will pay the
balance.*

*Our prayers have been answered! I will make my
travel preparations and look forward to the day when I
will see your smiling face. Continue to stay strong until
freedom is finally yours again.*

*Yours very truly,
Jim Green*

*P.S. Now that I am free, I needed to take a second
name. How do you like it?*

Emma looks at me in disbelief at what I have just read. Her
mouth opens and closes like a fish on the shore. She's speechless, and
I'm just the same. She gently pulls the letter from my fingers and reads
it to herself.

I look around me at the plantation. The slaves work their way in
rows through the rice fields, looking from a distance like an army of

ants. In the other direction, Master's house sits empty in the lush meadow, its trellises thick with green vines and yellow trumpet-shaped Jessamine flowers.

"Is it really true?" Emma asks.

"It would seem so," I say and take the letter back for another look. "October."

Emma looks out over the plantation now.

"October," she giggles.

I fold the letter and slip it back into the envelope. Standing, I bend over and kiss Emma. It's hard not to feel giddy, too.

"I've got to get back to work now," I say. "You know we mustn't tell a word of this to anyone?"

"Yes, Mama." Emma nods dutifully. Her expression is serious again, but there's a glimmer in her eyes that I haven't seen in so long.

"October," I say, planting one more kiss on top of her head.

"October," she says.

Walking back to the hospital, I see Granny Gin coming up the path carrying a baby. My heart sinks.

"Poor thing's got the fever," she calls out to me.

I run to meet her and take the child from her arms. It's Jefferson, one of Hope's twins. Dressed only in his diaper cloth, his skin is hot to the touch.

"Oh, Granny Gin."

"I know, child. I know," she says. Granny places her hand on the baby's head and says a short prayer. Then she turns and limps back down the path, shaking her head.

Once the twins were old enough to be weaned from their mama's breast, they were placed in the care of Granny Gin. During the fall and winter, Hope and Eli were permitted to take the boys to the slaves' quarters on Sundays. But when spring returned and the Beanes made their preparations for Pawley's Island, Hope and Eli were informed they both would be making the trip this year.

"That's nearly five months," Hope had bawled. Mrs. Beane calmly explained how difficult the previous summer had been on the family without Hope's help at the island.

"The babies will be well cared for by Granny Gin," the Missus had said. "It would be selfish of you to expect another summer of leisure when there is so much work to be done."

So Hope and Eli left in May for the island. And now one of their precious boys is sick with the fever.

"Zeta," I call out as I reach the hospital. She swings the door open wide. I rush past her and lay Jefferson down on a cot. "What'll we do?"

The witch clutches at her necklace, chanting and launching into her ritual dance. Her eyes roll back into her head.

"Zeta!" *Dancing and chanting won't save this child.* I grab hold of the old woman and shake her. "What can we do?"

"Easy now," she says, pulling out of her self-induced trance.

"Sorry," I say, releasing my grip and stepping back. A wave of hopelessness suddenly washes over me. I look back at Jefferson and ask again, feebly, "What can we do?"

"Not much to do," Zeta says what I already know in my heart, "but to pray and try to make him more comfortable."

We launch into the routine we've undertaken dozens of times before. I pump some fresh cool water from the well. With a wet cloth, I dab at Jefferson's forehead, chest and arms, to cool the fever. Zeta chants and gyrates as she mixes up a poultice of chamomile and lavender and other soothing ingredients. Then she spreads the paste on the baby's chest and neck. He breathes in the fragrant aroma and his muscles relax.

He'll probably fight and hang on for a few more days. But his fate is sealed. We lose so many slaves to the fever every summer. The babies are the hardest to let go. Poor Hope and Eli won't even get a chance to say good-bye to their precious son.

I've been thinking about what I'd like to do when we leave the plantation. It's a nice way to pass the long hot days, but it's a luxury I haven't allowed myself until only recently.

Maybe there's still a way I can find out where John and Sam were sold. I could work as a seamstress, save up money to buy back their freedom. Then we could all move North and be a family again. It seems impossible. Then again I never dreamed it would be possible for Jim to become a free man and rescue Emma and me. Perhaps anything is truly possible.

Pennsylvania holds so many memories. It would be too painful to go back and try to somehow pick up where we left off there. I could never return to Mill Green, despite Mrs. Ashmore's renewed kindness.

New York would be wonderful. We could start a new life, rent an apartment in one of the brownstones in the heart of the city. How we'd get there is a mystery.

Jim's letter didn't say if he plans to return to Mill Green after emancipating us, or if he wants to move North, as I do. But I'm hoping he will have some ideas about where we can go and how we can get there.

Chapter 35

Mill Green, Maryland

For the first time in his life, Jim was going to leave Maryland. For the first time, he was going to step off Mrs. Ashmore's property and leave Mill Green as a free man.

In Havre de Grace he would board a steamboat and travel down the Chesapeake Bay and out along the coast to South Carolina. From there, he would walk or pay for passage by coach across South Carolina to the Beane Plantation.

Jim had never been on his own, but he was not naïve. A black man traveling alone in the Deep South would no doubt invite trouble. He counted his money, separating the bills and coins into piles of varying amounts. Then he carefully tucked the piles into various purses and billfolds. These would be stowed separately—in his bag, in his coat pocket, under his hat, hidden in his undershorts, tied around his calf beneath his pant leg. If he were to be robbed, the thieves would not get his entire fortune.

The morning of his departure, Jim packed his few possessions into a canvas rucksack—a worn cotton shirt and pants, a thin wool blanket, a wooden box containing quills and ink and pencils, an envelope stuffed with blank writing paper, maps and money purse, a pocketknife and the leather-bound copy of Dickens's *American Notes*. He tucked his emancipation papers in his coat pocket with a billfold containing twenty dollars.

He closed up the bag and slung it over his shoulder. Then he strode out of the small shed that had been his home for roughly 20 years. He did not look back.

"I'm heading off now, ma'am," Jim called out to Mrs. Ashmore from the front porch of her home.

She came through the doorway in a rush.

"Oh, it's so early yet. Won't you stay for some breakfast? How about a cup of coffee?"

Jim stood at the edge of the porch, his coat buttoned up, his floppy canvas hat atop his head. There was an energy about him the widow could almost feel. He flexed his grip on the strap at his shoulder. He looked up the road and squinted.

"I don't think so, ma'am. I'd like to get to Havre de Grace by noon."

"Yes. I understand."

The widow cast her eyes down, and the two stood quietly for a moment.

"You'll need food for the trip!" Mrs. Ashmore rushed back into the house. In almost no time, she reemerged onto the porch with a bundle tied up in an empty salt sack. She shrugged her shoulders. "It's just a few biscuits and some salt pork, but it should help keep a little hop in your step."

"That's so kind of you, ma'am."

Jim set down his bag, knelt beside it and carefully tucked the food bundle inside. When he stood again, the widow threw her arms around him in a tight embrace.

"Mrs. Ashmore!"

Jim patted her back tentatively and looked around.

"You're gonna get me hanged from the nearest tree, if anyone sees you hugging on me so."

The widow released him and smoothed invisible wrinkles from her apron.

"No," she said. "No harm is going to come to you, my boy. You're going to have a safe journey. I couldn't be more sure of it."

Jim nodded. He picked up his bag, then hurried down the porch steps and across the lawn.

When he reached the end of the yard, he stopped and looked back. The widow was watching him still. He flashed her a broad smile and waved.

"Good-bye!" She smiled and waved back, as he found his stride and disappeared down the road.

Havre de Grace was just a little more than 15 miles south east of Mill Green. Jim knew the way. He and the widow had traveled there by horse and wagon several times to sell candles. Walking there took considerably longer, but Jim enjoyed the journey nonetheless.

He kept a brisk pace, taking the occasional shortcut over and across the hillside. The early October air cooled his lungs as he huffed his way along. By midmorning, he reached the half-way point in Glenville and decided to break for lunch at Deer Creek.

"Let's just see what Mrs. Ashmore put all together here," Jim said to himself as he settled down on the creek bed.

He removed his tin cup and lunch from his rucksack. He dipped the cup into the flowing creek and took a big long drink. The water was cold and clear. Jim opened the bundle Mrs. Ashmore had prepared. It contained biscuits and salt pork, as promised. It also had two pieces of saltwater taffy from the box Susanna had given the widow on her birthday.

"Ah-ha," he laughed. "I knew she'd sneak in a little something special."

Jim ate the biscuits and meat, and drank down another full cup of water. Then he lay back on the gentle slope of the creek bed and tucked his hands behind his head. The autumn sun warmed his cheeks. The bubbling creek sang to him.

"So this is what it feels like," he whispered.

After a bit, he sat up and surveyed the land around him.

"I wonder what it would cost to buy a plot somewheres around here."

He pulled his free papers from his coat pocket and carefully unfolded them. He read them for the hundredth time. He imagined someday stowing them safely in a decorative cedar box along with land papers in the sitting room of his very own house. If you could buy a person for $300, Jim figured, a plot of land must surely cost less.

Jim arrived at the lock house at about two o'clock.

"I'd like to buy passage to South Carolina, please."

The young man at the ticket window looked up. His skin was badly scarred, likely from a childhood bout with small pox. He scratched at his head with dirty nails.

"Is that so?"

"Yessir," said Jim, shifting his weight from one foot to another.

"If you're on the run, it'd make more sense to go North, don't ya think?"

Jim couldn't tell if the young man was playing with him or not.

"I'm a free man, sir," Jim said. He pulled his papers from his coat pocket and set them on the counter.

The young man looked down at the papers, then called out to the lockmaster in the back room. A rotund fellow with thinning hair appeared and waddled up to the ticket counter. The young man relayed Jim's request.

"We only got boats going as far as Virginia today," the lockmaster said, squinting at Jim's papers. "You'd have to buy passage further south when you get there."

"That'd be just fine, sir," Jim replied.

The men seemed to be thinking it over. They looked alternately at Jim and his papers. Finally, the lockmaster pushed the documents back across the counter.

"It's $10 will get you to Virginia," he said.

"10?" Jim hastily folded his papers and tucked them away. He looked at the sign posted overhead. "It says there passage to Virginia is $4."

"Does it?" The young man leaned forward to look at the sign. "Well, that's the old price."

"The old price," Jim repeated cautiously.

"Yep," the lockmaster said firmly. "It's $10 will get you to Virginia today."

Jim nodded slowly. What choice did he have? He pulled his billfold from his pocket, removed $10 and placed the money on the counter. The men just looked at it.

"It's $10 will get me to Virginia today," Jim said.

The lockmaster finally nodded and retrieved the payment.

"Boat leaves in half an hour," he said, handing Jim the ticket. "Be on time, and stay below deck while you're on board. No Niggers allowed up top."

"Yessir."

Jim moved quickly to the boat dock. He didn't want to risk missing its departure, after having paid a king's ransom for passage across the bay. He stopped short at the boarding plank.

The steam boat bobbed lazily in the lock. The plank, three feet wide at best, stretched from the lock foundation across the water to the boat deck. It shifted and slid as the boat rocked and dipped. Jim eyed the plank. He eyed the boat. He thought of Jerry Morgan's final moments in life.

"Get a move on, Nigger!"

Jim swung around. A man and woman had come up behind him, waiting to board. The man had grown impatient with Jim's hesitation.

"Sorry sir," Jim blurted. "You go on ahead of me."

He stepped aside, and the couple strode past him up onto the boat.

Jim waited a moment more. Then he took in a deep breath and quickly crossed over the plank before breathing out again. Once safely on deck, he peered over the railing at the water below. It was dark. He couldn't see its depths.

"Ticket?" The ship's hand approached him.

Jim handed over the ticket. The man punched it, handed it back.

"No Niggers allowed up top," he said.

"No sir. I mean, yes sir," Jim stammered. "I mean, I'll go below deck straight away."

Jim headed for the stairwell. The cast iron spiral was so narrow he had to hold his rucksack above his head as he made his way down.

Below deck the air smelled of mold and animal waste. At the far end of the compartment, an assortment of crates containing chickens and ducks were stacked and secured with ropes. Lining the other walls were oak barrels, steamer trunks and cartons of various sizes. On the floor, in the middle of it all, sat about a dozen Negroes shackled together with heavy irons.

The human cargo took Jim by surprise. And he nearly fell over the top of them as he stepped off the staircase in the dim light.

"Pardon me," he mumbled, removing his hat.

There were no benches below deck. Jim eyed an open space in the corner. He scooted past the slaves and sank to the floor with his bag in his lap. His stomach churned with the sway of the boat. The chickens clucked softly. Jim closed his eyes and tried to imagine himself lying back on the creek bed with the sun on this face.

"How come you ain't in chains?" A child's voice broke the quiet.

Jim opened his eyes and met the child's stare.

"Shhh, baby," his mother scolded.

But Jim could see the question in her eyes, too. It was in each of their eyes—every man, woman and child burdened by the shackles in the cramped compartment. He felt his cheeks get hot. He cast his eyes down to avoid their stares.

"My master, he-he don't chain me when we travel by boat," Jim lied, ashamed to admit he was free.

It was dusk when the boat finally made port in Norfolk. Jim thanked the Lord he hadn't bought passage all the way to South Carolina. And he resolved to travel only by land from then on.

"Excuse me, sir. Can you tell me where the shipping yard is?" Jim asked one of the hands unloading luggage. His new plan was to hitch a ride on a wagon headed to Richmond.

"Take a left at the end of Congress Street," the man said, pointing the way.

Jim made his way quickly down Congress and turned into the shipping yard. A handful of men were gathered near some wagons already loaded with goods. They watched him approach.

"Good evening," Jim said. "I wonder, if I might ask, are any of these wagons headed to Richmond?"

A blond-haired man, skinny as a bean pole, spit a stream of dark tobacco juice onto the ground at Jim's feet. "Why you want to know?"

Jim resisted the urge to step away from the tobacco stain in the dirt. "I was hoping to get a ride. I'm happy to pay for my passage."

"Slaves don't have money to spend for nothing," the bean pole said. "Where'd you get money from? You steal it?"

Jim looked from one man to the next. This was harder than he had expected.

"I earned wages as a free man up in Maryland," he said.

A second man stepped up then and demanded to see Jim's free papers. Jim removed them from his coat pocket, unfolded the papers, and held them up for all to see. The man leaned in for a closer look.

"Well, boy, I got some bad news for you," he finally said, shaking his head. "Now, I know you can't read, 'cause you a Nigger. So I'm sorry to break it to you, but these papers don't actually say you're a free man."

Jim squinted slightly.

"What do they say?" the bean pole asked.

"They say he's the queen of Spain!"

With this, the group broke out in raucous laughter. Jim could smell whiskey on their breath. He stuffed his papers back into his pocket and pretended to laugh along. After a moment, the group settled down.

"I don't care if you are the queen of Spain, I'll give you ride," a horse-faced man said, moving in closer to Jim. "How much money did you say you got?"

The hairs on the back of Jim's neck began to prickle. He took a small step back.

"Oh, not that much, really. A couple dollars, I think."

The group closed in around him a bit tighter. The shroud of night had fallen completely. Jim took a couple more steps back.

"Only a couple dollars, huh?" the bean pole said. "Hell, that's okay by me. I'll give you a ride for a couple dollars."

"Let me take your bag for you," the horse-faced man said, tugging at Jim's shoulder strap. "We can get going right now if you want."

Jim jerked from the man's grip.

"Oh, no thank you," he blurted. "I wouldn't want to trouble you tonight. I'll just come back in the morning."

Jim turned and ran from the shipping yard. Ran as fast as he could. He heard the men laughing. Calling out to him to come on back. But he just kept running, blindly, down the dark road away from the city. The shipyard voices faded in the distance.

When he could run no more, Jim stumbled off the road and into a shallow ditch. He crawled farther away from the road, finding refuge in the bushes, and pulled his bag to his heaving chest. He waited for his pounding heart to settle down.

Things were not going at all like he had planned.

Chapter 36

Mill Green, Maryland

The bell above the door jingled as Mrs. Ashmore entered the newspaper office in Mill Green. A clerk emerged from the back room, greeting the widow with a courteous smile.

"How may I help you today, Mrs. Ashmore?" he said.

"I'd like to place an advertisement in the paper."

"For your candles?" he asked.

"No," the widow replied. "Help wanted."

She handed the clerk a note containing the verbiage for her ad:

Help wanted. Must be strong and able-bodied. Free board and monthly stipend will be provided in exchange for household repairs, weekly errands and maintenance of the woodpile, livestock and grounds at the Ashmore Estate. Interested parties may inquire at the premises after noon Monday through Friday.

The widow was learning to enjoy her newfound independence. Still, she realized that, getting on in age, there were many tasks which she could not complete herself. She would miss Jim's friendship terribly, but she was confident she could find a suitable replacement for the work that needed to be done.

"How long would you like it to run?" asked the clerk.

"Let's start with two weeks," she said. "The economy being what it is, I should think the position can be filled quickly. Wouldn't you agree?"

"Oh yes, ma'am," he said. "It's a fine job you're offering. Should take no time to fill. In fact, I've got a cousin who might be interested. I'll let him know about it straight away."

"I would appreciate that," Mrs. Ashmore said.

"If you don't mind my asking," the clerk added, "what happened to that Negro you had working up at your place?"

"He's free now."

"Oh," said the clerk. The young man seemed to struggle for words to continue the conversation. It was the same reaction most people had when they learned the widow had freed her only slave, and she had already become adept at changing the subject quickly.

"I'll look forward to meeting your cousin," she said. "What is his name?"

"Isaac, ma'am," said the clerk. "Isaac Ferryman is his name."

"Very good then," said the widow, turning toward the door. "Let Mr. Ferryman know that I'll be pleased to meet him, and thank you, again, for your assistance."

"Thank you, ma'am," said the clerk, waving as the old woman pulled open the door and left the office. "Good-bye now."

The widow made the rest of her usual errands while in town, checking on candle sales at the general store and stopping in at the post office. Jim had promised to write to her as soon as he arrived in South Carolina and had secured Margaret's freedom. They had said their good-byes nearly two weeks before, so she wasn't expecting word from him yet. In fact, she wasn't really expecting word from him at all. As she had watched Jim walk down the road away from her estate, Mrs. Ashmore had been struck with a powerful sense of finality. In her heart, she'd somehow known that she would never see nor hear from her friend again.

"Hiya, Nat," Jake said as Nathan Bemis strode into the tavern late one Friday night. "What can I get ya?"

"Something strong," Nat said, plopping onto a stool and tossing a folded newspaper down onto the bar.

Jake poured a shot of whiskey, and Nat downed it in one gulp.

"I'll take another."

The barkeep poured a second shot, carefully eyeing his customer.

"You all right there, Nat?" he asked. "Don't usually see you in here this late at night."

"Just hiding from the wife, Jake. She's been riding me all day, because of this damned thing."

Nat pushed the newspaper toward Jake, who picked it up and read the advertisement that had been circled.

"What happened to her Nigger?" Jake asked.

"What happened to her Nigger?" Nat repeated. "Well, I'll tell you what happened to him, Jake. First, Mother Ashmore goes and hands over her deed of property to him. Makes him a free man, without even asking for so much as a penny in return."

Nat tossed back his drink and exhaled heavily.

"And then we see this ad in the paper, and Susanna goes to ask her mother why she needs an extra hand at the estate," he continued. "Turns out, the Nigger decided he's going after Margaret Morgan down in South Carolina, to buy *her* freedom, and Mother Ashmore is helping to foot the bill!"

Jake whistled through his teeth. He pushed the paper back toward Nat.

"You better hide that," he warned. "Ed's outside taking a leak. If he catches wind of this . . . "

"If I catch wind of what?" Prigg bellowed from the doorway. A hush came over the tavern. He stormed over to the bar, snatched the newspaper out of Nat's hand and read the ad.

"How could you let this happen?" Prigg demanded, getting in Nat's face.

"Don't you start in on me, too, Ed," Nat returned. "One nagging wife is plenty!"

"After all I done," the bounty hunter bellowed. He picked up a stool and heaved it across the tavern. The usual patrons dodged and ducked for cover as the stool crashed against the wall and busted into pieces. "Son of a bitch!"

Nat jumped up from his seat.

"What? You think I'm doing a dance over this?" he hollered back. "After all you've done? What about everything I've done, Ed? This is bullshit, but there's nothing either one of us can do about it now."

"Look here, boys," Jake interrupted. "Settle on down. Have a seat."

Nat followed the barkeep's orders. He exhaled and slumped back onto his stool. But Prigg stood firm by the bar, his chest heaving, his fists clenched at his sides. This wasn't a fight he was willing to lose.

"Maybe there's nothing you can do about it, Nat," he said through clenched teeth. "But there's plenty I can do."

Jake didn't like the look in Prigg's eyes. It was the same wild, angry look he'd seen in the eyes of a feral hog he'd caught rooting through the trash behind the tavern. Jake had tried to frighten the hog off, but it wouldn't back down, so he'd had to put a bullet between its eyes.

"Set me up with another pint," Prigg ordered. "I've gotta think this through."

Prigg began pacing back and forth in front of the bar. Jake stood his ground. After a moment, Prigg realized his mug was still empty. He picked it up, turned it upside down with a sneer and then pounded it back down in front of Jake.

"Sorry, Ed, I can't serve you any more tonight," Jake said. "Why don't you go on home and sleep this off."

"Don't talk to me like I'm some kind of child," Prigg hissed, moving in closer. "Just do your job and give me a damn drink."

"Sorry, Ed." Jake discreetly reached below the bar and took hold of the wooden club he kept tucked away for such occasions.

"Sorry, my ass!" Prigg yelled. All at once, the drunk lashed out at everything around him. He hurled his mug across the bar and pushed Nat right off his stool. Then he spun around and overturned a table loaded with drinks and food. The men gathered around it jumped up and scurried out of arm's reach.

"That'll do!" Jake slammed his club down onto the bar like a lightning bolt. His voice boomed through the quiet that followed.

Prigg spun around. Spittle flew from his mouth as he panted and trembled with rage.

"You're pushing our friendship, Ed," Jake warned with calm deliberation. "You stop busting up my place right now, or I'll bust open your head like a walnut."

Tension crackled through the air as the tavern patrons stealthily maneuvered about the room, jockeying for safer positions. Nat hauled himself up from the floor, his palms raised to Prigg in a gesture he hoped would be interpreted as friendly. Prigg pointed a crooked finger at him.

"There *is* something that can be done about this," Prigg said.

Nat nodded, his arms still raised in surrender.

Prigg eyed the room, jabbing his finger through the air at each of the bar's patrons one by one.

"I'll tell you all exactly what can be done," he said.

The men froze in their tracks, like so many marble statues in an assortment of chaotic poses.

"I'm gonna track that Nigger down and make him regret the day he became a free man," Prigg said.

He resumed pacing, from one end of the bar to the other, back and forth. No one else dared speak.

"And then I'm gonna find Margaret Morgan," Prigg continued, "and make her pay for all the suffering her miserable existence has brought to my life."

Prigg picked up Nat's whiskey glass from the bar and threw back the drink in one swallow. Then he swaggered to the tavern door. He turned and pointed again at Nat, nodding.

"I'm going to end this," he vowed. "Once and for all."

Then he pounded the door open with his fist and strode out into the darkness.

The half-dozen or so men in the tavern remained frozen for a good minute, before one of them finally bent down to correct an upturned chair and another started picking up the bits and pieces of the broken stool.

"Should I follow him . . . make sure he gets home all right?" one fellow asked hesitantly.

"Nope," Jake said. "Where he's headed, you don't want to follow."

Chapter 37

Margaret

It's October again at the plantation.

The Beanes returned from Pawley's Island this afternoon. Once the wagons were unloaded, the slaves were discharged from their duties for the day.

Standing at the hospital porch, clutching my heart, I watch Hope bolt from the big house down the path to Granny Gin's to see her sons. A few minutes later, I can hear her wail, as Granny breaks the tragic news about Jefferson.

It brings me right back to the slave auction, as if it had happened just yesterday, watching my boys disappear in front of my very eyes. And I break down myself, right here on the hospital porch, into a heap of painful sobs—for Hope, for little Jefferson, for Jerry and my boys, for everything that has been lost to this wretched business of slavery.

Three weeks now since the Beanes returned, and I've had no word yet from Jim. His last letter came months ago.

At least things have quieted down at the hospital. The heavy rains of summer have eased, and the cooler temperatures are bringing some relief to the field hands as they finish up from the harvest.

I pass the time planting seeds for winter vegetables—cabbage, onions, mustard greens. I'm alone at my work in the garden today. Emma is down at Granny Gin's helping make up ash cakes for the little ones. Something catches my eye as I pull at the prickly weeds. I look up from the garden rows to see Mrs. Beane rushing Hope up the path. Her movements are frantic. I jump up and run to meet them.

"What happened?" I ask, seeing Hope's forearm wrapped in a blood-soaked towel.

"She cut herself polishing the silver!"

"Let's get her inside," I say.

We go into the hospital and Madame Zeta pulls around a stool for the patient. The missus hovers by the door, pale, nervous. Hope looks up at me, biting her lower lip.

"Easy now," I say, pulling back the bandage. "Let's just have a look."

The rag is soaked through with blood, but Hope's arm appears intact. I scan up and down her wrist. There is no injury. Our eyes meet. Without words, she tells me how much she has risked to come and see me today. I wrap the towel back over her arm and press down.

"It's just a nick," I say. "It'll take a bit of time to stitch that up, but you'll be fine."

"Take all the time you need," Mrs. Beane says.

Madame Zeta brings my sewing basket, watching me closely. It's amazing how we have all learned to say so much to one another without even uttering a single word. She understands perfectly what I need.

"Lemme walk you back on over to the big house, Missy Simone," the old witch says, then clucks through her teeth. "What a terrible ordeal this has been for ya. I'll make you a nice cuppa tea. Help settle your nerves."

Simone plays right into it. "Oh, thank you, Zeta."

I wait to make sure they are a safe distance down the path before I finally speak.

"What is this all about, Hope?"

"I had to come see you," she says. "It couldn't wait."

"And the blood?"

"Nanny's roasting a chicken for dinner." Hope grins slyly, but I'm not amused.

"Well, how am I supposed to stitch up a wound that doesn't exist? Master will want to have a look when we're through, you know."

Hope's eyes dart from me to her arm. "I hadn't thought of that," she says hesitantly. Then, after a moment of reflection, a look of determination comes to her face. "Cut me then."

"Oh, Hope, I can't."

"You have to."

I exhale and shake my head. She's right. So I lay out the items I'll need—my jackknife, needle and thread, fresh bandages. I tell her to look away, and I quickly slice a small mark into her lovely brown skin. She whimpers and bites her lip again, in real pain this time.

"So," I say, as I apply a poultice to ease the pain of her fresh wound. "Why don't you tell me what this is all about."

"A man came to see Master yesterday morning," she says. "A *colored* man."

She has my attention now. I stop working for just a moment, then continue tearing fresh strips of cloth for her bandage.

"They talked on the veranda. I was just inside the door polishing the silver, so I could hear most of what they was saying. He introduced himself as Mr. Green and said he come to make a fair offer in the purchase of two of Master's slaves. He wanted to buy you and Emma."

Hope pauses. She studies my face, searching for answers in my expression.

"Do you know him, Margaret? Did you know he was coming?"

I nod, mute. I want to kick up my heels and shout for joy. I want to tell her all about the letters and how good things come to those who persevere. But it has occurred to me that Hope didn't risk punishment and injury to come tell me any good news.

"Master laughed at him," Hope continues. "Said, as far as he knows, Niggers don't carry the title of Mister. So Mr. Green said he was a freeman from Maryland and he showed Master Beane some papers he had in his pocket."

"His free papers," I say, nodding. "Jerry never left the house without his."

"Oh, Margaret," Hope says. Her voice cracks and she clears her throat. I wait, but she doesn't continue.

"What happened, Hope?"

"Master turned him away," she blurts.

"He what?"

"Said he ain't in the business of selling slaves, especially to a lying piece of shit Nigger," Hope says. "And then he ripped up the man's papers, Margaret. Just ripped 'em up and threw 'em in the air and laughed."

"Damn him," I say. Anger bubbles up inside me like a hot spring. "Damn him straight to hell!"

I stare at the wall, taking in big deliberate breaths and releasing them slowly. How will we ever escape this infernal place? And how will poor Jim get home without his free papers?

Hope just sits there, watching me. After a minute or two, I hold my hand out in front of me, to test my steadiness. Can't sew with a shaky hand. My fingers hold steady, like stones in the stream.

"All right now," I say. "Look away again and let me get you stitched up. I'll be quick."

Hope flinches a little each time my needle pierces her skin, but she doesn't pull away. Her strength takes me by surprise.

"All done." I pump fresh water into the wash basin and begin my ritual of scrubbing and rinsing my hands and utensils.

"Are you gonna run?" Hope asks.

"W—what?"

"You heard me."

"Why would you ask such a thing?"

I continue at my washing, shaking my head back and forth. My heart pounds wildly. Neither of us speaks for a moment.

"You're the strongest person I ever met, Margaret. If anyone could get away from here, you could."

All I can do is shrug and keep scrubbing.

"Take Washington with you."

With that I turn and face her square on.

"What on God's green earth has gotten into you, Hope?"

She nods her head at me. "Eli and me talked about it last night. We want you to take him."

"No, Hope. I can't take the baby."

"You can, and you must." She walks to me now, takes my wet hands into hers. "You know what it's like, Margaret, to lose a child."

"Yes," I sigh. "I do."

A few more minutes pass as we stand holding hands in the hospital. My mind is racing. Should I run after all? And if I did, how could I possibly get away safely with Emma *and* a baby?

"It's too dangerous, Hope. Even if I could somehow manage it, what do you think Master would do to you and Eli when he found the baby gone?"

"Doesn't matter what he do to us. He can't cause me any more pain than I already got."

I pull her to me, hug her tight. Then I take hold of her shoulders and push her back out at arm's length.

"You're still grieving for Jefferson, honey, that's all," I say.

"Yes," Hope nods. "And are you trying to tell me that pain's gonna pass?"

I don't answer. She and I both know that it won't pass. Not ever.

"Please just think about it, Margaret. Will you do that for me?"

Against my better judgment, I nod, giving in to Hope's heartfelt plea. She hugs me again and hurries to leave. She pauses before slipping through the doorway.

"Don't tell me when, Margaret," she says. "Just take him. Just take him and don't look back."

It's impossible to sleep. You'd think it was the middle of July, the way I'm lying here sweating, suffocating. But it ain't the heat or the mugginess or the fever that torments me. It's the truth. It's knowing that I can never leave this wretched place in an honest way. I roll off my bed mat and tip-toe out of the hospital into the night.

I slink through the shadows down to the creek and sit beneath my old cypress tree. The half moon makes the water sparkle as it burbles along.

Sure, I've thought about running. Thought about it a hundred times or more. I have a pretty good idea how I'd pull it off, too. But it always seemed wrong to break the law that way, to steal my own daughter in the middle of the night and make criminals of us both. Then again, everything about this place is backwards and wrong. When I think of it that way, running makes perfect and logical sense. We were free. So the law has already been broken once. Maybe running would somehow set things right again.

The sky shifts to a deep pink that tells me the sun will break in another half hour or so. Down at the slaves' quarters, the field hands will soon be making their ashcakes for the day. The smoke of their communal fire travels on the breeze and jolts me into the new day. I jump up and hurry back to the hospital before the coming light gives me away.

"Just picked the last of the butter beans," Emma says to me as I come into the garden. She's kneeling beside a wide basket, already heaped full with the day's pickings.

"That'll make a nice soup for Granny and the children," I say. Emma agrees.

I kneel down beside her and place my hand on her thigh.

"I have bad news about Jim."

"He's not coming?" She looks up at me.

"No, honey, he came, just like he promised. Hope saw him at the big house day before yesterday. But Master turned him away, refused to sell us."

Emma eyes narrow. Her mouth draws into a knot.

"That isn't fair," she says with a huff. She looks around frantically, at the garden rows, at the hospital, at the fields. "What'll we do now?"

I reach out and cradle her chin in my hand, turn her face to mine. "We're going to run."

Her eyes go wide. She gasps.

"Really and truly?" she says.

I nod.

"But you said it was wrong to run, that we need to fight."

"That's true, baby. But now that I know Master won't ever sell us our freedom, not for any price, then running is the only way we *can* fight."

Emma nods in agreement. She brushes the dirt from her hands and springs to her feet. "When are we going?"

"Shhhh!" I reach up and grab her arm, pull her back down into the dirt with me. I look around, over my shoulders, praying we're truly alone. "For heaven's sake, child."

"Sorry, Mama," she giggles. Her determination, her optimism, her utter lack of fear make me proud and scared to death at the same time.

"Emma, honey, we have to be so careful. This won't be at all easy," I whisper. She settles back down, gives me her undivided attention again. "We'll have to wait until the spring, when the Beanes leave for the island again. It'll be safer then."

She exhales heavily. I'm disappointed, too. Seems like all we've been doing is waiting our lives away since the day Mr. Prigg crashed through our cabin door. The waiting is becoming intolerable. But she seems to understand. I can see the idea running through her mind. Finally, she gives one quick nod.

"Then we'll go in the spring," she says.

Chapter 38

Margaret

My eyes fly open in the darkness. Will I ever sleep through the night in this infernal place?

A hulking shadow of a figure looms over me. Am I dreaming after all? I reach out, expecting my hand to go right through the shadow and disprove my imagination. My hand collides with its solid chest! Long fingers, dirty and moist, clamp down over my mouth. It's impossible to scream. My heart pounds wildly and every inch of my skin seems to burn from the inside. My hands fly up to fight off the intruder.

"Easy, Miss Margaret. Shhhh. It's me, Jim, from Mill Green."

My muscles relax, and the shadow eases the tension over my mouth.

"Sorry I scared you," he whispers.

He removes his hand from my mouth, and I sit up. It's still hard to make him out in the dark, so I reach out to feel his face. I recognize his gentle smile beneath my fingertips.

"Oh, Jim," I whisper, wrapping my arms around him. "Dear, Jim. You shouldn't have come back. It isn't safe."

I take his hand and lead him to the hospital door. Peeking out, I look around in the dim moonlight. All is quiet.

"Follow me." I crouch low and run for the cover of my cypress tree. He stays close behind. When we are safely hidden beside the creek bed, I give him another hug.

"I heard what happened the other day, with your free papers. I'm so sorry, Jim, to have gotten you into this mess. I should never have let you come here."

"It ain't your fault, Margaret. Don't you talk like that."

"But why did you come back, Jim? You must go back to Mill Green just as quickly as you can, so Mrs. Ashmore can renew your papers."

Jim shakes his head solemnly.

"No, it's too late for all that now."

"What do you mean?"

"After I left the plantation the other day, I was so scared, Margaret. I know what happened to you without any papers, and I was so worried I'd get kidnapped and shipped even deeper south."

It's a rational fear. I put my hand to his cheek, nod.

"But I thought I might be safe for a time if I returned to the stable in town where I'd spent the night before. The blacksmith there already saw my papers. For a dollar a night, he let me sleep in the stable and wash up in the trough in the morning. Anyways, I was lying there in one of the stalls and I heard some men talking outside."

Jim takes my hands in his. He seems at a loss for words.

"Mr. Prigg followed me here, Margaret."

"What? Why would he do that?"

"He's telling people he's on the hunt for a runaway Nigger with forged free papers, goes by the name Jim Green."

"Oh, dear God," I say.

"It gets worse. Mr. Prigg's saying he came here for you, too, Margaret. That you're wanted for murder in Mill Green, and he's gonna take you back there for trial."

"I don't understand. Why would he say all that?"

Jim doesn't answer. He just shrugs, shakes his head. Doesn't matter, anyway. Prigg will come to the plantation and tell his lies, and Master Beane will gladly believe him. There's no telling what Prigg has in mind for when he gets his hands on me again. But I'm sure it can't be anything good.

"We got to run, Margaret," Jim finally says. "And we don't have much time."

He's right. We must flee tonight. But we have nothing prepared, no rations packed. The night is half gone, which won't give us much of a head start. We'll need to create some sort of distraction.

Jim smiles at me. "You've got a plan."

"Yes," I say, smiling back, in spite of myself. "I have a plan."

There's an old row boat down by the levees on the west side of the rice fields. I noticed it a few months ago, when I was delivering garlic to the field hands. It was in good condition, though long neglected. When no one was watching, I covered it with fern branches and Indian grass. It was never reported missing, and the overseer never went looking for it.

"We'll take the boat into the swamp," I explain. "No one will even miss it."

Jim's eyes grow wide. "No, no, Margaret. There must be some other way than that."

"It's perfect. The dogs won't be able to track our scent through the water, and the swamp will take us west. Master and everyone else will expect us to run north."

"But I can't swim," he says, a panicked look taking hold of his face.

"Then you better stay in the boat," I say bluntly. He half chuckles and nods in agreement.

I give Jim directions down to the boat, telling him to stay to the bridges and walkways in the fields. He takes off across the creek, and I run back to the hospital.

Inside, I quietly fill my sewing basket with a handful of onions and cucumbers Emma picked from the garden this morning. A small jar of honey goes in last. Then I roll up my blanket and pad back toward the door.

"Planning a midnight picnic, Miss Margaret?"

Madame Zeta is sitting up in her cot. She must have been watching me the whole time. How could I have missed it?

"Oh . . . I . . . uh . . . "

"Make sure you take some garlic with ya, too," she whispers, pointing to her table of potions. "It'll help ward off the gator ghosts."

"Oh, Zeta," I say, rushing to her side and collapsing on the ground at her feet. I put my head on her lap, hug her crooked legs. "Thank you."

She strokes my hair for a brief moment, then tells me to hurry along. There's no time to waste. With my basket loaded down, I sprint out of the hospital and down the path to Granny Gin's.

Emma is startled when I wake her, but she snaps to fast. I quickly tell her about Jim and Mr. Prigg and why we must leave tonight. The dear thing. She's delighted that we're leaving sooner than planned! She doesn't understand how much more dangerous this early departure will make our journey.

"Take little Washington and meet me down by the boat. Jim is already there," I say, putting the honey jar in her hand. "If the baby cries, put a little of this on his fingers to quiet him."

"Where are *you* going?" Emma asks, a trace of alarm creeping into her voice.

"I've got to create a distraction, so Master won't notice we're gone right away."

"I'm going with you," she says.

"No, Emma, you have to make sure the baby stays safe." I pull her in for a good tight hug. "I'll be all right. I'll see you at the boat. You be ready."

"Ok, Mama."

I wait outside, behind the children's shack, until I see Emma safely exit and dart to the trees with her precious bundle in her arms. Then I run through the shadows toward the barn.

The horses whinny softly, alerted to my scent as I slip into the barn. A church hymn suddenly comes to mind, and I sing, ever so quietly, while I feel around in the dark for the lamp and flint stones the barn hands keep in a box by the door.

Heaven's bell a-ringing.
I know the road.
Jesus is sittin' on the waterside.
Do come along.
Do let us go.
Jesus is sittin' on the waterside.

The animals quiet down, but stay alert, their hooves shifting in their stalls. My eyes slowly adjust to the dark inside. I slide a bale of hay toward the front by the lantern. Then, with handfuls of hay, I create a trail to the back of the barn. Finally, I soak the trail with oil from the lamp. All the while, my midnight serenade to the horses continues.

I push the barn doors open wide, looking around to make sure I'm still alone. The rest will have to happen fast. I unlatch each stall and nudge and coax the animals toward the open door. A couple horses take to a gentle trot and head out to pasture without much prodding. Two others meander more slowly, one stopping to munch on the hay bale at the door. I grab the flint stones and retreat once again to the back of the barn. Then with a snap and a spark, the end of the hay trail ignites and a crackle of flames moves quickly down the line. The remaining horses need no further prodding. They whinny and bolt from the barn, with me close on their tails.

Down the hill, across the pasture, to the cypress-lined creek bed, my feet seem to carry me with a force all their own. I drop to one knee behind a broad fern bush, try to breathe through the cramp in my side. An orange glow wells up bright inside the barn. Won't be but a few minutes more before the whole structure lights up and the pasture will be teeming with slaves and bucket lines from the creek.

My second wind comes to me, and I splash across the creek toward the rice fields. I take the same route I had dictated to Jim and Emma. Their wet foot prints still linger on the walkways, preserved by the humid night air. Up ahead, Jim paces back and forth at the levee.

"You didn't say anything about bringing a baby along," he whispers at me frantically. "You've got another son?"

"I do now."

My tone is calm, matter-of-fact. But I feel just as frantic on the inside.

Emma is seated in the boat, Washington asleep in her lap. I step down into the boat with one foot and place my basket in the bottom. Then I untie the rope. "You coming?" I reach my hand out to Jim.

In a huff of exasperation, he nods and takes my hand, stepping gingerly into the boat. I pick up an oar and use it to balance myself as I push off from the levee with my other foot.

We glide for a moment before I settle down on the bench at the back. Dipping the oar into the dark water, I guide our vessel toward the cover of the black gum trees deep in the swamp. The glow of the barn fire soon disappears from sight, as we are swallowed up by the massive trunks of pine and cypress standing firm in the water. Somewhere in the distance ahead, Zeta's gator ghosts moan.

The warm sun rising at our backs is a welcome miracle. We seemed to glide through the dark swamp forever, too afraid to speak or even breathe. It's such a relief to know we were heading the right direction, and that there are likely a few miles now between us and the plantation.

Emma and the baby lie sleeping in the bottom of the boat. Jim sits at the front, his back straight, his eyes taking in the strange landscape. He stands slowly, hands reaching to the heavens, to stretch his stiff muscles.

The boat bumps against a fallen tree and rocks just a bit. Jim's eyes fly open wide. His arms flail. In a sudden panic, he overcompensates to the movement of the boat and topples right over the edge into the water.

"Jim!"

I clamor to my knees and extend the oar for him to grab hold. He's too far away, flailing in the water, gasping for air. The children are jolted awake. Washington cries fearfully and Emma immediately pulls him close for comfort.

"Hold tight," I say to Emma, and I leap into the water.

My knees sink into the mud, but my head is dry. The water's only a few feet deep! I rise to my feet, while Jim continues to sputter and splash.

"Stand up, Jim! Stand up!"

I trod through the murky water, sinking almost to my ankles into the ooze of the swamp bed. Finally reaching him, I grab hold of his shirt and yank him to his feet. He coughs and wheezes, as we stand together, thigh deep in water. We exchange bewildered looks.

"Come on," I say, knowing the swamp holds more dangers than drowning. "Back into the boat. Quickly, now."

Jim sprawls into the boat, all arms and legs, while I hold the edge. Emma steadies herself, and I climb in next. We sit here, staring at one another, all dazed, dripping and muddied.

"Heh heh," Jim chuckles, a goofy smile spreading across his face.

"Jim, you idiot," I scold. "This isn't the slightest bit funny."

He continues to laugh at himself, more heartily. *Damn fool!* Emma tries to be somber, but it doesn't last. She breaks down laughing with him. I give them my most stern look. Little Washington smiles broadly, watching them both, and starts in with his hiccupy baby giggle.

Oh, here we go. It's contagious! I can't help but join in the laughter. And the stress, the fear, the tension of the night seems to melt away.

"You damn fool," I say, laughing hard now, reaching out for Jim's hand. He takes hold, squeezes tight.

A bird cries in the distance, piercing through the swamp, a stark reminder of where we are and how we got here. Its warning call is clear to all of us at once. We quiet ourselves, wipe the tears from our cheeks and continue on our journey in silence.

Emma pulls an ash cake from her pocket. She hands it to Washington and he gnaws at it with great delight.

Jim smiles at her.

"Smart girl."

Emma opens my basket next, examining its contents carefully. She removes a cucumber and my jackknife. Expertly cutting the gourd into three pieces, she hands one to me and one to Jim. We all crunch into the juicy green flesh, satisfying both our hunger and our thirst.

The sun has broken completely now. Steam rises from the water.

"Should we find a place to take cover until dark?" Jim asks in a hushed tone.

I think for a moment before answering.

"The swamp's safer in daylight," I finally whisper. "Let's keep going and put more distance between us and the plantation."

Jim nods in agreement. "Why don't you see if you can sleep for a bit. We'll take turns."

He takes the oar from me and eases the boat forward, one long stroke on the left, one long stroke on the right.

I lie back, resting my head on the blanket roll, watching the cover of bald cypress branches glide by overhead. Here and there, tiny patches of light peek through the needle-like leaves, sending rays of sunshine down on to the water. The boat rocks gently, side to side, as Jim steers us through the swamp. My eyelids give in to the weight of our travels.

Chapter 39

Margaret

It's late afternoon now. We've all had naps and another meal of cucumbers. Emma plays peek-a-boo with the baby to keep him from getting too restless. It's my turn to row, and Jim keeps a lookout behind us.

As we glide along, my mind is filled with thoughts of what might be happening back at the plantation. Did the barn fire spread to the out buildings? Did Master notice I'm gone? I can almost see him, storming around, barking out orders, counting heads. *Have you seen Margaret?* he would ask one person, then another. *Where the hell is Margaret?*

Hope and Eli would have figured out what was happening right away. *She's probably up at the hospital getting supplies in case anyone gets hurt,* Eli might have told Master to throw him off track for a while. *I think I saw her in the bucket line down by the creek,* Hope would have lied.

A chill runs up my back when I think what will happen to them when Master learns the truth. Will they have made the ultimate sacrifice to save their son? *Dear God, please protect them.*

The swamp is changing as we push forward. A thick layer of slime coats the surface of the water here. Almost looks as though we could step out of the boat and walk right along it without sinking. The trees have changed, too, from knobby-kneed cypress to massive oaks, some trunks as wide as six feet. Their leaves have already begun to turn—the golds and reds and oranges making a sharp contrast to the green blanket on the water. All manner of insects hum and buzz in the air.

"How much further to the edge of the swamp?" Jim asks.

"I'm not sure."

"But you're sure we're still headed west?"

It's been tough navigating through the bushes and thick stands of trees in the water. We've had to veer off course a few times to get around. Once you start to zig and zag about, it's hard to know if and when you're back on track. Could be going in circles and never know it. But now that the sun is beginning to set, it's clear we're headed due west.

"Mm-hmm." I nod. "I'm following the sun now. But if we don't reach the edge before dark, we should tie off for the night."

A flutter of birds suddenly take to the sky with a symphony of warning cries in the distance behind us. We stop cold, listen. The faint neigh of a horse carries through the air.

Jim looks around quickly, then points to a stand of trees not far to the left of us. I try to steer the boat in that direction, but it's hard to move the oar through the thick water. The noise gets closer. If we can just make it to the trees, we might be able to hide.

The birds continue to flee, and the sound of something large splashing through the water gets closer, closer.

Jim reaches over the side to help push us long with his hands.

"No!" I shout, then whisper, "Keep your hands out of the water."

He pulls back his arm, looks at me helplessly.

"Hurry, Margaret," he whispers.

"I'm trying. I'm trying."

Within arm's reach of the trees, Jim grabs hold of the branches. He pulls our vessel back behind the massive trunks. Vines hang down from the limbs overhead, providing even more cover between us and the open swamp.

I pull in the oar, and we sit motionless as the water ripples around us. *Please, Lord, settle the water so it doesn't give us away.*

Suddenly, a man on horseback charges through a cluster of ferns about fifty yards away. "Whoa!" he shouts, bringing his horse to a stop in the murky water. I peer through the vines, catch a slender glimpse of him. That voice, that posture. I'd know him from a hundred miles away.

Prigg. I mouth the name silently to Jim, and he nods grimly.

Prigg scans the area and then continues forward on a slow advance. He's headed straight for us, his rifle laid across his lap in the saddle.

I look behind us, but there's nowhere to go. There's nothing to do but watch him approach and pray he doesn't see us. Emma's whole body begins to tremble. I put my hand on her thigh, and she relaxes just a bit. She can't feel how I'm trembling on the inside.

The horse whinnies and rears its head as Prigg nears our stand of trees. Its muscles ripple and quiver along its neck and back. Something in the swamp has it spooked.

"Easy," he yells. "Take it easy you ignorant beast."

Prigg jerks back hard on the reins, pulls the horse into submission, and they veer off in the opposite direction. He guides the horse further ahead through the watery clearing and disappears into the trees.

We don't dare move. We don't dare breathe.

After an eternity of silence, I finally work up the courage to speak, if only in a whisper.

"We're going to be okay," I say, trying to reassure myself as much as anyone else.

"What do we do now?" Jim asks softly.

I shake my head. I don't know. Night is falling fast.

"It will be more dangerous to travel through the swamp in the dark," I finally say. "But we need to put more distance between us and Prigg."

Jim nods in agreement, and so does Emma.

We wait just a few minutes more, then gently ease our way out from behind the trees. The night chorus of the swamp begins to make itself heard in its low menacing moan.

"The gator ghosts," Emma whispers, surveying the dark closing in around us.

"The what?" Jim asks uneasily.

"Never you mind," I say firmly to the both of them.

We drift along in silence. Just a hint of sunlight peeks through the trees, bringing an eerie glow to the swamp.

I dip my oar in the water to move us forward more quickly, and I hit something solid. The ridges of a gator slither past us in the green water. Its tail thumps against the side of the boat as it goes by. Emma gasps. Jim's eyes get wide.

"It's okay. It's okay." I just keep saying it. It's all I can do.

Something rustles in the brush behind us, and we all turn sharply to the sound. My heart jumps into my throat as Prigg emerges on horseback through the trees, not fifty feet away. He must have circled back around!

"Well, look at what we got here," Prigg says as he draws closer. "Remember me?"

None of us answers.

"Oh, I'm sure you do," he continues. "We've got such a lovely history together, don't we, Margaret?"

My eyes dart around, hoping against hope there's some way to escape him.

"Nowhere to run," he says, patting the rifle in his lap. He laughs.

"How did you find us?" Jim asks.

I wish he wouldn't say a word. What's the point of encouraging the son-of-a-bitch to gloat?

"What? You think a handful of dumb Niggers can fool me?" Prigg laughs again.

"I saw the smoke for miles when I rode into the plantation this morning," he explains. "I knew it was too much to be a coincidence, and I was right. Wasn't I, Margaret? They had the fire pretty much put out by the time I got there, but Mr. Beane was still plenty hot. I asked him if he done a headcount of his slaves, and he asked me who the hell I was."

Prigg just sits there, high atop his horse. He's quite the storyteller. No doubt he's looking forward to a day when he can sit back at the tavern in Mill Green, with a pint in his hand, and regale his story over and again in more detail.

"Funny thing is, Margaret, when I made introductions, he knew me. Ed Prigg, the bounty hunter. You see, darling, I've become quite famous since the day I dragged your sorry ass back to Mill Green. Famous across this whole damned country."

Emma reaches for my hand. I take it, hoping to provide some comfort. But her hand isn't empty. She presses the cold handle of the folded jackknife into my palm. Ours eyes meet for a split second, as I contemplate my options.

"Famous, huh?" Jim asks. "What for?"

I understand now. Jim is stalling, leading Prigg along in his bragging to buy us some precious time to think. Good, that's good. Now *think*, Margaret.

"My record as a bounty hunter is perfect," Prigg boasts. "I always get my man, or woman, as it were."

He pauses, puffing out his chest, so proud of himself.

"You still never said how you found us?" Emma asks, as I slip the jackknife into my knickers behind my back.

"That was easy," he says. "Once Beane figured out you were on the run, he sent out the hounds. But they couldn't pick up a trail anywhere. So I started nosing around the creek and the fields. Picked up on your footprints pretty quick, led me right to the swamp."

Prigg grins widely and spits into the murky water. "Beane was busy cleaning up the mess you left behind. He was all too happy to hire me to hunt you down. Like I said, my track record is perfect."

"But how did you know which direction to go?" Jim continues to bait him.

"You might not think you leave a trail in the water, but you do," he says. "It's easy for an expert hunter like me to track his prey. I see a broken branch here, moss scraped from the rocks by a boat over there."

"But . . . "

"Enough with your damned questions already!" Prigg bellows.

He unfastens a rope coil from his saddle and hurls it into the boat. My mind flashes back to our cabin in York, to when he tied my babies up. Back to when this whole wretched nightmare first began. *I've got to do something!* I can't let this happen again.

Prigg aims his rifle straight at Washington.

"All right now, girly, you tie up your mama and big Jim there, or I'll blow that baby's head clean off."

Emma picks up the rope, uncoils it slowly. She looks to me, searching my face for the plan. But my mind is blank.

"Make sure it's good and tight, now," Prigg hisses.

The horse shakes its head, and Prigg steadies the reins with one hand. It prances in the water, then rears back, whinnies loudly. Not far off behind him, I catch sight of black ridges gliding through the green slime.

Prigg struggles to gain control of his animal. But the horse will not be contained. It rears back again, kicking wildly with its front legs, throwing Prigg off and into the murky water. The rifle lands some feet away and sinks into the muck. In a flash and fury, the horse gallops away into the depths of the swamp and disappears.

"Damned animal!" Prigg gropes around in the murky water for his weapon.

"Let's get him," Jim yells, with the oar in hand, ready to attack.

"No!" I shout. "Don't go in the water!"

Prigg looks up at us in confusion. Emma screams, points. Suddenly, giant jaws lurch up from the muck, grab hold of Prigg's arm and drag him under water. The boat rocks with the waves as Prigg and the beast roll and thrash about. Time seems to stand still while we watch Prigg fight for his life.

"We have to do something!" Emma cries. "It'll kill him!"

"So be it," Jim answers. I nod in silent agreement.

"Mama, no," Emma says, pulling at my arms, pleading. Tears stream down her face. "We're not like *him*. We're better than that. We have to help. Please!"

Prigg rears up out of the water for a second, screaming wildly, punching at the beast with his free arm. Then he disappears again into the water, now dark red.

Washington screams in terror, clings to Emma for dear life. All the while, Emma begs me to do something.

"God help me!" I shout, drawing the jackknife and leaping into the water. I turn and point at Emma. "Stay in that boat!"

Jim shouts a chorus of foul words and splashes down into the shallow water beside me, the oar in his hands. We push our way toward Prigg. The gator thrashes, lurches and rolls. Its giant tail sweeps toward us, knocks me clean off my feet and into the water. Jim pounds at its armored back with the oar, but the beast is unfazed. It won't let go.

"Go for the eyes, Jim. The eyes!"

I get back to my feet. With a banshee cry, I lunge forward and stab at the gator's head, sinking my blade into its eye. In an instant, the beast releases its prey and swims off into the cover of the swamp, my knife still jutting from its head.

Jim and I stare at each other in disbelief. Then we look around.

"Now what?" he shouts.

"Let's get him over there," I say, pointing to a fallen oak.

We grab hold of Prigg and drag him to the massive trunk near the stand of trees where we had waited in hiding just a few minutes before. Jim hands off the oar to Emma, and she guides the boat closer in.

"Lift him up," I say. Together, Jim and I manage to pull Prigg completely from the water and lay him across the log. We climb up on either side of him, straddling the log and feeling quite relieved to be out of the water.

Prigg's arm is almost completely torn away. About six inches of the bone is exposed, all white and smooth beneath the shredded blood-red skin and muscle.

"Is he gonna die?" Jim asks.

"I might be able to stop the bleeding with a tourniquet. Hand me that rope."

Emma hands it up to me, and I lean over the patient. Prigg moans as I take hold of his arm.

"N-n-o," he says, trying to pull away.

"I have to stop the bleeding."

I lean in again. Prigg turns his face toward me and spits. Emma gasps.

"I'd rather die," Prigg says feebly, "than owe my life to a dirty Nigger."

Jim shakes his head. Emma holds Washington close to her, crying softly. I sit back on my feet, watch him in disbelief. I'm tempted to give him his wish, to roll him right off the log and back into the murky water.

Prigg moans again. His body convulses for a moment, then he stills. His breathing is shallow, labored.

"He won't be long," I say. "Too much blood is lost."

Jim whistles through his teeth. He looks at me, still shaking his head, as if to ask why a man would choose to die this way. It just doesn't make any sense.

"I'll see you . . . in hell," Prigg hisses at me under his breath.

"I've already been to hell, thanks to you, Mr. Prigg," I say. "I'm not going back."

He coughs, and his head rears back. Then his body relaxes, and he's gone. I put my hand on his face, close his eyes.

"It's over," I say.

We sit for a minute or two. The swamp is still again, but for the constant hum of the insects. Emma takes in a deep breath and lets it go. She wipes the tears from her face with the back of her hand.

"The poor man," she whispers. "Nobody deserves to die that way, not even somebody as bad as him. God have mercy on his soul."

With that Jim breaks down, burying his face in his hands. His shoulders quiver as he sobs. This emotional collapse, now of all times, baffles me.

"What is it, Jim?"

He sniffles and looks up at me, his face contorted by grief or maybe joy or both. He looks over at Emma, than back at me again.

"Forgiveness," he says.

My chest wells with pride. I understand. It *is* a miraculous thing—true forgiveness—the kind that comes only from God himself, through the eyes and the heart of an innocent child.

I climb down from the log into the boat and reclaim my position at the rear.

"Come now. It's time for us to move on."

Jim nods and ambles in. Once we're all settled, I push off the log with the oar, aiming the boat westward.

We glide along for just a minute or so when another gator slinks past us. We look back over our shoulders and watch as the beast pulls Prigg's body down into the water and disappears.

Chapter 40

Margaret

The edge of the swamp is finally in sight. We climb out of the boat when the water is about knee deep and gather up our few belongings.

"Better make sure no one finds it," I say, nodding at the boat.

"Good idea," Jim says.

He pulls a knife from his sack and jabs away at the bottom of the boat. Then he gives the small vessel a good hard shove. It floats back off into the swamp, water bubbling up through the hole, and slowly sinks out of sight. We watch in silence as it vanishes.

"Okay," I say finally. "Let's get ourselves to dry land."

We walk about 100 yards through the marsh over to a small stand of cypress trees. Night has fallen completely now. I suggest we make a fire to cook dinner, dry our clothes, and keep the gators away.

"But won't the fire give us away to the search party?" Jim asks.

"I don't think anyone else will be looking for us. Prigg was so arrogant with his 'perfect record' of tracking slaves. I'm betting he came alone."

"You think?" Jim asks.

"It'll probably be a couple days before Master will even start to worry about not receiving any word from old Prigg," I say, nodding with confidence. Emma smiles. She spreads out the blanket and sits down. Washington toddles over and plops down beside her. Jim sets off in search of dry wood. I pull four onions from the basket, peel away the husks.

In no time, we have a small fire going. We roast the onions on sticks over the crackling flames. When they're good and brown, we enjoy a hot meal.

After dinner, Washington rolls onto his belly and stuffs his thumb in his mouth, content. He's asleep in only a minute, and the three of us just watch as he breathes in and out, in and out. I suggest Emma take a nap, too. We'll need to push on again in a couple hours. Whether they're looking for us or not, it's still safer to travel at night. Emma gives me no argument. It's been such a long journey already, and she falls asleep quickly.

"Jim," I whisper. "Do you have any paper with you?"

"Yes," he says, opening up his sack. "And quills and ink, too."

"Perfect. May I have them, please?"

Jim hands them over without question. Using the basket lid as my desk, I set my best script to paper. When I complete the first page, I hand it to Jim for inspection.

"How does that look?"

He takes the paper and quietly reads it aloud.

"To all people to whom these documents may present: I, the Honorable William Archer, by the power vested in me by the State of Maryland and the County of Harford, do certify that on this day, May 20, 1844, Mrs. Margaret Ashmore of Mill Green has granted full and complete freedom from her ownership to this Negro, Jim, also of Mill Green . . ."

Jim's eyes grow wide and a smile spreads across his face. "Looks just like the real thing. It's beautiful."

I knew exactly what to write. I had read Jerry's free papers a hundred times or more, wishing I had had some of my own. No more wishing for me.

"I'll make some for me and the children next. These should help us make our way if we get into a pinch."

Jim nods. He folds his paper and tucks it carefully into his shirt pocket.

"I still have about $400 dollars," Jim says. "That should come in handy."

"I'll say!"

We laugh. It feels good. I work a bit more at my forgery. Then I pause.

"You can buy us some shirts and pants when we get to the next town," I say. "I'll cut my hair and Emma's, too. People will be less suspicious, I think, of men and boys traveling together."

"Mm-hmm," Jim agrees. "I'll see if I can buy us a hand-cart, too. It'll be easier to carry the baby that way. And we'll need food supplies. Corn meal and beans, maybe some raisins and salt pork."

"That sounds wonderful, Jim."

He nods. I can almost see the wheels turning in his head, as he plans out the rest of our journey.

"We should travel by night as much as we can," he says, speaking slowly, deliberately. "And just keep heading west until we get to the territories. We can take the Overland Trails to New Mexico. It'll take about five months on foot. And making our way in the winter will be hard. It'll be really . . . "

His voice trails off. He doesn't finish his thought. Our eyes fall on Emma and Washington.

"How will we ever make it, Jim?"

"Ahh, it'll be simple as pie," he suddenly brightens up. "They'll be expecting us to go North, just like you said. And you'll be surprised to see how easy it is to move through the night, invisible like the shadows. I guarantee you it will be easier than making our way through that swamp and wrestling with gator ghosts!"

We share a quiet laugh, careful not to wake the children. I resolve to believe him. We've overcome so much already.

I finish writing the other documents and hand them over, one by one, to Jim for inspection. He nods his approval.

"Your penmanship really is quite something, Margaret. It looks just like Mrs. Ashmore's you know."

"Well, she was the one who taught me."

Jim admires my work a few minutes more, then carefully folds the papers and tucks them away in his bag.

The fire dances. We watch the flames and listen to the children snore.

"I don't suppose you were able to learn anything more about my boys," I say after a bit more time passes.

Jim exhales, shakes his head no.

"I didn't really expect that you had."

"I'm so sorry, Margaret."

I look at him. His eyes stay fixed on the fire. He has sacrificed so much to end up sitting beside this tiny fire in a South Carolina swamp just for me. I suddenly feel ashamed for having asked any more of him.

"No, Jim. It's me that's sorry. You've done so much for us, and I'm so grateful."

I reach for his hand. He smiles and shrugs his shoulders.

"That's what friends do," he says. "*You* taught me that, Margaret."

The fire is starting to dwindle.

"Should I put on another log?" Jim asks.

"No. We should get moving," I say. "We can walk for a few hours and take cover again at daybreak."

Jim nods. He douses and covers the fire, while I pack up our things. Then I wake the children. Jim carries the basket and blanket roll along with his own bag. I scoop up Washington and set him on my hip. Emma takes hold of my other hand.

Together, we walk by the faint light of the stars.

Maybe Mama was wrong about Wednesdays after all. Seems to me, good and bad, God is watching every day.

The sun is breaking on the horizon behind us now, casting a deep orange glow onto the landscape, onto to our path westward. Now I understand—no matter what other obstacles still lay ahead, no matter what anybody else might say—we are free.

The End

Author's Note

Nat Turner, Frederick Douglass, Harriett Tubman, Dred Scott—just a few of the names most Americans associate with the abolition of slavery. Who ever heard of Margaret Morgan?

All Different Kinds of Free was inspired by many true events, by the actual Supreme Court case of *Prigg v. Pennsylvania*, and by what little is known of the real-life Margaret Morgan. It is a work of fiction, but it contains many historical truths.

The references you will find to *Prigg v. Pennsylvania* in history books are typically brief and lack details about the people involved. They generally emphasize that its controversial ruling fanned the early sparks of contention that eventually led to the Civil War. The history books will have you believe that is why the story of *Prigg v. Pennsylvania* is important.

Yet, from the moment I first learned of *Prigg v. Pennsylvania*, I believed the story was important because it began with Margaret—with one woman's fight, against all odds, to hold her family together.

According to the published Supreme Court opinion for *Prigg v. Pennsylvania*, Margaret Morgan escaped a life of slavery in Maryland when she fled to Pennsylvania in 1832. She lived there several years before being abducted by Edward Prigg and returned, along with her children, to her owner Margaret Ashmore. Prigg was brought up on charges for violating the Pennsylvania Personal Liberty Law, which had been created to protect free blacks from kidnapping.

According to several other public records, however, Margaret had lived her entire life as a free woman. The court opinion failed to note that she had married a free black man from Pennsylvania many years before she left Maryland and that she had not been listed on John Ashmore's deed of property at the time of his death. Margaret was not itemized as part of the inheritance to his widow or his daughter, as was all his other property. In fact, in the 1830 U.S. census, she, her husband and their children were recorded as "free blacks" by the county sheriff.

These facts never came to light during Margaret's life. She did, in real life, take Mrs. Ashmore to court in Maryland to fight for her freedom (roughly 20 years before Dred Scott attempted the same); and she lost her case.

The kidnapping ruling against Prigg was in fact overturned by the Supreme Court, on the grounds that the Pennsylvania Personal Liberty Law was unconstitutional because it violated the federal Fugitive Slave Law of 1787. It was the first time a major branch of the federal government had made a proslavery stand.

Despite the real lives at stake—Ed Prigg's and Margaret Morgan's among them—the court case was not about these people. It had become a showdown between the North and the South, between states' rights and the nationalization of government.

Little is known about Margaret's life before she was kidnapped, and even less is known about her life afterward. Only a handful of brief, conflicting newspaper articles were published at the time—one reported that Margaret and the children were sold to Southern slave traders; another stated they were returned to Mrs. Ashmore, who then set them free.

Yet, in the end, Prigg was deemed innocent, Margaret and her children were likely condemned to a life of slavery, and the issue of Margaret's true freedom was, apparently, irrelevant. These facts are amazing, almost unbelievable, when considered in modern context. The event was largely overlooked by the media. There were no front page exposés, in-depth interviews or profiles of Margaret. No one stepped up to tell Margaret's side of the story.

All Different Kinds of Free finally tells her story, a story shared by thousands of women just like her—generations of wives and mothers who fought for their families and their freedom during the dark period of slavery in America.

Reader's Guide

1. Margaret noted early in her story that there are all different kinds of free and later that there are all different kinds of bondage, too. How do you think Margaret's experiences shaped her beliefs about what freedom truly means?

2. Emma matured dramatically, under dramatic circumstances, during the course of just a few years. What events in your own childhood were turning points in your maturity?

3. Were you surprised to learn that slaves were routinely bought and sold in Washington, D.C.? Why or why not?

4. Do you consider the Supreme Court's ruling in *Prigg v. Pennsylvania* to have been an endorsement of slavery? Or was it simply a defense of the U.S. Constitution?

5. How you do think the court case impacted the national dialogue about state's rights and federal power in the years before the Civil War? Do you see any similarities in national dialogue taking place today?

6. When Widow Ashmore told Jim the story about a bird that dropped its twig in the pond, what do you think she was really trying to say to him?

7. Jim's relationship with the widow evolved from one of interdependence to one of self-reliance and empowerment for them both. Do you think he and Mrs. Ashmore had become genuine friends? Do you think he missed her when he left Maryland?

8. When Ed Prigg learned Mrs. Ashmore had freed her one remaining slave, he was livid and vowed revenge on Margaret Morgan. Why do you think Prigg was so angry? At what or with whom was he angry?

9. Why do you think Margaret took Hope's son with her when she escaped? What might you have done?

10. The author chose to write Margaret's voice in present tense. How did this technical decision affect the story's urgency and pacing? Did it allow you to connect more closely to the main character? How might your response have been different if the entire story had been told by a narrator in past tense (as the other chapters were written)?

11. How has slavery and its abolition affected the character of our country? What does Margaret's life and her story tell us about the importance of civil liberties? How many other "Margaret" stories do you think exist that have never been told?

About the Author

Jessica McCann, a professional freelance writer and novelist, lives with her family in Phoenix, AZ. Her nonfiction work has been published in *Business Week*, *The Writer* and *Phoenix* magazines, among others. *All Different Kinds of Free* is her first novel. Please visit her website at www.jessicamccann.com or follow her on Twitter at @JMcCannWriter.